LYREBIRD HILL

Also by Anna Romer

Thornwood House

LYREBIRD HILL

Anna Romer

SIMON &
SCHUSTER

London · New York · Sydney · Toronto · New Delhi

A CBS COMPANY

LYREBIRD HILL
First published in Australia in 2014 by
Simon & Schuster (Australia) Pty Limited
Suite 19A, Level 1, 450 Miller Street, Cammeray, NSW 2062

10 9 8 7 6 5 4 3 2 1

A CBS Company
Sydney New York London Toronto New Delhi
Visit our website at www.simonandschuster.com.au

National Library of Australia Cataloguing-in-Publication entry
Author: Romer, Anna, author.
Title: Lyrebird Hill/Anna Romer.
ISBN: 9781922052421 (paperback)
                 9781922052445 (ebook)
Subjects: Sisters – Death – Fiction.
                 Suspense fiction.
Dewey Number: A823.4

Cover design: Christabella Designs
Cover image: © Mark Owen/Trevillion Images
Typeset by Midland Typesetters, Australia
Printed and bound in Australia by Griffin Press

FSC
www.fsc.org
MIX
Paper from
responsible sources
FSC® C009448

The paper this book is printed on is certified
against the Forest Stewardship Council®
Standards. Griffin Press holds FSC chain
of custody certification SGS-COC-005088.
FSC promotes environmentally responsible,
socially beneficial and economically viable
management of the world's forests.

For my beautiful Katie,
with an ocean of love

You are a ruby in the heart of granite,
how long will you try to deceive us?
We can see the truth in your eyes.

RUMI

Prologue

August 1898

It is midnight. I am hunched on the cold floor of the library, scratching these words by the light of a candle stub. Wind rattles the panes, and the air is heavy with the smell of gunpowder.

The men with guns are drawing near. I can hear their shouts as they trample the bracken at the forest edge. Soon they will thunder along the drive and through the trees to the house. Their dogs will catch the scent of blood and they will find us.

A man lies on the floor beside me, covered with my cloak. A dark patch of blood seeps through the grey wool.

'Love,' I whisper near to his ear, 'can you hear me?'

He does not reply. I hear only the wind sighing in the red gums outside and the distant baying of hounds. I watch him in the moonlight, taking in the wide mouth bracketed by lines, the regal nose, the pale skin. His is a face that traps the gaze, draws the unwary observer into a state of curiosity. Then intrigue. And then, upon closer acquaintance, into a sort of fearful obsession.

I shut my eyes, but it does no good to wish away the past. My yearning is like a knife carving into the soft hollows of my heart. My sorrow feels fatal. All I want now is to die here in the dark in the presence of love.

I huddle closer. A coppery scent saturates the air. My father used to say that blood has the gutsy odour of raw iron, but I disagree. To me it is sour, like the rotting shadows of the casuarina tree I played under as a child; it smells of brine and ash, of snakes sliding beneath the old house, of metal buried too long in the earth.

So much blood.

My glance strays deeper into the room, but I cannot quite bring myself to focus on the other motionless body slumped in the shadows. My attention scurries around it, mouse-like and evasive. It is not that his death grieves me; quite the contrary, he was my bitterest enemy and I have good reason to rejoice in his parting. I only regret that, by dying, he has condemned us all.

Gathering my skirts, I lie down beside my love and link my hot fingers into his large cool ones. My sob fractures the stillness. Then silence returns.

I try to dredge up a prayer. Not for my own soul, for I am past saving – but for the loved ones I have lost, the ones who now haunt me. The Lord hears every prayer, my father liked to say; even the prayers of sinners. I try to summon the words but nothing comes. Perhaps my sins are too great after all, even for the Lord's forgiving ears.

It strikes me then, how far I have travelled. Not only across a rough sea and into the heart of an unfamiliar land – but within those miles I have made the journey from girl to woman, and then more. Along the way my old self died, and this new, unknown self was born. She is an unfamiliar entity, a creature who makes me nervous and oftentimes afraid. Yet I feel more at home in her skin than I did in that of the naive young girl I used to be.

I edge closer to the body of the man beside me, trapping his stillness in my arms, wishing I could warm him back to life. Once, he told me that love has the power to create miracles. If that is true, then surely love will grant me this one last wish?

Come back, I beg him. *Please come back.*

There is so much to tell – so many lies to unravel, deceptions to unburden, truths I want so desperately for him to hear. Before he is lost, too.

But where to begin?

My breath draws deep, my thoughts race back to an earlier, happier time. The time before fate called me here; before love turned me into a murderer.

'I come from a wild, harsh part of the country,' I tell him softly, 'where bare granite outcrops stretch for miles, and tea-trees form forests so thick that a cat cannot slip among them, a place where billabongs swelter in the blistering sunshine, and the mighty Muluerindie rushes inland from the sea, a place where black ironbarks rise into a sky so vast and blue it hurts the eyes . . .'

1

Those of us who fear the truth and dwell in a state of denial,
have missed the purpose of living.
– ROB THISTLETON, *LET GO AND LIVE*

Ruby, April 2013

'Hello . . . what's this?'

I was standing in my cluttered bedroom, near the window in a patch of early light, my pulse tripping uncertainly. In one hand I held my boyfriend's suit jacket; the crisply tailored charcoal-grey Armani he'd been wearing when he came in last night.

In my other hand was a scrap of black lace – a tiny, sexy bra, I realised. It had spaghetti-thin straps and a miniature gold horseshoe sewn into the lace between the cups. I'd found it in Rob's jacket pocket. Not that I'd been snooping. He'd hung the Armani near my open window, presumably to air it while he was in the shower. When I went to investigate, I'd caught a barely-there whiff of smoke. Cigarette smoke, I thought, which puzzled me because Rob never allowed his patients to light up anywhere near the therapy rooms.

His voice drifted through the bathroom door. He was singing

'Rhinestone Cowboy', which surprised me. I'd known Rob for nearly three years, and in all that time I'd never picked him as a Glen Campbell fan. Maybe that's what sparked my curiosity. Rob was a classical enthusiast. Brahms, Mozart, Liszt. If he was feeling in the groove, he might pull out some Shostakovich. Meanwhile I was mad about seventies folk – seventies anything, really – which I knew Rob considered terribly lowbrow. I'd been at him for some time to meet in the middle, compromise on both sides and find something we could both enjoy . . . but Glen Campbell? At any other time, I'd have been impressed.

I frowned at the bra.

Rob might have bought it for me as a gift. Which was crazy – I had curves, and lots of them; no one in their right mind would expect me to fit into such a tiny garment.

My heart clenched into itself. Who was I kidding? As the ache of realisation swept through me, I tried to contain it by standing very still. Holding my breath. Groping around in my mind for another, less horrible explanation, but finding none.

The shower stopped. Rob clattered around in the ensuite, whistling as he dried off. I imagined marching in there and demanding that he tell me what he'd *really* been up to last night – but fear kept me frozen in place. What if he admitted he'd met someone else; what if he broke up with me?

The flimsy bra dangled from my fingers like a dead kitten.

I sniffed it. Definitely cigarette smoke. And perfume: 'Poison' by Christian Dior. I knew it well; I had a large purple bottle sitting on my dressing table. I'd only used it once or twice to please Rob. He'd presented it to me soon after we started dating, gift-wrapped and tied with a glittery card that said, *Thanks for the happiest three months of my life.*

Our first few months *had* been happy. For me, deliriously so. I'd been single most of my adult life and secretly ashamed of the fact. I was thirty, and while all my girlfriends were getting married and popping out kids, I'd been following my dream.

That was my justification, anyway. People were always asking when I was going to get my act together, meet someone nice and settle down. Start a family of my own. I never had the heart to tell them that babies and husbands just weren't my thing, so I'd waffle on about career, and the miracles of modern medicine, and how women these days were delaying motherhood even into their forties.

I stared at the bra, then at the doorway that separated me from the man I loved. He was still whistling and banging things around, and each tiny sound made me feel increasingly alone.

Until I met Rob, my small bookshop had been my life. I'd worked hard to set it up from scratch, scrimping and saving and mapping out my plan with the precision of a military strategist. I had gravitated towards what I loved best, and somehow it had all fallen neatly into place. I stocked the latest bestsellers, but mostly the books were second-hand – with a scattering of music CDs and audio books to keep things interesting. I had a clutch of regular customers, most of whom I'd become close to over the years. I'd made a lot of friends that way – fellow bookworms who, like me, loved nothing more than sitting around the dinner table after a great meal, guzzling red wine and rambling on for endless hours about books.

Back then, those bookish dinner parties had kept my loneliness at bay. The shop helped, too. Even so, there'd been days when I found myself gazing through the window out at the sunny footpaths, scrutinising the passers-by. Plenty of gorgeous men, but they all seemed attached or gay or in too much of a rush to stop in and browse my books. I rarely went on dates; there'd been a few set-ups, but nothing had ever lasted past the three-week mark.

That was, until I met Rob.

I had liked his face the moment I saw it on the flyleaf of his first bestselling book, *Let Go and Live*. He had a wide, friendly smile and a rugged boyishness. I was drawn to him and wanted to meet him, so I devised the plan of holding an author signing at my shop.

To my surprise, Rob agreed.

The signing was a tremendous success, and Rob had lingered afterwards over a glass of wine. He was even more gorgeous in the flesh: tall and lean, impeccably groomed. Of course, he wasn't perfect – he had a scar beside his left nostril, and his thinning hair was trimmed close to his scalp – but he had a way of speaking, a mesmerising attentiveness that disarmed me.

Not long after that, he asked me out.

'Ruby?'

I startled from my thoughts. Tucking the bra into my dressing gown pocket, I made a lunge for the bed.

Steam billowed into my room as the ensuite door opened. Rob stood in the swirling vapours, his body gleaming and damp, his chest hair glittering with water droplets. He looked every bit the gorgeous buffed underwear model – without the underwear.

'Still not dressed?' His voice was smooth, but there was an undertow of irritation. 'We're leaving on the dot of eight, don't forget.' Reaching back around the door, he took a clean towel and scrubbed it over his head. 'I couldn't find my aftershave. Did you move it?'

'I . . . ah, I was cleaning up. It's in the—'

I swallowed the lump in my throat, unable to get the image of the bra out of my head. *Ask him now. Demand an explanation.* My lips parted, and the question took shape in my mind, but I couldn't get my tongue around the words.

Are you having an affair?

'Never mind.' Rob said, and I thought I heard him sigh. 'Really, babe, I wish you'd let me hire you a housekeeper. Or at least one of those organising experts. A man could vanish into your clutter and never be heard from again.'

He winked to let me know he was joking, and I forced a smile. But inside my dressing gown pocket my fingers had knotted themselves into the bra strap. The elastic grew tighter and tighter, strangling the blood flow to my fingertips.

'Rob,' I began, but again my courage faltered. Now wasn't the time. I was in bed in my dressing gown, my face bare of make-up. My hair was unbrushed, and long wisps clung to my damp neck under my collar. Worse, my breasts and belly and bottom and thighs were without the advantage of support wear. A heavy feeling settled over me. All of a sudden the idea of a confrontation – especially one that might involve a doll-sized rival – seemed too daunting. I would have to wait. Wait until my heart stopped hammering and I could speak coherently. Wait until I was looking my best. Wait until I could confront Rob from a place of certainty.

'What's that, honey?' Rob was adjusting his tie in my antique cheval mirror, intent on his reflection.

'Do you—' I cleared my throat and tried again. 'Do you think she'll be happy to see me? Mum, I mean?'

Rob glanced at me via the mirror. 'She sent you an invitation, didn't she?'

'I guess.'

I inched deeper into the bed, wanting to vanish. I'd been surprised to receive an invitation to my mother's latest art exhibition in Armidale. Mum and I had never seen eye to eye, even when my sister Jamie was alive. After Jamie died, I'd left home at the earliest opportunity, and Mum and I had drifted even further apart. Our current relationship consisted of occasional random phone calls for birthday or Christmas, and infrequent postcards.

I glanced over to find Rob watching me. His brown eyes looked nearly black in the early light, and for an instant – a heartbeat, a breath – he wore an expression I hadn't seen before; intense, focused . . . and unnerving. I shifted on the bed, drawing my fluffy gown tighter about me.

Then he smiled, and the intensity vanished.

'You're nervous, babe. That's all. You haven't seen your mother in – what, three years?'

'Four,' I reminded him, searching his face for a sign that anything was amiss; but if he felt any guilt about the bra, it didn't show. 'What if it's awful, Rob? What if we argue like last time?'

'Honey, it's natural to have qualms. This is just one of those curve balls that life throws you once in a while. You've got to learn to deal with it. What do I always tell you?'

'Stop catastrophising. Embrace the fear. Let it go.'

He went back to his reflection. 'Problem solved.'

I stared at him. Muscles rippled beneath the pristine white shirt. His skin gleamed, and droplets of water clung to the stubble on his scalp. He licked his lips and began to sing again, but this time I didn't recognise the song. My chest tightened. Rob was a decent man, a good man. A respected therapist and author, a loyal friend. He'd never cheat, never do anything to hurt me.

Would he?

Stop panicking, I chastised myself. *When I confess my fears, Rob will probably just shake his head in dismay. He'll offer a logical explanation and we'll have a good old laugh. He'll call me his little worrywart and tousle my hair, then we'll go to bed and everything between us will be roses again.*

But the thin elastic of the bra strap continued to cut off my circulation. The prickling hotness in my fingers grew more intense. It spread into my hands, up my arms and through my shoulders. It burned across my chest and burrowed deeper until it settled like a sickness around my heart.

'I thought you said your mother was sixty?'

I searched the crowd. The gallery was a huge converted warehouse on the outskirts of Armidale. The high, whitewashed walls were as smooth as icing, their pristine surface broken only by my mother's huge colourful canvasses. At the epicentre of the cavernous room, surrounded by admirers, stood a willowy figure in a shimmering evening dress.

'She *is* sixty.'

'You'd never know it.' Rob swallowed a mouthful of Heineken. 'She looks amazing.'

The admiration in his voice irked me. I shuffled uncomfortably as old insecurities flocked back. Yes, my mother was slim and gorgeous; no, I didn't resemble her. And I didn't remember hearing Rob enthuse about *my* appearance tonight. I glanced down at my all-black clothes. Why hadn't I worn something less businesslike? The pantsuit I'd bought now seemed severe and unimaginative; worse, my new shoes were eating my toes, and the elasticised shape-wear that was supposed to sculpt my flesh into pleasing curves was cutting off my blood supply.

Sweat trickled along my spine as I watched my mother flutter from patron to patron like an elegant turquoise butterfly. She'd pulled her dark auburn locks into a stylish chignon and her skin gleamed like porcelain. The sequinned fabric of her dress hugged her slender figure, glittering riotously as she moved through the crowd. I'd long suspected that people attended Mum's shows as much to see her as to view her latest paintings. She glowed, vibrant and mesmerisingly alive, a flaming supernova against the static backdrop of her canvases.

'Hey.' Rob nudged me with his elbow. 'Stop looking so glum. Remember what we talked about?'

I stared at him blankly.

He sighed. 'Let it go, okay?'

'Sure,' I muttered, fretfully tugging a strand of dark hair loose from my ponytail. 'I'll try.'

Rob smiled indulgently and kissed the top of my head, then returned his attention to the crowd. I glared at him from the corner of my eye. He looked good. No trace of tiredness after the drive from the coast, not a button out of place. The navy suit and crisp shirt made his eyes seem bluer, his teeth whiter. I sighed. I'd been looking forward to this moment for weeks; looking forward to showing Rob off, proving to Mum that I'd got my act together, stepped up in the world, done well for myself. Met a man who was not only hunky, but successful as well. I should have been triumphant; I should have been holding my head high, pink-cheeked with happiness.

Instead, I was a wreck.

Rob nudged me again. 'Here she comes.'

A glimmer of turquoise, the flash of a familiar smile. Mum paused to greet a bald man and they spoke quietly for a while, nodding and looking mutually fascinated. Suddenly Mum threw back her head and laughed.

The warbling bell-like sound of it caught me off guard.

Suddenly I was a child again, a gangly twelve-year-old standing in the kitchen of our old house. The air smelled charred from the toast Mum had just burned. She'd been gaunt and grey-faced back then, her eyes shadowed by grief, her mouth turned down. Her hair had been long and unkempt, and she'd smelled of alcohol. There'd been no smiles, no hint of warbling laughter. Tears were all she had to give. Tears and blame.

What happened that day, Ruby? Why can't you remember?

Jamie was Mum's firstborn, her favourite. Three years older than me, Jamie had inherited our mother's fine features and slim frame. She'd also been outgoing and bubbly, the way Mum was. My sister and I were both dark-haired, but that was where the resemblance ended. I'd always been weighty, even as a child. I was shy and wore glasses. Books saved me, but neither my sister nor my mother ever really understood my addiction to reading. They didn't exactly disapprove, but the word 'bookworm' always seemed to be spoken in a way that made me squirm.

After Jamie died, amid my pain and confusion and guilt, I'd entertained the hope that Mum's favour would transfer to me.

I waited through the tearful years; waited for Mum's grief to wear thin, for her smile to return, for her trilling laugh to once again ring through our house. Eventually it did, and there even came a time when she could look at me without crying. But I'd given up waiting for Mum's favour. Jamie had died, but she had never been forgotten.

'Ruby!' Mum waved. She excused herself from the bald man and hurried over. 'Darling, how lovely to see you!' She pecked my cheek and gave me a swift hug, then stood back to appraise me. Her smile slipped. 'I see you've let your hair grow. A pity, it looked so nice short.'

'Hi, Mum.' I attempted a smile, but there followed an awkward moment in which I couldn't think of anything else to say.

Mum turned her attention to the man beside me. 'Hello there, you must be Rob?'

Rob beamed, engulfing my mother's slender hand in his large one, pulling her imperceptibly closer. 'Delighted to meet you, Mrs Cardel. Ruby has told me so much about you.'

'Please, call me Margaret.' She smiled, then seemed to hesitate, as if uncertain. 'You look familiar, Rob. Have we met?'

Rob gave a sexy chuckle. 'If we had, I'd certainly have remembered. You've probably seen my ugly mug in a bookshop window somewhere. My third book's just come out, *Emotional Rescue*. Maybe you've noticed it around?'

'Not yet, but I insist on hearing all about it. You've obviously taken time out of your busy schedule to travel up here to see my show. I must say I'm flattered.'

'Wouldn't have missed it for the world, Margaret. Ruby speaks so glowingly about your paintings that I had to see them for myself. Very impressive they are, too. Good thing I brought my chequebook,' he added, patting his pocket.

Mum linked her arm through his. 'Then I must show you my favourite piece before someone else snaffles it up. It's a still life, the subject is a wonderful old Singer sewing machine I inherited from my grandmother. It dates to before the first world war. Are you interested in family history, Rob?'

His smile smouldered. 'It's one of my passions. In all honesty, I can't think of a more fascinating topic.'

I softened at his words; Rob loved history, all right – other people's history. He never spoke much about his own family. He'd tried once and got all choked up.

In the first chapter of *Let Go and Live* Rob described his childhood. A mother too smacked-out to care if he went hungry. A string of violent 'fathers'. Stints in remand homes. And then, life on the Sydney streets. Drugs, car theft, destitution. One stormy night, huddled under a bridge in a sea of mud and shattered glass and syringes, sixteen-year-old Rob had felt himself crushed by hopelessness. The pain of his existence threatened to swallow him. He picked up a broken bottle and pressed it against his wrist, thinking death would bring relief . . . but then a voice had spoken softly to him through the haze of his despair.

Let go, Rob. Let go of the pain and find a way to live.

He felt a spark of hope – he later wrote – as if a light had winked on in his heart. He dropped the bottle, got to his feet, and walked through the long night, letting the rain wash away the mud and blood and loneliness. After that, he turned his life around. He'd gone to uni and majored in psychology, but then branched off with his own radical ideas. Contrary to popular opinion, Rob believed that dredging up old wounds was counterproductive. His resulting book, *Let Go and Live,* was an overnight hit.

The trick is not to resist your fear, he'd written. *You have to smell it, taste it, embrace it, allow it to overwhelm you. And then simply let it go.*

Rob's sexy laugh lifted above the babble of voices, followed by my mother's musical trill. I sighed and turned away from the crowd. Mum's cool reception of me hadn't been a surprise; she was always aloof when we met, which I supposed was how she protected herself from my nagging curiosity about the past. But sweeping Rob away and leaving me standing around like a wallflower – well, that hurt.

Did Rob even care? Clutching my bag against me, I thought about the tangle of black lace crammed beneath my usual layers of dross. Tonight, I silently promised, I would confront him and learn the truth.

I headed for the outskirts of the room.

Bright halogens illuminated Mum's paintings, making them focal points in the otherwise dimly lit gallery. A quick scan told me they were all interiors, but it wasn't until I'd approached the first one – a large room furnished only with a bay-fronted 1940s desk – that my breath caught. The huge canvases were eerily beautiful, their jewel colours seeming to breathe under the intense illumination, as though they'd been rendered from living light rather than mere paint. There was a stillness about the rooms they depicted, a sense of quietude and desolation that drew me in.

I wandered from image to image, spellbound. The gallery around me faded. The chatter grew muffled, the clink of glasses ceased. I might have been alone, moving through those familiar rooms in silence.

There was the kitchen where Jamie and Mum and I had eaten breakfast. And there was our old lounge room. Years ago, it had been cluttered with tables and a piano and a wrought-iron day bed upholstered in brown linen. In the painting, it seemed almost bare; the clutter had been cleared away, the only furniture was a lonely pair of ornate chairs.

Further along was a smaller canvas showing the bedroom I'd once shared with Jamie, with its cabinet of spooky antique dolls and light-filled window shedding sunbeams onto a pair of neat single beds.

Ghostly fragments of memory wafted back to me, formless and elusive. Two little girls running through the long grass. Sunshine warming bare arms and legs. The sweet, spicy scent of stringybark blossoms. My sister's voice, whispering with heart-breaking clarity in the back of my mind.

Hey Ruby, you wanna collect wildflowers? I found some rock orchids near the river; we could press them and make a card for Mum. Bring your togs, we'll go for a dip while we're there . . .

Best friends. Doting sisters. Thick as thieves, Mum had called us.

I dug under my hair, rubbing the sudden knot of tension. Jamie had died a long time ago, I reminded myself. Eighteen years. I should have put her behind me by now, made peace with her death, and moved on – but she haunted me even now, and probably always would.

The next painting was Mum's old sewing machine, the one she'd been so eager to show Rob. It was smaller than the other canvases, more intensely colourful. The antique Singer sat on its cabinet in a narrow room, the window above it aglow with after-noon sun. The black curves of the machine's body were chipped and scarred by age, its flywheel worn shiny by the touch of count-less fingers. The decorative scrollwork was picked out in gold leaf, which glimmered softly under the lights.

I went closer, drinking in the gummy faintness of oil paint, the sharp tang of turpentine. Closer still, until the sewing room was no longer merely a painted image, but breathtakingly real.

Mum had used that old Singer to make our clothes. Floral tank tops and hippy pants, dresses in crazy patterns. Pink for Jamie, green for me. We'd teamed everything with boots and thick socks, even the dresses. It was an unusual fashion combo, but Mum had always insisted we dress sensibly in case of snakes.

You girls tread carefully in the long grass, she routinely warned. But Jamie and I always raced off, never listening. Down to the river, picking flowers and weaving hats from lomandra leaves. Ignoring Mum's calls that dinner was on the table going cold. We'd hide beneath the gnarly casuarina that grew on the bank, bluebells and purple-pea trampled beneath our feet, giggling madly with our heads together concocting wild stories, or belting out outlandish made-up songs.

The tension at the back of my head returned, and I rubbed it absently. According to the doctors, my amnesia was the result of the head injury I'd sustained the day of Jamie's accident. The injury had earned me eleven stitches and three weeks in hospital, and a god-awful headache that lasted months. Afterwards, my brain had gone into lock-down, burying my recall of that year in an unyielding vault.

But now, as I drifted through the landscape of memories my mother had created, I felt the contents of that vault begin to stir.

The next painting was eerie, as beautiful as a dream. It was a garden panorama observed through the open kitchen window. Curtains billowed in the breeze, framing a perfectly manicured landscape. The garden had never been that well tended in my day; its beds were always choked with weeds and drifts of gum leaves and fallen banksia pods.

Here in the painting it resembled a picture postcard: roses frothed around the base of a nodding purple butterfly bush, and nearby a clump of spider dahlias bristled in the heat. On an elevated bank overlooking the vegetable garden grew a walnut tree, its bare branches festooned with last season's pods. At the foot of the trunk was a small mound of earth, like a new grave.

It was a lyrical painting, magical – a summer song rendered in pigment and light – but the wintry tree with its blackened pods and grave-like mound infused it with a sinister element.

'She's certainly got talent, hasn't she?'

An elderly woman had sidled up beside me. She was tiny, possibly in her nineties, and wore a red dress embroidered with white daisies, complemented by a knitted bag and gorgeous black patent shoes. Her snowy hair was braided into bunches behind her ears, and pinned to the neckline of her dress was a tiny bouquet of native daisies – yellow-buttons, we'd called them as kids. As she moved closer to the painting, the overhead lights gleamed off the antique silver locket she wore at her throat.

She bent forward and squinted at the printed legend attached to the wall at the base of the canvas.

'It's called *Inheritance*. An intriguing name for a garden vista.' She beamed, and her features shifted into a landscape of wonderful wrinkles. 'I suppose the mystery is what makes it so enjoyable to ponder.'

It was probably nostalgia brought on by seeing Mum's paintings, but this woman seemed ever so vaguely familiar. I wanted to ask her name, but I held back. The gaps in my memory made chatting about the old days awkward; from the age of twelve I'd habitually avoided talking about the past, and old habits were hard to break.

'I'm not a big fan of mysteries,' I admitted. 'I'm the type who lies awake all night worrying over them. I'm much more comfortable knowing the facts.'

The woman looked at me, openly curious. 'Then I feel for you, my dear. The way I see it, life is one big mystery. A person thinks they have it all figured out, that there's nothing left to learn, and that's usually the point when the next big question lands on their head like a bomb. You must spend many a sleepless night? I know I do,' she added with a laugh.

I couldn't help smiling. 'You've got me pegged. I'm a chronic insomniac.'

We both chuckled, and a warm feeling came over me. I felt as if I'd known this woman for years. Her gaze seemed so open and friendly, so filled with approval. And her voice made me think of cosy things: buttered scones, bookshelves crammed with well-thumbed volumes, hot chocolate and laughter. The moment was so sweet that I lost my qualms and had to ask.

'The artist is my mum. Are you a friend of hers?'

The woman looked pleased. 'Yes, dear. At least I was, many years ago. We were neighbours.'

'I *thought* you looked familiar! You're . . .' There was an embarrassing silence as I groped around for the name I'd obviously forgotten.

She smiled kindly. 'You might remember me as Mrs Hillard. But please, call me Esther. I bought Lyrebird Hill from your mother, after . . . well, after you both moved back to town. It's been a long time, Ruby. How old were you then – eleven, twelve?'

'Thirteen.'

'How's life been treating you?'

'Great!' I said too hastily, then floundered. Now wasn't the time to go into detail about how off-the-rails I'd been before I'd met Rob; how grief had driven a wedge between my mother and me; and how I still had the occasional nightmare about Jamie.

'I've got a cottage over on the coast in Sawtell,' I told her. 'And I've—' *Met a really nice man*, I'd been about to say, but again my words stalled. I recalled the bra at the bottom of my handbag, and decided the topic of work was the safer option. 'I have a little bookshop twenty minutes' from home in Coffs Harbour, the Busy Bookworm. Despite everyone going digital, it's been doing really well. I sell rare and second-hand books, as well as all the latest releases.'

Esther beamed. 'I simply adore books. I'd love to see your shop – but I'm afraid my days of travelling to the coast are over. That sea air is a bit too humid for my old lungs.' She patted her chest, and her bouquet released a sweet peppery scent.

It made me think of grassy slopes, and river water gurgling over stones, and the sound of children laughing. An image flashed into my mind: a room full of cluttered bookshelves, in which a grandmotherly woman sat in a patch of sunlight, reading from the volume in her lap. I saw two children perched at her feet, listening intently. I strained to bring their faces into focus; it was just a tiny glimpse of memory, but all of a sudden it seemed important. Yet even as I grasped for it, the scene slipped away like smoke.

Esther gestured at Mum's canvas. 'Margaret's done a splendid job, hasn't she? It's been fascinating to see how the old farmhouse must have looked when the three of you lived there.'

'It was more cluttered,' I admitted. 'Mum was quite a collector back then. She had stuff crammed into every corner.' Despite my reluctance to talk about the past, the memory of our unruly living spaces touched me like a smile. My shoulders relaxed and I found myself rushing on. 'Jamie and I were chronic hoarders, too. We filled the place with all the treasures we brought back from the bush – birds' nests, lumps of driftwood from the river, that sort of thing. Mum's paintings don't do justice to the chaos we created. She's made it all seem very empty.'

'I suppose that's how she remembers it,' Esther said gently.

A length of silence followed. I feigned absorption in the painting, trying to think of a question to ask my companion that would divert our conversation in a new direction. There were plenty of topics that didn't involve the past: Where had she bought her fabulous dress? Great shoes, too. And what was the story behind the lovely locket she wore? But standing there surrounded by my mother's enormous canvases depicting a place so closely associated with my childhood, the past seemed inescapable.

Besides, I'd been quiet for too long.

Esther looked at me carefully. 'You and your mother had a sad old time, didn't you?'

'Yeah,' I muttered, unable to stop the sinking feeling. 'We did.'

'I've thought of you both so often over the years. Poor Jamie, too. She was such a bright girl. It must have been awful never knowing what really happened to her. All those years, wondering and worrying. I don't know how Margaret coped.'

My face tightened in shock. 'What do you mean?'

Esther frowned and moved nearer. 'They never did find who was responsible, did they?'

'Responsible?' The nameless fear that had lain dormant in me for years stirred. I drew a steadying breath and centred myself. 'Esther, you must be mistaken. Jamie fell. She hit her head. No one was *responsible*. It was an accident.'

Esther searched my face, seeming to take in every pore and freckle and line, frowning as if my features were a puzzle she was unable to work out. 'Is that what your mother told you?'

I stared at her, trying to stem the panic. I had no memory of Jamie's death; I couldn't remember finding her on the rocks that day, or the aftermath of questions; nor could I remember her funeral, or the months that followed. Mum had sat me down one day and outlined a simplified version of events, no doubt hoping to unlock my memory. But when the vault refused to open, she'd given up trying.

'Mum said there was a lot of rain that day,' I explained, my words coming in a rush, leaving me breathless. 'The rocks were slippery, Jamie must have misjudged the incline and lost her footing. It was definitely an accident, Esther. Maybe you're thinking about someone else?'

Esther pressed her fingers to her earlobes. 'Oh, Ruby, I do beg your pardon. My memory isn't as good as it used to be. I'm sorry I've upset you.'

My lungs deflated, and I slumped. My limbs were suddenly shaky, my brain wired. A vague feeling of nausea swam around inside me.

'That's okay,' I said in a mouse voice. 'No harm done.'

Esther's keen eyes – so intently trained on me until that moment – darted away. I followed her gaze across the gallery. People were milling in smaller groups now, or had detached from the central cluster to wander around the walls admiring the artwork. I saw Mum standing in the midst of a small gathering at the nibblies table.

Fingers curled around my wrist. Esther's skin felt as smooth as ancient satin, but her grip was firm.

'Will you promise me something, Ruby?'

I frowned at her, still shaken by our exchange. *Any* request for a promise made me wary, let alone one put forth by someone I'd only just met.

Esther released my wrist, but her eyes pleaded with me until I nodded.

'Will you visit me at Lyrebird Hill?' she asked. 'Please say you will, my dear. We can continue our conversation in private. I have fond memories of you and Jamie as children. Perhaps they'll help you remember? Besides, I've got something for you. A book,' she added quietly.

Surprise made me ask, 'What sort of book?'

Esther glanced over her shoulder, then replied hastily. 'Now's not the time to talk, love. Please say you'll come and visit. I'll show you the new gardens I've planted, and the seedling nursery, which I know you'll adore. It'll be great, we can make a day of it.'

I blinked at her. Visit Lyrebird Hill? Return to the place I'd spent the past eighteen years running from? Immerse myself in all the sights and sounds and smells of my childhood home, and risk *remembering*? The mention of a book rang my alarm bells, too.

'I'll think about it,' I said reluctantly. 'The shop's pretty hectic at the moment. I might not be able to get away for a while.'

Esther adjusted her bag and smiled. 'Well, when you *can* manage a couple of days off, why don't you come and stay? There are plenty of spare bedrooms, as you know. Please do, Ruby. It would mean so much to me.' Unpinning the bouquet of wildflowers from her collar, she pressed it into my hand. 'Just turn up whenever you like, dear. Any time of night or day. My door's always open.'

She hesitated, as if wanting to say more. Instead, she kissed me lightly on the cheek, then turned to join a group of patrons heading towards the entryway. I watched until she reached the door, and caught a last glimpse of her white hair and red dress, before she disappeared outside.

'Ruby!'

I looked around. Rob was weaving his way towards me through the crowd, balancing glasses of wine and a mini cheese platter.

'There you are,' he said, handing me a glass and helping himself to the platter. 'Incredible turnout, isn't it? All of Armidale must be here. Margaret's sold just about everything, too. Having fun?'

'Not really,' I admitted, and gulped my wine. 'I've had enough. I'll say goodbye to Mum, and then meet you outside.' Before he had a chance to respond, I stalked away into the thinning muddle of people, making a beeline for my mother.

When she saw me approaching, she hurried over and took my arm, steering me towards a quiet corner of the gallery.

'I was wondering where you'd got to,' she said. Her face was flushed and her chignon had frayed from its pins. 'I'm afraid I've been caught up; did you get a chance to look around?'

'The paintings are beautiful, Mum. All from memory, I suppose?'

She nodded. 'Although I've spent the past four years cursing myself for not having the foresight to photograph the old place. It would have made my job a great deal easier.'

'I'm sure Mrs Hillard would have welcomed a visit.'

Mum tensed. 'You know how I feel about the place, Ruby. The paintings were a way for me to try and find a sort of closure. Actually going back there would have just opened up old wounds.' When I didn't reply, her eyes narrowed on my face. 'What's wrong, Ruby? You look pale.'

My pulse picked up, and I took a breath. 'Speaking of Esther Hillard, she was here.'

Mum glanced over my shoulder. 'Oh? I must say hello.'

'She had to leave.'

'That's a shame. I haven't seen her in ages. I'd love to catch up with her.' Mum seemed to ponder this, then said a bit too loudly, 'Had a good chat, did you?'

'We did, actually. She mentioned Jamie.'

Mum forced a smile, but her eyes were wary. 'Both you girls used to visit her when you were little. You went through a stage where you spent more time at her place than you did at home. She was very kind. To all of us.'

I did vaguely recall those early visits, but only one memory stood out. I thought of the flash I'd had while talking to Esther – the half-remembered room with its cluttered bookshelves and aroma of hot chocolate, and the cosy feeling of wellbeing.

'She told me something about Jamie. It freaked me out.'

Mum paled, and her fingertips went to her throat. 'Ruby, please,' she said in a half-whisper. 'Now's not the time. Why don't you drop by my place tomorrow, we can talk then.'

'We're going back to the coast tonight. I'm sorry, Mum, I know it's inconvenient, but I really need to—' I hesitated, glancing across the gallery. Rob was nowhere to be seen, and the room was emptying fast. Mum was probably anxious to catch people before they left, to thank them for coming and say her goodbyes, but I simply couldn't stop myself asking.

'Esther said Jamie's death wasn't an accident. Is that true?'

Mum seemed to deflate. For an instant, I glimpsed not the porcelain-skinned artist at the centre of everyone's attention, but the broken soul she'd been after my sister's death: ashen-faced, old beyond her years, engulfed by sadness.

'Oh, Ruby,' she said. 'You do this every time we see each other, poking and prodding about Jamie. No amount of digging up the past is going to bring her back. Why can't you let her rest?'

She glanced across the gallery. The crowd had begun to thin, and people drifted towards the exit, calling their goodbyes and complimenting my mother on her wonderful exhibition. It should have been a crowning moment for her, a triumph to savour.

'I'm sorry, Mum,' I said quietly, looking back at her. 'I don't want to wreck your night, but I really need to know.'

Mum drew air through her nostrils, and finally, with what seemed like a great effort, she looked at me.

'There was an investigation. As it turned out, Jamie's injuries were not caused by a fall, but police forensics couldn't confirm that anyone other than you and Jamie had been on the rocks that day. You see, it had been raining – any evidence that might have led us to the person responsible was washed away.'

I tried to breathe, suddenly lightheaded amid the cavernous gallery with its pockets of intense light, the vibrant paintings, the taste of wine on the back of my tongue . . . and the sight of my mother's face, pale now, her eyes huge and dark, her lips raw where she'd bitten them.

'Person responsible?' I managed.

Mum nodded.

My pulse began to hurtle, then abruptly slowed. The words drifted from me, as if from far away. 'They thought I did it, didn't they?'

Mum shook her head. 'No, Ruby. No one ever thought that. No one ever blamed you.'

You did, whispered a voice in my mind. *You blamed me.*

I shook my head to clear it. 'Why didn't you ever tell me?'

'I wanted to spare you the grief. You were just a kid. You idolised Jamie, and losing her was traumatic enough.'

'So you let me think it was an accident.' I stopped, distracted by the sudden din of my thoughts. I was angry that Mum had kept the truth from me, but it came as no real surprise. All these years I had sensed there was more lurking beneath the still waters of my amnesia; I'd instinctively *known* my sister's fall wasn't an accident.

The police could find no trace that anyone other than you and Jamie had been on the rocks that day.

Suddenly I wanted to be outside in the cool air, away from the chatter and clink of glasses, away from the paintings that stirred to life a past I had no desire to remember. And away from my mother who had, with her years of silence, just resurrected my darkest fear.

'Earth to Ruby . . . Anyone home in there?'

We were standing in the car park outside the gallery. The only car left was Rob's Jaguar, gleaming blackly in the floodlights. My mother had invited us to join her at the post-exhibition party, but I could tell her heart wasn't in the offer. Our talk about Jamie had frazzled us both, and I knew she was relieved to see me go.

'Ruby, are you okay?' Rob said, watching me.

I was beyond tired. The wine had gone to my head. The nerves that had been fraying away all day were suddenly ragged. All I wanted at that moment was the quiet solitude of a dark space, somewhere cosy and safe, preferably my bed, where I could hide, barricade myself against the day's events. Anywhere but here, in the empty car park with its stark security lighting.

Rob jangled his car keys. 'Babe?'

Drawing a deep breath, I dug in my bag and pulled out the scrap of black lace.

'How do you explain this?'

Rob stared from my face to the bra, then back to my face, apparently bewildered. He shrugged, palms up. 'What are you talking about?'

'You're seeing someone else, aren't you?'

His eyes narrowed and he grew wary. 'Now, hold on a minute, Ruby. You've lost me. You'd better start at the beginning.'

My cheeks burned and my heart swooped around my rib cage, my lungs suddenly too tight to breathe. 'This morning while you were in the shower, I smelled cigarette smoke on your jacket. I picked it up to shake it out, and this' – I waved the bra aloft – 'fell out of your pocket.'

Rob's lips quirked up into a smile, but he didn't look happy. 'And based on that, you've now surmised that I'm cheating on you?'

I nodded.

He pinched the bridge of his nose. 'I stopped at the bar on my way back to your place last night. A couple of the lads were there. Maybe one of them slipped it in as a joke. You know what they're like, childish idiots sometimes. Stupid pranks like that—' He gestured at the bra and rolled his eyes. 'It's just their way of letting off steam.'

My hands shook. The bra quivered in my fingers. My legs were jelly.

'I don't believe you.'

Rob looked pained. 'How can you say that? How can you even think it?'

I shook the bra. 'I've got proof.'

'Oh hell, Ruby. When are you going to get it through your thick skull – there's no one else.'

I searched his face for falsehood. The gallery light silvered the edges of his cheekbone and jaw, making him seem godlike and inhuman, as distant as a star. Then he moved and the illusion broke apart. He was just Rob again, big gentle Rob with his tailored suit and strong pale hands, shaking his head in worry.

'You're the only girl I want. Ever since I met you – love at first sight, remember? You're the only girl I'll *ever* want.'

Cramming the bra back in my handbag and out of sight, I couldn't stop myself asking, 'Why? You could have anyone – why *me*?'

Rob actually laughed. 'Why? Because you're suspicious and untrusting and you always think the worst. You whinge relent-lessly when you're sick, you interrupt when I'm trying to tell you something, and you scrape your plate all through the news. Oh . . . and you snore.'

'I do not.'

He nodded. 'Afraid you do, babe.'

I shuffled precariously in my tight shoes, feeling my argument deflate. An exhausted, vaguely tipsy numbness settled over me, urging me to surrender. I sighed.

'Is that it? You like me because I'm so hopelessly flawed?'

He smiled seductively. 'Well, you do have a rather glorious bottom.'

'Ugh.' I gave him my sourest look. 'You're so shallow.'

His smile fell away. Closing the gap between us, he cupped my face in his hands and drew me against him.

'You're the girl of my dreams, Ruby. Haven't I told you that a million times? I used to dream about you before we met, and since that day in the bookshop, you're all I think about.' He kissed me tenderly, then murmured against my lips, 'Don't you know how much I love you, Ruby?'

The words came at me so softly, so unexpectedly, that I flinched.

For the past three years I'd longed for him to open up, to tell me how he truly felt – if indeed he felt anything at all. I knew better than to rush him, knew better than to press the issue, but three years felt like an eternity for love to go unspoken. I had tried to be understanding, tried to remember that despite Rob's outward strength he still carried the scars of his own troubled past. So, I'd waited. And told myself that although Rob had a knack for extracting personal confessions from other people, the workings of his own heart were a tightly guarded secret.

Until now.

I love you, he'd finally said. *I love you.*

I gazed into his eyes. His irises were dark, nearly black. As fathomless as the sea. Though we had shared only three years of history, it felt to me at that moment that there lay an eternity between us.

I love you, Ruby.

I groped for the appropriate answer, but none came. Maybe later, I reasoned; maybe after a strong cup of tea and a good night's sleep. Tipsy was no state from which to declare anything of importance, least of all love.

Pulling away from him, I stared up at the sky. A full moon drifted weightlessly above us, haloed by misty clouds. Rain was coming. A day away, maybe two.

I shivered. Despite Rob's words, despite his tender kiss and confession of love, I sensed a shift. A boundary had been crossed, a layer torn away.

All day I'd been dreading his honesty, making myself sick with worry in anticipation of hearing the truth. What I hadn't counted on was the possibility of a lie.

The headlights bored a tunnel into the darkness as we sped back to Coffs. Roadside trees thrashed in the wind, and the sky was a starless black wasteland of ragged clouds. Beethoven's 'Moonlight Sonata' drifted from the dashboard speakers, its bittersweet piano casting a spell of melancholy over me.

I'd intended to doze until Ebor, where we would stop to eat, but I was too wound up. Every time I shut my eyes I was standing in front of Mum's walnut-tree painting, hearing Esther's voice.

They never did find out who was responsible, did they?

The stereo lights shimmered. Dark waves of music rushed at me. Gone was the sweet melancholy; the tempo was now pure agitation and it made me jumpy.

'Mind if I change this?'

'Go ahead,' Rob said, not taking his eyes off the road.

Flicking on the overhead, I scrabbled through the CDs in the glovebox. Mozart, Shostakovich, Liszt. I would have loved to hear some Roky Erickson right then – his quirky lyrics and gravelly voice always managed to lift my mood – but a blast of psychedelia from the seventies would have really blown Rob out of the water. I chose a soothing Brahms instead, but as I pulled it from the pile another disc toppled out.

I looked at the cover in surprise.

A young woman in jeans, with a gingham shirt tied jauntily at her waist, open at the cleavage. She had bottle-blonde hair and spider-black lashes and was sitting on the backboard of a dusty ute nursing a huge Dobro guitar. Her smile was broad and friendly; the gap between her front teeth made me like her.

Removing Beethoven, I fumbled this new CD into the player. The woman's voice filled the cabin. Her guitar style was laid-back, a bluesy metallic twang that suited her clear, strong vocals.

'Ainslie Nash,' I read from the cover, then looked at Rob. He was staring straight ahead at the road, apparently lost in his thoughts. 'I never picked you as a country fan.'

Rob's fingers tightened on the wheel. 'You're always telling me to broaden my musical horizons.'

I frowned. In three years Rob had never strayed from the classical. Why now? I tried to tell myself I was edgy after Mum's show and my conversation with Esther, and after my drama with the bra this morning – but the heaviness in my chest warned me that something was off. Rob sounded defensive. His mouth was pinched in a line, and the furrow between his brows was deeper than usual.

I looked back at the CD. Ainslie Nash's smile was no longer quite so friendly. She was very slim, I noticed. Her milk-coloured hair was gathered at the back of her head, spilling long tendrils over her shoulders. She had small breasts, and just above the swell of them – beneath the collar of her gingham shirt – peeped what might have been an edge of black lace. Peering closer, I tilted the CD cover this way and that in the overhead light. Then I looked at Rob.

'Where did you get this?'

He didn't answer. Pressing the volume switch, he killed the music and drove in silence. A minute dragged by. Two minutes. Still, he didn't speak.

'Rob?'

A weary sigh. 'Give it a rest, Ruby. It's been a long day.'

'I can't let it rest. Did someone give it to you, a girl?'

For a long while – an eternity, to be exact – he frowned at the road, his fingers white-knuckled around the wheel. When he finally spoke, his voice was resigned.

'I bought it for you. You like female vocalists, and I know you're a fan of Glen Campbell too. So, when I saw the CD in Sanity the other day, I thought of you. I kept it in the glovebox, played it a couple of times. I wanted to be sure it was your kind of thing.'

A flush of heat spread down my throat. 'Oh.'

Flicking off the overhead, I stared out at the dark country-side. It was thoughtful of Rob to have bought me the CD. But why had he let me make a fuss before admitting he'd intended it as a gift? I wished I could shrug off my suspicions and trust him; I wanted desperately to believe his explanation about the bra. But something nagged in the back of my mind. Nothing I could explain; more a sense of uneasiness, as if, now that the cat of suspicion was out of the bag, it was tearing around out of my control.

We were passing the trout hatchery and the road had entered a dark tunnel of overhanging trees. In daylight this section of the trip was leafy and pretty, but now – draped in shadows that seemed to race beside the car in pursuit – the nightscape felt hostile, threatening.

Rob looked across at me. 'I meant what I said in the carpark, you know.'

'Yeah.' My voice came out duller than I'd meant. 'It just feels wrong somehow.'

'What does?'

My fingers dug into the lambskin seat cover and knotted themselves in the pile. 'I can't pinpoint it, exactly. I just feel something's not right.'

'Between us?'

My brows ached from frowning. I rubbed them but it didn't help.

'I don't know.'

Rob sighed. 'Honey, it's not healthy to be so paranoid and obsessive all the time. You'll worry yourself into a heart attack one of these days. I care about you, Ruby. I really do. I just wish you'd accept that.'

I looked at him warily. 'I'm not paranoid.'

'Babe, you blow a simple misunderstanding out of proportion. Then you start looking for evidence, trying to catch me out . . . and why? Because you're scared of letting anyone close. Scared of letting *me* close. The minute things get good between us, you pull away. You concoct all these issues between us, when the real issue is that you're scared of love.'

I felt my cheeks go hot and was grateful for the dark. 'You don't know me as well as you think you do, Rob.'

'You're an open book to me, Ruby. One look at your face and I know exactly what page you're on. I probably know you a far sight better than you know yourself.'

Gripping my elbows, I said through my teeth, 'So, what am I thinking now?'

He glanced at me, then looked back at the road. 'Your eyes are like saucers in the dark. You're leaning away from me, arms crossed, knees pointed to the door. I'd bet my last dollar you're thinking I'm a prize-winning dickhead and you wish you'd never met me.'

Spot-on as usual, I thought sourly. Jamming my hands by my sides, I glared at his smug profile, and in that moment I hated him. I hated his clean good looks and crisp white shirt and manicured hands. I hated his smooth confidence and charm. I hated the way he considered the inner workings of my mind to be public property for him to sift through and analyse any time he chose. I hated hearing his voice whenever I stood in front of a mirror. *A few kilos lighter, Ruby girl, and you'd be a real honey.* And I hated seeing the same question again and again in other women's eyes: *What's a tasty dish like Rob Thistleton doing with a blimp like her?*

I stared out at the sky.

Rob had a knack for reading people, picking up on their vibe and making snap judgements. But was I really the person he'd described? Paranoid. Obsessive. Fearful of love. I hadn't meant to turn out that way, but looking back I could see the truth of it: my troubled relationship with Mum; my lonely years before Rob; and now, when I had finally found someone to love me, I was more unhappy than ever.

Rob always said that too many people were searching outside themselves for answers, when the only true guidance they could rely on came from within. Pricking my ears, I listened. Wind hissed under the tyres and the motor purred quietly – but there was no word from my subconscious, no murmur from my inner self, not even a whisper.

I searched the landscape beyond my window. The roadside trees still swayed in the night wind. Stars glittered in their velvet dome. Somewhere out there, the ghost of a girl ran barefoot through the night; the darkness her friend, the riverbank her playground, the wild grasslands and dense thickets of tea-tree her home. What had become of her?

As it turned out, Jamie's injuries were not caused by a fall.

A rope of fear tightened around my insides. My skin felt too tight, as if I'd crawled into an ill-fitting garment and got stuck. I wanted to get out of myself, find the person I'd been before guilt and self-doubt had warped me out of shape.

Suddenly I was possessed by the urge to shove open my door and throw myself from the moving car. And in that moment of craziness, I glimpsed something about myself that had, until now, eluded me.

I was like a house – my doors bolted against the night, my windows shuttered to keep out the wind and rain. But all the while, the thing I feared most dwelled inside me, stalking my hallways and moving restlessly inside my rooms. I wanted to open up my doors and windows, let the elements flush away the ghosts and dust and disorder. I wanted to spring clean, to de-clutter, to strip away everything that didn't belong so that I could show my *real* face.

But how could I, when my fear of the truth was holding me captive?

2

Brenna, March 1898

Hurrying along the dirt track towards the Aboriginal encampment, wishing I had wings to fly there faster, I skipped over the stony track, clutching my dillybag to my side, dizzy with expectation. The day was brilliantly hot, the sun a scorching ball in the blue dome of the sky. The morning air was thick with bush flies, and the faint aroma of charred kangaroo.

My buttoned boots were dusty, and the hem of my tweed walking skirt was dotted with grass seeds; my hat kept flying off my head, and an annoying itch of sweat had worked its way under the high neck of my blouse – but what did I care? I was nineteen, strong of limb, and brimming with excitement. I was on my way to see my 'wild friends' as Aunt Ida called them, and anticipation sang loud in my heart.

The encampment was on the southernmost corner of my father's three thousand acre property. My father estimated that there were sixty or more Aborigines living in the area permanently, while another hundred or so migrated along their traditional routes – travelling the western slopes and up onto the tablelands, then along the eastern falls. As traditional hunting grounds were being grazed flat, and worse, being zealously patrolled by cattlemen with guns, food was becoming scarce for the people.

As I approached the camp, a thin woman of about forty walked out to greet me. She wore a dusty yellow European-style dress that my aunt had given her. Behind her, a cluster of bark huts surrounded a charcoal pit, which still smouldered after last night's meal. Marsupial pelts were strung on the low branches of a nearby salmon gum, among them the hide of a large grey kangaroo.

I felt a thrill of pleasure to see my friend. As I dashed along the track towards her, my hat bobbed off its ribbon and I felt the full warmth of the sun touch my face; Aunt Ida would disapprove, but at that moment the farmhouse with all its rules and proprieties seemed a world away.

'Aunty good?' Jindera wanted to know.

It was always her first question, although Aunt Ida had never been to the camp – at least not as far as I knew – and Jindera never ventured up to the house. Yet whenever I queried this, Jindera always insisted that she and my aunt were friends.

'Aunt Ida is well,' I said, hanging my hat on a branch beneath the drying pelts. Shaking out my hair, I lifted my face to the sun, savouring the fragrant air. 'But she'll be in a sour mood when she gets out of her bath and finds me gone.'

'You stay short time.' Jindera's voice was reedy and melodic, and she spoke the English language with a shy sort of exuberance. 'Get back before Aunty know you gone.'

'We'll see,' I said, laughing. Jindera's idea of a 'short time' stretched anywhere between five minutes and five days – which suited my way of thinking nicely. As we stood smiling in the shade of that old salmon gum, a feeling of peace settled over me. I wanted to pull off my boots and stockings and go barefoot like Jindera, burrow my toes into the soft dirt and feel the pulsing bedrock beneath me. I wanted to lie on the ground so the scent of gumnuts and yellow-buttons and warm granite would cling to my skin and be with me always.

Instead, I looked around the camp. 'Where's Mee Mee?'

'She collecting seed.' Jindera smiled, pointing to the prickly grass pips stuck to my hem. 'Like you, Bunna.'

I laughed in pleasure at her observation, but found myself gazing wistfully at the spot under the shady red gum where Mee Mee liked to sit with her grinding stones. Mee Mee was Jindera's mother, a lanky woman with huge liquid-black eyes and a quick smile who always fussed over me when I visited.

Jindera gestured to the bag slung over my shoulder. 'You bring book?'

My dillybag was roughly the shape and size of a large flattened nightcap, with a single strap that fitted comfortably across my chest. Jindera had woven it for me from grass fibres, coloured with red and black and yellow dyes made from barks and berries. Besides my book of botanical drawings with its pages of notes and thoughts, it was my most treasured possession.

Taking out the leather-bound journal, I placed it in Jindera's hands and we walked back to the encampment.

As we approached her hut, a gaggle of children raced into the camp from the direction of the river. They yelled happily when they saw me, and I dug into my dillybag again, this time pulling out a handful of unshelled almonds. In their haste to secure a few nuts, the children knocked them from my hands and had to scrabble in the dirt for them, jostling each other good-humouredly before running off laughing and shouting to crack open their dusty prizes with river stones.

I paused for a moment, watching them dart away through the trees towards the embankment. Some nights, I dreamed about that embankment. It was a magical place by day, when the current gurgled over the stones and then rushed over a deep natural spillway to the rocks below. But in my dream, the voice of the river was dark and desolate. It sang of death, and figures looming on horseback, and screams that seemed to rise up out of the earth and echo against the night sky. There was always the smell of burning – flesh and hair, bones. And the sense that I was trapped in the dark, my small body shuddering in fear.

I turned to see Jindera watching me, as she often did, from the darkness of her hut. Her eyes were velvet-black, her smile warm. She beckoned me in.

A sweet, pungent odour lingered in the confined space, perhaps kangaroo from last night's feast. Jindera spread a beaten bark mat across the dirt floor and we sat upon it. Placing my journal between us on the mat, she reached for a hide pouch of water and passed it to me. I drank thirstily, then handed the pouch back to Jindera and wiped my lips. Jindera drank, then set the pouch aside and took up my book.

Carefully she opened to the page I had been working on. It was a rock orchid, its delicate pink throat freckled with brown markings. It was common to this area, springing up in early summer, its brilliant colouring leaping from the grey-green foliage of the bush.

Jindera did not speak, but pleasure radiated from her. I knew she wasn't admiring the drawings for their beauty. She had often tried to explain that her people's drawings captured the spirit of the creatures and plant life they depicted. She said their paintings called to those spirits in the language of dreams.

My paintings – the flowers and seedpods, orchids and ferns and gumnuts that proliferated on the rocky granite slopes of Lyrebird Hill – were of interest to Jindera because she understood my passion for learning about their healing or dietary properties. Although the subjects of my botanical drawings were beautiful and oftentimes strange, they were not for decoration alone.

Since the age of fifteen, I had spent every moment of my spare time compiling notes and creating detailed watercolours that catalogued all the edible and medicinal plants known to Jindera. She had asked permission from the clan elders, who had at first forbidden her to speak to me. *Much danger*, they had warned, but how much danger could there be in the friendship between two women? Besides, Jindera had existed on the periphery of my life since I was a baby. My frequent visits to the camp had begun when I was fourteen, when we had formed a strong and unbreakable bond. So Jindera had persisted with the elders, and finally – after I presented them with my father's old muzzleloader, with which they could shoot wallaby – they eventually agreed.

Jindera paused at a sketch of tubular pink blossoms. Her fingers hovered over the neat lines of copperplate. Though she had no use for reading, I suspected she knew those words by rote. I'd read them aloud to her so many times, page after page until my throat was hoarse. We'd picked over each description in our stolen hours together, Jindera making corrections, adding new facts that occurred to her, snippets of memory, old stories from the vast reserves passed on to her by Mee Mee or one of the other elders. Meanwhile I scribbled frantically – dashing out notes, refining my descriptions, clarifying names – in a bid to keep up with her.

I tapped the page she was studying.

'That's the correa we found on the flatlands that day, on the place where the clan fought that southern tribe, do you remember?'

Jindera shook her head and laughed, her eyes gleaming. Reaching out, she gently squeezed my wrist. 'You got good memory, Bunna. That happen twenty year before you born.'

I turned another page and pointed to a drawing of clustered leaves in the shape of four-leaf clovers.

'And this fern, it was sprouting from a pile of wombat bones after the big rain last year.'

Jindera nodded. 'Nardoo. Hard time food.'

I found myself going through the pages, pointing out drawings I considered particularly successful, or reading anecdotes that held special memories for us of shared adventures.

Jindera reached for the water skin, and again we both drank. My heart was large with her unspoken approval. In our own way, we had fought an important battle – not with spears and nulla-nullas, but with brush and ink, with knowledge and quiet observation. My collection of drawings and Jindera's vast store of experience that accompanied them were a testament to our friendship. We had refused to let fear dampen our alliance, and we were both the richer for it.

'Brenna?' came a voice from outside.

A shadow darkened the hut's doorway, and I caught a whiff of horse sweat and tannery leather, rifle oil and gunpowder; scents that did not belong in the tranquil darkness of Jindera's hut.

I emerged into the sunlight, Jindera close on my heels, to find my foster brother, Owen, dismounting his horse. He was tall for a twelve-year-old, and lean; the grey shirt and breeches he wore seemed to hang off his skinny frame. The sun had bleached his hair, and his eyes shone blue as lagoon water.

Owen's face lit up when he saw my companion.

'G'day there, Jindera.'

'Hello, young Owen. You be good boy for Aunty?'

'I try.'

'How them fish biting upriver?'

'I caught a couple of turtles this week, but no trout.'

They bantered for a while in their easy way, while I bundled my journal into my dillybag, only half listening.

Owen had been orphaned a decade ago when an accident on a neighbouring farm took his parents. My father – Fa Fa, to those close to him – had found the little boy wandering along the road in the dark, hungry and as skinny as a stray dog. Fa Fa brought him back to the farmhouse, where our Aboriginal housekeeper Millie fed and bathed him and swaddled him in one of Fa Fa's old shirts. Owen soon became my father's shadow, perched on the saddle behind him when he rode out to check the fences, sitting at his feet when he smoked his evening pipe, sleeping at the foot of his bed. He had been a cherub of a child, eager to run errands or lend a hand with chores, a golden boy we all adored.

'Is Aunt Ida on the war path?' I asked warily.

'Afraid so, Sis. You have a visitor, and he wasn't all that pleased to arrive and find you not there.'

'Oh dear.' My heart kicked over. 'It's Mr Whitby, isn't it?'

Owen made a face and nodded.

I sighed. Poor Mr Whitby. Owen disliked him intensely, despite the fact that Whitby was one of my father's oldest and most trusted friends. Whitby lived in Tasmania on a large property, but often travelled to New South Wales on business. He had bought nearly a dozen holdings on the New England tablelands after the property crash in 1893, and liked to keep his finger in the pie of their management and occasional sale. Although he was in his mid-forties – a few years younger than my father – he had never married. Aunt Ida said that he was wed to his work, but my father scoffed at this. *Carsten is a private man*, he would declare, *he keeps his personal affairs close to his heart.*

'Where is Whitby now,' I asked with more calm than I felt. 'At the house? Has he brought news of Fa Fa?'

Owen examined a hangnail and took his time to answer. 'Fa Fa is still at the auctions in Newcastle. Aunt Ida's bailed up Whitby in the parlour. She's feeding him leftover Christmas cake and bottled apricots. Whitby seemed anxious for you to join them.'

Jindera was frowning at me, her eyes dark with quiet disapproval. She shared Owen's lack of esteem for Carsten Whitby, although she would never admit as much. Whenever I told her that he had visited, or if I enthused about his polished manners or fine looks, Jindera always managed to find something of greater interest – a gumnut fallen from a tree, or snake tracks in the dirt, or the dusty wrinkles that time had drawn across the palm of her hand.

We said goodbye to Jindera, and Owen climbed on his horse and hauled me up behind him. He clicked his tongue, and the mare plodded along the track towards home. I hooked one arm around Owen's middle and settled myself for the ride back to the house.

'Did Whitby mention the nature of his visit?' I asked.

My brother shook his head, and nudged the horse into a trot. I twisted around, trying to see Jindera's shadow in the doorway of her hut, hoping to give her a wave.

The only movement was a breeze ruffling the animal hides strung on the branches. The camp looked deserted, as though its inhabitants had fled.

Sitting at my dressing table, I hurriedly brushed my hair. It was more tangled than usual, and soon my brush was full of knots. I emptied some sweet almond oil from a bottle into my hands, and smoothed the oil over my wayward strands. As I pinned my chignon, I heard a shuffle in the doorway.

Aunt Ida moved into my bedroom, clutching a jar of cornflour. Pink blotches coloured each sharp cheekbone, and her eyes were as sharp as a bird's. 'I declare, Brenna. The sooner you're married off and away from those people, the better for all of us.'

I made a sour face in the mirror. 'Jindera's my friend. I've no intention of staying away from her.'

Aunt Ida's frown carved crevices between her brows. 'I've got Carsten Whitby in the room downstairs, of which I'm sure you are aware. I've spent the last hour apologising for your absence.'

Taking out a handkerchief, I wiped it over my face, getting rid of the dusty smears. 'Did he bring news of my father? When is he coming home?'

'Whitby didn't say.'

Something in her voice made me glance at her. It was no secret that she disapproved of my frequent visits to the encampment, and we often had words. But today she seemed subdued, almost depressed.

'What is it, Aunt?'

There was a long silence. Finally she said quietly, 'The clan doesn't want you there. Jindera is indulging you by letting you visit, but the elders resent your presence. They see you as a threat. You might not care about putting yourself at risk, but when are you going to learn to think about others?'

'Fa Fa lets me go.'

Aunt Ida shook her head, and placed the jar of cornflower on my dresser. 'Rub that into your face. You've neglected to wear your hat again. You've already got colour on your cheeks. My word, Brenna, don't you ever listen? Your Mama's last words to me were to keep you out of the sun, so you wouldn't end up—' She made a clearing sound in her throat. 'And look at your hair! I'd not be surprised if Whitby caught one glimpse of you and ran for the hills.'

Tucking away my handkerchief, I opened the jar of cornflour. White clouds puffed out as I swirled my wad of lamb's wool in the powder, then daubed it on my face. Sitting back, I examined the effect in the mirror, tilting my head to the side.

'What brings Whitby here, anyway?'

'He has come to speak to you.'

I whirled on my seat. 'Whatever about?'

My aunt's lips thinned against her teeth, but she did not reply.

Lately, the topic of Whitby had become something of an obsession for her; she sang his praises at every opportunity, and was constantly reminding me of his various virtues. *Did you know*, she would say, her eyebrows shooting up as if the thought had just occurred to her, *Whitby has a stable of fine horses? You like horses, don't you, Brenna?*

Why was she suddenly so restrained?

As I changed out of my dusty clothes, I studied her in the mirror. Sweat patches had formed on her blouse, and her face looked puffy and unusually pale. She was frowning fixedly at the cornflour, as if it were somehow responsible for her woes.

I sighed. 'Oh Aunt, I do wish you'd stop worrying. I'm sure you're wrong about Jindera's clan. They don't mind me being there.'

Aunt Ida stood silently for a time, then hurried out the door and vanished into the shadows of the hallway, the volume of her skirts whispering after her like an eddy of dry leaves. A moment later she returned carrying a small burlap-wrapped parcel.

'Here,' she said, placing the bundle on my dressing table. 'If you insist on visiting the encampment, then for heaven's sake keep your wits about you. And make sure you carry *that* on you at all times.'

I caught a whiff of gun oil, and my heart sank. Lifting a corner of burlap, I examined the contents.

'It was your father's,' Aunt Ida informed me. 'Before he saw fit to invest in a rifle. It's smaller than the weapon you and Owen learned on, but the principles of loading and firing are the same.'

'Why now?' I said. 'Why today?'

My aunt's face tightened. 'Whitby brought news of another killing on the plains. Further west from here, but you know how nervous people get when word spreads. Since you insist on wandering the far corners of this property, I'd feel better if you had a means of protecting yourself should anything happen.'

I lifted my chin. 'Jindera's clan would never hurt me.'

'It's not the clan I'm worried about,' Aunt said quietly, then turned and went out.

Closing the burlap over my father's revolver, I hid the package in my bottom drawer. My aunt's fears had shaken me, but I refused to let them dampen my mood. Standing before the mirror, I regarded myself. Aunt Ida was right. The sun had touched my skin, putting colour on my cheeks.

My oval face was framed by unruly brown hair, which was almost as dark as my eyes. A light sprinkling of freckles lay across my tawny complexion, despite Aunt Ida's regular reminders about wearing my hat. Fa Fa liked to say that I had inherited my looks from his grandmother, who had been born in Spain; both he and Ida were fair, so I supposed the Spanish blood had skipped a generation.

I wore my best black skirt, an ivory shirtwaist and a jacket of dark red wool with black trim. The day was hot for such heavy attire, but I had not chosen my outfit for comfort but, rather, to impress Mr Whitby.

For many months I had entertained the fancy that Whitby might fall in love with me. He was more than two decades older, but even Aunt Ida considered him a most desirable match. Yet it wasn't his wealth and social standing that interested me. After his visits, my heart always beat faster at the memory of his intelligent grey eyes, and the way his gaze always seemed to single me out and light up when I appeared.

I ran a handkerchief over my boots to banish the last of the dust, and hurried downstairs.

Sunlight streamed into the parlour, and a breeze blew through the French doors, bringing with it the musky scent of the shearing sheds. I stood in the doorway, taking in the scene. The spacious room appeared overcrowded, but in fact there were barely a handful of people present.

My aunt was by the fireplace, speaking intently to a muscular man clad all in black. Carsten Whitby was perfectly poised, straight-backed as a soldier, his handsome features serious as he nodded at Ida's commentary about the drought, and the farm, and the poor conditions for shearing. Yet he seemed distracted, his interest apparently caught by the painting above the mantle.

Nearby stood Owen, gazing as he always did in Fa Fa's absence towards the front gate. At his feet, my father's shaggy old wolf-hound Harold slept, oblivious to Aunt Ida's stream of chatter.

Millie fussed over the dining table, which had been laid with a red tablecloth and Aunt Ida's best tea rose china. On a tray beside several glasses sat a crystal decanter of the sherry Whitby favoured. There was also a cake stand full of iced cakes, and a large platter of sandwiches.

Nerves rumbled in my belly, and I wondered if food might calm them. I looked across at Millie and the tray of meatloaf she was placing on the table. She caught my eye, and beamed.

She was a tiny woman of thirty with a round face and enormous brown eyes. She had been with our family since the age of ten. Her parents were once part of Jindera's clan, but they had died two decades ago. My own mother had been ill at the time, so Aunt Ida – who'd never married – was pleased to acquire Millie's extra set of hands. For years, my father had been encouraging Millie to find a husband, perhaps even visit the encampment and ask Jindera's help, but Millie always refused, insisting she was content to live at the back of the farmhouse in a lean-to, where, she always claimed, she could breathe the sweet air that flowed up from the river.

She hurried over. 'How's Jindera?'

'Good. They had kangaroo last night.'

A wistful look came into her eyes, but it vanished quickly. 'When you finish here,' she told me, 'come out to the kitchen. I'll save you a couple slices of meatloaf.' Her dark gaze shifted, and she looked over my shoulder. 'Look out, Fa Fa's friend is on his way over.'

She moved away, back to the table, and I turned to see Mr Whitby heading my way.

'Miss Magavin, you are breathtaking as usual.'

I felt a blush creep up, and found myself beaming. 'Thank you, Mr Whitby. I trust your journey from Wynyard was a pleasant one?'

'Indeed, it went swiftly enough.' He bowed sharply and took my fingers, grazing his lips over my knuckles.

A shiver ran up my arm. He was a striking man, his dark hair and beard closely cropped, his skin pale; but most arresting were his expressive grey eyes, framed by black lashes and strong brows, and a gaze that always lingered searchingly on my face. He wore a snug-fitting double-breasted black frock coat that showed off his muscular physique, and a crisp throttling collar that made him seem taller and more upright.

'I trust all is well in Tasmania?' I asked.

'My sister has been unwell.'

'I'm sorry to hear it.' Although I didn't personally know Adele Whitby, my regret was genuine. I understood the heartbreak of watching a loved one wither away before your eyes. My mother had died from a weak heart when I was small, leaving a shadow over those of us who remained. 'I hope she enjoys a swift recovery.'

Twin spots of red suffused Whitby's craggy cheekbones. The lines around his mouth softened. 'That is most kind, Miss Magavin.'

'Aunt told me you saw my father in Newcastle,' I ventured, eager for news. 'Did he happen to mention when he'll be returning?'

Whitby shifted beside me. 'Miss Magavin, I'm afraid I have some bad news.'

I looked back at him, hoping I'd misheard.

Whitby lifted his hand, signalling to Millie. A moment later she was at his side, her tray crowded with glasses and the decanter that glinted vermilion as sunbeams speared through the sherry. Whitby took a glass and swallowed the sickly liquor in one gulp. Millie poured him another, then retreated to the kitchen.

Whitby frowned at me. 'Due to fluctuations in the wool market, your father's bales didn't clear his reserve. Any other year, he may have recovered the deficit the following season. But he has already suffered too many years of deficit. Recovering this latest loss is out of the question.'

I stood very still; my fingertips were suddenly cold, and my pulse drummed in my ears. Glancing across the room, I saw that Owen had wandered out to the yard, and Aunt Ida was presumably with Millie in the kitchen.

'I don't quite understand.'

'When I left Michael in Newcastle yesterday, his position was bleak. You know that his financier has been struggling since the crash in ninety-one?'

A knot of worry tightened in the back of my neck. 'Fa Fa's bank is currently being taken over, but the new bank has assured him that it wouldn't affect him.'

'Miss Magavin, there seems to have been a misunderstanding. Owing to the economic collapse and the bank's need to free up substantial quantities of cash, they have requested immediate payment. They have given your father thirty days to pay his default.'

'Thirty days? But the sum owing is considerable. We won't be able to pay.'

Whitby's bleak expression was his only reply.

I felt sure he was wrong. If my father's situation was so dire, Fa Fa would have mentioned it before now – wouldn't he? I gripped my hands together to stop them trembling.

'Why hasn't my father spoken of this to us?'

Whitby grimaced, pushing his fingertips through the stubble of his thin beard. 'I expect he was hoping to turn the situation around, before alarming anyone. Michael is a proud man, my dear. This predicament has taken its toll on him, but until now he was loath to share the burden.'

I shook my head, still trying to draw forth a solution. 'But even if my father had sold his bales above reserve, the earnings would never touch the amount he owes. And now that we've made a loss on the wool, how are we going to . . . ?' My words dropped away as the seriousness of our situation began to sink in.

Whitby drew out a silver watch and weighed it absently in his palm. 'Michael's been struggling to meet his repayments for years. He's not the only one. There's talk of unrest in Southern Africa again, and all over the country people are reluctant to part with their coin. Times are hard.' Secreting the fob watch back in his pocket, he looked at me. 'And as you know, there are those in the community who dislike Michael because of his political leanings.'

Whitby's words touched a nerve, and I drew up to my full height. 'You mean because he speaks out against murder? Because he talks about the rights of the tribal people to carry spears so they may hunt? Because he criticises the overgrazing of land, and the indiscriminate felling of trees?' My cheeks were burning, my heart racing dangerously fast. I was overstepping the same line that had earned my father the dislike of which Whitby spoke, but I didn't care. 'The clans that migrate through this area are no threat to anyone. They only want to be left alone and be allowed to feed their families.'

Whitby's eyes narrowed. 'Michael's actions here have made him unpopular. He has more than a few enemies in this town. If he went under, no one would extend a helping hand. Your father is ruined, Miss Magavin. You understand what that means, don't you?'

I *did* understand, only too well. And as that understanding deepened, something dark and deathly crawled along my spine. My skin went cold, the room tilted under me. I thought I might fall.

I remembered a long-ago quarrel, one between my father and Aunt Ida. They'd been in the dining room at opposite ends of the table, their faces lit by candlelight, speaking in a hush. From my vantage point beneath the table – I'd been twelve and hiding from Millie – their voices were cracked and distorted with emotion.

Oh Michael, you're a fool to borrow more money, my aunt had fumed. *You're digging yourself deeper into debt. There's nothing left of our inheritance, and you already owe the bank so much. For heaven's sake, Michael – if you* must *purchase those merinos, why don't you finance them by selling off a few hundred acres of land?*

I won't sell the land, my father had replied, his voice as jagged as a crow's. *Not an acre of it, not even a square inch. Don't ask me again, Ida. I won't sell.*

A long silence ensued, and I'd thought the argument done. But then Aunt Ida's words had bitten into the darkness. *You still think of her, don't you, Michael? You can't forget her. You'd rather drag us all to ruin than sell a chain of her precious land.*

'Miss Magavin?'

I forced myself to meet Whitby's measuring gaze. 'My father will never sell Lyrebird Hill. The loss—' I had to finish on a whisper. 'The loss of it would kill him.'

Whitby shifted uncomfortably. 'My dear, I understand your distress. It's a hateful thing to contemplate the loss of your home. However, don't alarm yourself. All is not lost. When I saw Michael yesterday, we discussed many possible scenarios, all of them unsatisfactory. So, after much thought, I put forth a proposal with the potential to benefit us all.'

His gaze skated around the room then alighted on the portrait over the fireplace: my mother in a pale pink dress, her golden hair spilling over her shoulders, her blue eyes huge against the waxy pallor of her face.

Whitby's lips tightened. He pondered the portrait for a moment, as if not really seeing its subject, but rather something that existed beyond its shallow surface of paint. When he looked back at me his face seemed aged, as if the lines around his mouth had grown deeper, his skin become thinner, and the gleam in his eyes faded.

In a weary voice, he said, 'My family originally came from Armidale. They were horse breeders, and very successful. When my father died fifteen years ago, he left everything to me. Of course, by that time I'd set up my own enterprise in Tasmania, but over the years I was able to greatly increase the worth of my inheritance by purchasing land holdings in this region.'

He flushed, and his eyes shone with intensity. 'Miss Magavin, I don't tell you this to impress you, but merely to explain myself. You see, while my businesses thrived, my personal life floundered. I have never married, and therefore lack an heir to whom I may pass on my estates. What I desire more than anything else in the world is a son.'

He regarded me closely as if to gauge my reaction.

I became very still. I understood where Whitby's fine speech was taking him, and part of me rejoiced. He was about to offer a solution to our problem; a way to save the property we relied upon for a livelihood, a property we loved. But another, smaller and more selfish part of me dreaded the words I sensed were about to spill from Mr Whitby's charming lips. Although I liked Whitby, the prospect of forsaking my home – and my freedom – dismayed me. I held my breath and anchored my fingernails into my palms, reaching inside myself for courage.

'My proposal is this,' Whitby said slowly, as though cautiously weighing his words. 'I will pay the default against Lyrebird Hill if you will agree to wed me, and bear me a son. Once the child is born, if you should find yourself unhappy in the arrangement, then I will freely release you to return home, on the condition that the boy stay with me.'

The sound of smashing crockery erupted from the kitchen, and Whitby glanced across the room towards the parlour door. A pulse of perfect silence beat around us, then I heard the scraping of the dust pan and the quick babble of hushed voices. I became aware of a vein pounding in my throat, and when I looked back at Whitby, I saw that he had noticed it, too.

Taking a breath, I forced myself to meet his eyes.

'You will pay the default?' I asked, hating the quaver in my voice. 'You will save our farm – if we are wed?'

Whitby inclined his head. 'Consider it my wedding gift to you, my dear. As well as my promise to do all I can to make you happy. But of course, you need not reply this instant. Please, Miss Magavin, take some time to consider your feelings on the matter.'

I stared into his fine grey eyes, seeing reflected in them a smaller, vastly diminished version of myself. *My feelings?* Whitby was not proposing a union between two people who adored one another, nor even between people who shared the hopeful purpose of building fond relations in the future.

He was simply proposing a business deal.

My gaze went briefly to the window. Beyond the grassy slope of our garden, rambled three thousand acres of bushland. Some of it was grazed by my father's flocks; much of it was wild and untouched. Westwards, along the river's rocky course, was the Aboriginal encampment. Was my freedom too great a price to save Lyrebird Hill?

I didn't need to ponder. Taking a shaky breath, I looked at Whitby and nodded.

'I agree.'

Whitby appeared momentarily at a loss; his pupils dilated and his nostrils flared, but then he smiled. It was a wonderful smile, unguarded, full of surprise and delight. The sight of his face captivated me, and I realised that until this moment I had never seen him so pleased.

He leaned towards me, and I wondered if he meant to kiss me. Instead, he grasped my fingers and I found myself shaking hands with my future husband, sealing the business deal we had just negotiated.

On Sunday evening my father arrived home, weary after his weeks in Newcastle. After dinner, we sat together at the dining table. Millie brewed strong tea and placed a dish of oatmeal biscuits on the table. Fa Fa packed a pipe and lit it, then settled back in his chair and regarded me.

'Whitby has promised me he will care for you,' my father said at last. 'Do you think you could grow to love him, Brenna girl?'

'He is twice my age.'

'He's a fine-looking man. At least, according to Ida he is.'

'Looks are not everything.'

'He is devoted to his sister. When her fiancé died, he paid for the young man's funeral, and then moved Adele into his house, the better to provide for her.'

'Will he be devoted to me?'

'Of course, my sparrow.'

I couldn't withhold a snort. 'Fa Fa, we shook hands. I wasn't expecting fireworks, not exactly – but am I foolish to assume that when a woman accepts a man's proposal of marriage, she is entitled to a kiss?'

Fa Fa lifted his brows and gave a weary sigh. 'Carsten has many admirable qualities. Unfortunately, social grace is not one of them.'

'But shaking hands?'

My father's face softened. 'You don't have to marry him, Brenna. It's not too late to write to him and admit a change of heart.'

A breeze lifted the curtains. The peppery scent of wildflowers mingled with the smell of tobacco. Drifts of native flowers had naturalised around the house. Nodding chocolate orchids, bluebells and golden hibbertia. My father loved them, and I'd crammed an armful into a Fowlers jar on the table especially to cheer him.

'There's been no change of heart, Fa Fa. I made a promise, and I intend to keep it. Anyway, what is love, when the fate of our home is at stake?'

Fa Fa tapped his pipe and relit it, then drew on the stem until the embers burned bright in the gloom.

'That's easy enough to say now. But how will you feel after the passing of a year? Of a decade? Time will dim your enthusiasm. Married life will limit your freedom, and tax your inner resources. You will have new obligations, and new restrictions. After a while, my sparrow, you may well come to regret your sacrifice.'

I sensed my father was speaking from experience, and for the first time wondered about his marriage to Mama. I had always thought them content; was it possible that Fa Fa had been secretly unhappy?

'I don't believe I'm making a sacrifice,' I told him. 'I'm simply doing what needs to be done.'

I could see by my father's frown that he wasn't convinced. His features looked pinched, his eyes dark with worry, and I realised he was more troubled than he was letting on. Beneath our discussion of marriage, lurked a deeper fear – a fear that I understood perfectly.

I went to the window, gazing past my reflection to the darkness outside. I could scarcely believe that a week ago I'd been unable to think of anything but my botanical pictures. I had rushed through my chores, bolted my food, and stayed up late drawing by candlelight. Whenever I could, I escaped to visit Jindera, consulting with her over my newest collection of specimens. Flowers, seed pods, frills of lichen; finch eggs, the blue-green feathers shed by a kingfisher, a wallaby skull.

Nothing had seemed more important.

Until now.

'Do you remember that squatter?' I asked Fa Fa, turning to face him. 'The one who paid his Aboriginal workers with loaves of damper, which turned out to be laced with arsenic?'

My father winced and looked away. 'I remember.'

'And do you recall that Aboriginal boy who was clubbed and left to die by the roadside?'

Silence.

My fingers trembled, but I couldn't stop. 'A few days ago, Aunt Ida told me about another killing, west of here.'

Pain rumpled my father's face.

I hated torturing him this way, but a fever of purpose had taken hold of me. He must understand; he must know that despite my reluctance to leave home, staying and watching it be sold off and ultimately destroyed would be far worse.

'Whole clans are starving because their hunting grounds are grazed flat. They're forbidden to carry spears, so they can't hunt. They live in a state of worry and uncertainty.' I took a shaky breath. 'Could you bear to see those things happen here at Lyrebird Hill? Could you tolerate Jindera's band being treated that way?'

'No, my dove. You know I couldn't.'

'Then, as long as the people who belong here live and breathe, I will have no regrets.'

Tears glazed my father's eyes. I sensed that he carried in his memory far worse reports than the ones I'd just described. With the creaky slowness of an old man, he reached into his pocket. Out came an object of dark wood, which he fumbled and dropped on the floor.

I picked it up. It was a chess piece, a fine dark queen. Much care had gone into its carving. Where had my father happened upon such a piece? Had he acquired the rest of the set? If so, I was already longing to play. I'd been practising obsessively, and fancied that my game had improved. It seemed absurd to be thinking of a game when the future of the farm was uncertain, but chess was a passion and I yearned to lose my troubles for an hour or so in a hearty challenge. Besides, some of my best ideas came to me while labouring a strategic point.

I replaced the queen on the table.

'She's all I have left,' Fa Fa said.

I looked at him, not understanding.

'When your mama and I were married,' he explained, 'we honeymooned in London. It was a strange time for us. We were both young and in love, only not—' He hesitated, and gave me a cautious look, then hurried on. 'Anyway, one day I secured a fine chess set in Camden. The white pieces were carved from boar's bone, while the black were of ebony wood. Florence was a keen player, and I knew she would be pleased by my acquisition. But as I was making my way back to our apartments, I was robbed. The thieves took everything I owned – my purse and wedding ring, even my shoes. When I climbed to my feet and looked around, I saw this little player lying in the snow, overlooked.

'I picked her up, and when I saw it was the black queen, I recognised it as an omen. For the longest time I stood there in the middle of that deserted London street in my socks and waistcoat, and all I could think of was how I yearned to be home. With each passing day, my yearning grew more insufferable. But whenever I picked up this little queen and held her in my hand, home seemed somehow nearer.'

I searched my father's face, wondering why a solitary chess piece had the power to ease his homesickness. The tiny ebony player made me think of my friends at the encampment. I imagined Fa Fa had made that connection too.

Since Carsten's proposal, I had created my own talisman against homesickness. Pressed between the pages of my Bible were twenty or more gum leaves, picked fresh from the trees in an effort to preserve their aroma. I had gathered flowers, too: native orchids, hibbertia, and papery ammobium daisies that rustled like silk. I could already feel the ache of separation blossoming in me, a cold, empty ache that I knew would grow deeper with distance. Even so, I refused to resent my sacrifice; how could I, when it meant saving the land and the people I loved?

'I couldn't bear to lose Lyrebird Hill,' I told my father heatedly, then chose my next words with care. 'Not an acre of it, not even a square inch.'

Fa Fa looked at me for a long time, an odd light in his eyes. Then he averted his gaze back to the table, nudging the ebony queen with a finger that appeared to tremble.

'No, my beauty,' he whispered hoarsely, 'neither could I.'

3

The journey towards emotional freedom begins when
you start thinking more about where you're going,
and less about where you've been.
– ROB THISTLETON, *EMOTIONAL RESCUE*

Ruby, April 2013

The week following my return to the coast was hectic. Several large deliveries of books arrived at the shop, and I threw myself into unpacking and cataloguing and finding space for them in my already impossibly cluttered shelves.

On Friday night, I went home early. Although my bookshop was in the busy metropolis of Coffs Harbour on the north coast of New South Wales, I lived twenty minutes south of there in the small seaside village of Sawtell. My tiny cottage was perched on the hilltop overlooking the sandy curves of Murray's Beach. On a windy day the salty breath of the ocean whispered through my rooms, teasing the curtains and enticing me out onto the patio to inhale the view.

Kicking off my shoes, I unloaded my groceries in the kitchen, then went out to the garden and picked a handful of fresh greens. When Rob rang and asked me to dinner, I found myself making excuses. He had resumed his usual chirpiness after our tiff about the bra, but I found myself watching him more closely now, reading hidden meaning into his words, looking for a chink in the armour of his innocence. I'd even stalked him once or twice, getting myself all sweaty and worried, working myself into a mood – but he'd only been with clients, or at the bar with his mates, or picking up laundry from the woman who washed and ironed for him.

There's no one else, Ruby. When are you going to get that through your thick skull?

I was trying to be happy with that. But since Mum's opening and my chat with Mrs Hillard, things had changed.

I felt as if I'd fallen down a rabbit hole and emerged into a world that was, by all appearances, normal, but under that veneer of normalcy was a life I didn't recognise. Esther's slip about Jamie, and then her gentle backtracking to save my feelings, still haunted me. I understood why Mum had never told me the truth, and appreciated that she'd only been trying to protect me with her silence; but something niggled.

Going out to my bedroom, I opened the wardrobe and took down a shoebox. Wiping off a layer of dust, I removed the lid and stared at the old photos inside.

After Jamie died, Mum had boxed up all our childhood photos and put them away, unable to cope with the grief they inspired in her. Once, I had rescued a Polaroid of Jamie from Mum's hoard and hidden it in my room, bringing it out to get me through those times when Jamie's absence seemed too painful to bear.

Where had it gone?

Urgency gripped me. I shuffled through the snapshots, hoping I'd overlooked the Polaroid in my haste. But it wasn't in the box. All of a sudden, I needed desperately to find it. If I could see my sister's face, catch it in my mind and hold it there, I felt sure my restlessness would subside.

From under my bed, I dragged out an old suitcase. Inside was an assortment of knick-knacks and odd flotsam that didn't belong anywhere else – dog-eared certificates, cigar boxes stuffed with old stamps and coins – but there was no Polaroid. Next I went through my collection of vintage handbags; still no luck. As I was packing them away, I came across the dusty bouquet of wildflowers that Esther Hillard had given me the night of Mum's opening.

I picked it up, thinking about my promise to visit. I never would, of course. How could I? The idea of seeing the old farm-house again filled me with unease. It was one thing to see an idealised version of my childhood home in Mum's paintings; after all, they were only oil paint on canvas. But to actually venture into the landscape of my past was simply too daunting.

They never did find the person responsible, did they?

Absently, I lifted the bouquet to my nose and drank in its dusty, peppery, wildflower scent. And just like that, the vault slid open and the past rushed out to engulf me.

Our farmhouse was cold this time of year, colder today because Mum had left all the doors and windows wide open. I was huddled at the kitchen table, working on a school project – knitting a woollen beanie with pompoms – but my fingers were turning blue, and I kept fumbling the needles, dropping the wool on the floor, picking it up, and then dropping it again.

Mum came into the kitchen, a pair of scissors in her hand. She stared at me for a long time, then finally said, 'Come over here.'

Abandoning my wool scraps and half-finished pompoms, I got up and plodded over to her on frozen feet.

She grabbed my shoulders and dragged me around to face the doorway with my back to her. I stared across the verandah into the yard. The walnut tree had shed its leaves, and withered black pods clung to the naked branches. I felt a cold sensation drag across the back of my neck, and flinched. Mum yanked me back into place. *Snip*. Something slithered past my shoulder and landed feather-soft on my foot. I couldn't look down; Mum was gripping the top of my head, holding me steady. *Snip*. Another flutter on my arm. *Snip-snip*.

Finally she pulled me around to face her. Her eyes were red, her cheeks puffy and her lips looked as if she'd nibbled away half the skin.

'What happened on the rocks that day, Ruby?'

'I don't know.'

'Why were your arms covered in bruises? They looked like finger marks. Were they, Ruby? Were they marks made by someone's fingers?'

I looked down. My toes were curling over the ends of my sandals. They were last year's sandals, white with buckles across the ankle. My foot had grown an inch or so in that time, but I hadn't thought to remind Mum it was time for new shoes.

Mum shook me. 'How can you not remember those bruises? You were black and blue for weeks. Did Jamie put them there? Did you have a fight? What did you do to her?'

My eyes stung. *Please*, I prayed silently, *please don't let me cry. Not now.* I tried to pull away, but Mum's grip held firm.

'Ruby, I told you girls to stay at home that day. Why didn't you listen? You knew the rocks would be slippery after the rain. Why couldn't you have done what you were told for once?'

When I didn't reply, and she let me go. Crossing the kitchen, she returned the scissors to the utility drawer and went outside.

My head felt so light I thought it might topple off and roll away. Bruises. Finger marks. I couldn't remember. My skin itched. My limbs shook. I stood there a long time, staring at nothing, my heart turning small, as hard and dry as a walnut.

Hours passed before I dared to look in the mirror. My hair was cropped like a boy's. Short, prickly. Horrible. It showed off my freckly skin and round face to its worst advantage. Somehow my resemblance to Jamie had disappeared; in its place was a girl I didn't recognise. An ugly girl I found myself hating.

Outside, the trees were shedding their leaves. The sky was the colour of washed-out denim. The air had turned icy. Rosehips were out, and the bean pods hanging on the dry vines rattled in the wind like castanets.

It was the last Sunday in June.

I was thirteen.

The flowers dropped from my fingers and scattered on the floor. Pressing my knuckles against my lips, I stared at myself in the mirror. I was hunched over, with possum eyes and cheeks darkened by the shadow of my hair.

The memory had been so vivid that I could still smell the woodsmoke from our old farmhouse kitchen, still feel the icy floorboards under my feet. The scissors rasped, and my thick dark locks slithered over my shoulders as I tried not to cry.

What happened on the rocks that day, Ruby?

I searched my reflection, but there was no hint of the bright, beautiful sister I had idolised as a child. Just my own familiar face – brown eyes, sweeping brows, unruly dark hair. Jamie's hair had been waist length, her eyes golden and her skin paler than mine; if there had ever been a likeness, there was no sign of that resemblance now, at least none that I could see.

Mum, on the other hand, must still be aware of it. Hadn't she commented, only last week, how much nicer my hair looked short?

In translation: *With long hair, you remind me of Jamie.*

Rob's apartment in Coffs Harbour was on the top floor of an older style block on the hill. Inside, the renovations were extensive, and the suite now boasted a huge open plan area with windows overlooking the jetty and Muttonbird Island, and then beyond to the Pacific Ocean.

I shifted uncomfortably on the sleek leather sofa. I had a champagne flute in one hand and a stick of cucumber in the other, and my bare feet were buried in the thick pile of a black flokati rug.

I should have been in seventh heaven.

Instead, I was glaring at the back of Rob's head, quietly fuming.

Two weeks had passed since my mother's opening in Armidale. In that time we hadn't returned to the subject of the lace bra. For Rob, it seemed to have passed into ancient history; meanwhile, I continued to brood.

'How's that?' Rob asked, glancing over his shoulder. He'd hammered a nail into the wall and was attempting to straighten his new painting.

I shrugged. 'Maybe a bit to the left.'

He adjusted the painting, then moved back to assess the effect. Obviously pleased, he shuffled onto the couch beside me and poured himself a drink. Mum's exhibition had closed yesterday, and the painting Rob had bought – the antique Singer sewing machine – had arrived by courier at Rob's therapy rooms this morning. He had waited until I turned up before hanging it, and then insisted we celebrate the occasion with bubbly.

'You're very quiet,' he noted.

'I'm just not entirely convinced that it suits the decor. I mean, look at all your other stuff.' I waved my cucumber stick at the room. 'There's all this chrome and leather and smoked glass, it's all so mid-century. Mum's old Singer would be more at home in a place full of older-style furniture, and . . . you know, antiques and collectables, that sort of thing.'

'You mean, like *your* place?'

I slumped. Yes, of course I meant *my* place. And of course I couldn't say so, because that would make me look selfish. But I couldn't help feeling a twinge of resentment; Mum's painting seemed too personal to be displayed just anywhere. To me, it was more than just a work of art hung on the wall to enhance the decor; it was a fragment of my forgotten past, an image that held meaning for me. It was too fragile to be exchanged for money like ordinary merchandise. Too precious. Too full of memories.

My memories.

Abandoning my empty flute on the coffee table, I crossed the room to the balcony doors and stepped outside.

Rob caught up with me. 'You're not upset about the painting, are you, babe?'

'Of course not. It's just that . . .' In truth, I *was* upset. I didn't understand why he'd bought it and hung it on his feature wall, when he knew how conflicted I was about Mum. I gripped the railing and gazed unhappily at the street below. Light puddled beneath the street lamps, and two women in batik dresses laughed quietly as they hurried past. 'I can't stop thinking about seeing Mum, and then running into Esther Hillard. I know a fortnight's gone by, but it all keeps replaying in my mind. It's making me nuts.'

'You still haven't told me what you and your mum talked about.'

I shut my eyes, and when I opened them again, the world was still there; odd, I'd have sworn it had rocked off kilter for a moment. I felt woozy, cold. My fingers tightened around the rail.

'Mum told me Jamie's death wasn't accidental.'

Rob shifted beside me. 'I don't understand. I thought you said she fell.'

I stared out across the dark sea. 'There was an investigation,' I said quietly. 'Jamie's injuries weren't consistent with a fall, but the police never found any evidence of a third party. Apparently the only ones on the rocks that day were Jamie . . . and me.'

There was a stillness. I imagined I could hear Rob's brain ticking over; it made a sound like a typewriter dashing out sentences, the clackety-clack of keys increasing in speed until his assessment of what I'd just said was fully formed.

'Christ,' he said softly. 'Now I get your mood. Ruby, I'm sorry.'

'It's okay,' I said too quickly.

Rob ran his hand up my spine, rubbing gently between my shoulder blades 'Seeing your mum again really put a spin on things, didn't it?' he said gently.

'I guess.'

The wind picked up, and he slid his arm around me, tucking me close against his warmth. 'You know, babe, I hate to say this, but maybe you and Margaret aren't meant to be friends.'

I looked at him and frowned. 'What do you mean?'

'Maybe it's time to let her go.'

Breaking from him, I stared into his face. He was striking in the starlight, a man carved from granite rather than flesh and blood. All-wise, all-understanding. From the moment I met him three years ago, I had the sense that I'd known him forever; yet he still had the ability to take me by surprise.

'You mean never see her again?' I asked softly. 'Cut all ties with her . . . just like that?'

Rob nodded.

I turned my gaze to the sea. Beyond the jetty lights, it was a vast dark nothingness. Muttonbird Island had been swallowed by the night, and the waves were present in sound only, lapping the invisible shore with their wet sighing-song. The wind tasted of salt and seaweed and waterlogged wood; smells I'd grown accustomed to in the eleven years I'd lived here. Sharp, vigorous smells that had seeped into me and changed me, made me forget the subtle fragrance of the arid western slopes where I'd grown up.

When Mum sold Lyrebird Hill in 1996 and moved us to Armidale, I hadn't coped with the change. The sprawling university town was in the heart of the New England tablelands of northern New South Wales and its pace was laid-back – but to a girl who'd spent the last six years on a remote property, it was overwhelming. I'd cried for weeks, unable to adjust to life away from my beloved bushland. Away from the river, from the wild-flowers and the freedom. Away from my memories of Jamie. But as the months rolled away, so did my anxiety. Slowly, I came to love Armidale's leafy tree-lined streets and hustle-bustle of cars and pedestrians and whizzing bicycles. In many ways, the change had done me good.

And yet I'd never been able to shake the feeling of not belonging. Mum and I argued frequently; Jamie's absence hung heavily between us. The minute I turned eighteen, I packed my bags and escaped to the coast. I got a job in a bookshop, and discovered I was good at it; I worked hard, learned the ropes, and slowly built a life for myself.

A cat wailed in the street beneath us, and in the distance a truck changed gears as it ground uphill on the highway. From the corner of my eye I could see through the patio doors to the white wall where Rob had hung my mother's darkly colourful painting. A lot of love had gone into rendering that old Singer in such fastidious detail; talent, too, and years of practice. But mostly love.

Could Rob be right? Could it be time to close that chapter of my life and move on? And if so, could I really bear to cut ties with my mother, despite our ragged history?

Beside me, Rob shifted. 'It's getting cold, hon. You want to call it a night?'

When he slipped his arm around my shoulders and steered me back inside, I didn't resist. It was only when we passed the painting that I hesitated. My toes dug into the shagpile rug, anchoring me in place as I studied it. It was a fragment plucked from a world that no longer existed for me; an echo of happy times, a tenuous thread to my childhood. Logic said that Rob was right. Mum and I were in each other's too-hard basket. We were only making one another unhappy.

It was time to let go.

I tried to back away from the picture, but my toes wouldn't unclench their grip on the carpet. So I stood there, wishing for a quiet place out of earshot of the sighing waves; a place where I could curl up, shut out the world, and let my thoughts unravel.

Rob drew me back against his chest and pressed his lips into my hair.

I closed my eyes. Into the darkness came our old farmhouse. I could hear a swishing sound. Mum was sweeping the kitchen floor. I was standing in the doorway, thirteen again. The back of my neck prickled, and I kept rolling my head from side to side, trying to get used to the lightness that had replaced my long hair.

I narrowed my eyes at my mother.

I hate you, I said. *I hate you for cutting my hair. Jamie loved to braid it, her fingerprints still would've been on it. Now it's gone and I'll never have it back because you're sweeping it away. I hate you.*

Mum looked over and saw me standing there. She put her broom aside, and stepped over the pile of dusty hair, came towards me. I stood my ground. I wasn't afraid of her. I knew she hadn't heard the words I'd said. Only I'd heard, because I'd said them in my heart.

'Oh, Ruby.' Gathering me into her arms, she started to cry, hugging me tight, like she used to do when I was small. 'My sweet little girl, what have I done?' Her tears scalded my skin. She was soft and smelled like bottled apricots and honey. Once, I would have hugged her back, surprised and glad for the attention. But now I just stood there, listening as she sobbed my name over and over, as if she had lost not only Jamie, but me as well.

Rob left at dawn the following morning to catch a flight to Melbourne for five days of book promotion. I headed home to Sawtell, stopping by the supermarket on the way to grab some supplies. Despite it being Sunday, the shops were crammed with people and I was glad to escape back to the car.

My old Corolla chugged along at ninety, rattling and groaning and occasionally letting out a pop. She'd seen better days, and Rob was always warning about the perils of driving a relic four years older than I was. To my way of thinking, buying a new car seemed somehow disloyal. This old girl had been a faithful friend, and while she still had some life in her, I'd never dream of upgrading.

Pulling into my driveway, I climbed the stairs to the verandah. An enormous fluffy white cat was sunning herself in a patch of early light. She must have detected the contents of my grocery bag, because she curled around my legs, squeaking in excitement.

'Hello there, Sissy.'

She belonged to Earle Bradley, the retiree who helped me at the shop. Earle had returned home a couple of days ago, after the successful removal of a malignant sunspot. Sissy's appearance on my doorstep meant that Earle was out and about. He lived a few doors up the street, and I'd only seen him briefly since his return from Sydney, and was looking forward to catching up.

Hoisting Sissy onto my hip, I unlocked the door and went inside. The house was musty after being closed up overnight, so I put Sissy on the floor and walked through the house, opening windows. Kicking off my shoes, I retrieved my thongs from under the dining table, and took my groceries out to the kitchen.

Soon the aroma of sizzling bacon and fried tomato, melted cheese, eggs and toast filled my small cosmos. I collected a plate for myself, and one for the cat, and stacked them with bacon, then added cheese and tomato and a handful of wilted dandelion greens to mine. I was just about to retire to the patio when someone knocked on the back door.

'Yoo-hoo, Ruby, are you decent?'

'Come in, Earle,' I called, grabbing a third plate. 'We're in the kitchen. Hope you're hungry.'

A stooped man in a wide-brimmed hat and oversized tartan shorts shuffled in bearing an armload of pink roses. Earle was in his seventies, an ex-florist who had in retirement discovered a passion for books – which was how he'd ended up working part-time in the Busy Bookworm.

'How are you today, Earle?'

'Fighting fit, old girl.' Placing his flowers on the table, he grabbed Sissy and lifted her with some effort into his arms, rubbing her generous belly.

'What's this, Sis? You're skin and bone.' He kissed her pink nose, then eased her back onto the floor. 'Hurry up with that breakfast, Ruby. Poor old Sis looks like she's about to fade away to nothing.'

Sissy let out a yowl and ran to my legs.

'Stop teasing her, Earle. You'll give her a complex.'

Earle chuckled. 'Dear old Sis, I love her to bits no matter her size. She was my wife's cat. Did you know that, Ruby?'

I nodded. Earle's wife had died five years ago. He often talked about her with great affection, and I knew he missed her terribly. 'It must be good to have a link to her.'

'It is, old girl. Indeed it is.'

Rummaging under the sink, Earle located a vase and filled it with water. By the time I'd topped his plate with bacon and eggs, he'd arranged the roses into a delightful spray and given them pride of place on the kitchen table.

'They're gorgeous,' I said, passing his plate. 'You really are a gem, Earle.'

We adjourned to the patio, Sissy quick on our heels, meowing for her bacon. Earle wedged himself at the small picnic table that took up most of the limited space, while I pulled my chair into the only patch of shade.

Earle tucked into his eggs with relish. 'You look peaky, old thing. Been sleeping okay?'

I pulled a face. 'Not really.'

'You worry too much.'

'Tell me about it.'

'How's your young fella, is he behaving himself?'

I scraped my toast corner through a smear of egg yolk, and faked a bright smile. 'He's fine. On his way to Melbourne as we speak, promoting his book.'

'How long this time?'

Peeling off a bacon rind, I dropped it onto Sissy's plate. 'All week.'

Earle muttered something I didn't catch, then asked, 'How's the shop? Any of my customers complaining that they never see me?'

'They *all* miss you. Even that grouchy Mrs Altman.'

Earle rolled his eyes, and forked up a mushy tomato. 'I'll have to watch that one. I think she's taken a bit of a shine to me.'

'Oh Earle, I'm really glad the op was a success.' I lifted my tea cup. 'I propose a toast. To new skin. And new beginnings.'

'Hear, hear.'

We clinked, then ate for a while in silence. Sissy began her wash, the warm sea breeze ruffling her long hair. Earle mopped his plate with a bread crust, then sat back. His hat – which he rarely removed – shadowed his eyes, but I could sense his gaze on my face.

I feigned interest in the ocean but Rob's words continued to haunt me.

Maybe you and Margaret aren't meant to be friends.

In the dazzling morning light, with the sun bleaching the colour from the sky and the waves crashing on the beach below, his advice seemed rational, the logical ending to a relationship that had been fraught with conflict and resentment. But in the quiet darkness inside me, I ached with fear. Without her, I'd be cast adrift; a nobody, a nothing. A ghost. Anything was better than that. Even being in my mother's too-hard basket was preferable to being out of her life altogether.

'You all right, old girl?' Earle asked, watching me.

'Yeah,' I said, too brightly. Then I slumped. 'Well, no actually. I'm a bit out of sorts.'

'Thought so. Boyfriend trouble?'

I hadn't told Earle about the bra; I knew he didn't really approve of Rob, and I wanted to avoid a lecture, so I just shrugged.

'Not really.' I sighed.

'Then it can only be your mum.'

'Rob thinks I should cut ties with her.'

Earle sat back. 'Cut ties? That's a bit drastic, isn't it?'

'You don't know my mum.'

'I know *you*, and you're all right. Whoever raised you can't be that much of a dragon.'

I stared out to sea. A flock of gulls swarmed overhead and then dissipated in a squall of cries. Taking a deep breath, I told Earle about the conversations with Esther Hillard, and then my mother, and how they had left me feeling so unsettled.

Earle listened intently. When I finished speaking, he looked directly into my eyes and asked quietly, 'They think your sister was murdered?'

I hadn't heard those words spoken aloud until now. I searched Earle's face, terrified that he would join the dots and arrive at the same conclusion my mother had apparently come to all those years ago.

Did you have a fight? What did you do to her?

But Earle only shook his head and gave a low whistle. 'That puts a spin on things, doesn't it? What about suspects? Didn't the forensics crew find anything?'

'Mum said it rained that day, and any evidence was washed away.'

'Which means that the police would have given you and your mother the third degree. Do you remember being questioned?'

I shook my head. 'That whole year is a blank. At least, it was until recently.'

'You've remembered something?'

I nodded, and before I could change my mind I shared the awful memory that had returned: Mum and me, the hair scissors. Any resemblance I shared with my sister, gone. Cut away.

Sissy must have heard the tremor in my voice because she rubbed against my legs and started up her purr engines. Reaching down, I dragged her onto my lap and buried my face in the soft fur of her neck. Only then did I find the courage to go on. 'I think Mum believes I was the one who hurt Jamie.'

Earle studied my face, his frown scaring me. But his eyes were kind, and when he finally spoke his voice was gentle.

'And you've been carrying that burden all your life, haven't you, old girl.'

I hunched into myself, digging my fingertips into my ribs. The question burned, I couldn't hold it in any longer. 'What if it *was* my fault she died? What if I was the one who killed her?'

Earle collected the dishes and piled them in the centre of the table, then made a tower out of our tea cups. Resting his elbows on the table, he steepled his fingers against his mouth and regarded me.

'Seems to me like you have some remembering to do.'

'Rob says digging up the past is dangerous for some people.'

'Poppycock.'

'But he says—'

'*Living* in the past is dangerous, old thing. But in my humble view, *remembering* can be a way to heal. Especially when your wounds run deep.'

'But what if I remembered that I'm responsible for my sister's death?'

Earle examined my face a long while before speaking. 'Then you'd have to face the music and deal with it. But you can't pass judgement on yourself until you know the facts. Innocent until proven guilty, right?'

Below on the beach, the waves rushed along the shore, smoothing the tracks made by dog walkers and joggers and the lone man with his metal detector. They all seemed a world away from the bubble of confusion and fear in which I suddenly found myself.

'I wouldn't know where to begin,' I said.

Sissy head-butted me, then curled against my chest and began to settle in for a nap. She'd grown heavy and my legs had pins and needles.

Earle adjusted the tower of plates. 'Everything you need to know is locked away inside your old noggin. All you have to do is find the right key.'

'You make it sound easy.'

'If it was me,' Earle said, 'I'd be talking to that neighbour of yours, the one you ran into at the gallery.'

I shifted uncomfortably, trying to rearrange my legs under Sissy's tremendous weight. 'She *did* invite me to visit. She even suggested I stay a few days.'

'Then what are you waiting for?'

I slumped, still daunted by the idea of returning to my old home. 'Maybe for my courage to kick in?'

'Courage is overrated, old girl.'

'Not when you don't have any.'

Earle sighed. 'Ruby, do you want to spend the rest of eternity torturing yourself over what you may or may not have done? Don't waste your young life worrying about events you can't change. Just make the decision, take the first step, and then see what happens from there. You'll find a way to cope, I promise.'

Despite myself, I laughed. 'You sound like Rob.'

Earle shook his head and grimaced. 'Lord help me.'

The following Friday I pulled up outside Coffs Harbour airport. Rob was due back early that morning because he had a ten o'clock session in the clinic. What better way to welcome him home than with a healthy deli breakfast and a surprise pick-up from the airport?

I arrived right on eight. The terminal was small, which meant there were limited flights in and out every day. A plane had just come in from Sydney, and newly disembarked passengers were making their way across the tarmac. The single arrival-and-departure lounge faced the airstrip, and had a view beyond to grassy flatlands. I searched the stream of people but Rob wasn't among them.

Back in my car, I wondered if I'd got the day wrong.

Then again, maybe he'd arrived last night?

I drove back to the link road and followed it into Coffs, turning at the roundabout and heading east to the jetty. I found a park along an embankment of garden, and hurried up the street to Rob's apartment building. It was a balmy autumn day, the air from the ocean salty and fresh. Inside the building, I climbed the stairs and pressed Rob's buzzer, pleased when the intercom crackled to life and Rob answered.

'Rob, it's me.'

A pause. 'Hey, babe.'

Another moment passed, and I shuffled impatiently. 'Can I come up?'

Rob opened the door, fresh-faced and damp, as if he'd just stepped out of the shower. His cheeks were pink and he seemed a little breathless; judging by his suit pants and white shirt, he was on his way to the clinic.

'Surprise,' I said.

He smiled, but there was a hint of a frown in the equation.

'What are you doing here?'

'I thought you'd like breakfast,' I said, trying to swallow my disappointment. 'Fresh croissants and Jarlsberg and Earle's organic tomatoes. But I can see I'm too late. I thought your session wasn't until ten?'

'It was brought forward.'

I took my string bag of goodies to the kitchen. From the corner of my eye I glimpsed Mum's painting; it looked a little crooked on the wall, and I had to resist the urge to rush over and straighten it. The entire place was a tad untidy, which was unlike Rob. Maybe his cleaner was on holiday. I could smell coffee, and a faintly sweet, somehow familiar chemical smell, like insect repellent.

Dropping my car keys on the bench, I unpacked my bag and placed the croissants and cheese in the fridge. In the door was a bottle of Dom Pérignon, half-empty. I frowned.

'Good trip, was it?'

Rob went over to the sideboard and collected a coffee mug, then brought it back to the kitchen and stowed it in the dishwasher.

'A huge success. I sold a mountain of books, and the publisher is excited about my concept for the next one.'

'Did you wow them with your seminar ideas?'

He brushed a scattering of crumbs off the counter into his palm, and emptied them into the bin. Was it my imagination, or was he having trouble meeting my eyes?

'Not only did I wow them,' he said, sending a smile over my shoulder, 'but I had them eating out of my hand. And I'm pleased to report that I've got bookings for several big author events in Melbourne in the next few months.'

'Great.' My heart was sinking fast. Something was definitely off. 'Is everything okay?' I asked.

Rob stopped flustering around in tidy-mode, and sighed. 'I'm sorry, Ruby. I'm running late, I'm a bit keen to get going.' This time his smile was high beam, and it struck me full force. Wiping his hands on a tea towel, he crossed the kitchen to wrap me in his arms. 'Come here, you. Did you miss me?'

His hot-blooded kiss took me by surprise. He smelled clean after his shower, and normally I'd have eagerly kissed him back. Instead, I pulled away. I was confused by his behaviour. One minute cool, the next minute hot. What was going on?

Paranoia, that's what. Relax.

Melting back against him, I kissed his earlobe and breathed him in. I *had* missed him, I decided. Playfully tickling my fingers up under his shirt, I whispered just how much.

'Steady on there, cowgirl,' he said softly, disengaging himself from my embrace and readjusting his shirt. He pressed a kiss on my nose, then collected his briefcase from beside the lounge and headed for the door. 'It was really sweet of you to bring breakfast, but I've got to rush. I need to be at the clinic in exactly eight minutes, and the cleaner'll be turning up any moment.'

I stared after him, puzzled. Maybe I wasn't being paranoid, after all; maybe things between us were not as rosy as I'd thought.

Collecting my string bag from the counter, I headed for the front door, then paused. My nostrils flared. The sweet fly-spray smell I'd noticed earlier was stronger here. It seemed to be drifting from the bathroom. I looked over at Rob.

He made a show of checking his watch, then ran a hand over his mouth. 'Will I see you tonight, babe?'

I gazed back at him, mentally shuffling through the apparently random list of things that were out of place in his apartment. The champagne in the fridge, the scent I couldn't quite identify, the uncustomary disorder. And most of all, Rob's hot–cold behaviour, as if he couldn't decide whether he wanted me here or not.

He was watching me, probably wondering why I hadn't replied to his question. Our eyes met, and something in his expression made me suddenly wary. I went along the short hall to the bathroom, where the chemical smell got stronger.

It wasn't fly spray, I realised. And then I understood why it seemed familiar. It was perfume: 'Poison' by Dior. I hadn't worn it for months; I'd never had the heart to tell Rob that it didn't suit me. I'd grown up with a mother who daubed herself in essential oils and essences, and I had, somewhere along the way, adopted her preference.

Pushing open the bathroom door, I stopped.

A soggy towel lay abandoned on the floor. Another was draped over the side of the freestanding spa bath. Sitting on the rim of the tub were two champagne flutes. Even from the doorway I could see that one had a smear of crimson lipstick on its rim.

My lips parted. My skin flushed hot, then turned slowly to ice.

'What a mess,' Rob said, reaching past me to pull shut the door. I felt the heat of his body. He stood close. Too close. 'It's a good thing the cleaner's on her way. I had a couple staying here while I was in Melbourne, some old uni friends. Slobs,' he added. 'I won't be inviting them again anytime soon.'

I wanted to move, but I was locked in place. In my mind I was still seeing the champagne flute with its crimson smear. A dark fist of understanding wedged itself up under my ribcage and began to expand. Vaguely, I knew I was holding my breath, and it was making my heart thud unsteadily, but there was no room in my lungs to draw air.

'We'd best be off,' Rob said, and his voice broke the spell.

I turned on him and searched his perfect face. His mouth was tight, his gaze fixed on me; he must have registered my shock, but was resolutely ignoring it.

'You lied,' I said in a raw voice. 'I trusted you, and you lied.'

'No, babe.' He stared into my face, almost raptly, his eyes aglow, as if spellbound by the pain he must surely see there. 'You can't seriously think . . . Oh come on, Ruby, it's not what it looks like.'

'How could you?'

Pushing past, I went back along the hall to the front door and wrenched it open. Rob caught up with me and took hold of my arm. 'Ruby, you're making a mistake.'

I shrugged him off. 'My only mistake was believing you the first time. I never want to see you again. *Babe.*'

The minute I arrived home, I dragged my overnight bag from under the bed and began to pack.

Jeans, T-shirts, track pants. I hesitated over the black pantsuit I'd worn to Mum's opening, then tossed it aside and went through my other clothes. Dark-coloured skirts and crisp businesslike shirts, more pantsuits. Rob was always reminding me that black was classy and sophisticated; best of all, it was slimming. *You have to dress like the person you want to become*, he always added with a wink.

Rubbing the dampness off my cheeks, I kicked shut the wardrobe door. At that moment, I hardly knew who I *was*, let alone who I wanted to become. The only reliable person I had in my repertoire was the person I'd once been.

Going over to my dressing table, I slid open the bottom drawer. Inside, I found a dozen or more of my old dresses, neatly folded, intended for the op shop. I took out a one-time favourite and went to the mirror. It was reminiscent of the fifties, with a soft collar and capped sleeves, gathered at the waist so the skirt flared out at the knee; pretty, a bit kooky, brightly coloured – a world away from the subdued corporate-style clothes I'd adopted since meeting Rob.

A world away from Rob.

Slipping out of my work clothes, I put on the dress and instantly felt lighter, more at home in myself. Feeling almost defiant, I packed the remaining dresses in my bag, and was about to slide shut the drawer when I noticed a photo lying face down on the bottom. Not just any photo, but the Polaroid I'd been searching for. Turning it over, I drew a sharp breath.

'Jamie.'

She glowed against a background of trees, her dark hair falling loose around her shoulders, her gaze fixed on the photographer. Her face was breathtaking, a perfect oval, her delicate lips slightly parted, her almond-shaped eyes gazing with an intensity that was at once untamed and demure. She wore my mother's ivory wedding dress, and her posture made me think of a wild deer, startled by the appearance of a hunter.

Mum had made it clear a long time ago that the subject of my sister was taboo. *What's the good of making ourselves miserable by talking about her,* she always said. *Words aren't going to bring her back.*

But as I studied the photo, a feeling of urgency overtook me. Eighteen years had passed since Jamie died. The grief had taken decades to heal, and even now the scar tissue over it was thin. I still had nightmares. I still couldn't remember. I still felt waves of guilt when I tried to cast back to that day.

All of a sudden, I wanted desperately to understand why.

4

Brenna, March 1898

My father's wolfhound raced ahead of me along the river track, his big shaggy body quickly vanishing in the dense lomandra grass. It was only a few hours after dawn, but the morning was already hot. Spears of sunlight penetrated the valley shadows, making the dew shimmer in the trees and setting the grass alight with rainbows.

Ever since my acceptance of Carsten Whitby's proposal just over a week ago, I had been dreading this day. My wedding was fast approaching, but I still hadn't spoken to my friends at the encampment. I wanted desperately to see Jindera, to tell her my news; to explain about my father's debt and Whitby's offer, and my choice to leave Lyrebird Hill rather than see it fall into the wrong hands. But most of all, I wanted to see in Jindera's eyes that she understood I wasn't simply deserting her.

Harold began to bark. I glanced along the track, then up the hill, but couldn't see him. Ducking under a low-hanging bough, I pushed forward along the riverbank. When I heard the yelp, and then a sharp high-pitched series of yaps, my stomach started to churn a little. I picked up pace and began to run.

'Harold!'

I saw him up ahead, crouched with his haunches up and tail lashing from side to side, barking at something concealed from me on the other side of the grass. He released another sharp yip, then began to growl at what he had discovered in the grass.

'Come here to me, boy!'

Ignoring my command, he darted sideways then retreated. Several feet away, I spied a long black body with a tinge of red along its belly. Hands shaking, I dragged open my dillybag and took out the revolver Aunt Ida had given me. Cracking open the frame, I fumbled six cartridges into the cylinder and snapped shut the breech. Pulling back the hammer, I took aim at the snake and cautiously approached. My pulse began to crash noisily in my ears. As I cleared the lomandra, the snake raised its head and hissed softly as it prepared to strike.

Holding my breath, I took aim and fired.

Harold yelped and dashed behind me, cowering and shaking his head. His ears would ring for days, and he would be gun-shy for a while, but he was alive.

Not so the snake.

Its head was gone, severed cleanly. Although it was dead, the nerves that wove along its lengthy backbone continued to function. The glossy body lashed and coiled on itself, the delicate tail looping and whipping the ground, slippery black in the sunlight.

Finally the sleek body stilled.

I emptied the unspent cartridges and stowed the weapon back in my dillybag, then grasped the snake's tail and picked it up. Its skin was velvety smooth, its strong muscles now limp. Calling Harold to my side, I continued along the river towards the camp, my mood now even more sombre.

Mama used to say that all God's creatures valued their lives as much as we valued ours. My memories of her were hazy, but I'd never forgotten her gentle manners and kind, calming voice. She had loved all living things, and in my mind's eye

I imagined her shedding a tear for the creature whose life I had just ended.

My own eyes were dry as I made my way towards the camp, but I understood my mother's viewpoint. Deadly as it had been, the red-belly black had possessed a fierce beauty, and I couldn't help feeling a twinge of regret for its demise.

Jindera, on the other hand, would be delighted. It wasn't every day someone arrived with breakfast.

Jindera was crouched at the river's edge, collecting water in a bark dish. Her bony spine formed a ridge down the back of her yellow dress, and wisps of her hair lifted gently on the breeze. She was singing, her voice thin and eerie as it drifted in the still morning.

Further downstream a couple of boys were stalking the shady shallows, probably hunting turtles they would catch with their hands. Some girls were sitting along the banks weaving fishing nets from grass fibres. They looked over when they saw me, and one of them waved and called out to Jindera.

Jindera got to her feet and turned to greet me. When I lifted the snake for her to see, she smiled.

'Where you get that long fella?' she wanted to know.

'I shot him.'

'We hear gunfire. Boys go along track, see you. Why you shoot him?'

I pointed to Harold. 'The fool of a dog nearly got himself bitten.'

Jindera took the snake from my hand, calling to the other women as she held her prize aloft. Meera, an older girl with a tiny baby strapped to her back, ran ahead of us to stoke the campfire coals. Meera, like most of the others, wore only a string around her hips from which hung a scrap of wallaby hide. There had been a time when the people's nakedness had embarrassed me, but over the years I had stopped noticing. Jindera was the only one who wore European-style clothes, and I suspected that her choice had less to do with modesty, and more to do with the fact that her dress was a gift from my aunt.

As we headed back to the camp, Jindera was quiet. I knew she sensed my mood, and was waiting for me to speak, but it wasn't until we arrived at the perimeter of huts that I raised the courage to tell her.

I stopped walking. 'Jindera, I'm getting married.'

Her soft brown eyes held the question, but she remained silent.

'I've come to say goodbye,' I told her. 'I'll be going away for some time.'

Still Jindera said nothing. I knew she understood me, because she was holding her shoulders tight and a crease had appeared between her brows. She examined my face for a long time. At last she asked, 'Where you go?'

'Tasmania. It's far from here. Across the water to another land.'

Jindera frowned, then shook her head. 'No cross water Bunna. Danger there. Bad spirits.'

A wedge of sorrow lodged in my chest. 'I don't want to go,' I admitted. 'But Fa Fa is in trouble. He's lost a lot of money, and now the men from the bank want to take our land away—'

I stopped, unable to go on. Jindera's people had already lost their land – to us. But while ever my father owned this small pocket of wilderness there was at least a small haven for some of the Indigenous people. I thought of the poisoned damper, of the night raids and the cruel beatings, and I had to look away.

That was when I saw Jindera's mother, Mee Mee.

She was sitting on a cleared patch of earth beneath the salmon gum where the marsupial skins had hung the last time I had visited. She was bent over a flat grindstone, a bark dish of water on one side and bowl of fine black seeds on the other.

While I watched, she sifted a handful of seeds onto the grindstone, trickled it with water and then began to pound the seed
with a smaller stone. The seeds came from grasses, or the flat
succulent pigweed the native people called munyeroo. Later,
when the men arrived back after the day's hunt, the sticky balls
of seed meal would be placed on hot coals and baked. Mee Mee's
seed cakes were highly prized, and whenever they were freshly
made she always set a couple aside for me to take home.

'Mee Mee,' I called.

She looked up and beamed, then got to her feet. Rushing
over, she gripped my hand, tugging lightly on my arm as she
always did in greeting. She wore a possum skin tied about her
waist, and a fine layer of soft powdery dust. Her white hair
plumed around her face, and her large brown eyes shone as she
examined me.

It only took her a moment to register my feeble attempt at
a smile. She spoke to Jindera and they exchanged a few words,
then Mee Mee looked back to me.

'You go away?' she asked, her voice jagged with alarm.

'I am to be married.'

Again Mee Mee looked at Jindera, who spoke softly to her at
length. When Jindera stopped speaking, Mee Mee looked at me
with a cry. Her eyes welled, and huge tears began to spill down
her cheeks leaving damp trails on her dusty skin.

I clung to Mee Mee's hand. 'I will come back to see you,'
I assured her. 'I promise.'

Mee Mee mopped her wrist against her eyes, but the trickle
of tears seemed unstoppable. Reaching up, she cupped her palm
against my face and looked into my eyes so searchingly that
my heart wrenched. As I met her dark gaze, I became aware
of the stillness, the utter quietude around us, as if the breeze
had stopped blowing and the birds were poised without song,
and the rest of the world sat frozen in time and only we three
remained; I smelled burning on the air, and caught the musty

odour of damp stone; then, faintly, very faintly, I thought I heard the distant echo of screams—

Danger, whispered my mind. *Bad spirits.*

Jindera spoke sharply, and Mee Mee released my hand. I blinked, and the world washed back around us – the breeze sighed in the treetops, the river murmured along its primordial course. In a nearby tree, a lonely magpie stretched its throat and sent a volley of magical notes into the sky.

I felt Jindera's gaze on me. 'This your home,' she said, her fluty voice firm. 'You stay here with family, where belong. You tell man, no marry. No cross water to other land.'

'Oh Jindera, if only I—'

The thud of a horse's hoofs made us all look around. The group of girls who had followed us up from the river called out and pointed. My brother Owen was approaching in a cloud of dust.

'Brenna?' he called shakily.

I was unwilling to cut short my goodbye, but something in my brother's tone made me regard him more closely. His eyes were huge in his pale face, dark and frightened, and his lips were chalk-white.

'What's happened?' I said.

He dipped sideways off the saddle, then seemed to change his mind about dismounting, and stayed astride.

'Come quick, Brenna. Aunt Ida's been taken ill.'

Jindera clutched my arms. 'Hurry, Bunna. You go now.'

Hastily I kissed her cheek, and clasped Mee Mee briefly and tightly in my arms. Then somehow I was stumbling away from them, my boots thudding on the dusty earth, my vision blurred, my promise ringing hollowly in my head.

I will come back.

Owen hauled me up into the saddle behind him. Harold was already skittering along the track ahead of us, and Owen urged the mare to follow.

I twisted in the saddle to look back. Jindera and Mee Mee now stood in the midst of a small group of women who had gathered when they heard the horse. Jindera was shading her eyes as she stared after us. She was taller than the others, her yellow dress defining her like a column of sunlight; at her side, Mee Mee huddled like a shadow. I stared hard at them through the dust kicked up by the horse's hoofs, trying to memorise their faces, praying that this would not be the last time I saw them, yet unable to shake the feeling that it was.

'Brenna?'

My brother's voice was tight with fear, and it gave me cause to worry. 'What is it, Owen? How sick is she?'

A tremor rippled through his wiry body. 'It's bad. Heart attack, Fa Fa thinks. He's ridden for the doctor and Millie's at the bedside. Oh, Brenna,' Owen's voice cracked as he struggled out his next words, 'Fa Fa said she might die.'

Aunt Ida's bedroom was dark. The curtains were drawn and the air smelled of camphor and smelling salts, and of the bitter herbal tonic my aunt habitually drank.

In the days since her attack, she had been losing strength. Now, she only had the energy to occasionally raise her head and sip the broth Millie made for her.

A cotton nightgown was draped over a chair back, and there was a cup of cold, untouched tea on her bedside. Next to the cup was a glass of lemon water, and next to that a photo of my mother, who had once been Aunt Ida's dearest friend.

'Aunt?'

Removing the tea cup, I placed the bowl of broth on the nightstand. Aunt Ida lay motionless on her side, her head sunk deep into the feather pillow. Her face was hidden under a spray of frizzy hair.

'Aunt Ida? Are you awake?'

A pasty face peered around at me. 'Florence?'

'No, Aunt. It's Brenna. I've brought you some broth. You haven't eaten since yesterday. Why don't you try some?'

She grasped the coverlet with shaky fingers and drew it to her chin. 'You might distract me,' she said, her voice frail. 'Perhaps a chapter or two from the good book?'

Settling myself in the chair at her bedside, I took up the Bible that sat within easy reach of her pillow. Opening to the red silk tassel she used as a bookmark, I began to read from the Psalms.

Aunt Ida rolled onto her back and shut her eyes. Her face was grey, her cheeks deflated and creased with lines. While I read, her lips moved as though reciting the words along with me. But when I paused to turn the page, she continued whispering.

'I must tell. I won't go to the grave with a lie in my heart.'

I leaned closer. 'Aunt, what is it? What's troubling you?'

'Michael is such a stubborn man,' she rasped. 'He could put an end to this ridiculous game, but he refuses to.'

'Aunt, have you forgotten? I'm to marry Mr Whitby. Father's debts will be paid as a wedding gift.'

Aunt Ida coughed weakly. 'The fool would rather lose his only daughter than surrender a few acres of his precious Lyrebird Hill.'

'No, Aunt, you're mistaken. It was my idea to—'

'You must forgive him, Brenna. Listen now. What I'm about to tell you might shed light on his actions.' She reached for the water glass, which I held to her lips. Dabbing the corners of her mouth with her hanky, she beckoned me nearer. 'Your mother and I were friends,' she began, then nodded. 'Jindera, too.'

My ears pricked up. 'My mother knew Jindera?'

Aunt Ida's watery eyes regarded me. 'You are very like her, did you know that?'

I looked at the photograph on the bedside table. My mother had been tall and stout, with a strikingly pretty face. Her hair was so fair it was almost white; she had worn it bunched loosely at her shoulders, letting it fall in soft waves. Fa Fa used to say her eyes were the colour of bluebells.

I looked down at my hands. I had long fingers like Fa Fa, and skin the colour of tea. My hair was dark, my eyes umber. My father said I had the look of his grandmother about me, her dusky European blood skipping his veins to flow unchecked into mine. Yet it was clear I had inherited nothing from Mama.

Aunt Ida gestured at the photo. 'Do you remember how she and Michael met?'

'At the conservation society in Armidale.'

'I was treasurer,' she explained. 'And Florence's father had been a patron of the society for many years. Florence and I struck up a friendship, and then at one of our fundraising events, I brought my brother along. It was a match made in heaven . . . or so I first thought. I did not know it at the time, but my brother's affections already belonged to another.'

I held my breath, certain I'd misheard. 'Another?'

Aunt Ida sighed, struggling to sit up. I propped a pillow behind her, and she smoothed trembling fingers over her frizzy hair.

'When I was a girl,' she told me, 'your grandfather brought Michael and me here from Scotland after our mother died. He acquired this land, and named it after the beautiful birds that lived in the ferny gullies where the scrub was very thick. They were curious creatures, those lyrebirds, mimicking every noise they heard. Then Father started cutting down trees and burning back the scrub, and even imported a herd of robust sheep from his homeland to graze it. Soon, there were no more lyrebirds . . . but that didn't stop him. The property made him very wealthy, and when he died he left it to Michael. And Michael continued our father's work, only not as successfully.'

The bedside chair was suddenly too small, too hard. I shifted, trying to get comfortable. 'What did you mean before, when you said Fa Fa's affections belonged to another?'

Aunt Ida's gaze drifted to my face. 'I was once like you, dear Brenna. I ran wild, developed a passion for the bush. And like you, I had a fascination for the people who lived along the river gully at the bottom of our land. I used to creep out at night, drawn by the blaze of their fires to watch them dance. The songs entranced me, and I was compelled—' Her voice broke off. I lifted a glass of lemon water to her lips. She drank only a dribble, than wiped her mouth and continued her story.

'Compelled to join their celebration. I never did, of course, and yet I fancied to myself that the invitation was there. One day, two girls snuck up from behind and captured me. I was terrified they'd expose my spying to their elders, but they were more interested in examining my clothes and hair and especially my fair complexion. They were lighter than the others in the band, and I guessed there must have been some European blood in their lines; they seemed intrigued and pleased by my appearance, and I was equally fascinated by them. They were uncommonly beautiful, with luminous smiles, and minds that were quick and curious. We had no language in common, but slowly we began to learn. Soon, the three of us were steadfast friends.'

I remembered the yellow dress Aunt Ida had washed and ironed with such care a year or so ago, and then bundled into a parcel. I recalled, too, the packets of matches, the damper and fruitcake and bags of walnuts that she sent along whenever Millie visited the camp.

'Was one of those girls Jindera?'

Aunt Ida nodded. 'And the other was her sister, Yungara.'

'*Sister?*' I sat back heavily.

Jindera had never mentioned having a sister; nor had Mee Mee hinted there had been another daughter. Yet I could not bring myself to question my aunt's story. *Yungara.* My pulse began to race, and the echo of the name rushed through my blood. *Yungara.*

My aunt smiled sadly. 'The three of us were drawn together,

as if by an invisible bond. In those days, Michael spent a lot of time away with our father, so I was stuck at home and bored to tears with housework – much like you, my dear. My friendships with those girls saved me.'

My racing blood slowed, and warmth washed through me. 'Jindera always asks after you. Now I know why.'

'We were firm friends, Jindera and I.'

'Then why did you forbid me to see her?'

Aunt Ida shook her head. 'After what happened to her sister, it became clear to me that our two cultures were not yet ready to share the burden of friendship.'

I stared, seeing not my aunt, but another woman, a stranger. I'd always believed Ida to be stuffy and intolerant of Jindera's band. For years I had prided myself on disobeying her wishes, escaping to spend time with Jindera whenever I could. I was flabbergasted to realise that I hadn't been rebelling, after all, but simply following in my aunt's footsteps.

'What happened?' I asked.

A stillness entered the room. I heard finches twittering in the garden, and the distant murmur of the river. I waited for my aunt to speak, and when finally she did, her words were barely audible.

'Yungara died in 1879.'

A shadow slipped across my heart. 'That was the year after I was born.'

Aunt Ida coughed and dabbed her lips with her hanky. 'Jindera and I never spoke again. I told myself it was safer that way. Now, in hindsight, I realise that guilt kept me away.'

'Guilt?'

'One day – I was about sixteen by then – I let Michael accompany me to the camp. He was nineteen, a budding naturalist and keen to expand his knowledge of the local area. He had assumed that I visited the camp to study the people and their ancient customs. If only he'd seen the three of us giggling and gasping and rolling about in the grass like two-year-olds, he would have changed his tune.' She wiped the dampness from beneath her eyes.

'Michael was keen to learn something of the people and their ways. But when Jindera and her sister ran out to greet me, I sensed that I'd been wrong to bring him.'

'Why?'

'I was young, I suppose. Eager to impress my older brother.' Thin fingers came up and rested beneath her eyes. She patted the skin there, as if puzzled to find wrinkled pockets instead of the fine plump cheeks of a girl. 'I had never experienced the glow of love myself, but I was not completely naive to the sight of it in others. The moment your father saw Jindera's shy, sweet sister, something in him changed. He seemed to puff out his chest and stand taller. From that moment on, he took no notice of what either Jindera or I said. Yungara was very quiet, she was shy – but proud, too.' Aunt Ida smiled laughed fondly. 'Well, you know Jindera, the way she watches you with her soft brown eyes, so patient – when all the while she's thinking what a silly goose you are. Yungara was like that, too.'

'What did she think of my father?'

Aunt gave a soft sigh. 'Yungara's dark eyes never left Michael's face. Not even for a moment. Besotted, they were, the two of them. I knew then that there would be trouble.'

'Trouble?'

My aunt blinked suddenly. Tears gleamed in her eyes. 'Yungara,' she said softly. 'It feels good to speak her name again at last.'

I too wanted to say the name. It sat on my tongue like honey with the promise of sweetness that would fill me if I said it aloud; but I hesitated. Who had she been, this woman whose name had the power to quicken my blood, whose memory caused my aunt's tears to flow so freely? This woman who had once captured my father's heart.

My mouth was suddenly dry. Reaching for the lemon water, I drained the glass, and placed it back on the nightstand. Then I waited for my aunt to resume her story.

And waited.

Silence breathed around us.

I touched a pale hand. 'Aunt, are you awake?'

Waxy eyelids fluttered. My aunt's eyes opened. She had drifted somewhere. Not sleep . . . memory, perhaps. When she finally registered that I'd spoken, she blinked back at me, confused.

'Florence?'

I knew I should let her sleep. Her face was grey, her breathing shallow. But the name of Jindera's sister had entered my bloodstream, beating through my veins like a moth.

'You were saying there was trouble. Between my father and . . .' *Yungara*.

Aunt Ida nodded, and closed her eyes.

Her hand lay on the coverlet, and I took her fingers in mine. They were deathly pale against the soft tan of my own hand, and I found myself wondering about her story.

Aunt Ida often said that after my mother died, Fa Fa had suffered greatly. Mama had left us a week before her fortieth birthday; her fair hair showed no signs of grey, and her pale skin was as smooth and clear as a girl's. She had been frail for years, but her death was a horrible shock, and it had broken my father's heart.

It seemed impossible that he had once loved anyone else.

I stood up, intending to go downstairs and fetch Millie. Instead, I found myself standing by the window in the dying light. A whirlpool of unfamiliar feelings churned in me. I felt cold, but my skin was hot. Time seemed to unravel around me. The fabric of my life began to fray, develop holes. Through those holes I caught glimpses of a past I had not, until now, considered.

'Aunt?'

The corner of her eye twitched, but she was beyond hearing. Kissing her damp brow, I stole across the room and went out, closing the door gently behind me. Tomorrow, when she woke, I would ask her to continue her story. Now, it was time for her to sleep.

Aunt Ida did not wake again.

We buried her a few days later at the Presbyterian cemetery in Armidale. My father stood by the grave while the minister read from the Psalms. Black half-moons darkened Fa Fa's eyes and his flesh looked sunken, the bones retreating beneath.

Afterwards, he withdrew from us, locking himself in his study, only taking meals when Millie hammered on his door and insisted he eat. As far as I knew, he didn't sleep. I grew fearful that he would quickly sicken and die, just as Aunt Ida had. I began tiptoeing past his study at intervals during the night, listening at his door. I heard the shuffle of paper, the clink of glass, the gurgle of brandy being poured. Countless times a night I lifted my knuckles to rap on the door and go in, to ask him the questions that were burning a hole in my heart.

Who was this woman you loved? Who was she to me?

But the nights passed, and my courage failed; my questions went unanswered. My wedding day sped nearer, but still my father did not emerge from his study. Finally, on the eve of our departure for Armidale, I decided to confront him.

It was nearing midnight. Silence had settled over the house. I knocked softly on the door of my father's study. When there came no call to enter, I turned the knob and looked inside.

Fa Fa was slumped at his desk, in dim lamplight, his head in his hands. A brandy bottle sat before him, and an empty glass.

He looked so crushed beneath the weight of sorrow that my courage left me. I was about to quietly slip away, when he looked up and saw me, beckoned me in.

'How are you faring?' he asked.

My eyes were red and sore, and my lips bitten; I knew the question was his way of acknowledging my grief, so I simply said, 'I miss her.'

Retrieving a second glass from the sideboard, Fa Fa dashed in a measure of brandy and pushed it across the desk. I had never shared a drink with him, and I wondered if he had guessed the nature of my visit. Fa Fa swallowed his drink in a gulp, while I sipped mine. It burned my gullet, and the smell made my eyes water, but its invigorating effect was immediate. I took a breath.

'Aunt Ida told me something before she died. She said you once knew Jindera's sister . . . She said . . .' I hesitated, expecting Fa Fa to startle at my words, to jump to his feet and splutter a string of denials. So, when he simply nodded in a resigned way, my courage grew. 'She said you loved her.'

My father smiled sadly. 'Poor Ida. Years ago I made her promise to keep my secret close to her heart. I had hoped the passage of years would provide me the pluck to tell you myself, but of course time only buried the truth deeper.'

The gravity of his words added weight to my suspicion. 'My skin is darker than yours, Fa Fa. And Mama was fair. I have brown eyes, while yours are blue, as were Mama's. You used to say that I resembled your Spanish grandmother, but I can't help wondering why Aunt Ida would insist I hear your story . . . unless it had direct relevance to me.'

Fa Fa's mouth moved as if chewing over his thoughts. 'Ida was right, my sparrow. I once loved a young Aboriginal woman.' He circled his fingers around his brandy glass, but did not pick it up. 'You are very like her, you know.'

I sat immobile, listening to the clock mark out its minutes. Each tick was a shard of my old life, the life I had taken for granted, falling away, casting me adrift in a present that was no longer mine. After a while, I looked at my father; even he seemed a stranger to me in that moment, a stranger with a familiar face but whose heart and mind were suddenly mysterious. I gripped my elbows and bent forward over my lap.

'There are things I need to know,' I whispered.

My father's brow tightened, but he nodded for me to continue.

I dragged the air into my throat, and in a strained voice said, 'My mother was Yungara.'

'Yes.'

'Jindera is my aunt. And Mee Mee is . . .' My words stuck fast in my throat as I remembered her brown eyes wet with tears, and the searching way she had looked at me, as if *willing* me to know her, willing me to understand.

'She is your grandmother,' Fa Fa said.

My fingers trembled. I knotted them in my lap, forcing myself to calm. 'All these years I've been going to see Jindera, feeling drawn to the camp and never knowing why. And now, when I'm on the brink of leaving, I learn they are my kinfolk. I would . . .' My throat was suddenly tight and I couldn't finish. I sipped the brandy until my glass was empty, and said hastily, 'I would have liked to speak of it to Jindera.'

'And you will, my Brenna. When next you return to us for a visit.'

I tensed. Rather than reassure me, his sentiment was like an ill-played note, all wrong to my ears. As Whitby's wife, I might not return to Lyrebird Hill for a year or more; it seemed an eternity.

I went to the window and stared into the darkness.

The encampment was an hour's walk, up hills and over rocky outcrops, along the narrow river trail. Treacherous enough in daylight, but deadly in the dark. And yet I wanted to run through the night and find my aunt and grandmother, to embrace them with the open-heartedness of a family member, rather than with the shy awkwardness of a friend. Why hadn't I guessed before now? Why hadn't anyone told me?

I heard my father pour more brandy. The clink of glass on glass, the gurgle of liquid; the dry click of his throat as he swallowed. And in that moment, a chasm opened between us; it was only the merest breach, a fracture in the foundation of our bond, a hairline crack that might have gone unnoticed – but it was done now, that whisper of damage, and I did not know how it might ever be repaired.

I went back to my chair and sat stiffly. 'What was my real mother like?'

My father picked up his pipe and prodded the contents of the bowl, then abandoned it. He scratched the stubble on his jaw, clearly uncomfortable. Finally he sighed.

'Yungara . . .' A pause. 'Yungara was a proud girl with the courage of a warrior. And yet she could be tender and shy. She was strikingly beautiful, too – the first time I saw her, I was spellbound. But as I came to know her, I saw her gentleness with the elders, and the soft way she teased her sister, and her games with the little girls as she taught them which berries to gather, or how to weave fish traps, or cut fine lengths of hide to make twine. Her kind, clever spirit touched my soul. I wanted to marry her. I begged her to come away with me, to a place far from the judgemental eyes of the world, where we could live peacefully.'

'Why didn't you?'

'She wouldn't leave her clan. She insisted that her people and her land protected her. If we went to another place, she believed she would sicken and die.'

I recalled Jindera's plea that I stay where I belonged, and not go across the water to another land. *Danger there*, she had said. *Bad spirits.*

'But she died anyway.'

Fa Fa's lips tightened over his teeth. 'Eighteen years have passed since I lost her. In all that time, not a day goes by – not an hour, not even a minute – that I don't think of her. She haunts me. Every night I carry her memory into sleep. And every day I feel her presence beside me. But it brings no comfort. What use is a ghost, when I yearn to hold a woman of flesh and blood?'

The longing in his words touched me, and I ached for him; yet his admittance seemed somehow cruel, selfish. 'But Yungara was still alive when you married Mama?'

For a long time my father sat silently. I feared I'd lost him, that he would withdraw again and refuse to say more. When he finally looked up, his eyes were wet and pink. 'I told Florence everything before we were married. About Yungara, and about you. I gave her the choice to back out of the marriage. You see, she was in love with someone else, too. I never found out who he was, just that Florence had cared deeply for him. But her father had disliked the young man's family, and so influenced Florence to marry me instead.'

He slumped and rubbed his eyes. 'Florence and I were friends above all else, and we found sanctuary in our friendship. I suppose we thought we could make our marriage work. I vowed to be a good husband and avoid the encampment, to spare her feelings. We were wed, and took our honeymoon in London.'

Fa Fa paused, and stared across the room to the window. It was a black rectangle, and I wondered what he saw there. Mama's soft kind face, or Yungara's proud striking beauty; or perhaps he saw me in the darkness of his mind's eye – me as a baby, wriggling and laughing in my mother's tawny arms.

I pinched my lips to stop them trembling. 'But you never forgot—' *Yungara*, I'd meant to say, but her name caught in my throat. 'You never forgot my natural mother.'

'No.'

Clenching my hands in my lap, I breathed away my apprehension and asked, 'How did she die?'

'Men came one night,' he said quietly, choosing his words with care. 'They rode along the riverbank, armed with swords and hatchets and rifles. They rounded up the clan and herded them into a gully. Some boys escaped into the water, concealing themselves against the banks. Others fled into the trees. Millie was among them, a frightened ten-year-old who only survived because her elderly aunt drew the killers away from her, sacrificing herself to protect Millie's hiding place. The rest of the clan, nearly fifty in all, were cut down in cold blood.'

I sat very still. A vacuum had opened around me and for a few beats of my heart I could not breathe. Aunt Ida had told me that Yungara died – but now, to learn that she had been violently murdered, plunged me into a shadowland of fear and despair.

'How did Jindera get away?'

'Jindera and her mother, Yargul—' Fa Fa gestured at me. 'The woman you know as Mee Mee, your grandmother – well, they took you and crawled into a small cave, barely more than a fissure beneath an overhanging boulder. That cavity saved your lives, but at a high price.

'From their vantage point, they heard everything. The screams and pleas of their families, the dreadful noises of slaughter. Yargul and Jindera clung together, pressing you between their bodies to keep you from crying. Finally, came the silence.'

My father hung his head. For a long time he did not speak. His shoulders began to shake, and when he finally looked back at me, his eyes were dull and wet.

'When dawn climbed the treetops and fell into the valley, Jindera and Yargul smelled smoke. Later, after the men had gone, they emerged to find that the killers had built a pyre and thrown the bodies of their victims on it to burn.'

A tear dripped from my father's eye, leaving a dark blot on his sleeve.

I stared at the blot. I'd never seen him cry. I'd never seen him show any emotion other than good humour, and the thoughtful melancholy he'd displayed the night we spoke of Mr Whitby's proposal.

Now I understood why. A few tears were not enough to wash clean the horror of the night he had just described; the death of my mother required from him a river of tears that might never stop.

Fa Fa drew a thick breath. 'This all happened a week or so before Florence and I returned home from our honeymoon. Later, when Jindera brought you up to the house in a bundle of wallaby skins, Florence didn't hesitate. From the moment she unwrapped the fur rug and glimpsed your small tear-streaked face, she loved you as her own.'

I was filled with horror and pity, shocked by my father's distress. And yet I couldn't stop myself from asking.

'Why didn't Jindera keep me?'

Fa Fa tugged a silvery whisker, and attempted a smile. 'The Aboriginal people are very protective of their little ones. Each member of the band or clan plays a vital role in a child's upbringing, and the family bonds are very strong. Under normal circumstances, Jindera would have raised you as her own. But after the attack, she was frightened. She insisted you would be safer with me and Florence.'

I bit my lips to stop the tears, but they flowed anyway.

'Who were they?' I managed to ask. 'The men who came that night?'

My father shook his head. 'I don't know.'

The desolation in the room had grown too heavy to bear. I stood, intending to leave my father in peace. I wanted to return to the safe darkness of my own room, to curl in my bed like a child until the storm of my emotions was spent. But as I kissed Fa Fa goodnight, he grasped my hand and drew me back.

'You must promise never to speak of this again. Not to anyone.'

I frowned. 'Why?'

'Not everyone feels respect or even compassion for the native people of this land. There are those who would, if they knew the truth, judge you and cast you down. I've always encouraged

you to speak your mind, and to regard honesty as the highest
of all virtues. But on this subject, I beg you to keep it buried. It
must remain a secret, even from Carsten.'

'He doesn't know?'

'The year I married Florence was a busy time for Carsten.
Business kept him away from us for several years. By the time
he returned, your mama was dead and you were a couple of
years old. He doesn't know the truth about your natural mother,
Brenna – and I beg you, never tell him.'

For the first time, my faith in Whitby faltered. What manner
of man was he really? What sort of heart and spirit lay concealed
beneath his handsome exterior? If Fa Fa thought it best not to
enlighten him about such a significant part of myself, then
what sort of relationship was I about to enter into?

My father released my hand. I collected my candle and went
to the door, but then turned back.

'Fa Fa?'

He looked up, and in the lamp's sallow light his eyes were
once again dull. I knew he wasn't seeing me, but *her*. Perhaps
the way she'd been that night beside the river – a proud, fierce
warrior girl standing in the midst of her clan, preparing to
defend her family to the death.

'What's that, Brenna girl?'

'Why did you never tell me before tonight?'

'I had hoped to spare you the grief.' He hesitated, then said
in a voice that seemed to cost him much effort, 'Be gone with
you, my little love. You want to look fresh-faced tomorrow. Try
to get some sleep.'

Closing the door of his study, I went along the hall towards
my bedroom, following my candle's wavering light. Despite my
father's efforts to protect me, I had grieved anyway. My grief
had not taken the form of tears or outward lamenting; rather,
it had bubbled up from my depths in the shape of dreams.
In those dreams there was always darkness, and the smell of

burning. And bare bodies pressed close against me, moaning and shivering – but not from cold. My aunt and grandmother had trembled with emotions of a kind I could not imagine.

Taking out my journal, I loaded my pen with ink and turned to a fresh page.

I want to lash out, I wrote, *to rage against the injustice of my mother's murder and the senseless killing of her people. I want to avenge Jindera's sorrow and silence, and Mee Mee's grief. But how? Too much time has passed, two decades. Even so, the impossibility of my desire does not stop me from wishing.*

5

Mighty trees can fall in a storm, but a blade of grass will withstand a tempest – saved by its ability to be flexible.
– ROB THISTLETON, *FIND YOUR WAY*

Ruby, May 2013

By the time I reached Armidale, a rattle had taken up residence under the bonnet of my old Corolla. I had developed a corresponding miss-beat in the vicinity of my heart. My discovery that morning of Rob's infidelity weighed heavily on me, a huge black shadow that settled across my shoulders, bowing me over the wheel and constricting my lungs. My mind was a whirlpool, flooded with anger one moment, and grief the next. But as the sweet New England air began to infiltrate my system, I managed to steer my thoughts away from Rob, and instead focus on what lay ahead.

It was early afternoon. A bank of dark clouds hung on the horizon, but the remaining sky was clear blue. I decided to bypass Armidale – and my mother – and head straight to Lyrebird Hill. The river would be gurgling over the stones, and the eucalypt leaves would be scenting the air with their spicy perfume. Esther had said to drop in any time, and I calculated that if I took the back route along the old Bundarra Road, I could be there in time for afternoon tea.

My Corolla coughed as I changed gears and slowed at the turn-off. My palms were sweaty on the steering wheel, and a feeling of urgency pumped through me. My mouth was dry, and although I drank continuously from my water bottle, the thirst would not be quenched.

For eighteen years I'd believed that my sister died after falling from a treacherous river embankment. Then, two weeks ago, I'd learned that her death had not been considered an accident after all; my mother had spun that lie to save my feelings. Meanwhile, in a dusty police filing room somewhere, was an inconclusive report that suggested Jamie's death was homicide.

The truth about what had happened to my sister may have been locked inside my memory banks, but I had no control over what surfaced. The glimmer of memory the other morning had given me hope, but it had also scared me. What if I remembered something I couldn't cope with?

All I knew about the day Jamie died was what Mum had once told me. She'd arrived home one rainy Saturday afternoon to find the house empty and the back door wide open. Sensing all was not right, she'd rushed along the river track, where she found me wandering in a daze. The bloody wound on the side of my head made her think that I'd fallen, and when she was unable to make sense of my garbled account, she had raced off in search of Jamie.

Later came the questions – the counsellors and psychiatrists who had tried to crack open the shell of amnesia I had constructed around what I'd seen that day. But the shell was hard, uncrackable; resisting all attempts to free the terrible kernel it contained.

Mum had never spoken about what happened after that, and I'd always been too scared to ask. Two decades later, nothing much had changed.

When I came to a crossroad signposted Clearwater, I turned right. Immediately the way became overgrown, shaded by tall stringybarks and red gums draped with golden beards of parasitic mistletoe. I passed a sand quarry where the exposed rockface had turned the colour of sun-bleached bones, leaving the earth scarred. Stunted tea-trees pushed out of the parched soil; granite boulders littered the bare hills; willows choked eroded waterways.

It was harsh country, ugly to those who didn't know it.

To me, it was so eerily beautiful that my heart began to race.

Opening the window, I drank in the fresh air. Out west, I noticed a bank of stormclouds, but they were a long way off. Directly overhead the sky was clear blue, and the air blowing into the car was dry and smelled of wildflowers; there was no hint of rain in the atmosphere; just sunshine and dust and birdsong.

Soon I would be standing on the land I had loved passionately as a child, experiencing it with adult senses. Would memory rush back in one overwhelming hit, or would it continue to elude me? How would I respond to Esther's recollections – with regret, or sorrow? Had the farmhouse changed, was Mum's old vegie patch still there, how would it feel to stand on the threshold of the bedroom I had once shared with Jamie?

A thrill of nerves had me clutching the steering wheel.

Generations ago, Lyrebird Hill had been a sheep station. At the turn of the century, the land passed into the hands of my great-grandmother. She had been a recluse, hiding away in the bush, seeing no one for years at a time. She sold off the sheep, then flouted the commercial-minded philosophy of her day by allowing the property to revert to bushland. On her death she bequeathed the farm to her only son, my grandfather.

According to Mum, Grampy James had hated the place. He moved to Armidale, and after his death, my mother had inherited the property. She was married by then with two little girls and quite happy living in Uralla. It wasn't until my father's death later the same year that Mum decided to escape to the bush and try to rebuild her life.

When we arrived, the farmhouse had been close to derelict. No one had lived there since the 1970s. The bush had seeded itself back into the thin granite soil around the house. Tea-tree and cassinia had invaded the garden, and tall stringybark saplings had shot up everywhere. The only neighbours were kangaroos and possums, owls and cockatoos; the house was overrun by black skinks, and a great old sand goanna had taken up residence beneath the water tank.

We had a simple life. Lentils and brown rice, candlelight and incense, clothes hand-made and hand-washed. A wood-fired oven, and baths taken on the verandah in an old tin tub. There was no phone, and only a basic solar set-up to run our lights and radio. Each morning, Jamie and I walked along the trail to the school bus stop. It was a secluded existence, but for the most part we thrived. Just the three of us, the occasional influx of Mum's long-haired friends, and three thousand acres of wilderness . . .

I came back to the present with a jolt.

The sky had turned from blue to grey. The thunderclouds that had been hovering on the horizon half an hour ago were now swiftly approaching. They were huge and dark-bellied, bunching their muscles and growing blacker by the second.

I looked back at the road. As a kid, I'd come this way plenty of times with Mum, but this was the first time I had actually driven this road. In the changed light, nothing looked familiar. I reached another crossroads, and as I turned left, the rattle in the front of my car seemed to get a little worse.

'Great. That's all I need.'

I depressed the accelerator, hoping a bit of velocity would dislodge whatever was caught under the chassis. But rather than speed up, the car made a coughing sound and began to fail.

'Oh no.'

Pumping the gas, I shifted to a lower gear and pumped again. The engine spluttered, and the car slowed. I guided it onto the verge and a moment later the engine shuddered and died.

I sat for the longest time, trying to breathe away my panic. It was a Friday afternoon; the road was deserted. Rummaging for my mobile phone, I checked the display but there was no signal. Walking up the road, I studied the display again. Not even half a bar of reception.

Staring into the grey day, I hugged myself.

By my calculations, I was about forty kilometres west of the New England Highway. The road I stood on was single-lane, eroded by potholes and flanked by bushland – obviously nothing more than a forgotten back-way. There were no signposts, no branching side streets, not even a distinguishing landmark. I could be anywhere, stranded on a deserted stretch that no one ever used.

Thunder grumbled in the distance.

I saw lightning flicker on the hills, and briefly it illuminated a curiously shaped ridge. It snagged my attention, and as I pondered it, recognition trickled in.

We used to call it the Spine because, on misty mornings when the bush turned white, it looked exactly like a stegosaurus scratching its back against the sky.

All at once, I knew exactly where I was. Beyond the ridge, on the rim of a valley overlooking the river, was the farmhouse of my childhood. It was quite a distance; I estimated ten kilometres, which, even if I stuck to the roads, would still take me the rest of the afternoon. But as I walked back to the car to collect my belongings, the first few spots of rain began to fall.

'Oh.'

The bushes along the verge twitched and rustled. The rain grew heavier. Within seconds it had become a deluge. A thunderclap exploded directly over me. Racing back to the car, I leaped in and closed the windows, then sat glaring through the windscreen, shivering as my sodden clothes dripped into the footwell.

I thought about Esther, cosy and warm in the farmhouse; she would hear the rain on the tin roof and smile to herself. It was dry country out here and rain was always welcome. She would probably go out to the kitchen and make herself a cup of tea, grab a couple of biscuits. Maybe even light the old Warmbrite, the way Mum used to when it rained, to take the damp out of the air.

I looked out at the sky. It had turned the colour of porridge, and the clouds hung in dark clusters overhead. Rain battered the car roof, each droplet like a hammering fist. Thunder cracked overhead and the car shook. A moment later lightning speared across the horizon.

Reaching into the back seat, I grabbed the picnic rug, then unzipped my overnight bag and dragged out jeans, T-shirt, woolly cardigan. Peeling off my wet clothes, I struggled into the dry ones, then pulled the rug over me. Resting my head back on the seat, I closed my eyes.

Damp air wafted through the vents, bringing with it the scent of the bush. Eucalyptus, settling dust, earth and granite and wallaby dung. And the sharp, deliciously spicy scent of wildflowers.

I began to drift.

The sound of rain dimmed, the air grew warm. I was no longer in my car on a deserted road – but in a cosy room filled with the scent of buttery scones and hot chocolate, where a grandmotherly woman sat in a patch of sunlight bowed over a well-thumbed volume of fairytales.

'Once upon a time . . .'

Despite the rain, Granny H's little cottage was cheery and dry. Candles burned in the corners of the room, and she had lit a fire in the potbelly. She chose a book of fairytales from the cluttered shelf, and settled onto her chair. Opening to the marked page, she began to read.

'Once upon a time there lived a sheep farmer, whose greatest treasure was his lovely daughter. Beauty was her name, and her father worked hard to provide her with every comfort. They lived in a roomy house and dined on seed cakes and rabbit stew, and Beauty always had pretty clothes to wear. But one unfortunate day, wool prices bottomed out and the farmer found himself penniless. Beauty wanted to help her father, and so she accepted the proposal of a wealthy landowner who lived in a faraway part of the country. One fine morning, she set out for her new husband's estate . . .'

I was sitting cross-legged beside the Wolf on a thick rug at Granny's feet. Her latest instalment sent a ripple of goosebumps across my arms and up into my scalp. I looked at the Wolf from the corner of my eye. He was motionless, his gaze fixed on Granny H, his boy-mask hiding his true, fearless nature.

Granny turned the page and continued her tale. 'Knocking on the manor door, Beauty waited for her new husband to greet her. But when the door swung wide, she found herself staring – not at a handsome husband, but at a hideous creature. He wore a man's clothing but had the shaggy head of a bull and shoulders like boulders. His eyes burned hot-poker red. Curling back his lips to bare long yellow fangs, he spoke in a surprisingly genteel manner, which Beauty found most disconcerting.'

Here Granny paused, and then said in a deep gravelly voice, '"Welcome, dear Beauty. Welcome to my humble abode."'

I gasped, then giggled.

The Wolf caught my eye and winked.

We'd heard this same story a million times, but with each telling the Beast grew uglier and scarier. Sometimes he turned out to be not the handsome prince under a witch's spell, but the evil witch herself in a beast's disguise, tricking Beauty into a life of sorrow and slavery. Granny H knew all the fairytales, but she never told them properly. They always seemed darker and more thrilling than the ones we read in books.

Granny sat back in her chair and shut her eyes, signalling that the story – at least for today – was over. The roof creaked, and outside the wind swished in the treetops, but no one moved. The tale might be told, as Granny liked to say, but its spell lingered, laying claim on our hearts and making us yearn to find our way back into the magic.

I woke with a start. Lightning flickered around me, and rain continued to hammer the car roof. I'd been dozing, but the woman reading from the book of fairytales had not been a dream.

Granny H – the woman I now knew as Esther Hillard – had been our neighbour. Her husband was dead, and she lived alone in a little settlers' cottage a couple of kilometres upstream from our farmhouse, on the other side of the river. It was an easy thirty-minute hike, over a natural bridge of stepping stones and up into the trees.

She'd been a kind lady – a baker of scones, a champion brewer of hot chocolate, and a skilled storyteller. Her voice was reedy and expressive, and her stories had never failed to fill me with excited dread. In fact, now that I thought about it, her stories had tweaked my young imagination, lingering with me into adulthood, eventually inspiring me to open a bookshop.

I imagined her now, sitting in the lounge room at Lyrebird Hill, her glasses balanced on her nose, a paperback in her lap. She might read late into the night, like I was often prone to doing, finally trundling off to bed in the wee hours, bleary-eyed and replete.

Thunder rumbled overhead.

I was gripped by a desperate longing to warm myself in our wood-fired kitchen, sipping tea with the woman I'd once known as Granny H. Suddenly there was nowhere else I wanted to be:

just there, in my old home, nestled in the valley surrounded by bushland . . . listening to Granny's tales and spinning a few of my own, basking in the company of a woman who had, during the difficult years of my childhood, shown me much kindness.

Another drum roll of thunder vibrated the car. Seconds later, a dazzling starburst of pure light tore open the sky. As it soared upwards then swept past me, I realised it wasn't lightning – it was car headlights. I flashed my own headlights, but I was too late; the other car had passed.

Throwing open the door, I stumbled out into the rain and ran after the retreating tail-lights, waving my arms and yelling. As quickly as it had appeared, the vehicle vanished along the road. I stared after it. Rain pounded me. Within moments my clothes were sopping, my hair plastered over my face; my hopes of rescue sluiced away.

Getting back in the car, I slammed myself inside and then sat for a damp eternity listening to the water drip off my jeans legs and puddle in the footwell. The dashboard clock showed 10.30pm. There was no point trying to walk anywhere; it was too dark, too wet.

I pulled a warm jumper and track pants from my overnight bag, then climbed into the back seat. Manoeuvring myself to almost horizontal, I pulled the picnic rug up around my neck and stared through the misty window. My stomach grumbled. Thunder boomed in the distance. I pictured myself at home, burrowed under the covers of my queen-sized bed; I tried to imagine that the din of the rain was actually the ocean outside my bedroom window, pulling its waves back from the beach then rushing them in again.

For a moment it worked.

Then from somewhere drifted the spicy golden scent of bush flowers.

All of a sudden I was no longer in my own imagined bed. This new bed was narrow, the cotton sheets tucked tightly around me. Moonlight shone through tall windows, and on the far wall was a bookshelf crammed with antique dolls. With a jolt I realised I'd stumbled from one daydream into another – because here I was in the cramped room I'd once shared with my sister. I looked at the other bed.

It was empty.

I shivered. Dragging the rug up over my head, I squeezed shut my eyes.

Midnight finally came around. Mum and Jamie were asleep, even the rats in the roof were quiet. Climbing out of bed, I stripped off my pyjamas and replaced them with the old nighty.

The nighty was threadbare and reached nearly to my ankles. The neck and cuffs were trimmed with pearl buttons and lace. I'd found it in one of the upstairs bedrooms, crammed into a cardboard box with a bunch of other old-fashioned clothes. There were boxes everywhere up there, packed along the walls and piled to the ceiling, all covered in dust and grot. Upstairs was out of bounds to Jamie and me, but I loved sneaking up there and escaping into the dusty darkness, working my fingers under the box lids and pulling out the treasures packed tightly inside. Tattered books and jars of hairpins and moth-eaten silk hankies with embroidered flowers, even some little pans of dried-up watercolour paint.

And the nighty.

Sliding open my bedroom window, I climbed outside and ran to the woodshed where I kept my bike. Barefoot, I rode towards the Spine.

The track was dark, and as my bike rattled over stones and fallen sticks, my insides were like a milkshake. I was shivering, too – but not from cold. My shivers were from Granny's story. It made me want to run willy-nilly into the dark, to throw back my head and laugh like kookaburra.

But I kept quiet. That was Rule Number Three. I was allotted one shriek at the end of the game, but even that must be carefully disguised to sound like the bark of a fox. Until that moment, nothing was allowed to pass my lips, not even a sigh.

Leaving my bike at the bottom of the Spine, I entered the tea-tree forest and clawed my way through the brittle branches, stopping occasionally to free my hair or drag the nighty from the clutches of a sharp twig. I moved stealthily, rolling heel-to-toe then bounding for a step or two, trying to sound like a wallaby.

The Beast was near. I couldn't see him or hear him or smell him, but the skin on the back of my neck was crawling and I wanted to stop and wee. I didn't dare. The Beast was near, and soon he would find me.

I stopped, looking up through the network of tea-tree branches. The sky was black velvet, the stars flaming match heads. All around me, the grey midnight world of the bush was coming to life. Gum leaves rattled in the treetops, bats twittered as they swooped for moths and beetles. Cicadas, bullfrogs, the scuttle of a lizard in the leaf dross—

And the quiet crunch of approaching footfall.

My heart kicked once, then began to gallop. I stared over my shoulder, licking my dry lips. Darkness like a wall. The moon was a fingernail, shedding no light. Only the stars shone, picking out the frilly beards of moss that grew from the branches, making the ribbon gums glow white. Looking east I saw the knobbled Spine, arching against the sky like a dinosaur's backbone—

A crash of motion. A dark mass loomed. Twigs crunched, a branch splintered away from its trunk. I lurched sideways but the creature grabbed me, pinning me against his shaggy body. I twisted and tried to throw myself away from him. His grip faltered, his stranglehold loosened, and I tasted a moment's freedom ... but then the Beast's claws reclaimed me and dragged me back against him.

The momentum of our struggle pulled us over and we hit the ground in a tangle of limbs. I took the opportunity to sink my teeth into his arm. His skin was hairy and as tough as elephant hide, tasting of salt and old leather. The monster grunted in surprise, then rolled on top of me. He was heavy, I couldn't breathe. Through my eyelashes, I braved a look at my captor. He was staring down at me, a hideous monster with the head of a bull, and eyes that burned like fiery embers.

I gave another token struggle, but my heart wasn't in it. The Beast pinned my wrists over my head and bent closer, his face a finger-span from mine. I could smell his rank breath, feel the heat of his huge deformed body through the thin fabric of my nighty. I shivered. The night seemed suddenly too dark, too close. My position was hopeless, so I fell back in surrender.

This only seemed to excite the Beast. Lowering his muzzle, he pressed his lips to my ear.

'Welcome, dear Beauty,' he rasped. 'Welcome to my humble abode.'

When I woke, the storm had passed. Throwing off the rug, I struggled my feet into my soggy runners and got out of the car. For the longest time I stood on the wet road, drinking in the sweet, damp air, thinking about the dream.

I'd been racing through the bush at night, my arms and face scratched by tea-tree branches, my heart thudding wildly. A dark presence bounded after me, a hulking creature that ran stealthily, not wanting me to know it was there.

It was an old, recurring nightmare; I'd had it for as long as I could remember. I knew its cause: childish anxieties that had taken root after my father's death, occasionally returning to haunt me. Right on cue, the scar on my shoulder began to pang – a painful, twitchy itch down deep near the bone that no amount of rubbing could ease.

Ignoring it, I repacked my overnight bag; it was heavy, but I'd rather get blisters than do without toiletries and clean clothes. I'd have to leave my car here until I could arrange for a wrecker to pick it up; I had no delusions about getting it repaired, the faithful old girl was clearly un-revivable.

As I set out along the road, I surveyed the landscape.

Mist rose up from the muddy ground, and raindrops glinted on the trees as the sun began to emerge. The road was littered with fallen leaves, and puddles of water reflected the clouds.

I had no phone reception, no food, and the prospect of several hours' walk ahead of me – not exactly my idea of a good time. And yet I was surprisingly calm. It was seven o'clock, Saturday morning; in a couple of hours, Earle would be opening the shop, stacking books on the specials table, tidying up the antique postcard display. Rob would be in the gym, pumping iron to get the endorphins firing before a busy morning of consultations, and then an afternoon of chapter rewrites. My mind raced ahead, wondering what he had scheduled for tonight. A cosy nightcap in the spa with his new love; the slow removal of her slinky dress that reeked of 'Poison'; the seductive running of his hands over her gym-toned body to unclasp the tiny black lace bra and reveal pert, perfect breasts—

My heart shrank into a knot, and I gritted my teeth on a sob. What had I done wrong? Neglected to adore him enough? Forgotten to hang off his every word, or laugh at his feeble jokes? Disappointed him in bed? Rob had seemed to enjoy our intimacy, but how could I ever know for sure? I'd heard of women faking passion. Were men guilty of the same deception?

Maybe, I thought ruefully.

They were certainly capable of *other* lies.

Stopping, I placed my bag on a patch of gravel and scrubbed my hands over my face. I wouldn't cry, I decided. That would mean admitting the depth of my hurt. Rob was an arse; I had wasted three years of my life, and I wasn't going to waste a second more by dissolving into sobs whenever I thought of him. In fact, now might be a good time to swear off love for good; that way, I'd never have to risk feeling this shitty ever again.

I dabbed my eyes, blew my nose, and then picked up my bag. Mud squelched under my feet as I walked, and after a while the cool moist air lifted my spirits. A flock of cockatoos startled from a nearby red gum, shrieking away into the sky. I tracked their path, watching them soar across the washed-out blue, winging towards the distant line of hills.

That's when I saw the ridge.

It had come back into view, a knucklebone-shaped hillock against the horizon. The sight of it made me shiver. Somewhere out there, in the shadow of its flinty spine, was Lyrebird Hill.

Breathing deeply, I savoured the cold, sweet taste of rain-washed air. The mist was breaking up. Hazy clouds banked around the distant ridge then ebbed away, obscuring it one moment and parting to reveal it clearly the next. The ridge seemed to inhale, like an ancient creature unhurriedly stirring from a long sleep.

Locking my sights on its bony outline, I picked up my pace and hurried along the road towards it.

6

Brenna, April 1898

My wedding day was overcast. Drab clouds veiled the autumn sun, and the atmosphere was muggy and oppressive. My head was dull, full of my conversation with Fa Fa in his study last night; my eyes were red, and I felt somehow unravelled, my legs unsteady, my heart beating out of kilter.

I wore a fitted jacket of fine grey wool over my best walking skirt, my good kid boots, and a layer of nervous perspiration. The small bouquet Millie had helped me pick that morning wilted long before I set foot inside the Armidale Town Hall, but I kept raising it to my nose, clinging to the fragile wisp of scent that linked me to my home.

The dank foyer was cool; its heavy walls had trapped the smells of the street – horse dung and pipe smoke, and the human odours of the other people who congregated here to do official business. The ceremony was simple: a celebrant recited the vows from his book, Carsten and I muttered our promises, and when the pronouncement was made he kissed me hastily, on the cheek. Fa Fa and a man unknown to me signed the witness statements, while Owen looked on in silence. No glad tears were shed, nobody hugged me. I felt lost without Aunt Ida and Millie, but Carsten had pointed out that in light of my aunt's recent funeral, a small wedding party was more respectful, and so Millie had stayed at home.

When it was over, the four of us boarded the train to Newcastle. I sat by the window next to Carsten, who ignored me and instead engaged my father in a debate about the precarious position of local banks in a floundering economy.

Owen sat opposite, the freckles stark on his ruddy skin. As the train rattled out of Armidale and southwards towards the coast, he took a handkerchief-wrapped bundle from his pocket and passed it to me.

'Open it later,' he whispered. 'When you start to get homesick.'

A whiff of honey drifted from the bundle, and I guessed it contained a sprig of stringybark blossom. My lips trembled. Reaching for my brother's hand, I gave it a quick squeeze and nodded my thanks. I didn't dare tell the boy that I was already homesick, and that the blossoms he'd collected for me with love would only serve to make me more so.

I stowed the precious contents in my bag, and turned my attention to the window. I had decided to make the best of my situation. Mama and Fa Fa had not been in love when they married, but over the years their affection had deepened. If I bore a son for Carsten, and practised kindness and understanding, then surely we would grow to love one another.

The only landscape I had ever known rushed past the window. The New England tablelands withstood scorching summers, and driving snow in winter; flood, drought, and brutal hailstorms that shredded crops and buckled rooftops and killed lambs. Most of the tree species that grew here were drab, their foliage grey-green, their trunks unremarkable – but they were tough, designed to survive extremes of climate.

Carsten leaned forward to emphasise a point to my father, and the window briefly caught his reflection. He was more animated than I'd ever seen him, his eyes alight, his features somehow more striking, but gazing at his ghostly likeness on the glass brought me no joy.

Closing my eyes, I rested back in my seat. As the train rattled me along the track to my new life, I made another vow, a silent vow that was mine alone. I would be a tree – an angophora, an ironbark, a hardy wattle. Whatever storm blew my way, whatever hail or snow or scorching heatwave raged around me, I would stand my ground and find a way to endure.

The steamship *Mareeba* departed Newcastle at dusk, beneath a cloud of seagulls. Tugboats led us from Oyster Bank, then released us to the mercy of the open sea. I stood on the deck gripping the rail as I watched the pier, tasting the salty sea spray and holding my hat against the blustering wind. My gaze stayed fixed on the lonely figures of my father and Owen until they receded from view.

In my hand I held the treasure my father had slipped into my fingers moments before I boarded the steamer. He had leaned near and whispered into my ear, 'Not a day goes by – not an hour, not even a minute – that I don't think of her. Look after her for me, my sparrow.'

My fingers had tightened around the little queen, and I smiled my thanks to Fa Fa, overwhelmed by the preciousness of his gift.

Darkness fell quickly, devouring the tiny lights of the port. Soon all that remained of the world was an inky nothingness. My limbs were stiff and cold before I finally tore myself from the deck and went below.

Almost the moment I set foot in the cramped cabin I was to share with my husband, my stomach began to churn. And it did not stop churning for the next three days, the majority of which I spent with my head over a tin pan. Carsten removed himself to an adjoining cabin, and I didn't see him again until we docked at Port Melbourne.

From there our passage to Burnie on Tasmania's north coast took twenty-eight hours. The sea became increasingly rough as we went through the Rip, a concourse of currents that, according to the steward who kindly brought it upon himself to deliver me a hot broth, was turbulent even in the mildest weather.

'Never fear,' he reassured me. 'Only one other passenger has ever died of seasickness on this route, and oddly enough, they were in this very cabin!'

I curled on the bunk, the grey light from the porthole filling the room with watery shadows. Beneath the sound of waves rushing past the ship's flanks, I could hear the drone of the steamer's engine, a constant reminder of the distance growing between me and my home. All through the night I clutched the black queen my father had given me, and drew comfort from her.

When I drifted into a queasy half-sleep, I dreamt of the cave in which I had been hidden that long ago night with Jindera and my grandmother. Only, in my dream, there was no fear – we sat quietly around a small fire, roasting wood grubs over the flames. Beyond our shelter there were no screams, no violence or terror – just the soft call of owls and the murmur of the river Muluerindie as it rushed inland, always inland, far from the raging sea.

Several hours before dawn, we disembarked at Burnie. A man was waiting for us on the dock. He raised his hand in greeting as Carsten descended the gangway. The shadow of his battered black hat concealed his face, and his shoulders were hunched against the wind, which whipped the threadbare coat around his lean body. Something about his bearing attracted my instant curiosity.

Although the ocean no longer rolled beneath my feet, my head still swum giddily and my legs were rubber. The porter brought our luggage from the ship, and the man – whom my husband introduced as Lucien Fells, his manservant – shouldered my small trunk and picked up Carsten's portmanteau. The man cast me a quick look but made no greeting, then hastened along the pier towards a black carriage that waited in the street beyond.

'Don't mind Lucien,' Carsten said as we followed him along the jetty. 'He's not a great one for society, but he's a good lad. Pay no mind to his manners . . . nor to his appearance.'

I wondered at that last remark and was about to query him further, but we had reached the carriage. It was open-topped like my father's, but its woodwork was lacquered and gleamed wetly beneath the street lamp, and its trimmings were shining brass. Lucien secured our luggage at the rear of the dray and busied himself unhitching the horses.

Carsten helped me up the steps and gave me a rug to drape around my shoulders. I settled onto my seat, huddling into the blanket, breathing in the scent of wood polish and leather. Lucien sprang into the driver's seat, and Carsten climbed in beside him. A moment later the vehicle jerked from the kerb and rattled along the road.

'Try and get some sleep,' Carsten called over his shoulder. 'It'll take us several hours to reach Brayer House. I'll wake you when we get to Wynyard.'

As we travelled along the edge of the bay, the air grew wintry. I pulled the blanket tighter around me, but soon my fingers were numb and my feet had turned to ice. I wriggled my toes inside my boots and blew on my hands, snuggling deeper into the blanket. And yet despite my discomfort, I couldn't wish the journey over.

On the landward side, tall trees overshadowed the road, their trunks concealed beneath vigorous undergrowth. On the ocean side, the bay was an inky dark bowl; I couldn't see the water, only hear it rushing in and out against the shore, breathing its salty exhalations into the night. Stars winked in the blackness, and every once in a while I saw a pinprick of light far out at sea, perhaps a fishing vessel or a distant steamer, striking out for Melbourne or crossing the strait on its way to England or Africa.

The road became uneven and potholed. The carriage rattled and strained, and I clung to the brass handrail, my palms alight with cold. We travelled uphill for a way, and our progress slowed until we crested the rise and began to descend.

As my eyes adjusted to the gloom, the two men at the head of the carriage became more clearly visible. I caught a glimpse of Carsten's profile, and wondered what he'd meant by telling me to pay no mind to Lucien's appearance.

Intrigued, I studied the manservant.

He was a youth, perhaps of similar age to me, nineteen or twenty, I guessed. He sat tall in his seat, although not as tall as Carsten, and was more slightly built. His long hair was snagged back in a tail, with wild strands escaping over his shoulders. On the few occasions he turned his face to answer a query Carsten put to him, I glimpsed pale features that rivalled Carsten's striking good looks.

I settled back against the cushions and closed my eyes. Days had passed since the wedding ceremony at Armidale Town Hall; days that Carsten and I had spent travelling. While on the steamer he had necessarily kept his distance; but now that we were approaching home, our period of abstinence would end and my life as a married woman would begin.

Drawing the rug tighter, I tried to doze.

The clop of horses' hoofs on the road, and the rhythmic swish of the sea, were soothing sounds, interrupted at intervals by the quiet talk of the men. The two voices were distinct. Carsten's tones were clipped as he enquired after his farm, his questions commanding and formal. The young groomsman spoke with more reserve, and his voice – for which my ears seemed to listen more acutely – was rougher at the edges than his master's, a vague accent that I could not identify, which gave his words a pleasant lilt. More intriguing, were his replies. His choice of words held a strange poetry, as if, despite a lack of education, he was in the habit of thinking carefully before he spoke.

Why had Carsten advised me to pay no mind to the young man's appearance? I squinted at him, but there was too little light to see.

Snuggling under my blanket, I resigned myself to knowing soon enough.

'My dear?'

I blinked awake. The sun had crested the horizon, and in its pale glow I saw that the carriage had stopped in front of an imposing house. Built of cream-coloured sandstone, with decorative black wrought-iron festooning the ground and first-floor verandahs, it might have sprung from the pages of a sinister fairytale. The black roof was pricked with pointed finials, and the slate tiles gleamed like the scales of a mythical serpent. It seemed large and gloomy in the dawn light, saved only by the rambling garden of exotic plants and trees that surrounded it.

Carsten alighted from the carriage, but rather than offer his arm to me, he strode immediately towards the house, where two women waited. One of the women was tall and dark-haired; her ivory dress made her appear luminous. Her companion was short and heavily built, with a tower of dark hair perched precariously on her head; she wore a black dress with mutton sleeves, overlaid by a stark white apron.

Gripping the carriage rail, I was about to step down when the servant, Lucien Fells, came to my assistance. As he extended his arm for me to take, I glared at my husband, but it seemed rude to decline the young servant's offer, so I rested my fingers lightly on his forearm. I took the first step without mishap, but then my legs were taken again by the sea-wobbles and I was airborne.

Lucien grabbed me roughly by the arms, and set me on my feet. He didn't let me go immediately, and I looked up at him, startled by the unexpected contact, feeling bruised by his fingers.

I'd not been wrong in my earlier observation. He had a striking face, an angel's face with dark eyes that were stormy grey as the ocean; a regal nose and brows that made me think of eagle's wings. His wild hair had loosened from its tail and now coiled unrestrained around his shoulders, the colour of burnished copper. His fine bone structure pushed through skin that was pale and, for the most part, flawless. He might have been beautiful, had it not been for the cruel scar that carved along the left side of his face from temple to jaw, disappearing beneath his ear.

My breath escaped too quickly. 'Oh.'

He released me, and turned his attention to the luggage secured to the rear of the carriage. While he unbuckled it, he kept his back to me, as if unwilling to subject himself further to my scrutiny.

Shakily I trod along the path towards the house and joined my husband and the two women. Their chatter fell quiet as I approached.

Carsten took my arm. 'Brenna, this is my sister, Adele Whitby.'

The woman in the ivory dress was even more striking close up. She appeared to be in her early thirties, with chestnut hair and eyes rimmed by long lashes, and full lips that might have been brushed with carmine. Her smile was full of warmth.

'Welcome,' she said, taking my hand and kissing my cheek. She smelled of roses, but from beneath her floral perfume wafted the treacly bitterness of Minerva Tonic.

Carsten introduced the shorter woman as the housekeeper, Mrs Quinn. She examined me with a frown, then muttered a stiff apology and hurried back to the house, quickly vanishing into the dark interior.

Adele took my arm. 'Don't mind Quinn. She's been caring for Carsten and me since we were babes in arms. Once she warms to you, I promise you'll be friends for life. Now, my dear, you look tired. I can't say I blame you after your long trip. Come, let me show you to your room.'

Carsten hurried ahead of us and bounded up the stairs, two at a time as if he couldn't wait to get away. I heard a door clatter shut, and then the heavy tread of footsteps as he crossed the floor. There was a faint clink of glass, and I guessed he was washing down the journey's dust with a measure of sweet sherry.

Adele steered me up the stairs. On the first-floor landing, she paused at a small lacquered table and gestured for me to go ahead. When she followed a moment later, her breathing sounded laboured, and as we climbed the rest of the way I heard the rattle of a nasty cough. Carsten had mentioned she was poorly, and I wondered at the nature of her illness.

My room was at the very top of the house, at the end of a narrow hallway. Adele turned the doorknob, and I expected to step into a room that was as cramped and dark as a wardrobe – so I was taken aback to find it large and bright and airy.

An enormous oak armoire took up most of one wall, its carved doors gleaming in the gentle sunlight that peeped through a chink in the curtains. The huge bed was swamped by an exquisite quilt of pale ivory silk, topped by pillows embroidered with daisies, and near the window was a small blackwood desk.

'I hope you'll be comfortable here,' Adele was saying. She went over to the bed, dusting her fingers across the quilt, absently plumping the pillows. A bay window overlooked the back garden and, as I pressed my forehead to the glass, I couldn't contain a sigh of pleasure.

'It's just ... divine,' I marvelled. Adele joined me at the window and we stood in silence admiring the vista. The sun was creeping up over the horizon, daubing the treetops with pale light. Down in the garden, brick pathways wound between the trees and vanished in a tangle of undergrowth. There were black cypress pines, mingling with flowering camellia hedges and wrought-iron archways smothered in jasmine vine, and sunny patches featuring great mounds of glossy-leafed daphne.

I spied a rambling vegetable garden, and on the southern horizon a line of hills slowly turning from purple to blue. To the west, the forest thinned and the land dropped away. Beyond, glittering in the early light like an endless field of blue diamonds, was the sea.

I was itching to rush outside and explore, to capture that breathtaking sunrise with my paintbrush and colours and breathe the salty ocean air. But a clock began to strike; seven ponderous notes rang out, each one vibrating beneath my boots.

'My brother has been lonely,' Adele said softly. 'I have the feeling you will do him the world of good.'

'I hope so.' In the room's dim light, she and I might have been sisters. There was colour in her skin that spoke of a love of outdoors, accentuated by the pale ivory dress. Her lips were deep red, but the effect was achieved, not by tint from a bottle as I first suspected, but by her unconscious habit of biting them.

I liked her, I decided.

Outwardly, she appeared quite perfect. And yet I sensed in her a darkness, a faint shadow of sorrow or perhaps of grief, that mirrored my own.

'I shall leave you now,' she said warmly. 'Quinn will bring some wash water for you. You can change your dress and freshen up. Breakfast is at eight. As you've probably come to realise, my brother values punctuality.' Dimples appeared in her cheeks, and her teeth shone white against the pink fullness of her lips. She leaned towards me and whispered, 'Whatever you do, my dear, don't be late.'

Carsten did not show himself at breakfast, nor did he appear for lunch, but it wasn't until his absence at dinner that I began to suspect he was avoiding me. That night I retired early, exhausted after the long journey, but once in bed I found I couldn't sleep.

I perched on the edge of my bed, my knees pressed together beneath my nightgown, my heart thudding as I watched the door. Downstairs, the grandfather clock ticked away the minutes; I could feel its mechanical pulse throbbing up through the floorboards and into the soles of my feet.

Finally, I heard footsteps in the hallway outside.

I tried to recall Aunt Ida's instructions, but all common sense had flown from my head; my thoughts were suddenly jumbled, like bees disturbed from the hive and goaded into a buzzing frenzy.

The door opened. My husband stepped into the room. He was dishevelled, his dark hair raked about, his eyes bloodshot; the sticky smell of port wine wafted off him. He did not glance at me, but walked straight into the room and took his watch from his pocket, placing it with care on the little blackwood desk. Removing his waistcoat, then shirt and shoes, he crossed the room to the bedside and blew out the lamp.

The bed creaked as he climbed in beside me.

'Lie down,' he instructed.

I did as he asked and lay in the darkness, wide-eyed. My heart rammed against my ribs, my breath seemed loud in the stillness. A cold, sweaty trembling spread over me.

I had once seen a pair of snakes mating. They had risen onto their tails and twined about one another, hissing softly as they moved in sinewy accord. I'd been transfixed, so absorbed in trying to distinguish one snake from the other that I hadn't heard my father's approach. There was a click, then the crack of rifle fire. I lurched in fright, and then stared at what remained of the snakes. Blood and mess, where a moment ago had been a delicate play of love. My father dragged me away by the arm, scolding me for putting myself in danger and forcing him to waste gunpowder on a reptile.

Carsten rolled onto me and kissed my mouth. It wasn't the lingering sweetness I had anticipated, but rather a hard meeting of lips that was quickly over. My nostrils filled with the smell of wine and pipe tobacco. Carsten was heavy, and when I expelled his foreign odours from my lungs, the air was slow to draw back in. I was lightheaded, wanting to shove him off me so I could breathe, but I did not dare.

Carsten grunted and buried his face against my neck. Reaching down, he grasped a handful of my nightgown and dragged up the hem to my waist. I felt a shudder of heat as his skin pressed against mine. He forced his knee between my legs, and when he dropped his full weight on me and began to move, I let out a huff of surprise.

I thought about the snakes, and the memory of the gunshot blast that had ended their union, unable to forget the bloodied mess that had become of them.

Carsten went still. The bed creaked as he rolled off me. For a time, he sat on the edge of the mattress, his head in his hands. I lay very still, not understanding. I had grown up on a farm, where rams climbed on ewes, and stallions went over the mares, and shearers' dogs always seemed to be on heat. Of course, I reasoned that the human act must certainly be far more genteel than the goings on of a farmyard, but as far as I could tell, Carsten's attempt had not been successful.

The lamp came on. Carsten stood and trod across the room. His body was lean and pale, downy with soft dark hair. He dragged on his trousers and collected his shirt from the back of the chair.

I sat up. 'Carsten? Did I do something wrong?'

A handful of minutes passed. Carsten lingered in the dark, his unbuttoned shirt hanging open, the moonlight shining on his face. His cheeks gleamed, as if they were wet.

'It's nothing you've done,' he finally said in a thick voice. 'Go to sleep, it's been a long day. I'm tired, that's all. So very tired.'

He tucked in his shirt and buttoned it, then reached for his waistcoat. He put on his shoes, then picked up his watch and chain from the desk but didn't slip it into his pocket straightaway. Instead he cradled it in his palm, moving into a patch of moonlight the better to see, rubbing his thumb over its face as though engulfed by memory.

I thought I heard him murmur a name, and felt a spark of hopefulness that the subject of his thoughts was me. But before I had a chance to ask, he turned on his heel and went out the bedroom door, closing it silently behind him.

For a long time I lay still. My nightdress was bunched around my thighs, and I sensed a chill creeping into the room. A feeling of unease crept over me; Carsten had said little, but displeasure had radiated from him like gusts of foul air. I felt tainted by it, grubby and heartsore, yet unable to pinpoint exactly what had gone wrong between us.

After a while, I began to shiver. Getting out of bed, I collected my shawl and went to the window. The moon was full, gleaming through the trees, as bright as a sovereign. The downstairs clock struck midnight.

Below in the garden, a blur of white made me look down.

A woman was hurrying along the path. Like me, she was dressed only in a nightgown. Her feet were bare, and her dark hair cascaded over her shoulders.

Adele.

She stumbled, and began to cough, that same chest rattle I had heard earlier on the stairs. Then she recovered herself and rushed on. Reaching her arms in front of her, she began to snatch at the air as if trying to catch something that danced invisibly just ahead of her. In a heartbeat, she was gone.

For a long while I stood there, waiting for her to return. When she didn't, I grew worried. Going to the door, I pressed

my ear to the cold wood and listened for any sounds of distur-
bance. Somewhere along the hallway a door clicked softly
shut . . . but there were no raised voices, no rushing footfall, no
indication of things amiss.

Back at the window, I searched the dark garden. The trees
moved gently, their leaves stirred by a night breeze. Stars glittered in the inky sky. I waited, my feet growing numb on the icy
floor, my breathing shallow, my neck stiff with tension.

Then a man appeared. I recognised Lucien Fells immediately. He made haste along the pathway as Adele had done, but
when he was directly below my window, he looked up. I froze,
and if he saw me he made no show of it. Instead he rushed on,
taking the same fork in the path that Adele had taken.

I stood at the window until my feet grew numb. My room
had grown dark, the candle long burned away, but outside the
sky had begun to lighten. The grandfather clock downstairs
rumbled out another hour. My eyes were gritty from searching
the garden's dark shadows, but I knew that if I turned away now
and climbed into my bed, sleep would never come.

I waited at the window until dawn finally crested the
horizon.

Still, Lucien and Adele did not return.

7

The best therapy for a broken heart is love.
– ROB THISTLETON, *LET GO AND LIVE*

Ruby, May 2013

The air was cold and damp, still heavy with the weight of rain. I followed the steep driveway downhill into the valley. I could smell river water, and the spicy tang of trampled gum leaves, and as I emerged through the trees I found myself in a scene straight from childhood.

The garden was overgrown with wildflowers: purple peas, white ammobium daisies and native bluebells springing up among clumps of silvery grass. Beyond the garden was bushland. Feathery cassinia and ferns formed a thick understorey beneath contorted salmon gums and upright black ironbarks. Leaves fluttered gently in the uppermost boughs, ablaze with dawn light. Further down the slope, I saw the glint of water.

In the midst of this wild garden was a spacious double-storey stone house surrounded by a deep verandah. Wisteria snaked up peeling posts, each trunk as thick as my arm; leafy brackets grew up onto the roof, and the ground below was littered with fallen leaves.

The verandah decking looked recently swept, but an air of emptiness hung over the place. I saw no sign of a car, and all the windows were shut tight despite the sunshine. I wiped my muddy trainers on the bristle mat, then mounted the steps and offloaded my overnight bag. Then I knocked on the front door.

'Esther? It's Ruby Cardel, are you there?'

I waited to hear footsteps, but when none came I knocked again. Finches twittered in the grevillea, and the river burbled over its stony bed . . . but the house lay in silence.

I went around and knocked on the back door, but it was clear no one was home. Going down the steps, I wandered into the garden. The vegie patch was still in the same spot, halfway down the slope to the river. Its wire fence was buckled, and the posts were split by harsh weather. Huge mounds of zucchini and rambling pumpkin dominated the garden beds, and the crops growing between them – onions and eggplant, beans and tomatoes – were thriving.

Shivering in the morning air, I went back onto the verandah and cupped my eyes against the kitchen window. Inside lay a gloomy stillness. But as my eyes adjusted, my heart gave a lurch.

There was our old dining table, with the same mismatched wooden chairs, where Mum and Jamie and I had sat to eat breakfast. On the table beside a jar of wilting roses sat a big floral teapot; nearby was a book with a gardening glove marking the page, a wooden bowl containing a mound of shrivelled apples.

My stomach rumbled; the hollow ache I'd managed to ignore until now reminded me I hadn't eaten since lunchtime the day before.

I wiped my breath-fog off the kitchen window.

On the long walk here, I hadn't seen any cars; if Esther had driven into Armidale this morning, surely our paths would have crossed? I recalled the headlights I'd seen last night, and wondered if that had been her; maybe she'd gone on holiday?

Cupping my face again, I peered back into the kitchen.

The bowl of withered apples didn't appeal, but I spied a kettle. And surely there was a biscuit tin lurking in one of those cupboards.

I glanced over my shoulder.

Esther wouldn't want me to starve; there might be an awkward moment if she arrived home and found me ransacking her larder, but we'd probably just have a good old laugh about it. Besides, I was starting to feel faint.

Returning to the back verandah, I slipped out of my muddy runners and rolled the legs of my sodden track pants. I gave the door handle a twist and found it open – but I didn't go straight in. For an eternal moment, I teetered in that doorway, my pulse skipping lightly, my breath shallow. This had once been my home; Jamie's home, too. The last time I had stepped across this threshold I was thirteen years old, haunted by my sister's death, and confused by my mother's apparent rejection of me.

I was now thirty; not all that much else had changed.

The old house's dizzying silence crashed around me. Still I stood there, half-expecting to hear voices drifting along the hallway, or echoing from the upstairs rooms. Jamie's bright chatter, my mother's tinkling laughter. Maybe even my own adolescent voice, piping like a now-extinct bird from the back room. When I took a tentative breath, memory threw back the aromas of tea brewed bitterly strong, and freshly baked blackberry muffins and homemade sour cream.

In the kitchen, I found a full pantry.

Cans of beans, tomatoes, corn. Mushrooms, tuna. Peaches and apricot halves in syrup. Boxes of crackers, jars of jam and chutney. Grabbing a tin of peaches, I rummaged in the drawer for a can opener, then a spoon. I stood at the sink and ate, and I do believe those peaches were the sweetest thing I'd ever tasted. Going back to the pantry, I examined the array of tins. My stomach grumbled softly, urging me to open more peaches, but the apricots looked good, too, and would probably go down well

with a few of those crackers . . . and, forgive me for hallucinat-
ing, but was that a packet of Iced VoVos—

A muffled hum broke the stillness. I went to the window.
The sky was brilliant blue; no trace remained of yesterday's
thunderstorm. Sunlight cascaded through the trees, gilding the
leaves and turning the grass to silver.

A car motor, then?

I cleared the evidence of my crime: rinsed and dried the
spoon, wiped the opener and crammed it back in its crowded
drawer, deposited the empty peach tin in what I hoped was a
recycle bin under the sink. Then I flew across the kitchen, down
the hall and out the door, my stomach churning in protest.

Outside, my hearing sharpened. The sound was only marginally louder. There was no sign of a car, and no accompanying
dust cloud. The noise seemed to come from overhead.

I examined the sky. A streak of white trailed across the
pristine blue. It was a plane, quietly travelling to some port of
civilisation. A few seconds later it vanished, and its faraway
drone dwindled to silence.

I returned to the kitchen.

There was a gas stove, and I rummaged for matches then
set the kettle on the flame. Opening the apricots, I reclaimed
my spoon and tucked in while the water boiled. Then I rinsed
the floral teapot, freshening it with swills of scalding water.
When the tea was made, I loaded a tray with the pot, a cup, a
jar of sugar and the packet of biscuits, and headed out to the
verandah.

The sun – and a full belly – had made me sleepy. The mud on
my track pants had dried, and I'd brushed the worst of it off my
legs and feet. Settling back against the warm stones, I yawned.
Before long, I was drifting.

In the haze of half-sleep, I could hear someone digging.

It was Mum. She was under the walnut tree, jabbing a shovel into the compacted soil around the roots. She wore jeans and a colourful tie-dyed blouse. Strange. She never went in the garden in her good clothes. And why was she crying? I could hear her sobs, see the puffy redness of her face.

She wiped her eyes on the back of her hand, then kneeled beside the hole. From near the trunk of the walnut tree, she picked up what appeared to be a large flat biscuit tin and placed it in the ground. Again she wiped her eyes, then got to her feet and began shovelling dirt back into the hole. Crying, crying all the while.

I shook my head to clear the dream, and when I opened my eyes the first thing I saw was the walnut tree. The smooth bark of its contorted limbs glowed silver in the dappled morning sunlight, and shadows darkened the patchy grass at its base. It was far from the serene picture-postcard Mum had painted; the real garden around me was an overgrown shambles, and the screech of lorikeets and chatter of finches was anything but tranquil. Once, Mum had loved the wildness of this garden. I couldn't help wondering if her painting reflected a need to pare away the disorder and somehow make sense of Jamie's death; or at least portray our wilderness home as a place of harmony and stillness, a safe place that belonged on the lid of a chocolate box.

Or a biscuit tin.

I stood suddenly, remembering another element of the painting: the small, grave-like mound beneath the tree. There was no mound now, just grass littered with leaves and a few blackened pods.

Going around the house, I found the old barn. Native sarsaparilla rambled up its sides, but its stone walls and wide door were exactly as I remembered. At the far end, to my right, were three old stable stalls, now chock-full of wheelbarrows and garden tools and rolls of chain link fencing. Parked in front of the stalls was a beautifully restored vintage Morris Minor.

I was about to go in search of a spade when a noisy rumble entered the stillness. I ducked around the side of the house and stood in the shade of a red gum, waiting for the vehicle to appear.

A moment later a battered ute burst through the trees and clattered past, finally coming to rest in front of the barn. A man climbed out, followed closely by a pair of red kelpies. Leaving the car door open, he walked unsteadily to the house and sat on the verandah steps. The dogs bounded up to him, sniffing and whining as he sank his head in his hands.

Esther hadn't mentioned that she lived with anyone. Perhaps he was a relative; a nephew or grandson. Whoever he was, I knew I should have alerted him to my presence, but my mouth was suddenly dry. If I called out, the dogs would see me and rush over. Already they were sniffing beneath the kitchen window, noses keen to the ground. Any moment now they'd catch my scent.

The scar on my shoulder began to itch, a painful pricking that made me want to scratch until I drew blood. I took a fortifying breath, but instead of making a move towards the man as I'd planned, I shuffled deeper into the shade, wishing myself invisible.

Please don't see me.

Rob always said my dog phobia was normal, after the attack when I was a kid, but he'd also pointed out that I was using my fear as an emotional crutch, an excuse to avoid responsibility for the way my life was – for my anxiety and overeating and worrying. According to Rob, fears stemming from childhood were the hardest to let go of; and yet often they were the most irrational, too.

One of the dogs let out a question-mark whine. Then its head jerked in my direction. It gave a surprised, angry-sounding bark. Then, like demonic shadows from my own personal hell, both creatures began racing up the slope towards me.

My scream was brief, but shrill enough to crack glass.

The man shot to his feet and saw me. 'Stop!'

I froze in place. Even if I'd wanted to run, my legs were suddenly trembling so hard I wouldn't have managed two steps.

Then I realised his command had been directed at the dogs. They had halted in their tracks a couple of metres from where I stood. They continued to bark, but neither made a move to come any closer.

'Old Boy, Bardo,' the man said sharply.

The barking ceased. The man strode past the dogs and lifted his hand in greeting.

'Are you all right?'

I might have asked the same of him. His hair was a shaggy mess of light brown, streaked gold at the tips. His square face was half-hidden behind a beard. Most striking of all were his eyes; they were red-rimmed as if he'd been crying, but the irises were a pure bright kingfisher blue.

'I'm fine,' I said, glancing at the dogs. 'I got a bit of a shock, that's all.'

'They're harmless,' he said, scrubbing his palms over his face. 'Bark's worse than their bite, and all that.'

Under the beard, he had a friendly face; a bit weathered, freckled by the sun, a generous mouth, and cheeks dimpled with laugh lines. But it was his eyes that got me – not just the colour, but the way they were regarding me, warmly, almost intimately as if—

Impossible. I was sure I'd never seen him before. He was probably only staring because of my dishevelled appearance. My shoes and track pants were covered in mud, and after spending the night in the car, I'd been so intent on getting to Lyrebird Hill that I'd neglected to brush my hair. And if I'd bothered to check the mirror, I knew I would have found raccoon-like mascara-eyes.

'This'll sound crazy,' he said, 'but we've met before, haven't we?'

I stared at him in surprise. 'I don't think so.'

Was he flirting? I took a closer look, taking in the wide mouth, the windswept hair, and threadbare T-shirt and jeans; there *was* something about him, but I couldn't be sure.

He shook his head, apparently embarrassed, and it was suddenly clear to me that he *hadn't* been flirting, but genuinely curious. He didn't quite smile, but his eyes crinkled up in a friendly way. My heart did a double-beat. Maybe it was the power of suggestion, or maybe his regretful little half-smile sparked – not *recognition* exactly – rather, a tiny ember of wishing that I *had* met him before.

'Are you a relative of Esther's?' I asked.

'A friend,' he said quietly. 'I live on the next property. That is, I bought a hundred acres off Esther a few years back. I run a small nursery business – native trees, that sort of thing. On my days off, I'm Esther's gardener. At least I was,' he added quietly.

I was about to ask what he meant, when his gaze sharpened suddenly on my face. He smiled – an almost shy smile – and dimples appeared in his cheeks.

'Ruby?'

I blinked. 'I'm sorry, I don't—'

'I'm Pete,' he said. He must have registered my lost look, because he quickly added, 'We were at school together.'

I smiled, relieved. At least now I had a reference point.

'It's okay,' he said, shaking my hand in an oddly formal gesture, grasping my fingers snugly in his. 'I don't expect you to remember me. I was only in the area for six months. Esther told me ages ago that you lost your memory after your sister died. I never got to tell you how sorry I was about that.'

'Thanks.' I hesitated. 'Did you know Jamie?'

He shook his head. 'She was in high school by the time I came on the scene. You were the one I was—' He cut off, and shrugged. 'You know, close to.'

I searched his face, trying to summon the features of the boy he'd once been. Had we really been close? How was it possible to draw such a blank on someone I'd known?

'I've got a rotten memory,' I said, trying to make light of it. 'That's why I'm here, I was hoping to see Esther. Of course, on the way my old car broke down and I got stranded, had to walk here this morning, through the mud. I ran into Esther a few weeks ago in Armidale, and she invited me to stay. We got talking about the past. She said she might be able to help me remember.'

'Oh hell, Ruby.' Pete's face crumpled. 'I'm really sorry. Esther died last night.'

I stared, hoping I'd heard wrong.

Pete pointed down the slope that led to the river. 'She had a fall, slipped in the rain. I found her late last night on the river-bank. She'd been there for hours.' He slumped and seemed to shrink into himself. 'Listen, I've just got back from the hospital. I'm going to make a cuppa, are you up for one?'

'Sure,' I said shakily. Shock was taking hold, making an empty hollow around my heart. I flashed back to the gallery, to the vibrant woman I'd chatted with so easily; to her kind smile, and her bouquet of wildflowers, and her promise to help me navigate back through my forgotten past. If my car hadn't broken down, if there hadn't been a storm, if I'd arrived yesterday afternoon as intended – then Esther might have still been alive.

'Do you think,' I began, then cleared my throat. 'Do you think Esther might have something a little stronger than tea?'

Pete looked at me. 'I'm pretty sure there's some brandy stashed in the larder for just this sort of emergency.'

We climbed the verandah steps, and Pete opened the back door, then ushered me in and followed silently as I made my way out to the kitchen.

'As you know, the storm hit suddenly,' Pete told me. 'I waited until the worst of it was over, then drove here to see if there'd been any damage to the new seedlings we'd planted.'

We were sitting on the verandah, the tray between us crammed with tea and biscuits, brandy bottle, and two glasses. The dogs lay side by side at the foot of the stairs, their ears pricked to the soft murmur of our voices.

Pete continued. 'I guess I knew the minute I got out of the car that something was wrong.'

The raspy emotion in his voice made me look more closely at him. He could not have been more different to Rob. He was like some kind of wild bush mechanic, with his raggy jeans and crazy hair and beard. His hands were knotted and looked stiff from years of hard work, but he wasn't old. My age, maybe a year or so older. But while I had the rosy glow of a pampered town dweller, Pete seemed worn and somehow battered, as though the nicks and cuts and tiny scars on his hands went more than skin deep.

'Esther always had this uncanny sense of knowing I was on my way,' he said. 'Even if I walked over from my place, she'd be waiting on the verandah, as if she'd heard me approaching from a mile away. I even tried sneaking through the pine forest at the back of the house, or cutting along the river, but she was always there, dusting her hands on her apron, the kettle already on the boil.' He sighed. 'Last night, it must have been about eight, I ran through the house calling, but she wasn't here. That's when I really started to worry.'

'Why was she down at the river if it had been raining?'

'She liked to sit on the rocks when she had something on her mind. The sound of the river soothed her, she always said.'

Pete was quiet for a time. His big body trembled, and I felt my eyes well in sympathy. Despite our history as school friends, this man was a stranger to me, but as I watched him his evident sorrow touched a nerve in me and I found myself wanting to soothe him, or at least distract him.

'You found her on the riverbank?' I gently prompted.

Pete looked up, scrubbing away his tears. 'At first I thought she was dead. I carried her to the house. Her head was gashed and she was blue from cold, but still conscious. I wrapped her in a blanket and got her into the car and cranked the heater, then drove like billy-o to the hospital. They managed to stabilise her, but I guess the damage was already done. Just before midnight she drifted off to sleep, and didn't wake up. If only she'd carried the PLB I bought her, she could have signalled for help.'

I looked at him. 'PLB?'

'Personal locator beacon, bushwalkers carry them in case of life threatening falls or snakebite, that sort of thing. The device alerts emergency services via satellite. Esther didn't want to know about it, so it's gathering dust under my sink. She always insisted that something like that was an invasion of her privacy.'

After a while, Pete dragged out a hanky and blew his nose. 'You know the worse thing? If I'd turned up an hour earlier – hell, half an hour, fifteen minutes – then she'd still be here.'

'You can't know that.'

I heard a scuffle, and saw that one of the dogs, the sharp-featured female, had crept up the stairs and quietly settled herself against Pete's feet. Pete reached down and absently tugged her ears. She was comforting him, I realised, and although I shifted uneasily on the bench, I didn't have the heart to wish her away.

'Esther taught me not to beat myself up for my mistakes,' Pete said. 'But I've got a feeling this one's going to haunt me.'

He was blaming himself; I recognised the signs. The pinched lips, the distant-focused eyes, the way he sat hunched into himself as if unwilling to take up space; I'd been seeing those same signs in myself for years.

He got up. 'I'm sorry, Ruby, I'm rotten company at the moment. I'll go for a swim and lighten up, and get these dogs fed. You're probably starving, so I can make us breakfast. Then I'll get to work on the ute.'

I was still thinking about Esther, so his words took a moment to sink in.

'The ute?'

Pete sighed. 'I was upset coming home this morning, and I got careless. I swerved to miss a kangaroo and hit a rock, buggered up my front end. I wasn't sure the Holden would get me home, which is why I came here – it's closer to the main road than my place. By the sound of that rattle under the bonnet, I won't be driving anywhere until the wishbone's fixed.'

'Wishbone? Ouch.'

'Yeah, nasty. I can repair it – I've got the parts in the shed at my place – but it's tricky work. Fiddly and time-consuming. Once it's fixed, I'll drive you in to Armidale. I'd take you in Esther's car, but that's out of operation, too. If luck's on our side I might have the ute working by tomorrow afternoon. Although,' he added darkly, more to himself, 'I don't like my chances.'

'So, we're stranded.'

The blue eyes locked on mine for an instant, and his smile seemed somehow regretful. 'Nothing that drastic. There's a landline at my place. You can call a cab if you like. The Armidale drivers don't like coming out here – once you get past Clearwater, the road's a goat track at the best of times, and after last night's rain it'll be a mud nightmare. A taxi 'll cost a bomb, but at least you'll get back to civilisation. Are you in a rush to be somewhere?'

I thought about my cottage overlooking the beach with its breezy windows and inviting patio. There was mud cake in my freezer, new bubble bath to try out, fluffy slippers and clean pyjamas to snuggle into, fresh sheets on my bed – and a bottle of shiraz stashed in the linen press for an emergency. I thought about my friends and our late dinners and boozy book rambles. I thought about my little bookshop with its sweet papery aromas and tranquil atmosphere, and Earle happily fossicking among the shelves.

Then back came the sharp, sweet smell of Rob's bathroom, and the likelihood that he'd already forgotten me. We were finished, I realised. I'd be alone again. Trudging through the days of my life, empty and sad.

Pete was watching me, his eyes curious.

I drummed up a smile. 'I was planning to spend a few days here, anyway. Do you think that'd be all right?'

'Esther would have wanted you here, Ruby. I expect the solicitor will arrange her funeral for some time mid-week. I don't suppose you'd . . .'

'I'd love to.'

Pete seemed pleased, but his eyes stayed sad and he glanced down the slope towards the river. 'Poor old Esther,' he said softly. 'I wish she was here right now. You would have just made her day.'

8

Brenna, May 1898

Since my arrival at Brayer House three weeks earlier, I had seen Adele twice more escaping through the garden. And both times, Lucien had appeared on the path soon after and followed.

I did not know what to make of my new sister-in-law's nocturnal activities. In the short time we had spent together, we had become amiable companions. We occupied ourselves in the library, or studied fashion catalogues that Adele ordered from England, or wandered among the flowerbeds cutting daphne and hydrangeas and sprigs of abelia for the table. I was reluctant to suspect her of illicit meetings with her brother's manservant, but how else could I interpret what I'd seen?

I quickly settled into what was to become my routine as Carsten's wife. Each morning I rose early, bathed, and dressed in one of my plain shirtwaists and a wool skirt, and buttoned boots.

Adele liked to help me pin my hair, which soon became an excuse for us to engage in conversation – at first about general topics, such as the establishment of a municipal police force, or the proposed electric lighting in Hobart, or the ongoing debate about Federation. I soon noticed that Adele never spoke of the son Carsten hoped I would bear for him; nor did she ever ask how many children I wanted, or whether I was looking forward to the experience of motherhood. The topic of babies, I quickly understood, was taboo. And yet, her reserve was a relief to me; had she asked about my expectations regarding a child, I might not have known how to answer. Carsten rarely visited my room, and our intimate relations were still bafflingly non-existent.

An hour before breakfast, it became my habit to go downstairs to the kitchen and see if all was well with Quinn. The housekeeper routinely rose before dawn to bake the day's bread and prepare breakfast. The kitchen was always warm and full of delicious aromas. Some days I sat over the household account ledger, which was more a custom than a necessity, because Quinn kept it in perfect order.

Brayer House enjoyed every luxury: oriental carpets, and high walls hung with paintings in gilt frames, lacquered furniture, carved chairs and lounges upholstered with exotic silks. And yet, in a flash, I would have given it all away to be back at Lyrebird Hill; to be sitting at the scarred oak table with Fa Fa, or wading in the river with Owen, or sitting with Millie in her lean-to nibbling fruit cake; or running along the track to the encampment, catching sight of Jindera's smiling face, feeling the approval that radiated from her dark eyes, that were, with the benefit of hindsight, so similar to my own—

'Brenna?'

Adele was watching me across the breakfast table. Shadows circled her eyes, and she had barely touched her porridge. This morning we were eating alone, because Carsten had left the house early to ride into Wynyard on business.

'You're lost in your thoughts,' Adele chided. 'I do believe you're daydreaming about my brother.'

My cheeks burned. How could she know that my thoughts of Carsten were chaste, and that my daydreams more likely involved thoughts of her and Lucien, or my home at Lyrebird Hill? So I found myself spinning a tiny white lie.

'I was simply wondering what book I'll choose for us to read today.'

'Oh, Brenna, didn't I tell you?' Adele shoved away her plate. She drew a large handkerchief from her skirt pocket and coughed delicately into it. She dabbed it against her lips, and then said, 'I have an engagement in Launceston, I'm afraid I will be away for several days.'

My spirits deflated. Several days? I longed to ask why, but Adele was clearly reluctant to speak more of it. When she asked me to help her bathe and dress, I agreed with only half a heart. I sat on a wooden chair in the kitchen while Quinn drew a bath and helped Adele into it. Adele chatted almost nervously while Quinn sponged her arms, her back, her neck, and when she closed her eyes and let herself sink into the water, I found myself studying her. Without her fine clothes and jewelled necklets and elaborately pinned hair, she was even more beautiful. How lovely she must seem to a simple man like Lucien, as he follows her through the garden at midnight, perhaps to some secret trysting place.

Later, as the carriage rattled off down the driveway and through the gates onto the road, I told Quinn I was feeling poorly and stomped upstairs to my bed chamber. Seating myself at the window, I glared down into the garden. In daylight, it seemed empty. Without the darkness and shifting shadows, without the moonlight lacing the treetops with silver – without Adele – it was a dull and uninteresting place indeed.

Carsten spent little time at the house.

We had separate bedrooms, so my first glimpse of him every morning was at the breakfast table. At eight on the dot he would be there, Quinn fussing at his elbow, pouring the strong tea he loved, and filling his plate with bacon rashers and scrambled eggs and big chunks of toasted bread. After he had eaten, he would go down to the stables and check his horses. He was in the habit of riding out most days with Lucien.

Although he employed several stockmen, he liked to check the fences and feed troughs and any possible storm damage himself; farming was not his financial mainstay, but I came to see that he enjoyed being out in the fresh air, and there were many days when he and Lucien were gone until dusk. He always returned from these excursions sweaty and flushed in the face, and usually in a good mood.

After dinner, he retired to the library, where he pored over his account books, then smoked a pipe and drank sherry until midnight. Once the grandfather clock struck the hour of twelve, Carsten climbed the stairs to bed.

On those rare occasions he visited my room, we seemed to simply re-enact our first night together. He would instruct me to lift my nightgown, then half-heartedly roll on top of me. His efforts were always unsuccessful, so he would lie beside me in grim silence until the clock struck the half hour, then rise and dress himself, and go out.

Tonight, I had attempted to cheer the room with a vase of rosemary, which I had placed upon the little desk. Its sharp scent perfumed the air. I lay under the covers in my nightdress, listening for footsteps along the hall, wondering, as I did each evening, whether tonight I would finally know how it felt to be loved, and if perhaps that love might thaw my husband's frosty manner towards me.

There was a shuffle outside my door, then a quiet knock. Carsten entered the room. He checked his watch, as he habitually did, and placed it on the desk beside my jug of rosemary. He undressed and got into bed. For a long while he lay without moving. His body heat warmed me, and I began to doze.

'I'll be leaving for New South Wales in the morning,' he said. 'An offer has come for a farm of mine near Hillgrove, and I want to oversee the sale. I'll be away for three weeks.'

I rose on my elbows, my pulse taking flight. 'But Hillgrove is only a couple of hours from home.'

'If I see Michael, I'll give him your regards.'

I was trembling now; I could almost smell the wildflowers of home, and hear the soft sigh of the river. My longing gave me courage, and I dared to place my hand on my husband's chest. The muscles tightened at my touch and I withdrew.

'Carsten, please take me with you. I'd like to see my father.'

'It's business,' he said gruffly. 'You'd be in the way.'

'I could stay with Fa Fa, and then take the coach to Hillgrove once your sale has gone through. I wouldn't get in your way, you'd hardly know I was there.'

'Out of the question.'

The weight of disappointment settled over me, but my thoughts continued to race. My husband was a wealthy man, a man of influence. His business took him to many places, and saw him in the company of a range of people. Until now I had believed that seeking justice for the murder of my mother, Yungara, would be a pointless exercise; any evidence would be long gone. But if anyone had the means to locate and expose her killers, it was Carsten.

'Twenty years ago,' I began cautiously, 'there was a massacre at Lyrebird. An entire band of Aboriginal people were murdered.' I paused, noticing that Carsten lay very still. I took a breath and went on. 'Afterwards, my father was stricken down by grief, and I know the memory of it haunts him. It would bring him,' and *me*, I added privately, 'great relief to learn the identity of the men responsible. Carsten, you once promised to do all you could to make me happy.'

Carsten made a rough sound in his throat. 'What are you asking?'

'Someone must know who those men were. Perhaps you could broach the topic with your associates?'

He rolled away, punching flat his pillow. 'I'm a busy man, Brenna. I haven't time to chase your whims.'

I expected him to get out of bed and stalk from the room, but instead he settled beside me. Soon, his breathing slowed, became rhythmic. The clock downstairs struck the half-hour. I tried to sleep, but my eyes kept flying open, seeking Carsten's dark shape. He hadn't agreed to my request, yet nor had he outright refused. For the first time since I had learned about Yungara's fate, justice seemed more than a distant dream.

A while later, I needed to use the chamber pot. Lighting the lantern, I rolled quietly off the mattress and padded across the icy floorboards to the privacy screen. I was about to duck behind it when I caught sight of Carsten's fob watch sitting on the desk. It attracted my eye because of its odd shape. It was oval, and flatter than a watch ought to be. I went closer.

It was not a watch at all . . . but a lady's locket.

I glanced at the bed. Carsten hadn't moved.

As I crept closer to the writing desk, my pulse picked up. My breathing became shallow, and the rosemary that scented the air grew intensely sharp.

Bending closer to the object attached to Carsten's watch chain, I saw that it was indeed a large silver locket. On its face was the embossed design of a lyrebird's tail feathers. Perhaps Carsten had never registered the details of the design, for surely if he had, he'd have made a point of showing me.

Unless he had good reason not to?

In that instant I knew the locket must contain a portrait or curl of hair – why else would Carsten gaze at it with such fascination? Just before I reached for it, something made me look towards the bed.

Carsten stood naked beside it, watching me.

'What are you doing?' he said gruffly.

I tried to conceal my embarrassment at having been caught prying, and attempted a smile, gesturing behind me at the privacy screen. 'I had to use the commode.'

Carsten crossed the room. His gaze roamed over me, taking in the flimsy nightdress, my dishevelled curls, my bare throat.

His attention kept returning to my mouth, and I touched it absently, nervously. He moved nearer, and then in a quick, fluid motion he slipped his hand under my hair and gripped the back of my neck. I winced in pain and tried to pull away, but his fingers tightened.

'We have one rule in this house,' he told me quietly. 'What's yours is mine, and what's mine is my own.' Reaching past me, he collected the locket from the desktop and held it possessively in his palm, examining its ornate surface, as if fearing my scrutiny had done it harm. Then he tossed it onto the bed.

Turning back to me, his face softened.

'You are nothing like her,' he whispered, drawing his lips back from his teeth in a forced smile. 'And yet you have your own rough charm.'

Like who? I wanted to ask, but Carsten pulled me roughly against him, and kissed me with a violent ferocity, bruising my lips. His grip on my neck tightened, while his other hand slid down my back and took hold of my bottom, squeezing so hard the pain made me cry out.

'Carsten, you're hurting me.'

Grappling me around, he pushed me face down onto the desk. The jug of rosemary shattered on the floor, splashing water on my bare legs. He grabbed a handful of my hair, then wrenched up my nightgown. I tried to twist from his grasp, but his hold on me was too strong. Then, with a moan, he plunged himself into me.

A sob stuck in my throat. This was not how I envisaged our first time. Carsten was by nature a reserved man, and I had hoped for some gentleness, or at least some consideration for my inexperience.

Carsten began to move, crushing me beneath him as his thrusts grew more vigorous. The top of my head banged against the wall, my cheek rasped on the wooden desktop. I bit the side of my mouth and tasted blood.

Shadows swarmed. The smell of rosemary flooded my lungs, mingling with the sour odour of my husband's sweat. I felt drawn in twenty directions, quartered by force, a silent scream raking the back of my throat.

Was this what my aunt had tried to warn me about? Would this be my fate from now on? I tried to escape into memory, wanting only to find a place where I was safe from Carsten's assault. My mind flew to the steep granite hills of my home, down among the trees where the shadows swarmed between fallen logs and mossy outcrops. But even there, I found no sanctuary.

A pair of snakes, entwined together, their slender bodies writhing as though in ecstasy; then a rifle blast, and blood and deathly stillness—

Carsten moaned and fell against me, pinning me to the desk. He lay panting, the heat of his limbs burning my back, his sweat sticky on my skin.

Finally he released me.

I sank to the floor, dragging my nightgown over my nakedness. I watched him dress, watched him retrieve his locket from the tangle of bedcovers. He seemed to take an eternity to hook the watch chain to his waistcoat.

'I hate you,' I whispered hotly.

He crouched before me. I flinched as he reached out his hand, but he touched the side of my face lightly, almost tenderly, as he thumbed away my tears.

'That will change,' he said gently. 'You will come to enjoy our games.'

He leaned closer and kissed me – sweetly soft, the way I had once daydreamed a kiss should be. His mouth moved on mine with all the tenderness of a man in love, but when he pulled away, there was no cosy glow of satisfaction, no thrill of nearness – just the warm salty taste of my blood.

The following morning, I stood at the parlour window looking into the front garden. My eyes stung and my face felt bruised out of shape. I wore a high-necked black dress with mutton sleeves lengthy enough to hide the bruises on my wrists. I had only just emerged from my room; the clock struck the hour and I counted nine chimes. Breakfast had been and gone; with Adele away, there would have just been Carsten and me at the table. How could I face him after last night?

Outside, the carriage waited on the gravel drive. Lucien was securing my husband's leather portmanteau. I heard the front door open and slam shut, and Carsten's black-clad figure emerged from the house. He greeted Lucien with a slap on the back, then climbed into the carriage. Lucien sprang up to the driver's bench and snapped the reins. The horses lurched forward and the carriage jostled down the driveway, through the ornate gates and out onto the road.

At dawn, I had tried to pen a hasty note for my father, but my fingers had trembled so violently that the ink splashed from my pen and ruined the paper.

In the end, I had given up.

I stared along the driveway, down to the gate through which the carriage had disappeared. It was only March, but already some of the trees were beginning to turn. A confetti of yellow and crimson leaves swirled through the air. At the perimeter of the garden was a line of birches, and many of the branches were already bare; their naked limbs appeared vulnerable, like skeletal hands reaching into the cobalt dome of the sky.

After Carsten's departure, I spent the following two days in my room with the curtains drawn, feigning ill health. I sat on my bed, trailing my fingertips over my body, seeking my bruises, touching the sore spot on my lip where Carsten's rough kisses had torn the skin.

Jindera's warning echoed continually in my mind.

No cross water to other land, Bunna. Danger there. Bad spirits.

Closing my eyes, I imagined the valley at home, and followed the river northwest towards the encampment. Jindera and the other women would be rebuilding their fire, gathering their coolamons and dillybags and bark dishes in preparation for the morning's food gathering expedition.

At that moment, my heart was filled with such longing I thought it would burst.

Beyond the dark drapes that kept my room in twilight, the sun burned high in the sky. Birds whistled and warbled and chirped right outside my window, but their bright songs seemed a million miles away.

By the third day my spirit seemed restored, and I decided to fortify it further with an afternoon of sketching. In the kitchen, I solicited some bread and cheese and a wedge of fruitcake from Mrs Quinn, who wrapped it all in a cloth with a garnish of warning.

'You'll fade away to nothing, Mrs W. You're already a stick of a thing. Come the first winter wind, you'll be picked up like a scrap of chaff and blown out to sea.'

Despite my melancholy, her dramatic fancy made me smile. After reassuring her I would do no such thing, I returned to my room and collected my paint tin, my brushes, block of sketching paper, and a small wooden folding seat that I'd transported in my luggage from home. Hooking my dillybag across my shoulder and dragging on my sun hat, I hurried outside.

The day was warm, the sunshine intense.

I followed the path around the house, pausing when I came to a fork. Veering right, I walked for a while, and soon emerged on the other side of the garden. From there I meandered down the hill until I came to a gate. It was rusty and whined noisily as I pushed through. I skirted a low conifer hedge, and was surprised to find myself in a tiny graveyard.

There was only a handful of graves, each weatherworn granite headstone engraved simply with a name and a date. The newest addition was also the smallest, and its headstone bore a more elaborate inscription.

Thomas Whitby, 1889–1893
Mama's little angel, safe from harm,
Resting at peace in his father's arms.

A four-year-old boy, I marvelled, buried in this desolate spot. Thomas Whitby; I hadn't heard anyone mention his name. Kneeling by the grave, I tugged out the few scrawny weeds. There were white camellias in a vase, their petals starting to brown at the edges.

I recalled Adele's inclination to steer our conversations away from babies or children. I knew her fiancé had died, it seemed common knowledge; but no one had breathed a word about a child.

'Oh, Adele.'

I brushed away a few fallen camellia leaves, my heart aching for the sweet, compassionate woman who had become my friend. I sensed that the various mysteries that circulated about Adele – her days in Launceston, her midnight forays in the garden, and now the little boy buried in a secret graveyard – were somehow connected.

Retracing my steps to the garden, I bypassed the stables and slipped into the forest. The air was cool, smelling faintly of woodsmoke and pine sap. Tall hoop pines rubbed shoulders with trees that sprouted dense sprawling canopies. Green light speared through their branches, and soon I was in another world. The roar of the ocean grew dim, replaced by the chatter of birds and whirr of insect wings. I walked east, deeper into the forest until I came to a clearing.

At the base of a pine tree I found a clump of plants that at first I thought were delphiniums, but on closer inspection turned out to be a late-flowering aconitum, a herb sometimes known as wolfs-bane or monkshood. Each plant had a base of dark green leaves, from which grew a tall slender shoot topped by an array of hood-like blue flowers. The flowers hung delicately from their stems, and their deep indigo hue glowed softly in the pine trees' dank shade. It was a most attractive plant, but deadly. Even making skin contact with its leaves or flowers might make a person extremely ill; to imbibe any part of the plant could be fatal. Taking my sharpening knife from my bag, I cut half a dozen of the hooded purple flowers and folded them in my handkerchief; they would make a fine addition to my collection of pressed herbs.

Unfolding my wooden seat, I settled on it and took out my charcoal stick and sketching paper. The clearing was shel-tered from the sun, and the air was still and warm. Birdsong surrounded me, accompanied by the whisper of leaves in the canopy overhead.

Bowing over my paper, I quickly fell under the spell of my work, savouring the scratch of my charcoal, delighting in the patterns of light and dark as my wolfsbane began to emerge on the paper. I took out the vial of water and swirled my brush in a smear of umber, blocking in the shadows.

As the sun climbed higher, the air grew warm. While I worked, the odour of the glue with which I treated my paper to strengthen it lifted around me.

From somewhere behind me drifted a noise. I ignored it, too immersed in my work to give it much mind. Washing off the umber, I collected a tint of cerulean and soon leaves and a tall flower stalk emerged. As I rinsed my brush, I heard a low growl.

I froze, my brush midway to the water vial. Then a drawn-out howl broke the stillness.

I leaped to my feet, scattering paper and brushes and paints as I whirled around. On the opposite edge of the clearing stood a dog. His hide was white, speckled with brown and caramel markings, stretched tight over his bones; he had a black muzzle and large frightened chestnut-coloured eyes.

He howled again, a wretched haunting sound that teased up the hairs on the back of my neck. I had never heard my father's wolfhound howl that way, but I knew instantly what it meant.

From my dillybag I retrieved Mrs Quinn's bundle. Untying the cloth, I removed the lump of bread and tossed it to the dog. The animal whined and sniffed the morsel, then choked it down in an eye-blink. I threw the cheese, and then the cake, and both vanished as if by magic into the dog's gullet.

A wave of pity went through me. I wondered if the creature had ventured here from a neighbouring farm, but then decided that it must be a domestic dog gone feral. It was no dingo; the wiry native dogs ran wild across the mountainsides that flanked Lyrebird Hill, but none I'd seen had such a look of desolation.

'Poor old boy,' I said softly.

The dog pricked its ears at my voice. It watched me warily, almost expectantly, but made no move to come closer. I had no more food to offer, and was wondering how to tempt it back to the house, when a man's voice broke the stillness.

'Mrs Whitby?'

The dog cocked its head as the thud of footsteps approached. It whined, then about-faced and fled into the trees.

Lucien appeared at the edge of the glade. His gaze roamed the clearing, taking in my strewn papers and spilled box of paints and fallen drawing implements.

He looked at me. 'What happened?'

'Nothing.'

'Why are your things scattered about?'

'I got a fright, that's all. It was just a poor hungry dog, it must have been attracted by the smell of my paper.'

Lucien looked astonished. 'Why would a dog be attracted to paper?'

'It's prepared with rabbit-skin glue. When I apply my water-colours on it, the glue softens a bit. The sun's warmth lifts its scent.'

Lucien was staring at me, clearly baffled. He collected one of my fallen papers from the ground and brought it up to his nose, inhaling deeply.

'What did you say it was, rabbit skin?'

'Yes . . . well, no, not actual skin. It's a glue, made by boiling down a rabbit hide. I paint it onto my paper so the pigments stay true.'

Lucien's eyes grew wide. 'You're an artist?' he finally said.

'Yes.'

He collected a stick of charcoal from the ground and rolled it between his fingers. 'That's what you were doing just now, when you saw the dog?'

'I was drawing that wolfsbane over there.' I pointed to the plants, then went over and crouched beside them.

Lucien, kneeled beside me on the grass. 'That's no delphinium,' he observed.

'It's aconite, but often called wolfsbane because through history it was used to poison wolves. In the right quantities the toxins can take effect almost instantaneously. Be careful,' I said hastily as he reached out to touch one of the blue flowers. 'They are quite deadly, and you can absorb the poison through your skin—'

I stopped. Lucien seemed interested, but there was amusement in his eyes, too. He must have been having a private laugh to himself, thinking me peculiar for traipsing alone into the trees with my sketchpad, and then lecturing him about plants.

I got to my feet, my cheeks beginning to burn. 'I'm sure you're not here to discuss unusual flora. Has something happened back at the house?'

Lucien stood. 'Miss Adele is home. She's keen to see you.'

A rush of joy caught me alight. I began to retrieve my strewn brushes, while Lucien moved to collect the papers that lay scattered in the damp grass. Leaf by leaf, he stacked them into a pile. When they were gathered, he didn't return them to me immediately, but stood with his head bowed examining the top sheet.

I hurried over and took them from him. Retrieving my satchel from the ground, I crammed my papers inside. Then I picked up my pencils and sharpening knife and charcoal, and the wad of fresh bread dough that I used to lift mistakes from the page.

'You're very good,' Lucien said, and there was a tone of awe in his voice. 'At drawing, I mean. Your depictions are lifelike, yet poetic, too.'

I examined him, seeking evidence of mockery. He didn't shrink from my attention as he had done before, but stood tall in the dappled light, allowing me to fully observe his fine features and the scar that marred them. He had a regal nose, and a wide full mouth with a tiny splash of freckles along his top lip; more freckles clung to his cheeks and brow, but other-wise his skin was fair, considerably lighter than mine. I saw now that his eyes were not grey at all, but green, a clear strong green – more bright camellia leaf than greyish magnolia. When I looked into the depths I saw they held no sign of mockery; rather, I thought I perceived a sort of shy admiration.

He collected my folding seat, and flattened it and tucked it under his arm. We left the glade and walked back along the trail in the direction of the house.

'Will you finish your drawing later?' Lucien wanted to know.

'Perhaps.'

'I'd like to see it finished. That is, if you wouldn't mind.'

'I rarely show them to anyone.'

His eyes widened as if this revelation shocked him. 'But you have a marvellous talent. It's a waste to hide it away.'

I pretended not to hear, and picked up pace along the track towards the house, eager to see Adele. Lucien soon caught up with me, taking one stride for every two of mine, peering into my face with open curiosity.

'Do you ever draw animals?'

'I've drawn antechinus – the little marsupials everyone mistakes for rats – and a few possums. Insects, too. But botanical specimens are my specialty.'

'What about people?'

I shook my head. 'I like the honesty of plants. They are exactly what they appear to be – a clump of poa grass, or a delicate orchid, or a tangled sarsaparilla vine. Their beauty is uncomplicated. Nature has its own deceptions, but sometimes that is how it survives. Mankind, on the other hand—'

I stopped. My husband's face intruded into my mind's eye. As my tongue found the graze at the corner of my mouth, my thoughts turned bitter. 'Plants bear you no malice,' I said. 'Even deadly ones, like the wolfsbane I was drawing. Its compounds can be used to kill or to heal, but how you use them is of no consequence to the plant. It simply exists.'

Lucien smiled, his gaze full of green fire. The ugly whiplash scar on his face vanished into that smile, and I became aware only of the shining eyes that crinkled at the corners, the dimples bracketing his mouth, the fine cheekbones and brow framed by tendrils of bright red–gold hair.

'I believe the same is true of horses,' he said gently. 'They bear no one any ill will. I've spent a great deal of time observing them. If a horse is tricky, I can guarantee you there has been a cruel master in its history.'

I looked at Lucien from the corner of my eye, sensing that there was also a hidden meaning to his words, just as there had been to mine.

'If I was a great artist like you,' he went on, looking down at the grassy track we walked away, 'then I would want to uncover the secret nature of things.'

I gave him a sharp look. 'What do you mean, secret nature?'

A pink flush crept across his cheekbones. 'I suppose I mean the spirit in us. The good. The truth that lies beneath the false face we show to the world. We aren't like those orchids or vines you talked about. We are complicated. We are joy-seeking beings – and yet we bring harm to one another, lie and mistreat and prey on others' weaknesses for our own ends. But deception is its own reward. The only ones we truly hurt are ourselves. We get distracted by the mask, and forget that our true nature is love—'

These last sentences were spoken in a raspy whisper, but I clung to each word, enthralled by what he was saying. Once, Mee Mee had related a story about an old woman who killed and ate her son's young wife. The son was heartbroken because he believed his wife had deserted him, and his mother continued that deception. In the end, the son learned the truth, and banished his mother into the submerged root system of an ancient red gum.

Mee Mee's meaning had been clear, just as Lucien's meaning was now clear.

Deception is its own reward.

Lucien stopped walking and gave me a lopsided smile.

'Forgive me,' he said quietly. Splashes of colour danced on his cheekbones, glowing against his paleness and clashing with the copper tones of his hair. 'I've run off my mouth and made a fool of myself. Now you see why I keep my own company.'

I ventured a small smile. 'I enjoyed your train of thought. It's given me much to ponder.'

He dragged his fingers through his hair. 'You must think me a firebrand for ranting on that way.'

'Not at all.'

'Everyone else does.'

'I'm not everyone else.'

We stood regarding one another in the dappled sunlight. Adele was waiting at the house and I longed to see her; I knew I shouldn't dally here in the company of my husband's man-servant. But my head felt so suddenly light, I feared the slightest movement would send me drifting up into the clouds like a feathery wisp.

It wasn't Lucien's appearance that held me transfixed to the spot at that moment, but his words. Who was this wild boy who preferred the draughty stables to the warmth and comfort of a manor house? A boy who shrank from society, and yet spoke with such eloquent abandon of delving into the mysteries of human nature?

'I liked what you said,' I admitted. 'I can see sense in it.'

We walked on in silence. I was curious to hear more of his theorems, but already my mind was awhirl. I needed a quiet place to brew over what he'd said, absorb it. To absorb him.

He was no longer the humble stable-hand; he was a young man aglow with passion, his hair on fire, his dark eyes full of the ferocity of the sea. The sight of him, the idea of him, the very existence of him sent shivers across my skin. My spirit rose, soaring free on wings of possibility. For a moment I was as he said, a joy-seeking being in full flight . . .

But then my elation dimmed.

How must I appear to him? Next to Adele I was plain and drab, bookish and thin. I was the moon, while Adele was the brilliant, radiant sun. Anyway, why was I thinking these thoughts? I was a married woman now. For better or worse, I was bound by law to a man I was swiftly coming to despise.

We reached the perimeter of the garden. Shadows crawled among the birches. Through gaps in the tall straight trunks I could see the house, its stone walls glowing pale gold in the sunlight. And there on the eastern face was a tiny rectangular blot of darkness: my bedchamber window.

I said my farewells to Lucien, who set out along the path to the stables, while I hurried towards the house. In the short span of time it took me to reach the verandah, my mood had darkened. My meeting in the glade with Lucien glowed in my mind's eye like a bright gemstone, full of colour and light – contrasting all the more painfully with my memory of Carsten's rough treatment of me.

I paused in the shadows to glance back along the path. From this side of the house there was no view of the stable yard, just the copse of birches and the wilderness of garden beds between. Lucien was gone, but somehow he still lingered.

I was dimly aware that a change had occurred. My customary prudence and good sense had broken formation and flapped away like a flock of southbound geese. Outwardly I looked the same, but inside my secret nature stirred. The blood of my mother's people flowed through my veins; it was wild blood, blood that sang of open spaces and wide starry skies.

Hugging my elbows, I went into the house.

Carsten might take my body and do with it as he pleased, but he would never have my heart.

I found Adele sitting in a patch of sun on the jasmine bench. She was staring vacantly at a book that must have fallen from her lap onto the grass. Her eyes were shadowed by dark circles, and her lips bitten.

I rushed to her and kneeled at her feet. 'Adele, look at you. You're clearly unwell.'

She shook her head and went to speak, but instead began to cough. Drawing out a handkerchief, she covered her mouth until the fit subsided. Finally, she looked at me with glassy eyes.

'I'll be better tomorrow once I've rested. The journey back from Launceston always tires me. Will you sit with me awhile?'

It troubled me to see her ill, yet I sensed again that she did not wish to speak of what ailed her.

'I shall do better than that,' I told her, retrieving her fallen book.

It was an English translation of *Aucassin and Nicolette*, a charming French tale to which Adele had recently introduced me. The cover was printed in red and black on Japanese vellum, and the etched title page displayed a headpiece of sea creatures holding a tiny book between their entwined tails.

I opened to the page we had marked, and began to read.

Nicolette came to the postern gate, and unbarred it, and went out through the streets of Biaucaire, keeping always on the shadowy side, for the moon was shining right clear, and so wandered she till she came to the tower where her lover lay. The tower was flanked with buttresses, and she cowered under one of them, wrapped in her mantle. Then thrust she her head through a crevice of the tower that was old and worn, and so heard she Aucassin wailing within, and making dole and lament for the sweet lady he loved so well.

I stopped reading, overcome with emotion. Beside me, Adele had slipped into her own reverie, her eyes closed, her lips parted, her breath whispering in and out of her in soft sighs.

At the far edge of the garden, the sun sank towards the horizon. Shadows crept along the pathways, moving stealthily across the grass towards the jasmine bench where we sat. When the dark came down and I could no longer see the page, I closed the book and rested my head back on the vine-covered lattice. I recalled Lucien's words as we walked along the trail from the glade, and despite the beauty of what he'd said, a deep melancholy filled me.

Deception is its own reward.

In my heart, I felt the truth of his words; but it was a bitter truth, a truth that made me despair. I was riddled with deceptions. The lie behind which I hid my Aboriginal heritage; the false facade of my marriage. And now, most dangerously of all, my growing feelings for a man who could never be mine.

9

Happiness isn't an elusive grail to be pursued;
it's simply a choice you make.
– ROB THISTLETON, *EMOTIONAL RESCUE*

Ruby, May 2013

'How about that bath?' Pete settled back beside me on the verandah seat. 'I've just checked the water, and it's nice and hot.'

The brandy had taken the edge off my shock after hearing about Esther, and the tea had revived my spirits; even so, I felt weary and grubby from my night in the car and consequent trek through the mud.

'A bath would be perfect.'

I stood up, expecting to follow him along the verandah and back into the house, but instead he headed downhill across the garden. Mystified, I followed. When I'd lived here as a kid, Mum had boiled water on the gas cooker in the kitchen and bucketed it into an antique hip bath that had once belonged to Grampy James. I assumed that, after Esther moved in, she would have overseen the building of a new bathroom.

As it turned out, that was exactly what she'd done.

We walked down the hill a short way, then followed a narrow path into a grove of grevillea until we came to a small clearing. The clearing was surrounded on all sides by thick walls of bottle-brush, and cast into dappled shade by a lofty apple gum. In the centre was a huge claw-footed bathtub sitting on a base of granite pavers. Over the tub was a huge old shower rose, connected to a mad tangle of galvanised pipes and gate valves and pressure gauges. The pipes led uphill to a 44-gallon drum resting on a steel frame. Under the drum smouldered a wood fire, drifting smoke up into the clear sky. Further uphill was a rainwater tank, from which ran more pipes leading back downhill to the drum.

'Esther's donkey burner,' Pete explained, indicating the drum. 'A wood-fuelled hot-water system, courtesy of the river and a bit of ingenuity.' He went across to the tub and wrenched on a huge brass tap. Steaming water gushed out and the bath began to fill.

I gazed around in dismay. 'But it's outside.'

Pete grinned. 'There's no one around for miles. Even if there was, they'd never see anything through the bottlebrush.'

There's *you*, I wanted to say. And the bottlebrush trees were all very well, but they weren't *walls*. There was no door to lock. No roof. I looked up at the sky. What if a plane went overhead? And how was I supposed to undress in the open air, climb into a tub of steaming river water, and get even halfway clean while staying alert for prying eyes?

'There's a towel,' Pete said, dazzling me with a smile, 'and a fresh block of Esther's handmade soap. I'll leave you to it.'

I stared after him. Then I went over and looked into the tub. The water was greenish, and smelled faintly of pebbles. At least the white towel was soft and fluffy. I picked up the chunk of soap and sniffed it. Roses and lavender.

The bath was nearly full. Turning off the tap, I sat on the rim and slipped off my runners. Reluctant to muddy the fragrant water, I checked the gap in the hedge and then slid out of my filthy track pants. What the hell, I thought, and stripped down to bra and knickers. I dipped my toes in, then my feet. Hot, soothing water lapped my knees. I wet the soap and lathered it over my legs, and the heat of the water released the full heady perfume of roses.

I scanned the wall of bottlebrush, and realised that Pete had been right: even if someone was standing on the other side, they wouldn't have been able to see through the dense hedge of prickly foliage. I glanced at the break in the hedge, where Pete and I had entered the bathroom clearing. A dog sat there; I could just make out the reddy-brown haunches and white-tipped tail of the female, Bardo. Maybe it was the strangeness of bathing outdoors, or perhaps the weight of all I had on my mind – but her presence didn't seem to faze me.

Closing my eyes, I slid into the water and let myself drift.

Despite my best efforts to ignore it, the heaviness under my rib cage persisted. Partly, it owed to Rob's betrayal. My cheeks still flamed every time I thought about my discovery of the lipstick-smeared champagne glass in his bathroom. At the time, I'd been mute with shock – but my brain had since come alive with questions. Who was she? Where had they met, how long had Rob been seeing her? Did he love her, and if so why – *why* – had he kept insisting he loved me?

Sighing out the tension, I sank deeper into the water.

The ache in my chest was also for Esther.

It pained me that she was gone; pained me that she had lain out in the storm, injured and cold and alone. I bitterly regretted that we'd never had the chance to catch up and continue our conversation, as we'd planned. My memories of Granny H were still vague for the most part, but they were slowly trickling back.

Unlike my memories – or rather, non-memories – of Pete.

We were at school together, he'd said. And he *had* seemed hazily familiar; but I must have known him the year Jamie died, because any real recall of him eluded me. Although, as I inhaled the fragrant steam, there was a stirring in the back of my mind, a shadow; a glimpse of darkness and trees and silhouettes moving stealthily through the night—

I shut my eyes.

And then, taking a breath, I let myself slide under the water.

An hour later, I was sitting on the verandah blissing out. It felt good to be mud-free, wearing clean dry jeans and T-shirt, dozing in the sun, listening to the happy chatter of birds.

I had almost drifted off when I became aware of a faint crunching noise. It sounded like gnawing.

I looked across the grassy slope to where Pete was stoking the barbecue, feeding the glowing embers with twigs and leaves, sending great puffs of smoke billowing overhead. The kelpies – until now, ever-present in the vicinity – were absent. An uneasy prickling in my scalp told me they were nearby, but my careful scrutiny of the garden failed to detect them.

Suddenly I needed to identify the sound, pigeonhole it, place it in the box marked 'no threat'. Getting to my feet, I went down the verandah steps and around the side of the house. A bank of grevillea screened the house from the old stables, and the noise seemed to be coming from behind it.

As I crept past the trees, I saw them.

A pair of dogs with pelts that gleamed like dark honey, their legs and muzzles dipped in gold. The crunching sound was coming from them; each had a small carcass in its jaws, devouring it with evident relish.

I rubbed my shoulder. Why was I even standing here? Why wasn't I running helter-skelter back to the house, diving into bed and pulling the covers over my head?

In the back of my mind, I heard Rob's voice: *This is just one of those curve balls life throws you once in a while. You've got to learn to deal with it.*

I stared hard at the dogs, forcing myself to watch. Suddenly, it was Rob they were feasting on. Rob dismembered, his magnificent gym-toned body torn asunder, his flesh ravenously devoured; Rob's skeleton cracked apart and its marrow licked out by a pair of hungry dogs.

'So well deserved,' I muttered darkly, and in a murky, vengeful corner of my mind, I imagined I could hear the echo of his screams—

'There you are.'

I jerked around, my heart bounding.

'Rabbits,' Pete said, indicating the dogs with a tilt of his head. 'That's what they're eating. I caught a couple this morning. You're not squeamish, are you?'

'Of course not.'

Pete's eyes narrowed. 'It's not cruel, if that's what you're thinking. The rabbits don't suffer. I use box traps, and wring their necks in a flash. It's all very humane.'

'Right.'

'Come on,' he said, and touched my arm softly, briefly. His hair and beard glistened with droplets of water from his swim. 'There's bacon and eggs on the menu. Hope you're hungry.'

'Starving,' I muttered.

Leaving the dogs to their gruesome breakfast, I followed Pete back down the slope towards the house. On the way, we passed the chopping block where presumably Pete had butchered his catch: a length of tree stump, its top end scarred and stained with blood smears. Propped beside it was a small sharp-looking hatchet. Pete kept walking and vanished ahead of me around the grevilleas, but I lingered. The scarred old block made me pause, its pitted surface holding me transfixed.

'Ruby?'

My mother's voice drifted out of the past. Time seemed to slow, then teeter for a moment before looping back on itself, rewinding. The chopping block and hatchet hazed out, and I heard my mother calling, as if from far away.

‘Ruby?’

I shrank lower, trying to be invisible. I was sitting on a flat boulder near the clothesline, out of view of the house. I'd spent the morning scrubbing grass stains out of my nighty and it was taking forever to dry. Which was okay by me; the worst time of the day was approaching, and all I wanted was to stay out of Mum's way.

‘Ruby!’

The kids at school thought Mum was weird. Most of their parents were farmers – sheep for wool, or beef cattle. They all thought Mum was crazy for owning three thousand acres without even attempting to make money off it.

Which wasn't true, because all our money came from the orchard or the vegetable garden. Every Saturday Mum collected a big box of vegies and another two boxes of Fowlers jars crammed with preserves – apricots in honey, halved peaches, last year's apples cut into chunks and studded with cloves. It was my job to help Mum pack the boxes into her car early in the morning so she could take them to the growers' market in Armidale. Armidale was a couple of hours' drive from Lyrebird Hill, which meant that Mum wouldn't be home until mid-afternoon. That was the good thing about Saturdays – I got to spend most of the day doing as I pleased. The bad thing was dreading what we invariably had for dinner: roast chicken.

‘Ruby, I know you can hear me!’

To be honest, Mum *was* pretty weird. For one thing, she hated the modern world. She hated pollution and loud noise and garbage trucks and power lines. She even hated men – which always puzzled me because plenty of women contributed to the ecological disaster as well. Of course, Mum wasn't all doom and gloom. There were tons of things she was mad about – batik dresses and incense and Joan Baez and steamed vegies – but there were days when her list of dislikes seemed to eclipse everything else.

I shifted on my rock, picking my scabby knee. Mum thought she knew everything, but how could she? Life looked wonky through the bottom of a wine bottle. I knew because I'd checked. One day I'd held up one of Mum's empties and looked through it like a telescope. I'd seen a wibbly-wobbly world where objects sprang about. Near, then far . . . then near again. Interesting for a while, but then I'd gone a bit giddy and some wine had dribbled into my eye and made it sting.

I glanced at the clothesline, at the nighty flapping gently in the breeze. When I was with the Wolf, the world didn't spring about and make me giddy. It seemed bright and stable, a happy place. I never stuttered or mumbled or did stupid things when I was with the Wolf. I stood taller, felt somehow prettier, smarter. Able to do things I usually fumbled.

'Ruby, I need you here. Now!'

I stood up, brushing leaves off my jeans. Going around the bottlebrush hedge, I dragged my feet back to the house.

Mum was standing near the chook shed. My heart dropped. She was holding one of our hens upside down by the legs. Its body was as limp as a rag, brown feathers littering the ground. It was only when I got nearer that I saw the snowy tuft of tail feathers.

'Esmeralda!' I cried, running towards my mother, but I was too late. Mum was already positioning the little body across the chopping stump. She looked up and saw me.

'Get me the wood-handled cleaver, will you, Ruby? This one's blunt.'

I couldn't move. My arms went limp.

Mum looked at me and heaved out a sigh. 'Oh, Ruby, how many times have I warned you about getting attached to the chooks? Silly girl, you shouldn't have named them all. They're not pets, they're here to provide eggs and meat. And this one's stopped laying. Now fetch the cleaver before she goes cold.'

My eyes began to sting. Esmeralda hadn't been a pet . . . she'd been my friend. She'd followed me around the yard, pecking after my feet or letting me pick her up and cuddle her, all the while chattering in her special soft language.

'Don't just stand there gaping. Get the cleaver and stop this rot.'

I gulped back tears. What would the Wolf do? Certainly not break down and blubber like a baby. He'd let out a bloodcurdling growl and spring at my mother, ripping her body in half like a ragdoll and spilling her guts all over the place, maybe even chop off her head and legs with the cleaver, then hang her up on the fence to bleed – just as she was planning to do with Esmeralda.

'Bitch,' I muttered.

Mum flinched. 'What did you call me?'

'Bitch,' I said again. I thought of the Wolf and yelled, 'A horrible old bitch!' Then, before Mum had a chance to react, I turned and ran.

It took me twenty minutes to reach the old shearing sheds. They'd been abandoned nearly a hundred years ago, and had been overrun with tea-tree and cassinia, and tall silvery grasses that pushed through the derelict sheep ramps. Their iron sidings were buckled and eaten by rust, the paddocks surrounding them shaded with black-trunked ironbarks and red gums.

The Wolf was waiting by the shed.

'You're early, Roo . . . Hey, what's up?'

Normally I'd have felt a twinge of disappointment to find a boy where there should have been a dangerous beast – but today I was glad.

The Wolf took my hand and dragged me into the shade, his gaze serious, his eyes full of questions as he searched my face. I couldn't speak at first, due to the lump in my throat. As we leaned against the shed's corrugated siding, I bit my lips and tried not to cry.

'Mum killed Esmeralda.'

'Oh, Roo.'

I slid down shed wall and sat on the ground. The Wolf flopped beside me. 'What a blow,' he said softly.

'I hate her.'

The Wolf's face was pale beneath its splash of freckles. His dark hair stood on end. He looked fierce, much fiercer than a boy of twelve had any right to look.

'Poor old Kangaroo,' he said in a half-whisper, taking my hand. His fingers were calloused, warm. The way they curled carefully around mine made me feel a microscopic bit better.

I leaned against him.

We'd only known each other for a while, six months at the most. The Wolf had lived in Newcastle before coming to Clearwater, and was being fostered at Mrs Drake's house, but I felt as if I'd known him forever.

I shut my eyes.

Dear Esmeralda with her quick black eyes and excited chatter. From the time she'd been a tiny fluffy chick, I'd tickled her and talked to her and saved her the best scraps from the kitchen. In return, she'd laid a perfect brown egg most mornings for my breakfast. Only lately she hadn't laid many, which was why Mum had given her the chop.

'I'll ask Mrs Drake if you can have dinner with us tonight,' the Wolf said.

I blinked away my tears and looked at him. He was oddly formal sometimes, the way he called his foster mother 'Mrs Drake'. Doreen Drake was another casualty of my mother's dislike list, which was probably what made me decide to accept the Wolf's invitation. That, and the horror of what was being served at my own dinner table that night.

'Will she mind?'

The Wolf shrugged. 'Nah. She's glad of the company now that Bobby's at uni. Come on, Roo. It'll be fun.'

'Well . . . okay.' Then an idea came to me, and it made me feel another microscopic bit better. 'Do you think it's too late to visit Granny H?'

The Wolf narrowed his eyes. 'We were only there yesterday.'

'She said her door's always open.'

The Wolf let out a growl of pleasure and sprang to his feet, flashing a toothy smile. He pulled me to my feet, and suddenly I was smiling, too.

Running towards the trees, we took the uphill trail. Ten minutes later Granny H's cottage came into view. Wild jasmine spilled along the verandah, and her door gaped wide. The smell of freshly baked scones sweetened the air. And there was Granny H, her silhouette shifting in the doorway, as if she'd been expecting us. Dusting her hands on her apron, she lifted her arm to beckon us in.

'Hey, Ruby.'

Pete's voice snapped me back to the present. My eyes re-focused. I blinked at the chopping block with its scarred surface and smudges of blood.

The Wolf, I marvelled.

Remembering him was dreamlike, as if he were nothing more substantial than one of the imaginary friends who had germinated out of my childhood loneliness. As a kid, I'd clutched at anything to fill the void left by my father's death, and by my mother's withdrawal into grief. Jamie got caught up with her friends at school, but I wasn't outgoing like she was. Hence my inclination to invent friends of my own.

But the Wolf was no invention.

Shutting my eyes, I tried to summon him. He'd been my height, a wiry boy with a starved look about him. Freckles,

pale city skin, dark hair . . . and something else. Vague images
gathered like wisps of cloud, then broke apart. Tall trees silvered
by moonlight, and a ridge of boulders crowded at the base by
shadows . . . and deep in the darkness, a creature lurked, stealthy
and unseen as it prepared to pounce—

'Ruby, I don't suppose you're hungry?'

Following the aroma of frying bacon, I found Pete in a small
cleared area surrounded by a grove of photinia shrubs. These
red-tipped trees were not native to Australia, but I recalled they
had fire-retardant qualities. Appropriate, because at the centre
of the grove was a wild-looking barbecue constructed from a
44-gallon drum. The drum must have been filled with earth
or rocks because the fire burned just below its upper rim. Pete
had positioned a blackened grate over the fire, on which sat
an enormous cast-iron frypan. I glimpsed a scrummy-looking
fry-up: crispy bacon rashers, scrambled eggs, tomatoes, mushrooms and wedges of sizzling potato.

Settling onto a log seat near the fire, I accepted the tea Pete
handed me. He had ducked back to his cottage while I was in
the bath, and now wore a snug-fitting T-shirt that revealed a
strong-looking chest and muscular arms. Taking the bench
opposite, he sipped his tea, regarding me over the rim of his cup.

After a while, he said, 'Can I ask you something about your
amnesia?'

I shifted awkwardly on the bench. 'Sure.'

'How much time did you lose?'

'About a year.'

Scratching his beard, he fixed me with his blue gaze. 'I guess
that makes sense. I was only here for six months or so.'

He'd obviously been mulling over why I didn't remember
him, which struck me as odd; even without the amnesia compo-
nent, recalling every classmate from eighteen years ago might
prove a stretch for most people. Which made me wonder if there
was more to our story.

'Were we friends?' I asked.

He looked at his hands, and when he lifted his eyes again, they had turned dark. He nodded, and said huskily, 'Yeah. We were.'

Standing abruptly, he went over to the barbecue and served up. As he passed me a plate of bacon, tomatoes, fried potato and fluffy scrambled eggs, he seemed thoughtful.

'You said Esther was going to help you remember?' he said, resuming his seat opposite.

I slumped a moment, regretting those weeks I'd wasted after Mum's opening. If I had visited Esther sooner, instead of running scared, I might have learned something. About Jamie. About the day she died. And possibly even something about myself.

I tried to smile. 'Esther told me she had fond memories of my sister and me as kids. She thought her reminiscences might help jog the bits I'd forgotten. Of course, I put off coming to see her, and now it's too late . . . I guess I was scared.'

I glanced at Pete through my lashes, expecting him to question this, but he only nodded, his gaze intent on my face.

'Your sister's death must have been really traumatic for you,' he gently observed. 'Anyone would be scared of facing that. You don't want to remember everything in a rush, it would probably do your head in. Best to let the memories come naturally, not force them. Maybe being here will help,' he added, almost to himself.

Picking up my fork, I dug into the eggs, feeling better because of what he'd just said. His comment about not forcing my memories resonated with me; it made me relax a little, and recognise that my trip here hadn't been too far off the mark, after all. I found myself sneaking another look at him from behind the curtain of my hair.

The image of a boy with a square freckled face and ragged black hair and blue eyes nudged ever so gently against my awareness.

Once, as kids, we'd been friends.

All of a sudden, I understood why.

That night I stood in the darkness of the house, letting the silence wash around me. Shadows seemed to draw apart to make way for me, the floor and walls and ceiling shifting and opening as if in welcome. The onslaught of sensations I had experienced earlier in the day was gentler now. The echoing voices dimmed, the dusty aromas were barely there – Mum's grass-flavoured tea, her black-berry muffins and sour cream, and underneath it all, as if seeping from the rafters and walls, was the faint, haunting tang of apples.

I switched on the lights and walked through the house, admiring Esther's stylish touch. Leather lounge chairs were softened with crocheted cushions and throw rugs; colourful paintings decorated the walls and vibrant Turkish rugs warmed the floors.

And books.

Everywhere were bookshelves, crammed with row after row of wonderful old books.

Running my finger along the spines, I hoped to see a title that I recognised as once belonging to me, but none rang any bells. Again I wondered if the book Esther had mentioned was Jamie's diary; my sister had kept a diary for years, full of notes about what flowers appeared in spring, when we had rain, and little stories about the birds and lizards in the garden. As she got older, she had hidden her diaries away. Perhaps Esther had discovered one of these later journals secreted in the back of an old wardrobe?

I searched for a while, but there was no sign of any diary, so I collected my overnight bag from the hall and went along to my old room.

Esther's flair for decor was evident here, too. A narrow bed sat near the window, over which was spread a colourful patch-work quilt. There was an art deco wardrobe and a wooden chair serving as a bedside, and a bright rug on the floor; it was a cheery room, and I felt instantly at home.

I found fresh sheets in the linen cupboard in the hallway, and made up my bed. Stripping down to my underwear, I climbed in.

Sleep didn't come straight away.

My brain was in overdrive. Every time I shut my eyes, a different image would accost me. One of Mum's paintings. Or a dog-eared report of the investigation into Jamie's death. Or the memory of my mum with the scissors in the kitchen that wintry day. Then Rob would somehow appear, his handsome face flushed pink from the exertion of his betrayal; Rob, the one person who had kept me anchored, had now cast me adrift on a sea of lies.

I punched my pillow, then lay back. I felt off kilter, as if the protective armour I'd built around myself had broken open, leaving me exposed. I no longer recognised myself, and I sensed that the only way to be whole again was to find my way back to the truth.

In the dark I unzipped my overnight bag and took out the Polaroid of Jamie. Propping it on the bedside, I studied it in the moonlight. She seemed sad.

'What happened that day?' I asked quietly. 'Did we argue, did I push you against the rocks and hurt you?'

No answer came back, of course. No voice from within, no glimmer of memory. Slumping back onto the bed, I gazed through the window into the garden beyond.

Silver moonlight drenched the hillside. The old walnut tree was still and shadowlike. Its trunk glowed ivory, its leaves hung motionless; it might have been a dark version of Mum's painting.

Just before I drifted off, I wondered if Mum's tin was still buried beneath it.

The following morning I had a brisk wash in the outdoor bath-room, and pulled on soft jeans and a cardigan over my singlet top.

Taking a pot of tea to the verandah, I sat in a patch of dappled sunlight and listened to Pete clatter about as he attended to his ute's broken wishbone. The weathered decking felt smooth and cool beneath my bare feet, and my tea was hot and strong. The morning had all the ingredients of a total bliss-out – except for the bruised feeling around my heart that, despite my resolve not to think about Rob, still persisted. I realised I was beginning to dread my return to civilisation; the possibility of running into him gave me butterflies.

Pete was hoping to have the ute working the next day; he had some seedling deliveries to make to a nursery in Armidale and had offered to help me organise a tow truck for my car. It was also a good opportunity to visit Mum.

Whatever you do, I cautioned myself, *don't mention Jamie*.

I stared down the slope, feeling suddenly grim; if not Jamie, then what else did Mum and I have to talk about?

My gaze lingered on the walnut tree. The sun had risen over the hill, stitching a lacework of gold on the grassy slope beneath. Again, I thought of Mum digging under the winter-bare tree, her face wet with tears. Why would she bury an old tin? I'd gone in search of a spade the day before to see if it was still there, but Pete's arrival had side-tracked me. Now seemed the perfect time to get back to it.

I got up and skirted the house, making my way around to the barn. Pete's battered ute sat in front of the open doorway, speckled with shade. A pair of jeans-clad legs poked out from underneath it, and Old Boy sat nearby, chewing fleas out of his tail. Bardo had flopped in the doorway, and as I hurried past, her tail lifted and thumped the ground, as if in greeting.

At the back of the barn among Esther's tools, I found a spade. Carrying it back down the hill to the walnut tree, I began to dig. The soil was ropy with roots, a nightmare to excavate.

Sweat soon prickled my ribcage, and I had almost convinced my myself I was chasing a wild goose – when the spade struck something oddly yielding.

Clearing the loose earth, I crouched to examine what I'd found. A mouldy tarpaulin. My hopes deflated, and I almost filled the hole back in. Only the memory of my mother's tears made me reach down and lift a half-rotten corner. The inner layers of burlap were black with mould, riddled with cockroaches and worms. When the sunlight hit them, they detonated in all directions, black fragments of insect-shrapnel dissolving back into the earth.

Inside the rotted material was a large rectangular tin.

It was an old Arnott's biscuit tin, with a rosella on the lid. When I shook it, something slithered inside. Re-burying the tarpaulin, I filled the hole and carried the tin back to my spot on the verandah, bursting to know what it contained.

A bundle of letters, tied with black ribbon.

They were only slightly damaged by damp; the envelopes rippled where moisture had infiltrated the tin and absorbed into the thick paper, but they had somehow escaped the ravages of mould and were, for the most part, in good condition. Something of a miracle, considering they were dated between 1898 and 1899.

There were about thirty envelopes. One stood out from the others, so I started with that. It was addressed to Master James Whitby, at Brayer House, via Wynyard, Tasmania. It caught my eye because James Whitby had been my grandfather. He died when I was six, the same year I lost my father. My memories of Grampy James were fleeting: he'd been confined to bed when I'd known him, a thin man with a sallow face and a soft, almost whispery voice.

I took out four pages. Each page was decorated with wide margins of exquisite watercolour drawings – gum nuts and seedpods, blue daisies and bright crimson-capped mushrooms, birds and spiders and butterflies. In among the botanical studies danced tiny figures with wings: imps and fairies, a lizard in a bowler hat, and a beautiful lyrebird inside a cage, its long tail feathers sweeping through the bars. As I shuffled through the pages, the luminous images came alive in the sunlight.

Going back to the first page, I scanned the beautiful copper-plate handwriting, an artwork in itself, its swirling script tugging my eye across the page. But as I began to read, my pleasure turned to puzzlement.

18 June 1899

My darling little James,

By the time you are old enough to read this, you will have forgotten our few precious days together. You were such a tiny thing when we parted, your eyes unfocused, your little hands like starfish, your hair a dark fuzz on your head.

I want you to know that you once had a mother who loved you with all her heart, and that if fate had been kinder, she would never, ever have let you go. Sadly, I did let you go, but not by choice. I hope that one day, with your aunt's help, you will understand and forgive the events that caused our separation.

Your Aunty Adele is my dearest friend. Be good for her, and listen hard. I know she loves you as much as I do, because she has promised to look after you and raise you as her own. One day, she will tell you my story, and the story of your father – and how proud he would have been of his little man, had he lived to know you.

My dearest boy, you will always be in my heart. Never be afraid, my darling, for I shall watch over you from heaven, and my love will keep you safe always and forever.

Your loving Mama

I sat back heavily. *Aunty* Adele? My grandfather's mother had been Adele Whitby – but if she wasn't truly my great-grandmother, then why hadn't Mum ever told me?

I shuffled through the other envelopes. About half were addressed to Miss A. Whitby at Brayer House, while the others simply bore the name B. Whitby, and a number, care of Launceston Gaol. I opened one of the numbered envelopes, and scanned the rumpled page within.

9 July 1899

My dearest Brenna,

You will be comforted to know I have arranged to visit you in the next several days. My only regret with this arrangement is that I cannot bring James with me. He grows sweeter every day, a picture of his beautiful mama in miniature. However, I have resolved to bring an item of his clothing for you to cherish in your lonely days.

Brenna, my heart goes out to you, but it also sings that we were blessed by friendship. My life would have been grim indeed had I not known you. I can only pray that I have in some small way enriched yours, too.

All our love is with you now, mine and your son's.

Do not give up hope. There will be no void for you, my Brenna – only everlasting peace.

Always yours, Adele

For a long time I sat staring across the verandah, letting the tangled knot of my thoughts unravel. Brenna Whitby – and not Adele – had been my great-grandmother. A stranger, a woman whose name I had never heard before. Meanwhile the kindly woman my mother had called Nanna Adele was merely a great aunt, and possibly only related by marriage.

A strange hollowness settled over me. Mum had once shown me a photograph of Nanna Adele. She had dark eyes and pure white hair, and her weather-beaten face was a maze of wrinkles. Most striking of all was the sense of deep sadness that radiated from her. I couldn't help wondering if her sorrow had stemmed from the loss of her friend, Brenna . . . or perhaps from the scar left on her conscience by Brenna's crimes.

Adele's other letters were all in a similar vein: gentle, and full of reassurance for her friend. I sorted through the other letters, determined to find out more about Brenna and why she was in prison.

Her tone was dark and full of despair, and as I read my way through her correspondence, I grew increasingly chilled.

18 November 1898

Every night I wake in a cold sweat, crying out. This cell is like a tomb, the stone walls are dank, wintry to the touch. I have learned that a child grows in me. Once it is born, they will take it away – that is, the chaplain assures me, the only Christian thing to do. I feel nothing for this new life, how can I? For a creature born in the shadow of a murderer, I have nothing but pity.

10 February 1899

It is summertime, yet the walls of my cell are like ice. There is no window. Sometimes I hold my hand an inch from my face and stare at it, but I may as well be blind. I am an eyeless creature underground, no different to the little one growing inside me. What will become of my baby, Adele? I know you have promised to step into my shoes as mother, but I fear that my child's soul will now be tainted by the same darkness that taints my own.

3 May 1899

Oh Adele, my baby is a healthy boy. I have named him James, which was my father's middle name. The labour was twenty hours, and mercifully a woman came from the town to oversee it. I had been dreading the arrival of a child into such a dreary, forsaken place . . . but now that he is in my arms, he has brought the light back into my heart. I long for you to meet him, Adele. How soon can you visit?

21 June 1899

I am not sorry for what I have done, Adele. If given the choice, I would pull that trigger again, a thousand times, if I had to. I worry only that my crime will ripple outwards to engulf you and baby James. He is so precious, my friend, such a brave little soul, deserving of a good life. Which is why you must take him far away, go to Lyrebird Hill, start afresh. The air there is clear and dry, and you will both benefit. It is a good place, a healing place. I beg you, find a measure of happiness, and do your best to forget me.

6 July 1899

Shadows are crawling across the cell walls as I write. They have moved me to a new cell; this one has a window with a view down into the courtyard. I don't dare look. They have begun to build something, and although I know it cannot be a scaffold, my imagination seems untenable. The clang of hammers sends tremors through my heart. My mind is full of death. The wardens shuffle along the corridors, and I constantly fear they are coming to drag me to the gallows. If that time ever came, I would pray for the courage to step across the threshold of this life and into the next, but how could I ever say goodbye with a brave heart, knowing I will plunge into a cold void for my sins and be lost?

Goodbye, sweet Adele. Pray for me once in a while, and remember me to James with love.

Folding the letters carefully, I placed them back in their envelopes. Then I looked down the hill at the walnut tree, taking one deep breath after another until finally my trembling ceased.

My great-grandmother Brenna Whitby had committed murder, and been imprisoned for her crime. In light of that, Mum's long-ago interrogation of me in the kitchen that day seemed full of foreboding. I had always sensed that she held me responsible for my sister's death; after all, I'd been with Jamie that day, and apparently witnessed her accident – no one could blame my mother for wondering why I hadn't raised the alarm sooner.

Only, it hadn't been an accident, and Mum had known this all along. Someone had killed my sister, and according to the forensic report, I had been the only other person present. It seemed crazy to entertain the idea that I might have inherited some kind of violent tendency from my great-grandmother – but that was clearly the connection Mum had made.

My child's soul will now be tainted by the same darkness that taints my own . . .

I looked down at the river, letting my gaze travel westward. The outcrop of rocks where my sister died was not visible from here, but I could see it clearly in my mind's eye: an outcrop of boulders jutting over the water, shadowed between by deep crevices, dotted with lichens that grew slippery in the wet. A dangerous place, my mother had always warned; yet it had been our secret place, a place filled with fascination and excitement for a pair of adventurous sisters.

Hugging my knees to my chest, I shut my eyes. Until now, my fear of what I might have done that day had been nebulous, a shadowy thing that lurked ghostlike in the furthest reaches of my mind.

All of a sudden, it was very, very real.

10

Brenna, May 1898

The cold woke me. The wind that blew from the strait seemed to find its way into my bedroom through gaps in the window frames and walls. I felt it first on my face, then its icy tentacles infiltrated my bed covers, creeping the length of me and drawing goosebumps from my sleep-warmed skin.

I reached for my shawl and dragged it around my shoulders. Sliding from the bed, cramming my feet into my felt slippers, I dashed to the window. The outside world was grey, the sun not yet up. In the garden below my window, wet footprints cut along the brick pathway. I studied the tracks, trying to distinguish if one set might belong to Adele's slippered feet, and the other to Lucien's rough work boots.

Ever since my meeting with Lucien in the glade the week before, a feeling of urgency had possessed me. Each morning I rose early and plunged into my work. The wolfsbane study he had so admired was complete, but immediately I had deemed it imperfect and begun again, this time from memory. I was not used to working from memory, and my first attempts were awkward and stiff. Then, just yesterday, I had managed to capture the nodding blue flower heads to my satisfaction . . . and, I secretly hoped, to Lucien's, too.

Hauling my trunk from under the bed, I took out my paintbox and brushes and few remaining leaves of paper. The touch of my painting tools thrilled me. I breathed them in – the familiar odours of bitter pigment and oily guar gum and rabbit-skin glue were delicious to me. First I arranged the tiny blocks of paint on their ceramic tray, then unwrapped my brushes from their cotton cloth and laid them in a row. Tucking my favourite drafting sable behind my ear, I uncorked the water jar and got up to fetch the ewer, only to find it empty.

I glanced at the door; Quinn would be pounding out her bread dough, stoking the oven and dusting her trays, probably eager for a nice long chat. But if I bypassed the kitchen, I could slip along the hall and through the double doors into the garden, fill my jar at the pump, then be back in my room without anyone being the wiser.

Dressing hurriedly, I crept silently along the hall and down the stairs, but when I got to the landing I paused to look through the window. From here I had an unhindered view of the distant hills that jutted along the horizon like purple elbows, tinged with an aura of gold from the rising sun.

The sight reminded me of my home. I wondered if Carsten had seen my father yet, and perhaps pocketed a note for me.

I longed to see Fa Fa, to know how he was faring after losing, in quick succession, first, his dear sister Ida, and then me. I hadn't realised, until my talk with him in his study that night, how deeply and desperately he struggled with his private sorrows. What must it have been like for him to love my mother Yungara with such great passion, only to lose her so tragically? Exposure of her killers might bring my father little comfort after two decades – but it would ease the pain in my own heart, and I prayed that Carsten had taken it upon himself to enquire.

So lost was I in my thoughts that I did not hear the man bounding up the stairs towards me. In the dawn glow of the enclosed stairwell, Lucien loomed taller than he had in the open spaces of the glade. Though he stood on the step beneath me, which brought our faces eye-to-eye, he seemed expansive, as if the stuffy indoors were inadequate to contain him.

'You're about early, Mrs Whitby.'

I was so astonished to see him in the house, I did not reply.

'It's a fine cold day outside,' he went on, apparently unbothered by my silence. 'Will you be going out sketching?'

I collected my voice. 'Perhaps.'

'I have something for you, Mrs Whitby. A small gift. It's nothing much,' he added quickly, seeing my frown, 'just a token.' Drawing a flat parcel from his coat pocket, he held it out to me. 'I was going to leave it by your door this morning, but I must say I'm glad we met in person.'

I hesitated. Exchanging banter in the glade was one thing, but accepting a gift? It seemed too intimate, too personal, and I had to glance away.

Beyond the window, the sun had capped the hills. The stockmen were emerging from their quarters, walking trails through the wet grass, their voices ringing sharply in the air.

I looked back to find Lucien watching me. I lifted my hand, intending to smooth my unbrushed hair, but instead dislodged the paintbrush tucked behind my ear.

It clattered onto the step at Lucien's feet.

He swooped to retrieve it, and as he passed it back he slid his parcel into my hands at the same time.

'Please take it,' he said quietly. 'It's such a small thing. I thought you might be glad of it.'

As I accepted the package, his rough fingers grazed mine. I was surprised at the warmth of his skin despite the cold and the early hour of the day. Surprised too, by the thrill of nerves that shot through me at his touch.

I looked down, and a breath of shock escaped.

Covering his fingers and knuckles was a cross-hatching of scars that rendered the already pallid skin into a kind of lacework. Some of the scars gouged deep into the flesh, leaving shiny dips of pink tissue; others were raised and knotted like twists of fine silk. I felt suddenly ill, and my eyes went back to his face before I had time to conceal my horror and pity.

He seemed to shrink into himself, pull away from me as though our proximity threatened him. Hastily he bowed, then turned on his heel and thudded back down the stairs, vanishing a moment later in the gloom.

I looked down at the parcel. It was wrapped in brown paper and secured with string, which I hastily untied. Twenty sheets of fine, smooth rag paper lay inside the humble packaging. It might have cost him a week's pay, and certainly a trip to Launceston – for where, in the tiny town of Wynyard, would he have found such a costly and unusual commodity?

And why had he given *me* a gift, when I had imagined that it was Adele who occupied his secret affections? Was the parcel of paper merely a ploy, in case he was caught creeping to Adele's room at this early hour? It seemed a lot of trouble and expense to go to for a distraction. Could it be that my husband's grooms-man had feelings for *me*?

I shivered, suddenly cold. But the chill didn't come from the icy air drifting into the stairwell from outside. It didn't come from the draught leaking through the gaps around the windowpane to freeze my skin and redden my nose and bite my fingertips.

The lonely, pervading chill I felt at that moment on the stairs came from deep inside me, blowing up from a dark, desolate place that until now I had not known existed.

Later that morning, after breakfast and then rushing through my few household duties, I took my paints to the garden. In a secluded spot, I unfolded my seat and arranged my colour blocks, brushes and vial of water. Then I opened the package of paper Lucien had given me.

After much thought about my predicament, I had decided to paint a portrait of my husband as a peace offering. A week had passed since Carsten's departure. The bruises had faded from my skin, and the abrasions seemingly healed; but each tiny injury had settled inwards, scarring my soul, causing a festering resentment. Today, I decided, I would put that resentment behind me and try to see my marriage through more pragmatic eyes.

I did not love Carsten, and the rough liberties he had taken with my body repulsed me. But we had made an agreement. And for the sake of my father, and for the land I loved, I would find a way to endure.

I sketched quickly, finding my husband's likeness in my memory. Features began to emerge on the paper, the charcoal lines almost too faint to see at first, like marks made by the random fluttering of dusty moth wings. As my thoughts drifted, the press of my charcoal stick gained force and a face began to emerge on the paper's smooth surface.

Lucien's face.

I shivered. His beauty might have been sublime had it not been for the whiplash mark carving his cheek. If he had been spared the defect, would he have been quite so intriguing to me? Didn't imperfection lend a depth to beauty that took the gaze deeper? Suffering and humility, my father always said, were qualities that made the man. I hadn't really known what he'd meant – until now.

Alone with Lucien in the glade, I'd seen another side to him. Gone was the gruff servant who hid his face in shadows; he had spoken openly, revealing his private views, and showing interest in mine. I had never before conversed with anyone in that manner, not even my father. And as we returned to the house along the shady path, I had never before felt so alive.

Warmth settled over me, banishing my shivers. I had been dazzled by Carsten's wealth and poise; blinded by his fine

clothes and beguiling eyes, easily believing he was a man of
honour. But strip away the outer, and what was exposed? A
man who rarely smiled, who lacked sensitivity to other people's
feelings; a man with a brutal streak.

Lucien's outer might have been scarred and unkempt,
strange to the eye of genteel society, but I sensed, after our few
brief moments alone, that behind his rough facade was a gentle
boy whose heart shone pure and strong.

A heart that, I suspected, beat a little faster when I was near.

Sitting back, I studied my drawing. The paper was now a
dark mass of charcoal markings and smudges, and gazing back
at me from those turbulent lines was a face that intrigued me.

But it was not my husband's face.

I should destroy the drawing, smear my hand across the
charcoal lines and blur the face out of recognition; perhaps even
burn the paper so no prying eye might guess the subject I had
rendered with such passion, but something stayed me.

Reaching for my paintbox, I wet my brush and began to add
colour to my sketch. I worked feverishly, with a resolve I'd never
before experienced. Soon the familiar features came to life on
the page – his pale skin, his straight nose, his stubborn jaw,
his full lips and intense green eyes. And all about that striking
face, in a halo of wild snakelike tangles, his hair gleamed deep
alizarin red.

Adele sat at her dressing table, watching me in the mirror. I had
loosely braided her hair and was winding it up onto her crown,
ready to secure with hairpins.

I had been unsettled since Carsten's departure, and our
encounter was still fresh in my mind. *You are nothing like her*,
he had said, confirming my suspicions that he harboured secret
affections for another; the woman, I guessed, whose portrait he
carried in his locket.

I fumbled the pin container and dropped it on the floor. Hairpins sprayed over the carpet, and I kneeled to retrieve them. I had not intended to ask the question aloud, but found myself saying, 'Why is it, Adele, that your brother has never married before now?'

Adele's smile fell away and a look of bleakness came over her. She turned back to the mirror.

'There was a woman my brother once loved. Many years ago. They were sweethearts, and Carsten wanted to marry her. However, by the time he gathered the courage to ask, she had received another offer – an offer so favourable to the girl's parents that they influenced her to accept. Carsten was destroyed. He vowed never to give his heart to another woman as long as he lived.'

I thought of Carsten with his fine dark eyes and unsmiling mouth, and the trust I had placed in him by agreeing to become his wife and leaving my home to dwell in his; I thought of the way he had used me so roughly that last night, and of his refusal to take me with him so I could visit my father – and I felt a pinch of gladness that he had suffered.

You are nothing like her.

'That locket he carries: it's a portrait of *her*, isn't it?'

Adele regarded me warily. 'I must confess I don't know. There is much I don't know about him. My brother is a private man, as you must be coming to understand. Some would even call him secretive. But he means no harm, it is just his way.'

'He looks at it often.'

She regarded her reflection thoughtfully, then twisted in her seat and reached for my hand, her smile full of reassurance. 'You mustn't let it bother you, Brenna. There was a time when he hated her, when the hurt she'd caused him was all he thought about. He became bitter, and fell into a dark despair that lasted many years. One night, when we were still living at Hillgrove, he came home reeking of drink, his clothes bloodied and torn.

He said he'd been waylaid by thieves, but the incident left him moody and wretched. Soon after, he bought Brayer House and moved here. In time, his despair lifted, and I suppose he forgave her. But I am certain of one thing.'

'What's that?'

'She haunts him. Perhaps she always will. Which is why,' she added, taking the container of hairpins from my fingers and peering into my face, 'you must make him forget her by giving him a son.'

The clock struck eleven. Moonlight drifted through my bedroom window, and a blustery squall rattled the panes. I shivered and drew my wrap more tightly around my shoulders, gazing across the grey landscape of the garden.

From the far end of the hall, drifted the intermittent hack-hack of Adele's coughing.

For the most part, Adele was rosy-cheeked and full of good humour. But several times a week, her eyes became dull, her hair lacklustre, her skin sallow. On those days, she retired to her bed, and for many hours the sound of her rattling cough echoed through the house. Quinn tiptoed along the hall, her broad face rumpled in concern as she supplied Adele with bowls of hot broth and laudanum mixture. By morning, Adele would be recovered, and brush off my enquiries as to her health.

The clock downstairs chimed the half-hour. Adele's hacking finally stopped.

The roof beams creaked, and the wintry breeze knocked softly against the windowpane. I nestled into my shawl, relieved that Adele had fallen asleep.

Meanwhile, I remained wide-eyed awake.

In a few days, Carsten would arrive home, and just the thought of seeing him slicked my sides with anxious sweat. In his absence, the household had come alive. Most evenings after dinner, Adele played the piano and sang, and sometimes Quinn read poetry – not the insipid rhymes I'd learned at school in Armidale, but rousing stories of adventure and romance and danger. Once, Quinn had bellowed out a Scottish rebel song and declared – to the amazed delight of her audience – that since her rebel father's blood ran in her veins, she was a rebel, too. Even I had been enticed to perform. Standing nervously before the others, I found myself singing a song Jindera had taught me in her language. Encouraged by the eager applause, I had then launched into a description of how the clan built fish traps in the river shallows, and rolled their catch in mud for baking over hot coals.

I gazed across the trees, remembering my resolve to endure; not just for the sake of my father and Lyrebird Hill, but for my own peace of mind. The moon had risen higher, drenching the garden in silver light. Camellias glowed like pearly beacons, and the sea whispered in the bay.

A blur of white appeared on the path below.

Adele. She was not asleep, after all, but down there in the garden, barefoot, wearing only a nightdress. Her dark hair hung around her shoulders, and as she hurried along the path in the direction of the stables, her hands reached ahead of her, her fingers clenching and flexing as if trying to snatch something from the darkness.

Then Lucien stepped from the shadows and quickly approached. He took Adele's arm, but she wrenched away from him and continued along the dark path. Lucien followed, and as he turned his back to me I saw the frayed ponytail that hung between his shoulder blades; wild in the moonlight, but bleached of its true dark copper-red.

I frowned. Where was Adele going? And why was Lucien trying to stop her?

Pulling my coat about my shoulders, I rushed from the room and silently descended the staircase. The house was tomblike at this hour. Grey light flooded through the library windows, but under the furniture and in the corners of the room lurked the blackest shadows. Pushing through the French doors, I ran along the path towards the rear of the building.

There was no sign of Adele or Lucien, so I hurried in the direction of the stables. From somewhere nearby came a cry, then a frantic babble of words that could only be Adele. I raced towards the sound, stones bruising my feet, the lapels of my coat flapping around me like wings.

I found them huddled on a garden bench. Adele's face was a death mask in the gloom. Lucien sat close beside her, his body bent protectively, Adele's hands clasped in his own.

Momentarily, my heart sank into my stomach as my suspicions flared; had I had stumbled upon Adele and her lover in a secret tryst? Then I saw that her cheeks were wet with tears. Her face turned towards me, but I saw no sign of recognition in her eyes. Tearing her hands from Lucien's grasp, she began to clench her fingers in front of her in that odd way. This was no tryst.

I rushed to my friend and kneeled at her feet. 'Adele, what is it?' I cried softly. 'What's happened?'

She blinked. More tears splashed her cheeks. 'I want to see him,' she said. 'He's weeping, I want gather him up. There—' She twisted her head as if startled by a distant noise. 'Can you hear him?'

I looked at Lucien, and my mouth must have fallen agape, because he shook his head and put a finger to his lips.

'Miss Adele,' he said softly. 'Your sister is here now. She's going to help you back to the house.'

'I don't want to go back to the house. I dreamed he died. My poor little boy, alone in the earth, so cold and afraid. I must go to him.' She began to cry. Then, a cough broke from her, one of her deep, chest-rattling barks that shuddered through her slight frame. Dragging off my coat, I settled it around her shoulders.

'Come with me, Adele,' I said. 'You can sleep in my bed tonight, it's nice and warm. I'll read to you a while, if you like?'

She seemed to regain herself a little. Her convulsing fingers relaxed. 'Read to me? Yes, read me a story. That will calm me. I had a dream, you see. I wanted . . . I only wanted—' Again, that racking cough, and a fresh spill of tears.

'It's all right, Adele.' I gently grasped her fingers. 'Come on now, let's get back to the house where it's warm. I'll brew you some chamomile flowers to help you sleep.'

She sat forward on the bench, and I helped her to her feet. She was shaky, but she gripped my forearm with surprising force. Lucien took her other arm and we walked a couple of steps across the damp grass. Then Adele stopped.

'Lucien,' she said in a voice more her own, 'it happened again, didn't it?'

'Yes, Miss Adele, but there's no harm done. You'll be toasty warm in a moment, and we don't ever need to mention it again.'

'You won't tell Carsten?'

'No, miss. There's no need to trouble your brother.'

She appeared calmer, and allowed us to lead her back to the house. Lucien helped me navigate the dark stairs, and then along the passageway to my room. He removed my coat from Adele's shoulders and hung it behind the door, while I settled Adele beneath the coverlet on my bed. For a moment, she clung to my hand.

'Promise you won't tell Carsten.'

'Not a word.'

She smiled, and her pale beautiful face was as trusting as a child's. Then she closed her eyes and burrowed into the pillow. Soon her breathing slowed and she did not stir.

I crossed the room to where Lucien lingered in the doorway. 'What happened tonight?' I asked softly, although I was beginning to guess. 'Where was she going?'

Lucien looked at the bed, then beckoned me into the hall. We stood in the darkness, illuminated by candlelight.

'She was sleepwalking, Mrs Whitby.'

I let out a breath, remembering the other nights I'd glimpsed Adele running through the garden in her nightgown. I looked across at her and she seemed small under the great weight of the covers. My heart swelled with pity.

'She mentioned a little boy. Is he the child buried in the graveyard beyond the garden?'

'Yes, Mrs Whitby.'

My throat clenched, and tears pricked the backs of my eyes. 'Oh, Adele.'

'He was a sickly wee boy,' Lucien said kindly. 'Never made it to his fourth birthday. Soon after he was buried, I found Miss Adele one stormy night on his grave, face down in the mud, trying to shelter him from the rain. She was sick after. We thought she might die. It weakened her lungs. She won't speak of her illness, but since then—' He gestured at the doorway. 'She can't seem to find any peace, Mrs Whitby.'

I shivered, gripping my elbows, feeling bruised by what I had just learned. Of all people, Adele Whitby did not deserve the burden of sorrow; I wanted to go to her, hold her near me and reassure her – but I sensed that the subject of her son must, for now, remain unspoken.

I looked up at Lucien. 'Carsten doesn't know about the sleep-walking, does he?'

'No, miss.'

I should have wished him goodnight then and shut the door, but I hesitated, letting my attention linger. In the gloom, it was easy to overlook the scar that had ruined his face; I saw him as he would have been without it. Dark-eyed, with sharp cheekbones and a regal nose, a jaw that hinted at stubbornness, and a mouth that made me wonder how it might feel to touch my lips there.

I realised I'd been staring, and my gaze flew back to his eyes. He was staring, too; not in a guarded way, but openly, almost intimately. I tried to unlock my gaze from his, but something in those dark green depths held me captive. Was he letting me glimpse behind the mask of his face, to the true nature that dwelled beneath? And was he, in turn, seeing behind mine? I felt naked, wide open, exposed; but rather than disturb me as it should have, that brief recognition between us sent a spear of fierce joy into the core of my soul. My pulse flew, crashing so violently through my veins that surely it was loud enough to wake Adele.

Reaching for the doorframe, I gripped it tightly, aware that I wore only a thin nightgown. An unnatural heat was blossoming through me, and I feared that Lucien might see the flush in my face and guess my thoughts.

'Goodnight, Mr Fells,' I said more abruptly than I had intended.

Bowing his head, Lucien retreated silently into the dark hallway and quickly vanished in the gloom, his footsteps eerie and dislocated as he trod quietly along the floorboards. A moment later, he reappeared at the top of the stairs. Moonlight caught him again as he descended, a slender young man with a shock of wild hair and a scarred but heartbreakingly beautiful face.

'Goodnight, Lucien,' I whispered into the darkness, then hurriedly shut the door.

11

*Scars remind us of our suffering and pain; they are also
evidence of our body's greatest gift – the miracle of healing.*
– ROB THISTLETON, *LET GO AND LIVE*

Ruby, May 2013

We were sitting in Mum's kitchen at the back of her house, on opposite sides of an enormous dining table. The sun streamed in colourful ribbons through a nearby leadlight window, highlighting the gold details on Mum's good teapot.

Mum sat stiffly in her chair, a frown carving her normally smooth brow as she gazed at the pile of letters in front of her.

'I can't believe you remembered me burying them.'

I hesitated. 'Bits and pieces are coming back.'

Mum folded the letters and began tucking them back into their envelopes. 'Do you think it's because you're staying out at Lyrebird Hill?'

I shifted on the wooden chair, knotting my fingers on the table. I had spent the morning with Pete, organising a tow truck to collect my car from the roadside and take it to the wreckers in Armidale, then Pete had dropped me here at Mum's. She seemed

196

unfazed by my revelation about the letters, but she was pale and red blotches flamed on her cheeks.

'Actually,' I said warily, 'the memories started filtering back when I saw your paintings.'

Mum looked up, clearly surprised. 'I hope it wasn't too horrible, Ruby. I'm sorry, I had no idea they would have that effect—'

'No, no,' I said hastily. 'It was okay.'

'You were upset about your sister that night.' A vague tone of accusation clung to her words, and I could see by the tightness around her mouth that she thought I was blaming her.

I slumped, wondering if we were heading for another Jamie fight. I chose my next words carefully, but they still sounded wooden. 'It was a shock to find out that Jamie didn't die from a fall. I understand why you kept it from me, but . . .' My words dwindled off, and I swallowed, tried again. 'I guess I was hurt.'

Mum pushed the letters into the centre of the table. 'I didn't mean to hurt you, Ruby. It just seemed easier to pretend that it was an accident. They never found . . . well, you know all that now.' She reached for the teapot, then hesitated and withdrew her hand.

'What else are you remembering?'

'Nothing too exciting.' I thought about her wringing the neck of my favourite chicken, and cutting my hair – but decided to keep it light. I wasn't here to start flinging grievances; what I really wanted was answers.

'What made you bury the letters, Mum?'

Finally she poured the tea, and as she pushed my cup across the expanse of table, her fingers trembled. 'I was upset to find out that Nanna Adele wasn't actually my grandmother. And then to learn that my *real* grandmother had been convicted for murder.' She sighed. 'We'd already been through so much. Our family was shadowed by more than its fair share of death. Discovering this new drama seemed unbelievable at first, but then a few dots began to join. I couldn't stop myself wondering if all the deaths in our family were somehow connected.'

It took me a moment to understand what she was saying. 'You mean, like a curse?'

Her eyes widened, and in the afternoon light they were somehow wet and vulnerable. 'Nothing so dramatic, Ruby. Although the notion of bad genes had crossed my mind. I was heartsick, finding those letters. They made me question myself and everyone around me. I started thinking about your father's death, and all the old guilt bubbled up. And then when we lost Jamie—'

She stood up and went to the window. In the harsh light from outside, I caught a glimpse of strain around her mouth and eyes, and a few threads of grey in her auburn hair.

I couldn't help asking. 'Was Brenna executed?'

Mum shook her head. 'I looked on the internet – the last female execution in Tasmania happened in the 1860s. Brenna must have died of natural causes. She'd recently given birth, and I imagine prison conditions were harsh.'

'So, she gave up her baby – our Grampy James – to her sister-in-law Adele Whitby?'

Mum nodded. 'And Nanna Adele raised James as her own son.'

'Those letters are family history, Mum. Why didn't you just tuck them away somewhere, out of sight?'

'I thought about it, but I knew you were always nosing around where you shouldn't. I didn't want you to find them, but I couldn't bear to destroy them, either. The drawings decorating their pages were so beautiful . . . and so sad.'

'Why didn't you want me to find them?'

She hesitated, then said in an almost-whisper, 'I had my reasons.'

'Mum, you're doing my head in.'

She sighed. 'You went through a lot, after Jamie died. There were so many questions. So much poking and prodding and trying to get you to remember. Detectives, and social workers, and child behavioural analysts. I was probably being paranoid, but at the time I thought it best that the letters not fall into the wrong hands.'

That threw me. 'Wrong hands?'

'The media, I suppose. Or the police. We were in the midst of an inquiry. One of my daughters died, and the other one was seriously injured. And after your father . . . well, I was under suspicion, as were you. Can you imagine what a meal the media would have made out of a bundle of old letters disclosing that my grandmother was a murderer?'

I could hardly believe what she was saying.

'Mum, the letters were already antique when I was a kid. Why would anyone care about a crime that some poor woman committed in 1898?'

'Ruby, she wasn't just "some poor woman". She was your great-grandmother. I just felt it would have reflected badly on us.' She touched the tips of her long fingers under her eyes, as if patting away invisible tears. For a while she sat still and tense, then finally got to her feet.

'I'm sorry, Ruby.' She glanced at the wall clock. 'I've got to run. The gallery has a buyer for some earlier works of mine, and they've asked me to be there. I hate kicking you out, but I can't be late.'

She walked me along the hallway to the door, then turned back and looked at me, her face in silhouette, the sunlight streaming through the flywire drenching her in golden light.

'I'm pleased you came to see me, Ruby. Don't leave it so long next time, okay?'

She pecked my cheek, and we said goodbye. I went along the path, and when I reached the gate I turned to wave, but Mum had already disappeared back inside. I studied her closed door.

I was under suspicion, as were you.

The seed of doubt I'd been storing in the back of my mind for the past eighteen years finally slid into fertile soil and began to germinate. My feelings of guilt; my conviction that Mum secretly blamed me; my fear of recall – all of it skirting the real issue of that one forgotten event that, if remembered, would shatter me from the inside and leave me broken forever—

There was a clatter of glass further along the street as someone emptied their recycling. I squinted into the blinding sunlight, rubbing my temple. I had a sick, sinking feeling, and then the leafy footpath, my mother's house with its picket fence and landcaped garden, and the sleepy bustle of the Armidale street vanished. I blinked, and there I was instead, a twelve-year-old sitting down to breakfast in the kitchen of my childhood home.

A single boiled egg sat on my plate, the last of Esmeralda's. I was planning to scoop it out of its shell and mash it across a piece of wholemeal toast, but I was still deciding how to eat it. Should I scoff hungrily like I usually did, or take my time and savour every bite?

I was picking up my knife when Jamie's voice drifted through the open kitchen window.

'I saw them up on the ridge last night,' she was saying. 'Ruby . . . and a *boy*.'

She must have been standing behind the water tank talking to Mum, who'd gone out to the vegie patch to pick greens for our school sandwiches.

'What boy?' Mum asked.

'That foster kid staying with Mrs Drake.'

'What were they doing?'

Jamie's reply was muffled by birdsong, but something in her tone made me nervous. Picking up my knife, I cut open the egg and scooped it onto my toast.

Mum came into the kitchen looking flushed, as if she'd spent too long in the sun. She took a colander from its hook on the wall and rinsed the greens under the tap.

'What were you doing with the Mrs Drake's foster boy last night?' she asked without looking around. 'Jamie said she saw the two of you out after dark.'

I glared at Jamie. She'd followed Mum in and was examining the plate of scones, her eyes all big and innocent. She chose the largest, I noticed, and broke it into bits on her plate.

Mum shook the colander into the sink. 'Well, Ruby?'

'Nothing.'

She turned to look at me. 'What's got into you lately? You used to be such a quiet girl. Your grades were good, the teachers only ever had praise for you. Now there are notes sent home every week about your attitude. And as for your outburst yesterday – I understand you were upset, but swearing? I think that foster boy is a bad influence.'

I sat up straight. 'No, he's—'

'You'd better stay away from him.'

I opened my mouth to argue, but a loud clatter cut me off. All eyes went to the far end of the table. Jamie had dropped her butter knife.

'Sorry,' she said sheepishly, but when Mum turned her attention back to the greens, Jamie pulled a face.

I glowered back.

A couple of years ago we'd been best friends. Swimming in the river together, fishing for yabbies. Collecting ferns and yellow-buttons and everlastings to dry in the flower press we'd found in the barn. Jamie had written stories, and I'd drawn pictures to go with them. We'd been a team, thick as thieves, best mates.

Then Jamie started high school in Armidale. She began experimenting with make-up, and saved up to buy her own clothes. She got in with the cool crowd. All of a sudden, in her eyes I was a baby. Boring. *A regular yawn*, she'd written in her diary.

And that wasn't all she'd written.

I can't believe I've got a boyfriend. Mum would freak if she knew, so I only ever meet him at our secret place. Yesterday we kissed for the first time . . . sigh, I think I'm in love.

I looked at Mum. She was frowning at four slices of brown bread arranged on the benchtop. They were slathered in homemade mayonnaise, and Mum began arranging sorrel leaves in rows across the yellow gloop. A mound of grated carrot sat nearby, awaiting its fate as sandwich filling.

Scraping back my chair, I got to my feet. I was shaking so hard I knocked over my glass, splashing milk across the tablecloth.

'You think Jamie's so perfect?' I yelled at Mum. 'You think she never does anything wrong? You always blame me for mucking things up, but if you knew the truth about *her*, you'd get a rude shock.'

Mum frowned at Jamie, then at me. 'What are you talking about?'

I stared at Jamie in triumph. But all of a sudden, her face was pale and her big golden eyes were pleading at me. She was no longer the sophisticated teenager, but a kid just like me; her freckles popped against her creamy skin and she looked about to start blubbering.

Mum was waiting, her dark hair frayed into wisps around her face. The empty colander dangled from her fingers.

'Well?'

I opened my mouth, but no words came. I didn't want to hurt Jamie. Despite her awfulness to me sometimes, I still loved her. And I still secretly hoped that one day we would be friends again, just as we'd been before she started high school.

So I said nothing.

Later that night after dinner, I saw her sneak into the yard. The incinerator was still smouldering from when Mum had burned a load of blackberry canes. Jamie stoked the ashes until the fire licked the incinerator rim, then she threw something in.

She stayed there a long time, a shadow in the darkness, staring at the blaze, her face painted gold and crimson by the flames.

When the fire died and Jamie came inside, I went to investigate. At first, I saw only ashes. But when I prodded the ash with a stick, I upturned a blackened blob of metal that, on closer inspection, turned out to be the remains of a tiny padlock.

My sister had burned her diary.

The flashback, on top of my conversation with my mother, had left me feeling drained. For the longest time, I stood at the gate outside Mum's, gazing back, trying to summon the energy to retrace my steps along the pathway and knock on her door.

In the end, it seemed too hard.

And too unlikely that Mum would be much bothered by my recollection of a snippet from so long ago; besides, she'd probably already known about Jamie's one-time boyfriend. I swallowed a lump of disappointment about the diary, too; the book Esther had mentioned was probably just a volume of fairytales after all.

The sun was high and bright overhead, the air had turned warm. I had promised to meet Pete at the mechanic's in Marsh Street at 2pm, which meant I had a couple of hours to kill; shopping was the last thing I felt like doing, so instead I walked. Soon I had blisters on my heels, and a little while later they became painful. I found a park bench, and sat for an hour watching a family of magpies pick over drifts of rubbish around the picnic tables.

Something Mum said about the letters wasn't adding up.

Had she really only been trying to protect me from the shock of discovering my great-grandmother was a murderer? Or to prevent the letters being sensationalised by the press? Or was she motivated by reasons of a more private nature?

The notion of bad genes had crossed my mind.

Bad genes. Traits passed from one generation to the next. Could Mum really believe that? I was about to discount it as simply too outlandish, when I remembered the title of the painting that had led me to the walnut tree in the first place.

Inheritance.

I went hot, and then every molecule of heat drained out of my body and my blood turned ice cold. Slowly, the truth dawned. Mum didn't just blame me for Jamie's death; she didn't simply hold me responsible for not getting help fast enough, or for not remembering important facts that might have helped the police catch Jamie's killer.

Mum believed I *was* Jamie's killer.

Sliding my hand down to my instep, I found a blister that had worn tender beneath my sandal strap. When I dug my fingernails into the watery bubble, it burst and leaked fluid. I dug harder, and the slow ooze of blood rose under my nail.

. . . no trace that anyone other than you and Jamie had been on the rocks that day.

I peeled off the blistered piece of skin and let it drop in the grass. Was Mum right? How would I ever know for certain? And if I never knew, how could I live with myself?

The answer to that was simple: I couldn't.

By the time I asked directions to the mechanic's, promptly got lost and asked again, then finally found my way to the motor repair shop, it was well after two o'clock. There was no sign of a woolly-haired man with two kelpies, or his old ute. Just a car yard full of demo vehicles, a garage littered with engine parts, and an office hidden behind smoked glass.

My phone buzzed. I looked at the display, it was another message from Rob. I deleted it, then typed a reply.

Leave me alone.

But when I tried to press send, my fingers fumbled and the message disappeared. Rather than try to retrieve it, I just stood there, hunched over my phone, feeling so suddenly weary that I actually considered curling in a ball and resting my head on the warm concrete.

'Ruby?'

Pete had emerged from the office and was walking towards me. 'Hey,' he said, 'are you okay?'

'Not really. My boyfriend – that is, my ex-boyfriend – cheated on me. Now he wants to talk. And Mum thinks . . . she thinks I—' My words choked off. All I could do was stare into Pete's impossibly blue eyes and fight back the tears.

Taking the phone from my fingers, Pete slid it into my bag and grasped my hand. Then, gently, he led me around the side of the building where his ute was waiting. Bardo and Old Boy were on the back tray. They'd been sitting quietly, but the moment they saw me they sprang to their feet and began to whine excitedly, straining their chains. Bardo's tail wagged with such vigour that her entire back end twisted to and fro.

Pete opened the passenger door and I got in. A moment later he was settling into the driver's seat, buckling up. He looked at me, his big freckled hands loosely grasping the wheel, his dark hair raked into wild tufts, his blue eyes shadowed with concern. He was clearly curious about what had shaken me loose, but had the restraint not to ask. Instead he reached for my hand. His fingers were warm and calloused, and the way they curled cautiously around mine made me feel marginally better.

After a moment, he withdrew and started up the car.

'What is it about you and those dogs?' he marvelled. 'You ignore them, avoid them, and generally act as if they're not there – which from a dog's perspective is somewhat upsetting. And yet they hero-worship you.'

I shrugged, and ventured a small smile.

But as we drove up Marsh Street and then hooked right at Rusden, I caught myself turning my head ever so slightly. The cab window was directly behind me, but if I peeked from the corner of my eye I could just see two pointed, furry faces with ears pricked and tongues lolling and lips pulled into sloppy grins. Their moist noses were pressed near the glass, and both dogs were watching me, their golden eyes brimming with happy fascination.

'You're bleeding.'

Dusk was falling, and one by one the stars were coming out. I shifted on the log bench, sliding one foot behind the other, out of sight. 'It's nothing. Just a blister.'

'Blister, my arse.' Pete removed the tea towel he'd tucked into his jeans as a makeshift apron, and kneeled at my feet. With surprising gentleness, he cupped his fingers around my ankle and stretched out my leg, bending nearer to examine my instep. 'It looks more like you've been gored by a wild boar. I'm afraid I'm going to have to operate.'

'What about dinner?' I asked, looking hopefully over at the barbecue. Tonight we were having roasted garlic salmon with vegetables and salad, and the aroma wafting from the cast-iron bush oven was driving me to distraction.

'Food will have to wait,' Pete said. 'Don't move, I'll be back in a flash.'

He ducked into the house and was back a moment later with a large first aid kid. He took out gauze bandage, nursing scissors and a tiny bottle of Betadine.

'I'm just going to give it a squirt with this,' he explained, unscrewing the Betadine. 'It might sting, so don't say you weren't warned.'

I shut my eyes.

You're bleeding.

The antiseptic liquid burned my raw skin. I shifted focus: the warm rough squeeze of Pete's fingers on my ankle as he applied a strip of gauze; the tickle of his hair against my bare leg when he bent to retrieve the scissors; the rhythm of his touch as he wound the bandage gently, smoothly, and with infinite care, around my injured foot.

The murmur of wind in the casuarinas reached me, and my attention wandered. All of a sudden I was twelve again, racing along the river's edge and up the hill, into the dark shadows of the pine forest.

'Hey, Roo. You're bleeding.'

The Wolf pointed at my T-shirt sleeve. 'Did you cut yourself?'

We were sitting in the patchy shade of a black cypress pine that grew at the base of the Spine. The ground beneath us was carpeted brown with needles and dotted with hard little pinecones.

I examined the splodge of blood on my sleeve. 'It's nothing.'

The Wolf frowned and leaned closer, bumping his bony shoulder against mine. 'You'd better let me have a look,' he said. 'You might need stitches.'

I shoved him away, and the words popped out before I could stop them. 'I've just scratched my scar.'

Curiosity lit the Wolf's eyes. 'You have a scar? Let's see.'

'No way.'

'Come on. I'll show you mine.'

'Yeah, right. As if you'd have anything *this* ugly.'

The Wolf wiggled his eyebrows. 'You'd be surprised.'

'And *you'd* be grossed out.'

The Wolf hitched up his jeans leg to reveal a shiny coin-sized patch below his knee, pink against the tanned skin. 'Snakebite,' he said proudly.

My breath got stuck in my throat. 'How come you didn't die?'

'I cut across the bite with my penknife and sucked out the venom.'

I couldn't stop staring. 'Mum says you shouldn't cut a snake-bite. She says you have to bandage up the limb and wait for help.'

The Wolf pulled a face. 'Hard to wait for help when you're deep in the scrub and no one knows where you are. Anyway, check this one out.'

He slid down his sock to expose his ankle, revealing a zigzag like a red lightning bolt. 'Croc attack,' he boasted. 'A real monster of a thing, too. Dragged me right under, had me in the death-roll. I only survived on account of being a champion swimmer.'

A glimmer of disbelief made me scrunch up my face. 'Really?'

The Wolf flashed his canines in a devious smile. 'Would I lie to you, Roo?'

'Yes!' I rolled my eyes, but secretly I was impressed. I looked hopefully back at his leg. 'Any more?'

Rolling up his T-shirt, he displayed a tanned stomach where a pink line hooked around his right hip. 'This one nearly finished me,' he said seriously. 'Fifteen stitches. I was in hospital for yonks.'

'What happened?'

He waggled his eyebrows again. 'It'll cost you.'

I had twigged by now that he might – just *might* – be pulling my leg about how he got all those scars. But it didn't matter; he had *scars*. None as bad as mine, but it was a relief to know he wasn't perfect.

'All right, I'll show you.'

'Promise?'

'Cross my heart and spit in your eye.' I nodded at the pink line on his hip. 'So, how'd you get it?'

'Wild boar.'

My mouth fell open. 'Get away!'

'It's true.'

'What happened?'

'We were pig hunting. My brother's dog flushed some piglets from a hollow, and the sow went wild. Me and my brother ran like buggery, but just when I thought I was safe, the sow charged out from behind a tree and went for me.'

My brows shot up. 'You have a brother?'

The Wolf picked up a pinecone and snapped off a spur. 'Sure. He's twenty-five. I haven't seen him in yonks. He's in jail for armed robbery.'

I stared. 'What about your mum and dad?'

'Mum died. I still see Dad sometimes.'

'Why don't you live with him, instead of with Mrs Drake?'

'He's mad.'

I stared at the Wolf in amazement. A million questions were suddenly hammering my brain, but the Wolf had gone very still, apparently fascinated by his pinecone. A weird sort of silence spun around us. I felt uncomfortable – not because of what the Wolf had told me about his family, but because of the deep frown carved into his normally cheerful face.

The silence between us grew. Currawongs burbled in the branches of a nearby tumbledown gum, and from the distance came the quiet roar of the rapids.

'I like Mrs Drake,' the Wolf said suddenly. 'She bought me these jeans. I've never had new jeans before.'

'They're cool.'

'She gave me all this other stuff, too. Gear that Bobby grew out of, football jumpers, T-shirts, that sort of thing. I've even got my own room.'

Mrs Drake lived on the other side of the Hillard farm, and mostly kept to herself. Her husband had died a long time ago, before Mum and Jamie and I came here to live.

'What's Bobby like?' I asked.

The Wolf shook his head. 'Up himself.'

'How do you stand living there, then?'

'Most of the time it's just me and Mrs Drake. Bobby's hardly ever home, he's too caught up at uni. Anyway, I'd much rather be there than at the home.'

That was the first time I'd ever heard the Wolf mention the boys' home in Newcastle. I waited for him to give details, but he was staring pointedly at the sleeve of my T-shirt.

'Come on, Roo,' he reminded me. 'I showed you mine.'

Taking a deep breath, I lifted my sleeve. The Wolf shifted nearer, and let out a soft whistle.

'What a beauty! How'd you get it?'

'A dog bit me.'

The Wolf pulled away and looked at my face. 'Cripes, that must've hurt. How old were you?'

'Six.'

His eyes went wide. 'I bet you had a gazillion stitches.'

'Only twenty-five. And surgery. And lots of time in hospital.'

He whistled again. 'I can't believe I've known you all this time and you've never shown me before. Whose dog was it?'

'My dad's.'

'Did it get put down for attacking you?'

'Well, my dad . . . it was . . . I mean, he—' I hung my head, suddenly faint. Clawing my fingers into my jeans legs, I tried to breathe away the memory.

'You okay, Roo?'

I nodded, but I wasn't okay. Not really.

When I was little, Mum took Jamie and me to see a puppet show in Armidale for the school holidays. There'd been a brightly painted stage with trees and a lake, and wooden puppet-girls wearing swan costumes. The puppets – marionettes, Mum had called them – had danced across the painted lake, faster and faster as the music rose. Then one of the swan-girl puppets got tangled and her strings broke. She fell limp, her wooden body hitting the stage with a clatter.

That's how I felt now. As if my strings had been snipped.

'Roo, what's up? You've gone all pale and quiet.'

I gulped a breath and opened my eyes – when had I shut them? The Wolf was staring at me, his eyes a hand span from mine. He collected a strand of my hair and wound it around his finger, gave it a gentle tug and smiled.

'I thought you went somewhere.'

'I did . . . kind of. I'm back now.'

He gave a soft growl, then sprang nimbly to his feet. He reached for my hand, and as we stood in the shade of the cypress he began to transform.

'I didn't bring the nighty,' I admitted. 'Do you think the Beast will mind if I wear jeans?'

The Wolf considered this. His change was almost complete; he was no longer a boy. His eyes blazed and fur was beginning to sprout on his face. His nose was long and sharp and he had whiskers.

Baring his teeth, he snarled. 'You've got ten minutes to escape.'

Without wasting another breath, I turned my back on the terrifying creature and ran for my life.

Pete finished tying off the bandage and stood up, his shadow rippling over me. 'This time tomorrow, you'll be right as rain.'

I looked up at him, shading my eyes from the sun.

'Have you ever been bitten by a snake?'

I don't know why I said it; the question kind of blurted out of its own accord. Pete must have thought me crazy, but I couldn't shake the feeling that the boy emerging from my forgotten past and into the brighter light of these new incoming memories had grown into the man who now stood before me.

Pete's brow went up, then he grinned. 'Nah. Their fangs'd snap off in my leathery old hide. Why do you ask?'

'Never mind.'

He narrowed his eyes, and his lips twitched into a secretive little smile. 'Although I did,' he added quietly, 'get attacked by a crocodile one time.'

'Nasty.'

As he went back to the barbecue I thought I heard him mutter something about being a champion swimmer.

A flush shot into my cheeks, and I busied myself inspecting the dressing he'd just applied to my foot, picking at the edges of the bandage, loosening a thread and worrying it free.

Of course, I couldn't just come right out and ask.

What if he said yes? What if he remembered everything that had once happened between us, while I was still mostly in the dark? When I was twelve, life had been precarious. I wasn't popular like my sister. Rather, I was tubby little Ruby Cardel, always the last one picked for a team, the weird, quiet girl at the back of the class, the one who sat alone at lunchtime.

I glanced at Pete from the corner of my eye.

He was whistling – not a happy tune, but some disjointed rendition of a Nirvana song that made it sound like a dirge – as he scrutinised the sizzling salmon, then reached for more twigs to fuel the barbecue flames.

If my suspicions were right – and Pete was in fact my childhood friend the Wolf – then my stay at Lyrebird Hill had the potential to become tricky.

I drew the loose thread from the bandage weave and rolled it between my fingers. Gradually, my recall was trickling back, but I wasn't yet ready to play my hand without knowing the full score. Something had definitely happened between us; the only trouble was, I couldn't remember if it had been good . . . or better off forgotten.

At dusk, we walked down the grassy slope to the river's edge. Water babbled through the rocks. The tall she-oaks leaning from the banks shed their needles into the current. Pete was quiet, and I guessed he was thinking about Esther.

Picking up a stone, I skimmed it across the water.

There was a splash. Bardo flew past me into the shallows, biting at the ripples where the pebble had vanished. I stiffened and looked at Pete.

'Sorry about that,' he said, and called the dog to him. But Bardo only grinned at us, clearly ignoring his command. Her tongue lolled in excitement, and her amber eyes darted from me to Pete then back again.

Her expression was so comic that it made me blink, and the muscles in my neck relaxed. Picking up another stone, I sent it further than the first one. Bardo bounded after it, snapping at the ripples again and letting out a joyful yelp.

'She's a strange one,' I observed

'You'll never catch her chasing after a ball,' Pete explained, and there was a waver of caution in his voice. 'But throw a stone in the river, and she'll be your friend for life.'

I searched inside myself for the anxiety that this remark should have inspired, but couldn't find it. In its place, was a faint feeling of completeness, as if a tiny, overlooked puzzle piece had slotted perfectly into the larger picture of who I really was. Breathing deeply, I collected another stone to skim, and was about to hurl it when a whine came from behind. Pete and I looked around.

Old Boy was pawing a large flat rock jutting from the pebbly embankment, as if trying to overturn it.

'Does he want to play too?' I asked, my heart bounding only a little.

'No,' Pete said thoughtfully. 'I think he's found something.'

Wedged almost out of sight beneath the rock was a silver chain. I drew it out. It was attached to an ornate locket, which was embossed with a design of lyrebird tail-feathers.

'That's Esther's,' Pete said. 'She must have lost it here. '

I weighed the locket in my palm, suddenly overcome with sorrow. 'She was wearing it at the gallery.'

'Poor old girl,' Pete said softly. 'She must have dropped it when she slipped that night.' Taking it from my fingers, he carefully prised it open. 'Look, there's a little painting inside, she showed me once.'

It was a woman; she was ghostlike, with colourless eyes and ashen eyebrows, and white-blonde hair piled high on her crown; the only colour was in her cheeks, which bloomed the soft deep pink of summer roses.

'She's lovely,' I observed. 'Was she Esther's mother?'

Pete shook his head. 'Esther found the locket at the farmhouse a few years ago, forgotten behind a bookcase. Apparently she asked your mum about it, but it wasn't hers, so Esther kept it. Here,' he said, taking my hand and pressing the locket gently into my palm. 'Something to remember her by.'

I was about to resist, then hesitated. I turned the locket over in my hands. There was something about it that intrigued me; maybe it was because it had been Esther's. Then again, maybe it was simply the pretty way its ornate face gleamed softly in the dying sunlight, almost like a silver raindrop.

Almost like a fragment from long ago dream . . . or memory.

12

Brenna, June 1898

What started as an accidental dalliance quickly became my obsession. Under the pretence of sleeping late, I latched my door and brought out my paints and brushes, balancing my drafting board on my knees at the window.

Some mornings, Lucien appeared in the garden to scythe away the long grass that grew up around the fruit trees, or to deliver barrow loads of manure to the flowerbeds. I hovered unseen in the shadows of my room, my artist's eye taking note of his copper hair in the sunlight, or the flex of a muscular arm, or the curve of his jawbone beneath the broad brim hat.

Other days he did not appear.

Still, I sensed him out there as he moved through the morning, raking spent straw from the stable, replacing fresh hay in the racks, bruising the oats for the older horses, ensuring they were all watered and fed. If the carriage had recently been in use, he would rise early to wash and dry it and polish its varnished surface with soft leather and sweet oil.

Those days I drew him from memory.

As the murky dawn light shone through my window, and the rest of the house slept, Lucien's likeness materialised on my pages. My fingers trembled as I worked, and my sides were wet with perspiration. Every creak of the roof or whisper of footfall outside my door made me lurch upright and hold my breath, listening until the imagined threat had passed. But I could not stop. I painted with a fire in my heart, snapping charcoal sticks in my haste, adding a frenzy of ink lines and vibrant colour washes, smearing the paper with fingerprints of alizarin, cardinal blue, sap green and cadmium.

Shame burned within me. It was wrong to feel such intense fascination for a man who was not my husband; but my shame was merely an ember, easy enough to ignore. Because I knew in my heart that if I could not stoke this secret fire each morning, then my spirit would most certainly wither and die.

Carsten arrived unexpectedly, late the following Friday evening.

He came to my bedroom in his travelling clothes, smelling of road dust and port wine and horses. He greeted me warmly, and in the candlelight I noted the flush in his cheeks and the shine of his eyes. He appeared to have forgotten the ill-humour he had suffered the night of his departure, and his soft words lulled me into believing he had forgiven my interest in his silver locket.

But when he undressed and met me under the covers, his violent passion resurfaced. He held me roughly, pressing my face against the mattress, twisting my arms until the joints flamed with pain; soon I was drenched in his sweat and bruised from top to toe, wishing only for our joining to end.

Sliding my hand along the edge of the mattress, I let my fingers curl around the bed frame. Somewhere below me, protected by shadows, was my travelling trunk. Inside, under piles of clothing and several pairs of cloth-wrapped shoes, was the bundle of paper Lucien had gifted me. Each leaf was now buckled by water and pigment, its surface darkened by charcoal lines and ink.

It brought me a strange kind of comfort to think that although Carsten could use my body, my thoughts were free to drift down into the dusty darkness and wander among my private gallery of stolen memories: Lucien watching quizzically while I babbled about wolfsbane that day in the glade; Lucien on the stairwell bathed in morning light as he presented me with a gift of his forbidden esteem; Lucien in the dark garden at midnight, sitting on the bench, his face eerily beautiful in the moonlight.

Lucien. Always Lucien.

I should have destroyed my secret portraits, but it was clear they were among my best work. Besides, they were well hidden; what cause would Carsten ever have to check beneath my bed?

For a long while after Carsten had spent himself and retired to his own room, I lay awake. When the clock chimed midnight and sleep continued to elude me, I made my way to the library.

While the household slept, I stalked the dusty walls of books, hoping that their lofty shelves and muffled quietude would soothe my inner chaos. Instead, the stillness drew my attention to the muffled ticking of the grandfather clock down the hall. Whenever it chimed – the hour, or half-hour – its tones roused my heartbeat with a sort of fearful expectation that I could not name. Earlier, in my bedroom, Carsten had made no mention of his trip, nor whether he had seen my father. I ached for news of home, but more pressingly was the other request I had asked of him.

There was a massacre, a band of Aboriginal people were murdered; someone must know who those men were—

'Brenna.'

I whipped around. Carsten stood in the doorway. His eyes were dull and his gaze slid past me to the sideboard where he kept his liquor.

'I couldn't sleep,' I told him, unable to keep the tremor from my voice. 'I was looking for a book . . .'

Carsten poured himself a sherry and downed it, then retrieved another glass. He topped this to the brim and brought it over to me.

'It always helps me sleep,' he said softly. 'Drink it down and get yourself back to bed.'

The gentleness in his voice roused my courage. I sipped the sherry and swallowed the sickly syrup, then cleared my throat.

'Your trip went well, I hope?'

He eyed me over his sherry glass. 'Well enough.'

'How is my father? Did he send a note?'

'There was no time for notes. We spoke briefly about business, then I had to board the Newcastle train.'

'So, you were not long in the New England?'

'A mere few days.'

'Did you . . .' I hesitated, sensing his impatience with my interrogation, but I had waited weeks and the question was eating at me. 'Did you have an opportunity to enquire after that matter we spoke of – those killings at Lyrebird Hill?'

Carsten looked grim. 'It was so long ago, no one remembers. Nor do they care to,' he added gruffly, then his face twisted into a sneer. 'They're wild blacks, not worth my energy chasing up their accursed history. Don't ask me again.'

'But it's important to me—'

'Enough!' Carsten moved quickly to close the door. When he turned back to me, his face was pale and hard. 'Those people deserved what they got in seventy-nine. They were stealing cattle, spearing stockmen – they were a danger then, and still are today – the sooner they're wiped out, the better.'

Wiped out. I staggered back. Dear Jindera and Mee Mee, *wiped out*? Yungara, my mother; the woman to whom my father had given his heart; the clan whose blood surged through my veins . . .

Wiped out.

A darkness swept through me, rushing up from my depths, bringing with it echoes of my dream – I smelled firesmoke, felt the press and tremble of frightened bodies, heard the anguished screams of my loved ones. I swallowed, trying to seize control of myself, knowing instinctively that my life depended upon my silence. I bit back my words with such force that I tasted blood, but they burst forth anyway.

'The people steal cattle because they're hungry,' I said, clenching my fists at my sides. 'And because the stock have grazed bare the grasslands where they once hunted kangaroo. And if they spear a stockman, it's because he has killed their wives and mothers and children for crimes that are not only petty, but the fault of the white settlers to begin with.'

Carsten's handsome face was ashen with shock. He stood rigid, his sherry glass forgotten in his hand, his eyes glinting darkly.

'Your words sicken me, Brenna,' he said, his voice hushed with warning. 'I'm beginning to think your father's foolish doctrines have addled your brain. Why should you care what happens to a camp full of blacks? Your interest in them strikes me as an unhealthy obsession. Women should stay out of matters they have no capacity to understand.'

'You speak of them as if they were no more than animals.'

He dashed his sherry glass to the floor; broken shards and blood-thick sherry sprayed across the boards. 'They are savages!' he cried, and staggered towards me. 'They live like beasts and deserve no better treatment.'

There was little more than an arm's length between us; I knew he wanted to see me cringe, to shrink away, but I held my ground and squared myself against him. 'You're wrong, Carsten. They live simply, but their inner lives are complex. In many ways, they are superior to those white brutes who—'

Carsten rushed at me and slapped my face. I went to hit back, but he grabbed my arms. His breath reeked of sherry, and his eyes were glassy and bloodshot, dark with anger.

'Get one thing straight. While under my roof, you'll keep a civil tongue. You won't address me again in so loose a manner, or I'll have you horsewhipped. Do you understand?'

I struggled to free myself, my eyes narrowed on his face. 'Whip me if you dare, but if you do, I'll walk out of here and never return.'

He gripped me under the arm and dragged me to the reading table. Sweeping the scattered piles of books onto the floor, he shoved me against the rim and pressed his mouth to my ear. 'You'll stay here where you belong,' he said, digging his fingers into my flesh. 'At least, until you give me an heir.'

He released me, but when I tried to spring away, he grasped a handful of my hair and forced me face down on the table. With his free hand, he lifted my skirt and insinuated his fingers into the leg of my drawers, dragging them aside.

'Not here,' I said harshly. 'Someone will find us. I'd die of shame.'

'Shame?' Carsten hissed, unbuttoning his trousers. 'Where's the shame in pleasing your husband in his own house? I want a son, Brenna, and you're going to give me one.'

He wrenched my arm back behind me, and I had to drag my teeth across my lips not to cry out. Hot tears pricked my eyes, tears of fury and pain that dulled my sense of danger; all I wanted was to lash out, to strike at him, to hurt him – but my only weapon was my words. 'I'll give you a son,' I whispered in a voice I barely recognised. 'A wild little boy with a savage's blood in his veins.'

Carsten froze. Hauling me around to face him, he grabbed my arms and shook me until my teeth rattled.

'What rot is this?'

I wrenched backwards and fell against the table. 'The people who were murdered in that massacre in seventy-nine were *my* people, Carsten. My family. And if I bear you the son you long for, they'll be *your* family, too.'

Sweat broke out on Carsten's brow. He grew still, his fury apparently deflated. 'You're lying.'

Slowly, I shook my head, savouring his evident distress. His lips had parted, his cheeks turned to hollows, his eyes seemed sunk in his head. I drank in the sight of him; never had I felt more afraid, nor more exhilarated. To finally speak the words I'd kept imprisoned within me for so long brought fierce joy to my heart.

'It's no lie. I was born before my father married. I went to live with him and Mama after my Aboriginal mother was murdered.'

Carsten stared at me, his face ragged with shock. 'But Michael told me Florence had a baby that year. I thought . . . I thought she was—'

He shook his head, as if to clear the realisation. His face had greyed, his mouth thin as a cut. He went to turn away, but then half-turned back. Clenching his fingers, he drew back his arm, and I stiffened, thinking he planned to strike my face – but instead, his fist drove into my belly.

I buckled over, the breath gone from my lungs as I went to my knees.

Carsten stared down at me, his face twisted in a mask of hatred. 'You agreed to give me a son. And your father took my money to save his godforsaken land, no doubt laughing all the while behind my back. By God, Michael has a bloody hide . . . but he'll be sorry. All of you, you'll all be sorry you crossed me.'

He swayed on his feet as though drunk, and his eyes turned hard. 'I have to go, I can't stay here. The sight of you sickens me. I'll leave immediately,' he added quietly, almost to himself. He spun on his heel and went to the door, and I heard him mutter, 'If I ride hard I'll catch the early steamer.'

He was going? I wanted to point out that he'd only just returned, but my thoughts were suddenly jumbled.

'What will you do?' I called after him. 'Will you send me home?'

Carsten stepped into the dark hallway, then looked back. I had the sense that he was already gone, that his mind and spirit had rushed ahead, and the man staring back at me was merely a shell.

'You'll stay here,' he said thoughtfully. 'But if you're unlucky enough to give me a son – or any child – I'll have it drowned before it draws its first breath. I'd rather burn this place to the ground than leave it in the hands of a savage.'

My racing heart woke me. I rolled over in bed, thinking someone had called my name, but it was only a choir of magpies in the tree outside my window. Then I heard the thud of hoofs on the drive, and knew my husband was departing.

I sat up, and the memory of last night's encounter in the library crashed back. Carsten's face appeared in my mind, flushed and contorted, his eyes alight with fury. I touched the sore spot near my ribs, and rolled my throbbing shoulder; mostly, though, I ached with the understanding that I had made a terrible mistake.

The day was already warm, but I found myself shivering, as if my marrow had turned to ice. Getting out of bed, I dressed hurriedly in my walking skirt and sturdy outdoor boots, and pinned my hair into a loose knot at my nape. As I reached for my hat, I saw, on the mantle, the black chess piece my father had given me the day of my wedding.

Picking up the little queen, I held her in my hand, remembering Fa Fa's words.

Twenty years have passed since I lost her. In all that time, not a day goes by – not an hour, not even a minute – that I don't think of her.

'Yungara,' I whispered. My fingers closed over the carved figure, gripping her, fusing her to my skin, wishing never to let her go. I squeezed shut my eyes to stem the tears, but they came anyway, childish tears that seemed to rush up from the well-spring of sorrow that I carried inside me.

Yungara's warm skin and gentle voice and girlish laughter were not quite a memory to me; rather, they were etched into my being, an echo – not of what I'd once had, but of what I'd lost. Tucking the little queen into my pocket, I made my way down the stairs, through the parlour, and out the double doors into the garden. I needed air of the freshest, brightest variety, so rather than heading into the forest where the atmosphere was misty and damp, I took the path that led westwards to the cape.

There on the headland I stood and gazed across the bay, towards the dark waters of the strait. The air was cold and salty, and as I drank it in I lifted my arms like wings and imagined myself flying away over the water, across the sparkling blue–green waves until I came to the far shore; then over roads I flew, and towns and hillocks grazed bare by cattle. I would veer to the west and drift over the granite plateau, and down onto the western slopes until I could see the heart-shaped land that was my home. My wings would quicken me earthwards, through the treetops, and I would breathe air made peppery by the scent of bush flowers and eucalypt blossoms, and cooled by the sweet breath of the river—

'Hello there.'

Snapping from my daydream, I lowered my arms and dug my hands into my pockets, twisting around to find a man standing several feet away. He was tall and lean, sharply cut in black. The rising sun was at his back and so his face was lost in shadows, but his hair betrayed him. Today it was loose, coiling waywardly over his shoulders, creating in my mind the indelible image of a male Medusa.

I tore my hand from my coat pocket to shade my eyes the better to see him – and so dislodged the small object I'd secreted there.

Lucien swooped on it. He made as if to give it back, but when I reached out my hand to take it, he hesitated.

'A chess piece,' he marvelled, then looked at me. 'Do you play?'

'Indeed,' I managed to say.

He was carved from shadows, and his windswept silhouette took my breath away. In the dim morning light, his eyes seemed to shine. He stepped nearer, and I found myself transfixed.

'May I challenge you to a game some time?' he said, as he dropped the little queen into my outstretched hand.

'Oh, no.' My reply came out harsher than I had intended, so I felt the need to explain. 'It might be best not to draw attention to our acquaintance. It might seem . . . improper.'

Before he could reply, I turned and hurried back along the headland in the direction of the house. I was sore and shaken after last night, feeling like a child who had been thrashed for wrongdoing; the last thing I wanted was to dig myself deeper into trouble. The wind cut across my path, bending the shrubs that grew there, pressing flat the silvery grass. As I retraced my footsteps, I could sense Lucien's presence behind me.

'Mrs Whitby, do you fear a challenge?'

I ignored him.

'A wager, then?'

I stopped walking. My breath scurried in and out from the brisk pace I'd taken along the headland. I looked back. Lucien's scar was stark white against his wind-flushed cheeks, and he stood very still, every bit a character from myth – but no longer a Medusa. He made me think of a Viking standing at the edge of his distant lands, gazing across the sea, his eyes reflecting the green ocean depths as he contemplated his realm.

I narrowed my gaze. 'What sort of wager?'

He considered this, pulling his lips against his teeth in that same unconscious way my father sometimes did.

'Anything you like,' he said at last. 'For instance, a carriage ride to Wynyard.'

'I don't need to wager you for that. I only have to give my order.' I made to turn away.

He called after me. 'Information, then?'

When I looked back, he was smiling, as if to deliberately taunt me; how had he known that a wager for information would tempt me so powerfully?

'What sort of information?'

'Hmm.' He rolled his eyes skywards, as if pondering the clouds. Then he looked back at me and laughed, a raspy musical rumble that rose out of his chest and made his eyes gleam roguishly. 'I know all the gossip that goes on at the house. And I've got a strong memory.'

He was teasing me. I could see it in his eyes that he expected me to blush and declare that I was the mistress of the house and therefore well above the sins of gossip.

But my mind was suddenly awhirl. I thought of Carsten's mysterious locket and his lost love; and I thought of the darkness in his past that Adele had hinted at – the answers to which Lucien, as Carsten's trusted manservant, would surely know.

'May I ask anything?'

If his offer had been a test of my integrity, then Lucien showed no surprise at my query. 'You may ask any question at all . . . but only one.'

'And you swear to answer honestly?'

He bowed low. 'My brain is yours to pick. That is, it will be if you win. I must warn you, Mrs Whitby, that chess is a passion of mine. If we play, the likelihood of your success is slim.'

His boldness pulled me from my sour mood. I almost laughed. A thrill went through me, and suddenly the salty air was filling my lungs and the sky was brilliant blue, and Lucien was smiling into my eyes and I found myself thrilling at the prospect of stealing time alone with him.

'We'll see about that,' I said, drawing on my gloves. 'Where shall our game take place?'

He seemed to hesitate, then his words rushed out. 'I have a set of players and a board at the stables, if you'd care to join me there. My quarters are humble, but clean.'

I nodded. 'It will have to be at night, while the household sleeps. I don't fancy trying to explain myself to Quinn.'

'Midnight?'

I nodded, savouring our moment of conspiracy. The wind whispered cold around us and the salt air stung my eyes and lips, but still I could not turn away. I captured Lucien in my mind's eye, already planning my new drawing. But then, in my moment of distraction, I realised I had not asked what Lucien wagered for.

'If,' I said pointedly, 'it should pass that I lose the game, what prize will I secure for you? Perhaps one of my husband's cast-off shirtwaists, or a parcel of food from the kitchen?'

'Quinn feeds me well enough, so I've no need of food. And I have no desire for my master's cast-offs.'

'What, then?'

He trod nearer, and I saw that his breath came sharply and his cheeks had flushed a deeper pink.

'A kiss,' he said quietly. 'From you.'

As his words sank in, I began to quake. Heat shot along my spine, while my fingertips seemed suddenly made of ice. My heart beat with such eager force, that for a moment I could not breathe.

Finally I found my voice. 'We can't,' I whispered. 'If Carsten found out . . .'

He watched me steadily. 'There's nothing else I want.'

My eyes widened. There was nothing else I wanted, either. Lucien was risking his position by speaking to me this way, but there was something irresistible in the notion of making a cuckold – even for the brief duration of the kiss – of the man who valued me so little.

'We have a deal,' I said. 'Tonight at midnight, prepare to have your brains picked.'

Lucien bowed, and then without another word he turned and stalked away along the headland, his tall, black-clad figure quickly swallowed by the mist.

A cold breeze billowed from the ocean, filling the midnight garden with a freshness that made my heart want to grow wings and soar out above it. This sea air was coarse and ripe with its heavy odours of rotting weed and fish and salt, and as I ran along the pathway and through the trees towards the stables, I felt it seep beneath my skin and fill my spirit.

Lucien was waiting inside the stable doors. He stood aside for me to enter, and as I passed his gaze caught mine. I saw my own excitement reflected in the stormy green of his eyes, and I saw the blush of passion in his cheeks, as he surely saw it in mine. I knew, in that fleeting moment, we were somehow locked together, two souls woven from the same fibre and bound by fascination, neither one able to tear away without harming the other. And with Carsten between us, this new path we trod was suddenly strewn with danger.

Lucien lit a candle and led me across the straw-littered stables to a small door in the far wall. We entered a long narrow room. At one end, a curtain concealed what I guessed must be Lucien's bed. There was a ladder against one wall, and a rickety-looking shelf crammed with tattered books. At the opposite end to the makeshift bedchamber was a small table and two chairs. The table was topped by a large chequered board, upon which sat a chess set beautifully carved from pale wood. The players lacked the intricate detail of my black queen, but they were flawless in their simplicity.

'What lovely players,' I told him. 'Wherever did you get them?'

Lucien watched me in the candlelight.

'I made them,' he said dismissively. 'Would you care for a drop of tea? It's freshly brewed.'

I nodded and took my place at the table. As I stared at the carved players sitting on their polished board, I drew out my ebony wood talisman and sat her at the edge of the table.

'For luck,' I told Lucien, as he arranged an enamel pot of tea and two tin mugs carefully on the tabletop.

'You'll be needing plenty of that,' he remarked as he poured the tea, and then gestured at the game. 'Black goes first.'

I moved my central pawn, rethinking my strategy. I would clear a path for my rook, take out Lucien's queen, and corner his king.

Lucien mirrored my move, and I gained confidence. Moving my second piece into the path of a white pawn, I watched as Lucien bypassed my bait and instead positioned his pawn in front of my bishop. I collected his piece, then realised I'd fallen into a trap.

My game went badly after that. Rather than attack, I seemed to continually move in a defensive manner. When I made a gap for my knight, Lucien positioned his bishop in readiness for the conquest. When I sent my queen out, she was immediately threatened by Lucien's rook.

Lucien sat back, examining the board. At last he looked up at me and smiled, then slipped his queen in direct line with my king.

'I've won your kiss,' he said softly.

I withdrew my hands to my lap; they were suddenly damp. My heart pumped so furiously that my roaring blood deafened me. I dared to peek at Lucien.

'You're supposed to say, "checkmate".'

His eyes gleamed in the candlelight. 'Whatever you call it, you owe me a kiss.'

My tea had gone cold, but I drained the cup in a long swallow. I looked at Lucien. His hair coiled over his collar and his dark eyes watched me intently. Since our meeting in the glade, I had daydreamed of a moment where we might be alone again; I had even constructed scenarios where he drew me near and kissed me.

Yet now that my dream was reality, I quaked with a sort of delicious fear.

'Where shall I collect my prize?' Lucien wanted to know.

My limbs were suddenly unreliable, so I gestured vaguely at the table. 'Here's as good a place as any, I suppose.'

Lucien got to his feet, and helped me to mine. I stood before him, just out of reach of the candlelight. My fingers shook, and warmth was rippling through me. I waited, leaning ever so slightly towards him.

Lucien gazed at my face, as if committing every detail to memory. Then he smiled regretfully. 'I enjoyed our game, Mrs Whitby. I'm pleased you agreed to play with me; you are a worthy opponent. Your company is enough reward for me. Come on, I'll walk you back to the house.'

I had not realised, until disappointment struck, how very much I had been looking forward to his touch; to feeling him, breathing him in; having him near.

'But we had a wager.'

The candle wavered in the draught. Lucien's smile seemed sad. 'I really didn't expect you to kiss me. I'm flattered that you're prepared to, but . . .' He shrugged, and his gaze softened. 'You're so very beautiful, Mrs Whitby. And I'm an ugly brute.'

I searched his face. In the muted light, he looked angelic, a boy with hair made ragged by the wind, and a bittersweet smile that, all of a sudden, filled me with warmth.

'But a deal is a deal, Mr Fells.'

Moving nearer, I stood on my toes and reached up, gently cupping his damaged face in my hand, intending to perhaps place a dry, motherly peck on his cheek. At my touch, his eyes locked to mine and his lips parted, and I felt my inhibitions fall away, replaced by a yearning of such power that it drew me to my toes and made me lift my mouth to his; but in the instant before our lips touched, Lucien jerked away from me and back-stepped into the shadows.

'You mock me,' he breathed, and his eyes gleamed with sudden tears.

'No,' I said, moving towards him, inexplicably desolate. 'I would never—'

'Please leave.' He backed away and turned his face from the candlelight so that shadows engulfed his features.

'Lucien . . .'

Moving through the shadows, he stalked to the other end of the room, where he slipped behind the heavy curtain and into his makeshift bedchamber.

Ashamed, I stared after him. When he didn't reappear, I gathered my skirts and hurried to the door.

13

*We'd all love to travel back in time and do it differently –
avoid those mistakes we're so ashamed of, work out more,
save more money, say the right thing to that special girl or guy.
Of course, time travel is a science-fiction dream; the only
thing you can change now is your future.*
– ROB THISTLETON, *FIND YOUR WAY*

Ruby, May 2013

There should have been rain for a funeral. Grey skies, thunder. Boggy lawns and a generally dank, dreary atmosphere. But Granny H had never been conventional in life; why would she have been any different in death? The sun blazed in a perfect blue dome, and rainbow lorikeets dive-bombed the acacias, screeching and fighting over seedpods. It was a raucous day, a bright and dazzling glory of a day, and I wished that Esther could have been here to enjoy it.

In her honour I chose a fifties-style dress – deep indigo with neat collar and sleeves and a full, flattering skirt. I pondered my reflection for a while, then realised that my face didn't match my outfit. Rummaging in the bottom of my make-up bag, I found a cherry-red lipstick that I hadn't worn for ages. It was an old favourite, but it hadn't coordinated with the slimming black or charcoal hues that now dominated my wardrobe. I daubed it on, blotted on a tissue, and then stood back to admire the effect.

At nine o'clock I went onto the verandah to wait for Pete.

The ute pulled up on time, and the dogs craned over the side of the tray and wagged their tails – but I barely recognised the man who stepped out and strode towards me.

The beard was gone. He seemed a little lost without it, and his unease made him enticingly vulnerable. He had a square jaw and full mouth that, even as I stared, softened into a smile. It was a slow, sad smile, and it made the breath catch in my throat.

'Hey,' he said as he approached, and then stood at the base of the steps, looking up at me. He had combed his hair, and his face and hands were spotlessly clean. He wore an expensive-looking navy shirt, which enhanced the blueness of his eyes. The suit was dated – maybe as far back as the 1970s, which impressed me enormously; it had wide lapels and a light pinstripe, snug-fitting around his muscular arms and chest.

'You scrub up well,' I told him, unable to keep the admiration out of my voice. I could hardly believe my eyes when a faint flush of colour infused his cheeks. The dimples came out, and his teeth were white and straight behind the embarrassed smile.

I rattled Esther's car keys from my pocket. Earlier in the week, Pete had given the old Morris a jumpstart and a clean-up. He'd handed over the keys, insisting that Esther wouldn't have wanted me to be stranded out here. Today, I had decided, we would forego the dusty old Holden and travel to Esther's funeral in style.

Two hours later, we were sitting at the front of the church, an arm's length from Esther's coffin. The casket was glossy black, simply decorated with a wreath of gumnuts and red roses.

While the minister spoke about a woman who had worked tire-lessly for the environment, and had given most generously of her time to Landcare, and to WIRES, and was a benefactor of the local Indigenous organisation, my thoughts drifted to the wonderful storyteller I'd known as a child.

She had kept her door open to a pair of misfit kids, and given them the gift of stories; she had baked scones and brewed hot chocolate, and transformed the simple act of reading a book into an experience so thrilling and rousing that it had inspired endless hours of enthralment – acting out the tales, talking about them, living and dreaming them.

I had barely thought of her in the last eighteen years, but suddenly I missed her terribly. I wanted to go over to the casket and lift the lid, and see her kind face one last time. I wanted to rain tears on her and wake her up, like in the fairytale. And I wanted to tell her that I was sorry that I'd run away and forgot-ten her; sorry that the whole Jamie mess had turned me into someone I didn't want to be, someone I'd hated so much that running was the only way I could stand to be around myself.

Sorry, too, that I'd huddled in my car and taken shelter from the storm beneath my cosy picnic rug, while she lay on the cold riverbank, pounded by the downpour, her blood trick-ling into the rocks. And later, while she lay dying in the sterile whiteness of the hospital, I had stalled and dithered, listening, in my mind's ear, to Esther's younger self as she related one final story.

Pete must have sensed the tremble that overtook me then, because he reached for my hand and enclosed it in his warm fingers. But although I felt a rush of gratitude for his kindness, I found myself withdrawing, giving his hand a quick light squeeze, then sliding it out of his grasp and back into my lap.

Pete was one of the pallbearers, so when he got up to attend the coffin, I trailed behind the stream of people making their way to the cemetery at the back of the church. Afterwards, Pete found me and we lingered by the graveside until everyone was assembled, then he stepped forward and read a short verse – not from the Bible, but from Bram Stoker.

How blessed are some people, whose lives have no fears, no dreads, to whom sleep is a blessing that comes nightly, and brings nothing but sweet dreams. Well, here I am tonight, hoping for sleep, and lying like Ophelia in the play . . . I feel sleep coming already. Goodnight, everybody.

He placed the book on the coffin and said quietly, 'Thanks for everything, old girl. Sleep in peace.'

Then he returned to his place by me, and as the coffin was lowered into the ground, he shifted so that his arm pressed against mine. We stood like that, shoulder to shoulder, while the minister recited the final benediction.

But it was Pete's short reading that lingered. The beautiful words had brought to mind a very different scenario. I was sitting in Granny H's tiny cottage, cross-legged on a mat on the floor, gazing up at Granny's flushed face as she recited those very same words to us.

. . . *sleep is a blessing that comes nightly, and brings nothing but sweet dreams.*

Beside me on the mat, his arm resting comfortably against mine, sat a boy. A boy with freckles and dark unruly hair, a cheeky grin, and eyes the colour of a kingfisher's wing.

I stole a look at Pete.

He hadn't changed so very much. The face was older, craggier, carrying a few more scars and fewer freckles. The hair was longer, and the beard had, until today, finished off the job of hiding his boyish identity – but I knew him, and now that recognition had kicked in, I wondered how there had ever been a time when I *hadn't* known him.

I tugged his sleeve.

He looked at me and his eyes were wet and his face raw with grief, yet somehow he found a smile for me.

'I remember,' I told him softly. 'I remember you.'

Tears welled up out of my eyes, and I reached for his hand. He squeezed my fingers, and for a moment his strength and warmth were an anchor that held me secure in the violent deluge of emotion. Then he released me and I floundered, but only for an instant; suddenly I was in his arms, held firm, engulfed by the scent of pinewood and motor oil and Esther's handmade rosemary soap.

And all the while, in my mind, the same words, over and over. *Why had I forgotten him? Why had I ever let him go?*

Jamie was standing in the kitchen. She was red-faced, out of breath. Her hair was a windblown mess.

'What's up?' I asked.

She ignored me.

Even when she was being a snobby cow, she was still the prettiest girl I'd ever seen. Once, her prettiness had made me feel proud; now, it only made me cranky. Answering her snub with a rude face, I went over to the sink and pulled out the strainer.

Mum came in from the garden with a basket of carrots and parsnips and leafy celery. She dropped the basket onto the benchtop and began unpacking the vegetables onto the sink. The silence must have alerted her that something was wrong, because she glanced around.

'For heaven's sake, Jamie. Look at your hair! What do you girls think it is, bush week?'

I gritted my teeth. It irked me how, if I did anything wrong, it was *Ruby, Ruby, Ruby*, but if Jamie acted up, it was *You girls*. I didn't say anything, though, just filled the sink with water and grabbed the vegie brush. Cutting off the carrot fronds, I started scrubbing away the dirt.

'Well?' Mum said to Jamie. 'Spit it out.'

Jamie flopped onto a chair with a loud sigh. Always the drama queen, making sure she had everyone's attention.

'You know that foster kid at Mrs Drake's?'

My ears pricked and I glared at Jamie, feeling a rush of possessiveness. The Wolf was *my* friend, not hers. And why did she keep glancing across at me, her normally smooth brow puckered in a frown?

'What about him?' Mum wanted to know.

'He's gone.' Jamie eyed me from under her lashes. 'They sent him back to Newcastle.'

I stopped scrubbing. 'He's not gone. I saw him at school on Friday.'

'For your information,' Jamie announced loftily, 'he was a thief. He got caught stealing, and Mrs Drake sent him back to the boys' home. Good riddance, I say. He was weird.'

'Stealing?' Mum said. 'That's a shame. The teachers always speak so highly of the boy, I must say I'm surprised.' She looked at me and frowned. 'Well, if anything good comes out of this, it might be that Ruby's grades pick up.'

'His brother's a jailbird,' Jamie said, 'and his dad's a loony tunes. He's no better. Everyone at school knows that bad blood runs in his veins.'

Mum frowned. 'Jamie, that's not a nice thing to say. It's not the boy's fault his family is dysfunctional. I won't have you speaking like that.' She turned back to the sink and dithered for a moment, then opened the pantry cupboard. Subject closed.

I felt the blood drain from my head. There must have been a mistake. The Wolf wasn't a thief. He couldn't be gone. My heart began to thrash like a rabbit in a trap. I had a picture of my life before the Wolf came along – sitting by myself at lunchtime, getting picked on at school, muttering and fumbling on account of my horrible shyness.

He couldn't be gone.

Jamie looked at me and smirked, twirling her finger near her ear. 'Loony,' she mouthed.

I threw the vegie brush in the sink and ran to the door. Stuff them, I thought, rubbing my eyes with gritty fingers as I raced along the path to where I'd left my bike. Stuff them both . . . they could scrub the blasted carrots themselves.

'I knew the very minute I saw you.'

Pete and I were sitting on an embankment beside the river, lounging on a tartan picnic rug. Old Boy and Bardo were dashing about in the water below us, chasing sticks that Pete periodically threw down to them.

I toyed with one of the sticks, picking at a sliver of loose bark.

'Not the *very* minute,' I said a little shyly. 'Come on, how long did it really take?'

'Really? Let's see . . . it took all of, oh, shall we say – a nanosecond?'

'No!'

'You haven't changed *that* much.'

I grimaced. 'Still the geeky twelve-year-old, eh?'

Pete snorted. 'Roo, you were anything but geeky. A bit of a tomboy, maybe. And a temper like a cut snake.'

'So Mum always claimed.'

His smile fell away. 'I have to confess, I was smitten.'

I gave him a shove. 'Get out of it.'

'Hey, it's true.'

I shook my head in mock disbelief, but inwardly I was chuffed. The Wolf . . . smitten with *me*?

'You don't believe me,' he said with a laugh. 'But I can prove it.'

My gaze drifted down to his mouth. Oh yes, I wanted him to prove it. Right now, the sooner the better. Because all of a sudden I needed proof, craved it like a drink on a parched day, longed for it the way a moth longs for the moon.

Which was wrong, very wrong. I'd given up on love, remember? Anyway, what did I really know about Pete – that we'd been friends as kids for six months while he'd been fostered on a neighbouring farm; and that he'd been sent back to the boys' home by his foster mother for stealing? Not the strongest foundations upon which to build a romance.

But then the Wolf was smiling at me from the face of a grown man, and it was such a friendly face, with intelligent blue eyes and a gaze that somehow turned the straw of my failings into gold, and lips that quirked at the corners in that cheeky way that made me want to lean forward, press my mouth to his, and lose myself in the forbidden pleasure that awaited me there.

Wicked thoughts. Fiendish. I had to stop thinking them.

But as I sat on the velvety green grass beside the river with Pete, tickled by shadows as the casuarinas swayed overhead in the warm breeze, I could feel the draw of my desire. And despite the cautioning voice in my head, I wanted to abandon myself, maybe even go a little wild. So, when Pete got to his feet and reached for my hand, and hauled me up beside him, it took me a moment to register what he'd just said.

'You're going to prove that you were once smitten with me?' I asked incredulously.

'You bet.' He waggled his eyebrows mysteriously. 'Follow me.'

High along the rocky slopes of the Spine, formed by the junction of neighbouring boulders, was a crevice. It didn't look like much, just another shady gap between big flaky rocks. But as Pete kneeled on the ground before it and reached his hand into the cool darkness, it brought back a flash.

Granite wears away like an onion, the Wolf had once told me. *Hundreds of years of frost and fire, sunlight and rain cause the surface to expand and contract. The constant stress causes the top layers to flake away, which is why it's called—*

'Onionskin weathering,' I remarked to no one in particular.

Pete looked over his shoulder and studied me a moment, then winked. 'That old memory of yours is sharpening up. It must be all the fresh air.'

Ridiculous, how an offhand comment and a wink had the power to make me glow. But as I stood in the shadows of the tall trees, basking in the warmth that radiated off the clustered boulders, I *did* glow.

Pete dragged a long rectangular steel box from the crevice, and grappled with the lid. 'Remember this?'

I nodded. The Wolf and I had been learning about time capsules at school, and had decided to make one of our own. Granny H had given us an old army ammunitions box in which she'd once stored broad beans. The box was rat-proof, water-proof, and – though Granny H had said not to quote her on this – fire-proof. She'd also donated a TV guide, a crocheted beanie and a paper bag of homemade shortbread – only the shortbread hadn't survived long enough to make it into our capsule.

'Open it.'

Wedging the ammo tin between his feet, Pete gripped the front handle with both hands and pulled. Finally, on the third try, the lid squealed open.

Inside was a tiny rocket ship the Wolf had built out of tin and wood and coloured glass – far too good to bury, I remembered arguing, but in it went anyway, along with a photo of the puppy the Wolf had had as a kid, and a packet of Smarties. My contribution had been a book. Not just any old book, but one I'd made myself with leftover paper from one of Mum's art projects. Mum had showed me how to stitch the spine and glue the binding boards, and on the cover I had painted a picture: Granny H's face as the sun, and her hair poking out around her like rays. She was beaming down on two small sunflowers, which were supposed to be the Wolf and me, but really were just blobs with eyes. My book was full of the stories Granny H had told us – all the crazy fairytales that grew out of shape and turned into something else entirely.

Right at the bottom, we found another book.

'Here,' Pete said, passing it to me. 'Proof.'

'I don't remember this going in.'

'I snuck back later and added it. I wanted to give you something to remember me by.'

'But it was meant to be a time capsule. We were supposed to wait fifty years before we opened it.'

'Yeah, well, we've just shot that plan to hell. Still, eighteen years isn't a bad effort.' He gestured at the book I held. 'Aren't you going to look inside?'

I turned the little book over in my hands. The cover was leather, and looked really old. A loop sewn into the edge of the back cover held a slim pencil. All its pages were blank. Except one.

When I opened the flyleaf, a soft brown feather wafted out.

'Esmeralda,' I marvelled, picking it up and beaming at Pete. 'I was gutted when Mum gave her the chop. I don't think I ever really forgave her.'

'You were pretty upset.'

'You held my hand.'

'There you go. More proof.'

I blinked quickly and looked back at the book, turning to the first page. Written in the Wolf's careful handwriting – smudged with a grubby fingerprint – were two short sentences that made me feel hot and cold, happy and sad all at once.

I'll never forget you, my lovely Kangaroo.
Your friend always, the Wolf.

'You called me your "lovely kangaroo"?' I pointed out. 'That's your idea of declaring eternal love?'

Pete frowned at the wobbly inscription. 'Hmm. I'm sure I remember filling the page with soppy devotion. At least, it felt pretty momentous when I wrote it. I definitely remember spending hours mulling over what I was going to write, what words best captured the depth of my feeling.' He grinned. 'Hey, stop laughing. "Lovely" is a pretty passionate word for a twelve-year-old!'

As we joked and bantered I couldn't help stealing secret glances. Pete had brought me here to unearth a fragment of our past – a time capsule that had waited in the dark for nearly two decades for our return. His inscription touched me, but more than that I felt a surge of warmth that he had remembered.

'Why are the pages blank?'

'For your stories.'

'What stories?'

'The ones you were always writing down on scraps of paper, or the backs of envelopes, or inside the covers of your exercise books.'

I shook my head. 'I never wrote stories.'

He picked up the book I'd handmade with Granny H's face on the cover, and flipped through it.

'Yeah, you did.'

'But they weren't *my* stories. Granny made them up, I just copied them down.'

He started packing our various treasures back into the ammo box, but kept the little leather-bound book out. Tucking the feather back in the flyleaf, he handed it to me.

'Well, now you've got another blank book to fill with someone else's stories. And maybe, occasionally, you'll turn to that first page and remember the boy who was once smitten with you.'

I took the book and smiled into his eyes, intending only to offer my silent thanks; instead, I found myself lingering in his gaze, melting into that clear, impossible blue. I tried to pull back, but there was something there I needed to see. A recognition, maybe. An acknowledgement that these first warm threads of feeling were real.

'Why did you vanish out of my life?' I asked quietly. 'After they sent you back to the home. Why didn't we stay in touch?'

He considered me, his head tilted, his smile at half-mast. 'I guess I went a little off the rails, after that.'

My own smile was shaky. 'Join the club.'

Pete wedged the ammo tin back in the crevice, making sure it was hidden under a sprinkling of leaves and twigs. Then he stood up and took my hand and led me over to the edge of the stone outcrop. We gazed across the rolling hills and valleys. Stretching in all directions was a sea of treetops, interrupted here and there by islands of bare stone. Closing my eyes, I leaned against Pete's warm shoulder and tilted my face to the sun. The insides of my eyelids turned blood-red and I could see tiny arteries. In a nearby stringybark, a butcherbird sang its fluty song.

Once, I had shown the Wolf my dog scar. And he, in return for the favour, had shown me his. He was kind even back then, I realised; even as a twelve-year-old foster kid from Newcastle. He had told me about crocodiles and snakes, and shown me the marks they had made; but now, in hindsight, I understood.

He'd been a gentle boy – with a wild streak, but what boy didn't? And yet someone had, judging by the scars on his legs and abdomen and arms, hurt him badly as a child. Was that why he now hid himself away in the bush with his dogs, living as far from other humans – Esther excluded – as possible?

I floated for a while, trying not to think about the world that lay beyond Lyrebird Hill – not my little cottage on the coast, not my bookshop, not even Earle who was probably starting to wonder where I was. Most of all, I tried not to think about Rob; whether he missed me, or whether he was finding comfort in the arms of a woman who wore a doll-sized black bra. He seemed suddenly far away, both in distance and in my thoughts.

Which suited me just fine.

Pete unlinked his fingers from mine, and we turned and walked back along the trail, leaving behind us the crevice, and the time capsule hidden in its darkness. Maybe only fifteen minutes – half an hour, at most – had gone by since we'd arrived at the Spine, but it felt as though years had whizzed past.

Maybe even a lifetime.

After dinner, Pete grabbed a torch and we walked up the dark hillside into the trees. The moon was full and low on the horizon, illuminating the bush into a silvery sort of daylight. We navigated our way between boulders and prickly stands of tea-tree, until we reached a bare shoulder of stone. For a while we stood on the rock plateau and gazed at the trees below.

'We used to meet up here,' Pete said. 'Mostly at midnight, which was pretty exciting. At least, it was for a twelve-year-old from the city.' He sprang onto a boulder, then turned back and reached for my hand, hauling me up beside him.

'It feels weird remembering,' I remarked, gazing out across the moonlit hills.

'Not too overwhelming, I hope?'

'Hmm. At first it's like having a dream come back, but then rather than fading like a normal dream, it becomes more concrete in my mind as time goes on. It takes some adjusting, but after a while it gets worn in, and I can't see how it was never part of me.'

'The memories have always been part of you. Just locked away out of sight.'

'I wonder what else is in here.'

Pete shifted closer and bumped his shoulder against mine. 'Your brain had good reason for blocking bits out. You'll remember in your own good time.'

The warmth of his arm against mine was comforting, but his words niggled. For me, there *was* a rush. Nothing tangible, no reason to think that time was running out – rather, a feeling that past and present were converging, and that if I didn't seize control soon, by remembering, then it'd be lost.

Somewhere below us the river flowed through the darkness. I could hear the rapids surging over the rocks, and the muted roar filled me with a strange longing. Drinking in the cool air, I tried to empty my mind, tried to make room for just one more memory to rush in. I waited, only to discover that my senses were too full of the man standing next to me – his solid warmth, his nearness. We'd once been friends, I felt it strongly; yet I couldn't help wondering why my brain had chosen to block *him* out.

'What's this amazing thing you said you wanted to show me?' I asked, breaking contact and moving away.

Pete pointed up the hillside. 'There's a cave up there. Are you game?'

'Of course.'

As we walked uphill, the slope grew steep. Huge crouching rock formations pushed up between the trees, freckled with pale circles of lichen the size of dinner plates which glowed faintly in the moonlight. The tall granite outcrop seemed to loom larger until it blocked out part of the sky. Nearing it, I noticed a black fissure of shadow between two huge boulders.

Pete ducked into the gap, and I followed him into the cave, which was long and narrow, similar in size to the interior of a bus. Pete flicked on his torch, and shadows jumped around the beam. At the far end of the cave, at eye level, we found a shelf of rock from which jutted a tangled mess of sticks. It was some kind of nest. The outer twigs were large and loosely woven together, becoming progressively smaller towards the centre. The hollow core of the nest was lined with intricately woven thin twigs and root fibres.

'Watch this,' Pete said, then moved the torch beneath the nest so that its beam shone upwards through the knot of sticks. Prickly shadows leaped across the cave walls. The torch moved slowly, and bizarre shapes danced and shrank around us, intricate cross-hatchings of shadow and coin-like spots of light burst and spread, then contracted like a constellation of spider legs.

'How beautiful,' I breathed. 'What sort of nest is it?'

'I'm not sure, but I like to think it was built by a lyrebird.'

'I thought lyrebirds only inhabited rainforest areas.'

'Mostly they do, although the Superb Lyrebird was very common all up and down the eastern mainland of Australia – even this far west, believe it or not. Sadly, there haven't been any sightings on this side of the range for more than fifty years. Which makes me think that this can't be a lyrebird's nest. It's not recent, but I don't think even a nest as well constructed as this one would withstand the elements for fifty years.'

'Why aren't lyrebirds seen out here anymore?'

'You know they're clever mimics?'

'Yeah. They can imitate other birds, barking dogs, human voices, car engines. Even chainsaws, I've heard.'

Pete switched off the torch and plunged us into silvery gloom. 'A lyrebird imitates the sounds it hears most often. And if that sound is a chainsaw, then it means someone in the vicinity is cutting down trees. The fewer trees there are, the fewer places the birds have to nest. And if they can't nest, or forage or hunt, they can't survive.'

'Jamie and I saw one once. At least, we thought we did. It was just a glimpse, a dark shape dashing through the trees down beside the river. At first I thought it was an escapee from the chook pen, but it was bigger than a chook and had long legs and a trailing tail. Jamie insisted it was a lyrebird.'

Pete shifted beside me. 'It's unlikely, but it might have been a female. They're drabber than the male, and they don't have the lyre-shaped tail feathers. That's the great thing about this property – it's big enough to provide a variety of habitats. But places like this are getting rare. That's why Esther's work here is so valuable. She was passionate about preserving habitat, as well as establishing the right environment to generate more.'

A soft beam of moonlight pushed through an overhead crevice and fell into our darkness. It turned the nest into a woven mass of shadows – but rather than splashing about the cave walls as they had done under Pete's torchlight, the shapes pulled tight, clustering among themselves, secretive and dark.

Pete was studying the nest, apparently lost in his thoughts.

I shifted nearer. In the stillness, I could feel warmth radiating from him. Shadows carved across his face, and I felt compelled to reach out and playfully tug a lock of his wayward hair or tickle my fingertips down the length of his arm. I thought about my reclaimed memories of us as kids: sitting in the shade of the shearing shed, or listening to Granny's fairytales. Our time together had been magical, dreamlike; tonight, here in the dark stillness of the little cave, some of that magic trickled back.

'So, if it's not a lyrebird nest,' I mused aloud, 'then what is it?'

Pete looked at me. 'I was hoping *you* might know.'

'Me?' I snorted. 'Yeah, right. I can just see the headlines. *City-girl morphs into David Attenborough overnight and identifies a new species of* . . . What did you say it was?'

Pete laughed, or rather, did this husky coughing thing that made me blink and then break into a fit of giggles. He leaned nearer, and nudged me gently with his shoulder.

'It's good to hear you laugh,' he said. 'I've missed it.' Then he took my hand and led me out of the cave, into the cool night air.

It felt good to be outside at night, somehow forbidden, the way it had felt as a kid. I had a vague recall of sneaking out my window and running through the dark bush with the Wolf.

Free and wild, as if the conventions that governed the rest of the world didn't reach this far; as if the moonlit landscape was part of a secret realm that belonged only to us. Pete's hand was warm, his skin calloused and his grip reassuringly firm. I wanted to lean against him, savour this enchanted moment for as long as possible.

So, when I saw we were heading back down the hill in the direction of the farmhouse, I couldn't stem a twinge of disappointment.

I wasn't ready to go back. Not yet.

I stopped walking. Leaning back against a tree, I shut my eyes and let my thoughts slide backwards into the past. I saw a creature springing from the shadows behind the shearing shed, a wolf-like animal on its hind legs with a shaggy face and fangs and a mane of windswept hair. I saw it grabbing my twelve-year-old self, clutching me against its body as I wriggled around to face it. A scream bubbled out of me as I looked into its fierce black eyes – but then the eyes turned golden and then somehow they were blue. The fangs withdrew and the hair receded from the creature's face. A boy appeared, and he was near, and then nearer still. Without meaning to, we bent our heads together and our lips touched, so briefly and so sweetly, it had taken a while – a day or two, at least – for me to look back without blushing and understand that we had kissed.

Pete had doubled back and now stood in front of me.

'I remember,' I whispered, and reached for him, gathering handfuls of his shirt and drawing him closer. 'I remember what you meant to me.'

He didn't smile, but the moonlight gleamed in his eyes and I thought I saw pleasure there. Sliding his hand under my hair, he cradled the back of my head and melted against me. Then his lips were on mine, firm and gentle all at once, his closeness intoxicating. Smoothing my hands across his shoulders, savouring the hard muscles of his back, I slid my fingers into the thick terrain of his hair and pressed fiercely against him. The silver moonlight transformed him into a creature of myth – part-flesh, part-dream. The thrill of our childhood escapades, and the strength of our young friendship acted as a magnet, drawing me inexorably to him. I became a river of desire, flowing around and through him. For a stolen handful of minutes there was no separation between us, no past or present, no other world than the one of darkness and starlight that we now inhabited.

'I don't mind that you forgot me,' he murmured, his lips hot on my skin. 'I never once stopped thinking about you.'

His words reached through the haze and jolted me back to reality. Another man's face came clearly and sharply into focus: Rob. And although Rob and I were finished, my heart was still bruised by the impact of his betrayal.

Pulling back, I untangled myself from Pete's arms and stepped away.

'I'm sorry,' I said huskily. 'It's not great timing for me.'

Pete searched my face. His lips looked bruised, and I felt a rush of possessive pleasure. I wasn't sorry I'd kissed him. I'd simply fallen under a spell of nostalgia for the boy I'd been so fond of as a kid. We'd been close, and the shock of remembering had momentarily skewed the boundaries.

'Hey, it's okay.' Pete attempted a smile. 'Still friends, right?'

'Right.'

But as we straightened our clothes and gathered ourselves back into a semblance of normalcy, I sensed that a shift had occurred. A line had been crossed, a portal opened; a different type of dream had been recalled and was now fast becoming concrete. A dream from which I desperately needed to wake.

We walked back down the slope in silence, the magic leaking out of us and draining away into the thin granite soil. All around us, eyes watched from the darkness: owls, possums, antechinus, wallabies, insects. The promise of frost chilled the air as we descended into the valley, and I shivered. My memory might well have been full of gaps, and big chunks of my childhood were gone forever, but after tonight one thing was certain: the kiss I'd shared with Pete in the shadows of that dark, silver-drenched hillside was now scored indelibly into my soul, and there was nothing – no injury, no passage of time, no amount of forgetting – that was strong enough to break me from its spell.

14

Brenna, June 1898

For the next two days my gloom deepened. Whenever I shut my eyes, I saw Lucien's face, stricken by my touch, his eyes dark with shock, and I cursed the recklessness that had compelled me to act unthinkingly.

My memories of the woman I had known all my life as Mama were as insubstantial as wisps of dream. When I cast back in time to seek her, she lay on her bed in her darkened room, wrapped in a shawl, smelling of camphor and bitter herbs. Only one memory stood out from the others. She was in the kitchen, showing a teenaged Millie how to stuff a chicken. I had been getting under their feet, teasing one of the kitchen skinks with a twig, blocking its escape for my childish amusement.

Mama stopped her lesson to kneel beside me.

Why are you tormenting that little creature? she'd asked in her kind voice, gathering me to her. *Don't you know it has feelings just as we do? It might be trying to return to its little family, and your game is waylaying it. Have you forgotten that all of us – Fa Fa and Aunt Ida and you and me and Millie are under God's eye? And that God also loves his little ones – his lizards and possums and finches and bush mice? Have a heart, my cherub . . . let it go.*

From that moment on, I cherished every living thing – not just the creatures, but the trees and gumnuts and flowers, and even the solid unmoving stone. Mama's quiet words wove a spell on my soul, and I began to study my bush surrounds with new eyes. I befriended the skinks, and got to know their quirky traits; the beetles and cicadas and colonies of brown ants drew me into their busy worlds. I started noticing orchids and the red balls of glistening sap that trickled from the apple gums. My awe had grown until it had inspired me to capture my new friends in ink and paint.

And yet, last night, I'd forgotten myself. I had overstepped the line of propriety. Lucien was not a wild creature to be toyed with; he was a young man with a full undercurrent of passions and fears and dreams. And I was a married woman.

I burned with shame.

But I could not find the will to stay away.

The following midnight I knocked softly on the door at the back of the stables. Shifting from foot to foot, I waited, fearing that Lucien was already deep asleep and deaf to my presence. But finally I heard a shuffle and Lucien opened the door. He was dishevelled, his face rumpled and sleepy, his hair a wild mane about his shoulders.

'Are you up for a challenge?' I said, pushing past him into the candlelit gloom of his chamber. 'I feel a lucky streak tonight, but in the unlikely event that you win, I've brought cake.'

I crossed to the table. Rather than the fine chess pieces I'd been expecting, I found a book. It was old and tattered, the pages gaping away from their threadbare binding. It appeared to be a ledger of sorts, and when I bent to read a section, my suspicions were confirmed.

'Why are you looking over a ledger?' I asked. 'It must be fifty years old. What use is it to you?'

Lucien cleared the book and began to set out his carved chess pieces.

'I've got to read something.'

'But a ledger?'

He shrugged. 'Books are a rare commodity. At least, they are for me. Besides, the old ledgers have their own fascination. For instance, did you know that in 1835, the garden produced fourteen barrels of white turnips? And that in 1847 the house-keeper placed an order for ladies' handkerchiefs from Launceston, but they never arrived? I often ponder who acquired those fine lawn hankies, and what became of them. Perhaps they were used to impress the wife of a lowly dockworker?'

My brow shot up. 'Or perhaps a bushranger?'

Lucien did not quite smile, but I saw the beginnings of forgiveness in his sea-green eyes. The kettle whistled softly and he hurried over to make the tea.

I set my bundle of cake on the edge of the table and took my seat, revising the tactics I'd planned for tonight's game. Since I had lost our previous game, I would use my apparent weakness to dupe my opponent; I would open with a folly, then strike hard and fast when he least expected.

My instinct proved correct; within the half-hour, I had cornered his king and declared a checkmate.

He looked at me. 'What would you like to know?'

I sat back in my chair, savouring my win. A little of my old self trickled back, and I allowed myself to smile into my teacup. At last I would uncover the secret of my husband's silver locket, and perhaps even learn the identity of the woman whose portrait I felt certain resided within.

But the question that sprang readily to my lips was very different to the one I had rehearsed, and it surprised us both.

'Do you remember your mother?'

Lucien's eyes went to saucers. I bit my tongue and winced. There, I'd done it again; allowed my recklessness to have the upper hand and lead me straight into trouble.

Lucien sat back in his chair and looked at me. 'You could ask anything, anything at all – and you want to know about my mother?'

I nodded.

Lucien scratched his head. 'I haven't thought of her in years.'

'But you remember her?'

'Yes.'

'What was she like?'

'Why do you want to know?'

I sighed. 'Our wager was that I could ask anything. I don't know exactly why I asked. Perhaps because I've been thinking about my own mother a lot lately.'

Lucien swept his hand across the tabletop and collected the fallen chess players. Then, with slow deliberation, he began to position them on their squares.

'Hair like polished copper.' He nudged the rook into place. 'Big square hands like a man, only a gentle touch.' The bishop found its spot, then the knight. 'A pair of threadbare slippers scuffing across the kitchen floor. Red lips clamped around a pipe stem. She always smelled of smoke and rum and sweat.' The king took up residence on his central square, and then finally the queen beside him. 'She taught me to read.'

'What happened to her?'

'I don't know. I remember getting home in the dark, the house in shambles. She was gone. Everything she owned was still there, but my mother was gone.'

'What did you do?'

'I found employment with a man who bred horses.'

I hesitated, then asked, 'Is he the one who scarred you?'

A startled pair of eyes lifted momentarily from the board to meet mine. Lucien nodded.

I barely dared to breathe, so when the word left me it was on a whisper. 'Why?'

Lucien took a deep breath and shut his eyes. 'One of the foals was born with a gammy leg. It always struggled to stand up, which riled the master. He took to it with a stick, and flogged it half to death. I grabbed the stick and gave him a taste of his own treatment. He saw that I got a few hundred lashes for my trouble, and promised that I would live to regret what I'd done to him. But he was wrong. That old horsewhip was my salvation. After it had done its job on me, Mr Whitby found me, and I came to live here. I get a feed and a warm bed, and best of all I get left alone.'

He rubbed the backs of his hands, as if only now seeing the crisscross of scars. Discomfort radiated from him, but he didn't shrink away as he had before. Looking up suddenly, he asked, 'Is your mama still alive?'

'No.'

'What do you remember of her?'

It was my turn to slump back in my chair. What *did* I remember? Sadly, too little. Yet I clung to those vague glimpses, and although they may have been more dream than memory, they were all I had. Wallaby fur, the tremble of warm bodies pressing close, the smell of smoke and the echo of screams. And my other mother in her bed, smelling of phosphorus tonic and unwashed hair.

'Not much,' I admitted with an ache in my heart, and it was the truth for both of my mothers. 'I was young when she died.'

Silence set up camp between us, but it was no longer uncomfortable; rather, the silence seemed to draw us nearer to one another, as if to a warm blaze on a winter night.

'Another game?' Lucien suggested.

The board was set up, so I agreed. I felt moody and unable to concentrate, so when – fifteen minutes later – Lucien declared checkmate, I wasn't surprised.

He reached for the cake I'd brought, but I got to my feet and rounded the table. Collecting a strand of Lucien's hair between my fingers, I tugged it playfully.

'The cake is payment for your last win,' I told him. 'This is tonight's prize.'

Bending to him, I placed my mouth on his. His lips met mine with hesitation, but when I pressed nearer and slid my hand onto his chest so that I might lean with more force upon him and pin him beneath me, he moaned softly and lifted his scarred hand to my face, drawing me nearer still.

I had expected to thrill a little at the revenge I was exacting upon my husband, so I was unprepared for my response to Lucien's touch. When his mouth began to move hungrily on mine, my nerve endings burst into flame, my body filled with light and longing. I seemed to fall from a great height, and then somehow I was in his lap, enclosed in his arms.

Breathless, I withdrew my lips but stayed close. We searched each other's eyes. I felt transfixed by his storm-coloured gaze, and by the face that was no longer ruined by its terrible scar but, rather, all the more beautiful for it. The candle crackled, our breathing steadied. Then, the soft whinny of a horse in the adjoining stable broke the spell. I moved away and got to my feet, feeling the chill of his absence close around me.

'Tomorrow night, then?' I whispered.

Lucien simply nodded.

He saw me to the door. We mumbled hurried goodbyes, and I swept away along the moonlit path towards the house. When I reached the verandah, I looked back. I couldn't see him, but there in the dark landscape of the garden, through the open stable doorway, I saw the faint fluttering candlelight and knew that he watched me still.

Adele had heavy eyes at breakfast. Her face was puffy and her cheeks blotched, but she chatted gaily about our plans for the day.

'Why don't we ask Quinn to pack us a picnic lunch and we could walk to the headland and spend the morning in the cove collecting shells?'

'That sounds lovely.'

'Or, if you'd prefer, we could take the carriage into Wynyard and watch the ships.'

'That sounds good, too.'

'Then again, Quinn mentioned there's a chance of rain this afternoon. Perhaps we should barricade ourselves in the library and pore through those botanical books you love so much?'

'Indeed, Adele, I shall be most content to spend the day with you regardless of our activity.'

She smiled at that, but then, as breakfast wore on, she began to wilt. She fell quiet and picked at her food, chasing the same crust around the plate with her fork.

'Are you well?' I asked at length, not wishing to pry but unable to ignore the lengthy bouts of ill health she seemed to be suffering.

'You are so kind to me. I never thanked you for . . . well, for assisting me when I wandered out that night. I am grateful to you, and it pained me to ask that you not tell Carsten. I don't like asking you to keep secrets from him.'

There were already many secrets I was keeping from my husband, dangerous secrets. Yet the one I should have kept closest to my chest – the truth of my link to Jindera's clan – had been spilled. I looked at the kind, sweet woman sitting opposite. I would be more careful with her secrets. I thought of the graveyard and its sad lure for her. We had never spoken of her lost child, but her silence, and her sleepwalking, confirmed the depth of her pain.

'Oh, Adele,' I said gently. 'You're not *forcing* me. I'm sure my husband has enough to worry about, without adding your night-time forays to his list. Besides, Aunt Ida used to say that if a man can't fix something, he'd rather not know about it.'

I had intended to lighten the mood between us, but Adele looked at me steadily.

'Lucien has always been kind, too.'

I shoved my plate away, dipping my head to hide the sudden blush that warmed my cheeks. 'I've got an idea about our day. Do you think Quinn has any knitting needles in her possession?'

Adele brightened, her eyes widening in curiosity. 'Knitting needles? Of course, she has an entire trunk full of needles and hooks and wool scraps. Why do you ask?'

'Winter is already upon us, but we still have time to knit ourselves a pair of decent shawls.'

Adele looked incredulous. 'Knit?'

Scraping back my chair, I got to my feet and went to the kitchen door. Calling to Quinn, I explained what I wanted and she bustled away upstairs to oblige. Ten minutes later she was back with a large cloth-wrapped bundle, and her customary warning.

'There you go, Mrs W. That should keep you and Miss Adele busy for the next fortnight or so. But if you knit yourselves into a corner, don't expect me to come and dig you out.'

We retired to the library, and I bade Adele remove her lacy shawl so we could scrutinise its stitchery. The delicate snowflake pattern had been achieved with a lace hook and finely spun silk fibre; we would not get the same effect from scrap wool, but the attempt would certainly provide a distraction.

'Brenna, dear?'

'Yes?'

'Why would I want to make my own shawl, when I can send Quinn into Launceston to buy one?'

'Because it's fun!' I said, laughing, and settled myself beside her, digging in Quinn's bag for the skeins of wool.

By early afternoon Adele had succeeded in crafting what looked like an elaborate knot. The soft red wool she'd chosen was fluffed and ragged from constant unpicking, and huge loose strands wavered delicately on the draught that ventured under the French doors. Adele tilted her head this way and that, then held up her handiwork, beaming.

'You're right, dear Brenna. This is certainly a pleasing way to spend the day. Now, tell me again about Aunt Ida's tame cockatoo, and how she taught it to speak.'

'Actually, Adele, I was hoping you might tell me something.'

'Of course, what would you like to know?'

'I fear it might be a bit indelicate of me to ask.'

She looked at me and smiled. 'Please ask. We are friends, are we not? And sisters.'

I halted my knitting, and picked absently at a loose tail of wool. I was slowly coming to know Lucien, but rather than quench my curiosity about him, the glimpses he gave me of his private life only made me thirst for more. But the topic of his past clearly caused him discomfort, and I was loath to repeat the blunder I'd made that first night with him.

I hesitated, choosing my next words with care. 'My husband's groomsman is badly scarred. He seems a gentle sort of man, not prone to fights or violent behaviour.' *Unlike his master*, I added privately to myself, then said, 'He told me he was beaten by his previous employer. Do you know much else about him?'

Adele set aside her knitting and shifted in her chair to face me. Glancing to the open doorway, she said in a low voice, 'Carsten arrived home with him about eight years ago; Lucien must have been eleven or twelve. As you said, he had been flogged brutally and left to die. If it hadn't been for Quinn's vigil at his bedside, and her expertise with a needle and thread and comfrey poultices, Lucien would most certainly have died.

'He didn't speak to anyone for nearly a year. He wouldn't even look at me or Quinn for ever so long. When he finally found it in himself to trust us enough, he declared that his name was Lucien Fells, and that he would like to live in the stables and look after the horses. And since that day, that's exactly what he's done.'

'Do you know of his family?'

'I'm not entirely certain there ever *was* a family, Brenna. If you'd seen the state of the boy when he arrived – not just the horrific injuries he sustained from the flogging, but his hair and eyes, his fingernails, his feet – you'd think he'd spent his young life in a pen with the pigs. Or, out there in the bush with the wild dogs and wallabies.'

I picked up my knitting, but my fingers were clumsy. Adele's account had shaken me. I did not pity Lucien for the rough life he had endured; rather, I felt my admiration for him deepen. Despite his hardships, I was certain he did not bear any malice for the man who had mistreated him. Lucien was blessed by a quality of peacefulness; he loved the simplicity of his life among the horses, and he loved the hard physical work of a life spent mostly outdoors. Instead of surrendering to bitterness, as so many would have done in his circumstances, he continued to believe in kindness, and truth, and love.

Most of all, love.

Adele drifted to another topic, and as I sat in the quiet room, struggling with my needles and wool, smiling and nodding and engaging in conversation, my secret heart flew through the window, growing wings in the cool air, speeding through the trees to the warm haven of the stables . . . and to the man who had suffered so much, and yet still believed in love.

At the end of the following week, I rapped softly on the stable door. It opened immediately, as though Lucien had been expecting me, which of course he had. Our wagers had become – at least while Carsten was away – a delicious habit that, with the chime of midnight passing, always drew me to the candlelit barn.

'I found these,' Lucien said by way of a greeting, dipping into his shirt pocket, drawing forth a crushed bouquet of green leaves. 'They're not in flower yet, but they smell good. They were growing near your little glade. When I saw them, I immediately thought of·you, which, I confess, is not unusual these days.'

'Yellow-buttons,' I said wonderingly, taking the leaves from his fingers and holding them against my nose, eagerly drinking their perfume. 'How did you know?'

Lucien looked puzzled. 'Know what?'

'That they grow at Lyrebird Hill. And that after the rain, or on a cold starry night, the air gets this wonderful scent about it, you just want to keep breathing deeper and deeper. Then the scent fades and you forget about it, but some time later when you least expect it, your nostrils flare and there it is again, all at once sweet and sharp and spicy and you breathe and breathe and wish with all your heart that it would never end. And now here it is . . . so far from home.'

Lucien was gazing at me with such tenderness that my breath caught. He captured my fingers and crushed them against his lips.

'I'd like to see your home one day,' he said quietly.

A look passed between us. He had spoken forbidden words, but my heart thrilled to hear them; I knew our secret meetings were wrong, but how could I deny the way I felt? Reaching up, I twined my fingers around a lock of Lucien's fire-gold hair, and drew him to me. Our kiss was strong and sweet, and binding; and it made me ache for what I knew I could never truly have.

One evening a week later, we sat on the floor in Adele's room by candlelight in front of a carved oak dressing table, our skirts billowing around us. Adele opened the deep bottom drawer, in which piles of infants clothes were neatly folded. Her usually pale face was flushed pink, and the infusion of colour made her eyes gleam. She leaned nearer, as if to impart a secret.

'Carsten insisted I get rid of them, but I couldn't.' She glanced at me warily, but I smiled encouragement. Carefully, she lifted out a tiny crocheted bonnet and matching dress. 'Aren't they precious?'

I took the delicate items from her fingers and examined the intricate lacework. 'They're lovely, Adele.'

'Quinn made them for me, the clever old thing. She made this, too.' She passed me a baby's knitted blanket of lacy, pale blue wool. 'You must think me sentimental for hanging on to them for so long, and I wouldn't blame you.'

'I think no such thing, Adele. It would have been a crime to throw out such exquisite little treasures. Besides, they are your link to happier times. It must have been hard for you when your fiancé died. Did you never have the opportunity to remarry?'

Adele smiled sadly. 'Malcolm was such a kind-hearted man, he would have made a wonderful husband and father. When he was taken from me – just a few weeks before our wedding day – I resolved never to love again.' She pulled more tiny garments and comforters from the drawer. 'My brother is very good to me, you know. Whatever trinket or bauble takes my fancy, whatever treasure or luxury my heart desires, I can send Quinn to acquire for me in Wynyard or Launceston, or order in from overseas. Fine soap, kid gloves, satin slippers, silk dresses, damask underthings. Face paint and powder, Irish linen for my bed, lace shawls from Europe.' She hung her head and smiled down at her hands. 'Anything I want is mine for the asking, Brenna, except the one thing I truly wish for.'

'What?' I barely whispered. 'What is it you wish for?'

'A child of my own. A little son or daughter to reach their chubby arms around my neck and kiss my cheek with their cherub lips. Alas, for me that day will never come. But it will for you, Brenna, dear. Which is why I want you to have these little clothes. When you have your own baby, you'll be glad of them. They're a wee bit outdated, but they're warm and clean and so very pretty.'

I grabbed her hand, unable to stop my eyes welling. 'Oh, Adele, they are simply lovely. I'd be honoured to have them, but only if you can bear to part with them?'

She nodded and quickly began pulling out more dainty clothes until the drawer was bare. When I noticed the tremble in her fingers, I reached for her hands and grasped them gently in mine.

'He wore them, didn't he? Your little boy.'

Adele searched my face, a worried frown wrinkling her forehead. 'You found the grave.'

'I didn't mean to pry, Adele. I only wanted to know where you went, those nights you walked in your sleep. You seemed so sad, and I thought there might be some way for me to help.'

Adele bit her lip, regarding me solemnly. 'Do you hate me, Brenna? Do you think me wicked?'

Impulsively, I brought her hand to my lips and kissed her knuckles. 'Of course not, silly. When I understood why you were so troubled, and what it was that drew you from the house and into the garden on your restless nights, I couldn't help but love you more. If you can bear to speak of him, Adele, I will gladly listen. There is no judgement between friends.'

Tears spilled over her lashes, glistening diamonds on her perfect skin. She squeezed my hands, then drew a hanky from her sleeve and dabbed her eyes. Tucking it away again, she began to fold the little outfits into a neat pile.

'Soon after Malcolm died, I found myself pregnant. Carsten and Mrs Quinn were the only ones who knew. My little boy lived for three and a half wonderful years. Then, one frosty morning in July, I went into the nursery and found the window wide open. The room was icy. Quinn swore that the window had been shut when she'd looked in upon him the night before. The only explanation I could think of was that I had wandered into the nursery in my sleep, and flung it open myself. My poor little

Thomas. I gathered him up and held him against my warmth, but he was cold and unmoving. A few days later, he was sleeping in the ground.'

'Oh, Adele.'

We sat in the stillness, adding our collective silence to the room's tomblike quietude. Then, somewhere downstairs a door slammed. Boots echoed on the floor below, then thudded up the stairs and along the hall towards Adele's bedroom.

'Brenna!' a man bellowed.

Adele jumped to her feet, scattering a snowfall of small garments about her. 'It's Carsten,' she whispered, grabbing up the knitted blanket we had been admiring and cramming it into the drawer. 'He's back early. Quickly, he mustn't see them.'

Hurriedly we collected the baby's clothes and shoved them into the drawer, jamming it shut just as the door burst open.

Carsten stood in the doorway, glowering. He pointed at me and yelled, 'Where is it? I want it back.'

I stared, dumbfounded.

Lucien appeared in the hall behind Carsten; his face was white, the scar stark in the flickering candlelight. Had he broken our pact of silence? Had he confessed to Carsten about our midnight chess games – or worse, our stolen kisses? Lucien must have anticipated my thoughts, because he shook his head.

'Well?' Carsten strode into the room and gripped me by the arm, shaking me so hard my teeth clattered. 'Where is it?'

'Where's *what*?'

Adele was beside me. 'Let her go, Carsten.'

'Stay out of this, Adele.'

'Please, Carsten, there's no need to shout. Whatever you think she's done, for heaven's sake hold your temper and speak like an adult.'

Carsten growled in fury. 'I'll speak to my thieving wife however I please.' Elbowing Adele aside, he dragged me through the door and along the hall to my room. Quinn had joined us, alerted by the fracas; her face was stiff with shock and her eyes kept darting protectively to Adele.

Again I tried to tear free of Carsten's grasp, but I only succeeded in bruising my wrist, and earning myself another severe shaking.

'I want her room searched,' Carsten told Lucien. Looking back at me, he snarled. 'And if I find it in your possession, God help me, Brenna, I'll have you horsewhipped.'

'I don't know what you're talking about,' I said. 'Let me go, you're hurting me.'

'Consider it a taste of what's to come, you treacherous bitch.'

Adele grabbed her brother's free arm and tried to hinder his progress down the hall. 'What have you lost, Carsten?'

Shaking her off, he barged into my bedroom. Thrusting me ahead of him, he towered over me, his face twisting, his eyes – the same intense eyes I'd once sighed over – fixed on me. I felt his hatred blaze out of him like fire.

'I've lost the only thing that matters,' he said rasped. 'You stole it away because you couldn't bear the truth of what it contained. But you'll be sorry. More sorry than you've ever been in your life.'

Carsten then turned and instructed Lucien to search my belongings.

'A silver locket on a fob chain,' he explained. 'Embossed on the face with a lyrebird tail. It's one of a kind, and of great personal value.'

Adele stood back and frowned at her brother. 'Could you have lost it on your travels, Carsten? That makes the most sense. You probably took it off and left it somewhere.'

Carsten glared at me. 'Brenna took it before I left. I saw her eyeing it, and one night I caught her trying to steal it. No indeed, my wife took it to spite me, I have no doubt of it.'

I glared back at him, my nerves alight with loathing. How could I forget that night? I'd been intrigued by the one object my husband appeared to treasure above all others, and had merely wanted to observe it at close range. But Carsten's vicious response to my prying had left me sore and bruised, and I had come to hate the sight of the locket – not only for being a reminder of that night, but because I knew it contained the portrait of my husband's lost love.

'I only wanted to know why you looked at it so frequently,' I told him through my teeth. 'But I didn't steal it, Carsten, I swear on my life. After that night I had no desire to touch it.'

Carsten ignored me. 'Lucien, go through everything.'

Lucien turned to me. His face was pale, his eyes – the dark hue of stormy waves at sea – observed me warily.

'Would you mind, Mrs Whitby?'

'It's not her choice,' Carsten barked. 'Just do as I instructed, man.'

Too angry for words, I turned my back on them all and went to the window. I tried to look down into the dark garden, but all I could see was Lucien's reflection in the glass, standing at my chest of drawers, illuminated by candlelight.

Out came my jackets and shawls, kid gloves, and dresses. Two drawers down were my underclothes, my blouses, my nightgowns and stockings. Right at the bottom he found my shameful secret – the collection of patched cotton bloomers and threadbare shirts and stockings darned at the toe and heel; all the old clothes I had brought with me from home and been unable to relinquish to the rag basket.

Carsten stood hawklike, his keen eyes missing nothing. When he was satisfied that his treasure was not concealed in my clothing, he pointed to my bed.

'Drag the mattress off and check it,' he instructed. 'I wouldn't put it past her to have buried it in the stuffing.'

Lucien did as he was bid, although from his demeanour it was clear he wasn't happy about it. But as the mattress was hauled from the bed's frame, Carsten pointed to the travelling trunk shoved into the shadows beneath.

'What's that?'

Before I could utter a protest, he had directed Lucien to bring the trunk out into the light and unlatch it.

If I had felt exposed when my underthings were made public, then the sight of Lucien reaching into my trunk made me want to shrivel and die. With a cry I made to rush over, intending to shut the lid and keep him from seeing the trunk's contents – but Quinn grabbed my arms and wrenched me away.

'Steady now, Mrs W. Mr Whitby just wants a look-see.'

Lucien appeared miserable as he withdrew the flat parcel from the bottom of the trunk. He might have recognised it as the one he had given me all those weeks ago, because his face paled. But the sheets of paper wrapped within were vastly transformed.

My breath became a solid mass in my lungs, I could not breathe. He must not see them. Carsten must not see. Tearing from Quinn's grip, I made a dash towards him, but my husband barred my way.

'Open it,' he told Lucien.

Unwrapping the brown paper, Lucien glanced at what lay within, then hastily wrapped it again and made to replace it in the trunk.

'What is it?' Carsten demanded.

Lucien looked at his master, his cheeks pink. 'It's nothing, Mr Whitby. There's no locket in there, just scraps of paper.'

But Carsten had – as we all had – taken note of Lucien's reaction. Poor Lucien had tried to keep his face impassive, but the deep flush in his cheeks and the shock of surprise that widened his eyes at the sight of the paper had given him away.

Carsten released me and stalked over to Lucien, snatching the parcel from his servant's hands. Taking it to the candle and tilting it to the light, Carsten peeled open the wrap. One by one he flicked through my sketches, examining each page for the longest time. Finally, he frowned at me.

'Did you draw these?'

I shut my eyes.

'Answer me, did you draw them?'

I nodded.

No one spoke or moved for several heartbeats. The air in the room was stuffy and warm, but I felt cold to the bone. Shame washed over me; I wished I could sink under the floorboards, down into the earth, and vanish beneath the weight of dirt and stones and rubble.

Carsten went to Lucien, and slapped his face. Then, without looking at me, he left the room.

Not one of us murmured a word; we barely breathed, only stood in our silence, listening to Carsten's footfall on the stairs, and then below us in the parlour. A door banged somewhere at the back of the house. A moment later, a cold blast blew along the hall and through my bedroom door, extinguishing Quinn's candle.

The sudden darkness disoriented me. Was it possible to die of heartache and shame, of fear? But of course I wasn't dead. Quinn rattled a box of vestas from her pocket and struck one of the wax matches alight. Reigniting her candle, she took up the candleholder and marched to the door.

'That was an ill wind if ever I saw one,' she intoned dramatically, then marched off along the hallway leaving Adele and Lucien and me to regard each other unhappily in the gloom.

15

Ghosts abound in the human psyche,
feeding and growing strong on our fear.
– ROB THISTLETON, *EMOTIONAL RESCUE*

Ruby, May 2013

It was nearly dawn. The mattress was full of lumps. Quills from the feather pillow pricked through the pillowcase, needling my cheeks and neck as I tossed from one side of the bed to the other in a bid to get comfortable.

My skin was super-sensitive, my lips swollen. I kept turning my head to check that the moon was still shining beyond my window. It had drifted across the sky, sliding inevitably closer to the western horizon, but its ghostly silver rays were still falling on the landscape below, just as they had fallen on Pete and me on the dark hillside. I wondered what he was doing at this exact moment – sleeping like the dead, or glaring up at the moon and thinking of me?

I hammered my pillow, then flopped back against it, my ill-fated words echoing in my mind.

Not great timing.

I moaned and shut my eyes. I'd promised myself that Rob

was ancient history, and he was. I'd already wasted three years of love on him, only to be repaid with lies and humiliation; it was time to move on. So why had I hesitated last night on the hillside with Pete? Why had I botched a perfectly lovely kiss in the moonlight by freaking out at the critical moment?

You're scared of letting anyone close . . . scared of love.

I sat up and opened the window. Cool air flowed in from the garden, and I expanded my lungs to absorb what I could of it. After a while my head stopped spinning.

I thought about Pete's smile, about the way it lit up those hypnotic kingfisher-blue eyes; I thought about his warmth, and the easy way we talked, and how his nearness tonight had made me quake with desire. He had kept his dogs out of my way, knowing my fear; and he had never once pushed me to remember him, despite clearly wishing I would. He was kind and dependable . . . and utterly gorgeous.

What was there to be scared of?

Leaping out of bed, I dragged on my jeans and a cardigan, slid my feet into my runners and dashed along the hall. When I burst onto the verandah, I looked at the sky. It was light enough to navigate through the bush, yet there still remained a hint of darkness in which to hold the magic – at least until I got to Pete's cottage, a twenty-minute hike on the other side of the river.

But as I rushed down the stairs, something fluttered past my cheek – a moth, a gust of air, a strand of my hair – whatever it was, it made me jerk back in surprise. And in the unexpected chaos of the moment, the vault door opened a crack and I found myself flashing back in time.

Since Esmeralda's death, I'd lost interest in the hens. Then Mum introduced a couple of new Isa Browns, and one of them, newly christened 'Chocolate', had quickly got under my skin. She was smaller than the others, with a fluffy white underbelly and caramel feathers. I knew the instant I saw her we would be first-rate friends – as long as I could keep her off the lunch menu. She had a pretty beaky face, although she was very small and her eyes lacked Esmeralda's clever twinkle. But as the Wolf was fond of saying, nobody was perfect.

Hmm. The Wolf.

Months had dragged by since he'd gone back to Newcastle. Still no letter came. The kids at school forgot about him. Somehow, my old life settled back into the hole created by his absence. I resumed my role as unwanted team member; I sat alone at lunchtime; and the teachers continued to reprimand me for getting lost in daydreams. To Mum's disappointment, my grades remained low.

I began to suspect that the Wolf hadn't been real at all, but a creature who had leaped from one of Granny H's fairytales.

I stopped in the middle of the yard. The girls flocked around me squawking excitedly, scratching the dirt for the treats they knew would soon fall from my colander.

If only we'd been able to say goodbye. If only I'd been able to look in his eyes and see that he was still the same dear, funny old Wolf. If only . . .

Stupid. 'If only' was for fairytales.

The truth was, the Wolf had forgotten me.

Picking the corn cobs and celery stalks out of the colander, I threw them about the yard. The girls darted after them, attacking their delicacies in a joyful frenzy.

I took the remaining scraps – mostly lemon skins and onion parings that were yucksville for a chook – over to the compost and scraped them into the bin.

A charred bit of paper caught my eye.

My first thought was: *Who'd put burned paper in the compost?* Whatever we incinerated was supposed to go in the ash bucket, and from there onto Mum's tomatoes to sweeten the yield. Everything we incinerated – pinecones, old bones, blackberry brambles and noxious weeds – made good ash for the garden and was never wasted.

My second thought was: *It looks like part of a letter, and I think I recognise the handwriting.*

Peeling the sooty scrap off the bottom of the colander, I smoothed off a smear of rockmelon and peered at the carefully printed words.

. . . know where I am, but you haven't written yet so maybe you think . . .

I gasped. It was a letter from the Wolf. At least, part of a letter. Why had it been burned and put in with the scraps? I tried to flatten it out, but the damp, scorched paper tore and disintegrated until nothing remained but grey confetti. I tried to ease the remains into my jeans pocket, but they drifted to the ground and were lost.

Whirling around, I glared at the house. 'Jamie!'

I stomped back inside. Voices drifted from the lounge room, where I found Mum listening to the radio, sorting through her folio of watercolours. Normally I'd hang about and watch. Mum was really clever, and I liked the pictures she painted – seed-pods she took from the bottlebrush trees, and colourful bird feathers, and the wildflowers that Jamie and I collected for her.

'Where's Jamie?' I asked.

Mum looked up and frowned. Her eyes were red-rimmed and puffy. On the table sat a glass of wine and a half-empty bottle.

'No idea,' she said, then looked back at her drawings.

'A letter came for me,' I told her. 'But it ended up burned in the compost. The mail is Jamie's job. Why did she burn my letter?'

Mum's bleary eyes focused on me. 'Oh Ruby, what is it with you and Jamie these days? Always at each other's throats, always at loggerheads. You used to be so close.' Reaching for her glass, she drained the contents. 'If you find her, could you tell her the solar battery needs checking? With all this sun, I expect the water needs a top-up.'

I didn't bother replying, just stomped along the hall and back out into the yard.

'Jamie!' I yelled as loudly as I could. Behind me in the house, a glass smashed. I cupped my hands around my mouth and yelled even louder. 'You rotten bitch, Jamie! You'll be sorry for burning my letter! *Really* sorry, and that's a promise!'

Mum's footsteps thumped along the hall, but I wasn't in the mood for another lecture about language. Running to the woodshed, I dragged out my bike, climbed on and pedalled up the slope into the trees. I rode uphill until I came to the goat trail that led to the Spine. Speeding through the pine forest, I bumped over cones half-hidden under the mat of needles, then veered along a smooth ledge of granite and into the tea-trees on the other side.

If there was one small glad thing adrift in this sea of shitty things, it was knowing that the Wolf *hadn't* forgotten me after all. But somehow that made me feel worse. He might have written other letters. He might have waited ages for a reply, and when none came assumed I didn't like him anymore – because of Mrs Drake's stolen locket.

. . . you haven't written yet so maybe you think . . .

A hollow feeling came over me. It got bigger and darker, a thundercloud growing against the inside of my chest.

I hated my sister.

I hated my mother.

I wanted to run away to Newcastle and find the Wolf. We could rent a little cottage on the edge of a forest somewhere and do as we pleased, playing the game all night if we wanted, eating ice-cream and cake for breakfast, and lemon meringue pie for lunch, fish and chips every night for tea. There'd be no more scrubbing carrots and grating Mum's horrible turnips – and no more waking up to the sour smell of empty wine bottles, no more getting roused on for things I didn't do. And best of all, there'd be no more smirking, gloating, smart-alec, ballet-dancing Jamie.

The sound of a car motor drew me back to the present. I peered along the track into the early light, expecting to see Pete's ute emerge through the trees. So when the sleek black Jaguar appeared and rolled to a stop in the circular drive, my heart kicked over.

Rob got out and walked towards me. He was wearing jeans and polo shirt, his gleaming Hugo Boss brogues unnaturally shiny in an environment that coated everything else in a fine layer of dust.

'Hey, babe.'

I tucked a strand of hair behind my ear, suddenly aware of my bruised and bitten lips; they felt swollen, chafed pink from stubble-burn. Folding my arms across my chest, I summoned a glare.

'It's six o'clock in the morning.'

Rob smiled. 'The best time to catch someone at home.'

'What you want?'

He sighed. 'You haven't returned any of my calls. I was getting worried. Look, Ruby, I feel wretched about what happened last week. You took off before I had a chance to explain.'

'What I saw in your bathroom was pretty self-explanatory.'

Rob dragged his fingers across his scalp, and his face was suddenly tight, furrowed with frown lines. 'Trust you to freak out like this. It was a mistake, okay? A stupid mistake. I'm really sorry.'

'And the bra?'

He sighed, and glanced along the track, his gaze roaming the shadows. 'I was an idiot, but when you walked out, I got a shock. I've spent the last week thinking about you. I don't want to lose you, Ruby. You're my world. Do you think you could try to forgive me . . . and come home?'

I pinched my lips together, feeling their rawness. I had a flash of silvery moonlight, and a hillside belonging to a mythical realm, full of shadows and promise. I glanced along the track at the sky. It was turning light, the night escaping.

Rob's presence here seemed suddenly invasive.

'You really hurt me,' I told him. 'I don't think I can forgive you. Besides, I'm not ready to go home.'

He studied me for a long time, then said quietly, 'You've started remembering, haven't you?'

I shrugged. 'So what if I have? It's not your problem anymore.'

He stepped closer, his gaze sharpening. 'Maybe not, but I still care about you, Ruby. And I still believe you're treading dangerous ground by coming back here.'

He had spoken those same words to me countless times before, but all of a sudden they sounded like a warning.

'What are you saying?'

'It's clear you're nowhere near ready to cope with your suppressed memories . . . or with the shock of what you might remember.'

He held my gaze, and I sensed that he wanted to say more but was holding back. His lips parted, and his eyes narrowed on my face. A feeling of unease swept over me, and I pulled my cardigan tighter across my chest.

'I might be more ready than you think.'

Rob let his gaze drift over to the house. 'You're out here alone, are you? Today, I mean,' he added quickly.

I didn't answer straight away; it seemed crazy that I should feel guilty about kissing Pete on the hillside last night, when Rob had just admitted his own infidelity. Old habits, I thought ruefully . . . and guilt was certainly one of mine.

Rob stepped closer, searching my face. I sensed that his uncanny body-language radar had switched to overdrive. Before I could move away, he reached towards me and cupped my cheek, pressing his thumb against my tender bottom lip. I flinched and stepped back.

'Oh Ruby,' he murmured, his voice husky with emotion. The pain of understanding dawned in his eyes, and his pupils grew dark. 'Don't give up on us so easily,' he whispered. 'I love you, babe. I couldn't bear to lose you.'

This was a side of Rob I rarely – if ever – saw. He had always been a master of drawing forth emotion from other people, meanwhile remaining calm in the midst of their teary outbursts. Seeing him like this, suddenly vulnerable, with welling eyes and uncertainty etched in his handsome features, made me hesitate.

But only for a moment. Rob and I had crossed a bridge of mistrust, and now stood on opposite banks of a vast divide. For me, at least, there was no going back.

'It's too late, Rob,' I said as gently as I could. 'You'd better go.'

Rob tensed, but then he nodded. 'I hope you know what you're doing, babe.'

Then he was striding back to his car, getting in, firing the engine and cruising slowly around the circular drive.

I stood there shivering in the farmhouse's shadow, hugging my cardigan about me, watching Rob's Jag disappear along the track and into the trees, heading back to the outside world. As the silence settled back into place around me, Rob's words replayed in my mind.

You're nowhere near ready to cope with the shock of what you might remember.

But he was wrong. I wanted to remember, and suddenly I felt ready to deal with whatever those memories revealed.

'Okay, Ruby, I'm going to count backwards from twenty and I'd like you to listen carefully to my voice. Are you comfortable?'

'Yep.'

'Good. Now settle back into your chair. Take a deep breath and let it out. Start to feel your limbs growing heavy and your eyes slowly drifting shut. That's it. We'll begin at twenty, feeling relaxed. Nineteen, letting go and drifting deeper . . . eighteen . . . seventeen . . .'

Rob's visit earlier that morning had rattled me. I wanted to prove him wrong, to prove that I *was* ready to face the past. So I hadn't gone to Pete's as I'd planned, but had instead taken Esther's car and driven into Armidale. Hypnotherapy was a long shot. It might dredge up the truth, yet there was every chance I would emerge from the experience empty-handed. Even so, I was swamped by a feeling of urgency, and was ready to try anything.

I was staring at the spot on the wall I'd chosen, but in my peripheral view I could see the deep red curtains drawn against the light, and the glass table upon which sat two tumblers and a jug of water. Nearby, seated on a huge leather armchair that matched the one I sat on, was Flora, the hypnotherapist I had picked out of the *Yellow Pages*. Her face was turned towards me, and her chair was pushed close to mine. I could have reached out and touched the sleeve of her smart pink suit. I didn't, of course, because my arm suddenly felt like a lump of stone. As I settled deeper into my chair, her words seemed to echo from inside my head.

'Fourteen . . . thirteen, your eyes are closed now, Ruby . . .'

Darkness then, but I didn't feel sleepy. Rather, I felt almost preternaturally alert, as if I were rigged up to a drip bag of coffee. I was twitchy, worrying I was doing it wrong, scared it wouldn't work, and terrified that it would.

'Nine . . . eight, you're walking down a staircase, it's very dark. Candles light your way. Seven, deeper now, the stairs are taking you very deep . . . six . . . five . . .'

Rats moving in the shadows. The scurry of motion, the echoey drip-drip of water. A damp smell, like moss on a riverbank. But they were just weird random images that had nothing to do with the past. I wondered if I should tell Flora that her hypnosis wasn't working; she might want to stop and try a different tack. I must have been one of those people who resisted any form of hypnotherapy, because I was fully alert, so on edge my blood was humming—

'Three . . . two . . .'

—and I was getting more jittery by the second. I really should tell Flora I wasn't responding; what if something went wrong? I engaged my neck muscles and attempted to turn my head, and—

'One.'

—I was standing on the riverbank. Below me, the river rushed past. Trees swayed in the shimmering air, the sky was littered with remnant storm clouds. All around me, the landscape hazed into a blur of brightness and light.

A human-like shape hovered before me. Slowly, it morphed into a girl, into Jamie. Her face was contorted as if she was shouting, but all I could hear was the hissing rush of the river. Jamie grabbed my arms, her fingers digging in as she tried to shove me away. I felt angry and afraid, and there was a great weight dragging at me, a shadow the size of the moon. As I tried to shake off the shadow, Jamie slipped from my grasp. She toppled backwards and her head cracked on the wall of stone behind her. I reached for her, but somehow her head hit the wall again. Her mouth opened, but her scream was silent and her head kept hitting the wall. Her face twisted in pain, and a bubble of blood came out of her mouth.

'Ruby, I'm going to start bringing you back now.'

The bright sunlight was suddenly blinding. Jamie began to dissolve into it, and I gripped her tighter, trying to hold onto her, but she was slipping—

'Counting from five . . . four . . .'

Struggling now, time was pulling me back to the present but I couldn't leave Jamie. I blinked hard but could see nothing in the dazzling light. Groping for her in the haze, trying to find her, fearing she'd already gone.

'Three . . . two . . . one . . . and – eyes open.'

My lungs expanded suddenly, and I dragged in a gasp of air. The room was dark, stained red by the murky late-afternoon sunlight that seeped through the curtains. My face was wet, and as I pulled breath after breath into my airless lungs, I heard my mother's voice inside my ear.

There were so many questions. So much poking and prodding and trying to get you to remember.

Later, as I walked along the street to where I'd parked Esther's car, my mother's voice became more insistent. Other snippets drifted back, snatches of conversation I'd overlooked at the time, or deemed unimportant, now seemed darkly significant.

. . . the notion of bad genes crossed my mind . . . I started thinking about your father's death, and all the old guilt bubbled up . . .

16

Brenna, June 1898

Cries drew me to the window. Flinging up the sash, I leaned out into the cold morning air and looked towards the stable yard.

Adele was calling to Carsten, and the shrill edge to her voice had me ducking back inside, dragging my coat over my nightdress and rushing down the stairs. As I burst through into the garden, Adele's distress reached a new pitch.

'Stop it!' she cried. 'Carsten, you'll kill him, please stop.'

Tearing along the path, I reached the stable yard and met a wretched sight.

Carsten held a stockwhip, and his shirt and trousers were flecked with blood.

It took me a moment to notice the man slumped behind him, against the tether rail in front of the stable barn. He had crumpled to his knees and fallen forward. His hands were roped above his head; he was bare from the hips up, his strong, lean torso scored with deep gashes that oozed dark-coloured blood.

'Lucien.'

I raced towards him, but Carsten intercepted me, grabbing a handful of my loose hair. He jerked me to my knees and bent to meet me face to face.

'Take a good look at your handiwork, Brenna. Do you think him so worthy of your artist's brush now?'

I could smell blood on him; salty, sweat-infused blood. Lucien's blood. My hand shot up and I clawed my nails at his face. He flinched back with a cry, and it was only when I felt the sticky warmth of blood between my fingers that I realised I had broken his skin. Spiteful gladness filled me.

'You wildcat,' he spat and slapped me sideways into the dirt. Gravel bit my palms and knees and the wind tugged open my coat and whipped my nightdress.

'I curse the day I married you,' Carsten said. 'My only solace is the pain I know is coming for you. Now get yourself back to the house, woman, before I take my lash to you, too.'

He strode away, the whip coiled loosely in his fist; the leather tail quivered as if with its master's agitation, its fine tip flicking droplets of blood onto the path in a sticky crimson trail.

The shock of Carsten's actions sent waves of unease rippling among us. No one said it aloud, but I knew from the silence that descended on the house that we were all thinking the same thing.

If Carsten had turned his anger on Lucien, whom he loved, then what might he do to any of us?

Lucien went about his duties in the stable yards without a nod or a word to anyone. Later, when I took him some salve I'd mixed from my store of dry herbs, he refused it and retreated to the dark safety of his barnyard lair. His eyes were huge and black in his pale face, his mouth set firm. Blood leaked through his clothes and dried into sweaty crusts, and at the end of the day he was forced to soak himself with water bucketed from the horses' trough in order to peel off his shirt so he could bathe.

I watched for him constantly.

Always from the corner of my eye, as I dared not let Carsten see me looking. If the occasion arose for me to venture outside, I hurried along with my head bowed, as if finding fascination with the ground. But always, always, watching for him.

Those blunt feelings aroused by my drawings had sharpened with time, honed by our stolen kisses in his barn dwelling, whetted by the feelings I now knew he reciprocated. At first his fractured beauty had inspired a challenge for my brush and pencils; now, upon more intimate acquaintance, I trembled just to see his shadow flit past me; I quaked to glimpse him moving about the distant stables. And on those brief occasions that I caught sight of his face, I ached with remorse, sick at heart to know his pain was my doing.

Carsten's suffering was clear. He looked suddenly old; his face had taken on a pinched aspect; he wore his mouth downcast, and his eyes had turned small and hard. Since that day in the stable yard when he had destroyed his only true friendship to spite me, he had become a human storm, torn by the black thunderclouds that churned within him. By all appearances he was filled with self loathing, regretting what he had done. And yet knowing Carsten as I now did, I feared that his underlying sentiments were not so noble; rather than reproach himself for what he had done, in truth my husband resented that law had restricted him from doing *more*.

In the weeks that followed Carsten's attack on Lucien, my husband had no business abroad, and his lingering presence kept us all on edge.

I barely saw Adele. Since Lucien's flogging, her health had suffered and she spent much of her time in her room.

Quinn had begun to reek of drink. Port wine and cooking sherry, and occasionally of cough syrup. The breakfast eggs were served half-blackened, the coffee was lukewarm, the milk curdled, the bread stale. Carsten rumbled about throwing her out, but Quinn paid him no mind; she simply turned her deaf ear towards him and made herself scarce.

Deliveries arrived in the early morning and were neglected. Hefty bags of flour and sugar and tea languished near the kitchen door, tripping us as we hurried in and out. Mail piled up on the table, and it wasn't until late on a Friday afternoon that I found the time to go through it.

One letter was addressed to me.

I hadn't received any correspondence for weeks, and was anxious to receive word from home. But the writing on the envelope was not that of my father. It had been penned in neat childlike handwriting, which could only mean it had come from my brother, Owen.

Mystified, I tore it open.

19 June 1898

Dear Brenna,

I am sorry to be the bearer of upsetting news. Fa Fa is unwell. The doc says his heart is weak, and fears for him. Please come home.

Always yours,
Owen

I went to Carsten and showed him the letter, but he waved me away.

'You'll not be going anywhere.'

'But my father's ill. I must go to him.'

'How can I trust you to return?'

'Of course I'll return. We have an agreement,' I reminded him bitterly. 'Or have you forgotten?'

Carsten drew up to his full height and glared at me. 'Your father got to keep his farm. In exchange, I gained a wife, who promised me a son. You'll stay here, Brenna, until you give me one. After that, you can go to the devil.'

I retreated to my bedroom and curled on the bed. At first I was too angry to cry. Darkness raged inside me, bruising my spirit as it thrashed from side to side. I had never felt hatred before, but suddenly I recognised it in myself.

But as I thought of my father, the rage died. Tears began to leak from my eyes, hot frightened tears that stung my skin and turned my lashes brittle. My father was gravely ill and my brother alone to care for him; it was a long difficult ride for the Clearwater doctor, and I feared my father would not get the care he needed.

Trees lashed outside my window, churned by the wind that shrieked up from the strait. A steady drizzle of icy rain battered the panes.

I went along the hall a little way, then saw that the library door was cracked open; Carsten would be keeping watch, his ears alert, his pistol at the ready. He had included the house-hold in his vigil, too: Adele had been given the order to sleep in my bed, to prevent me creeping out at night; Quinn had set herself up on a straw cot in the parlour, and would slumber, so she warned, with one eye open.

But the flesh is no match for the spirit, as my father was fond of saying; somehow, despite my husband's refusal to let me go, I resolved to defy him and find a way.

The night of my escape, Adele fussed around in the kitchen while Quinn prepared Carsten's nightcap; when the housekeeper was distracted by a pan of over-boiling milk, Adele placed a measure of laudanum in Carsten's drink as we had planned, and then stole back up to my room.

We waited until midnight, when Adele risked a peek into the library. My husband's snores drifted along the hall; he slept at his desk with his head on his arms, the empty mug at his side.

Before the grandfather clock had finished chiming the hour, I crept down the stairs, past the lump of Quinn's heavily sleeping body, through the night garden to the stables, where Lucien had prepared a swift black mare. He would ride with me to Launceston and see me safely on the steamer, and from there I would send word to Owen to meet me at the train once I arrived in Armidale.

In a few days, I would be home.

At Launceston, there was no time for a lingering goodbye.

'Look after Adele,' I told Lucien. 'Don't let her fret. I will return once I know my father is all right.'

Lucien took my hand and kissed it. 'Don't despair,' he whispered. 'Our love has the power to create miracles. I will wait for you.'

The cry came to board, and passengers began to migrate up the gangway, jostling and calling, their voices disembodied in the early mist. I felt myself tugged along, and a moment later Lucien was lost to me. I held him in my sights as long as I was able, and when the ship began to ease away from the pier, I watched his black-clad figure recede until it was a speck. And when the speck finally winked from my view, a sensation of loss folded over me.

Going below deck, I unpacked my journal and turned to a new page.

Tonight, I wrote, *I had hoped to find solace in writing, but the words refuse to flow and the ink has dried on the nib of my pen. I find myself turning back through these pages, rereading the entry I made after meeting Lucien that sunny afternoon in the glade. If there is ever a moment of a person's life that brings shelter in a time of inner storm, then that bright island of a day is mine.*

I took my black queen from my pocket and held her in my hand. She had never failed to soothe me; at least, not until now. But as the steamer forged across the reeling ocean, bringing distance between Lucien and me, the dark heaviness of loss did not abate. And as the day wore on, the burden of it became so leaden I thought I would die.

17

Ruby, May 2013

My mother regarded me from the dimness of her hallway, shielding herself behind the front door. She hesitated, then swung the door open to let me in.

'I wish you'd let Jamie rest in peace,' she said by way of a greeting. 'You weren't the only one devastated by her death. Why can't you simply let it go?'

'I haven't come to talk about Jamie.'

Mum looked surprised, then relieved. 'Good. Then this is a social call?'

'Actually, I was hoping we could talk about Dad.'

Even in a casual outfit of cropped jeans and rumpled linen shirt, with her dark auburn hair pulled back in a ponytail, she looked dazzling. But at the mention of my father, she seemed to fade.

'Come on then,' she said, resigned, and ushered me along the hall. We bypassed the kitchen and went out to a pergola-covered courtyard at the back of the house. There was no lawn, just concrete pavers and mondo grass edgings, and elegant palm trees in pots. A hedge of compact lemon trees grew along the pergola's perimeter, filling the courtyard with a citrusy scent. I must have interrupted Mum in the middle of pruning the lemons, because a bucket of leaves and pair of secateurs sat on the pavement nearby.

'Well,' she said, sitting at the big teak table and motioning me to take the seat opposite. 'Spit it out.'

At sixty, she had never looked lovelier. There was hardly a wrinkle on her face and her hair was threaded only lightly with silver. But as she waited for me to speak, she seemed inwardly drawn, smaller, as if battening down her hatches in preparation for bad news.

I took a breath. 'Last time I was here, we talked about Brenna's letters, and how the idea of bad genes had crossed your mind.'

'I remember.'

'You said how finding the letters made you question yourself and everyone around you, and that all the old guilt had bubbled up over Dad's death. I guess I'm just trying to fit all the pieces together.'

Mum stood suddenly and went inside, returning a minute later with two glasses and a decanter. At first I thought it was brandy, but it turned out to be iced tea. She splashed the amber liquid into each glass, then pushed mine towards me and downed her own.

'You were such a bright little girl, Ruby. So curious about everything. Jamie used to love dressing you up like a doll. And you *were* a doll, with your mop of curly brown hair and big caramel eyes. But after the dog attack, you changed. Became more withdrawn, less certain of yourself. As the months wore on and your wounds began to heal, I realised that my chirpy little daughter had been replaced by a girl who was terribly shy and apprehensive.'

She fiddled with her empty glass, then finally poured more tea. 'How much do you remember about what happened?' she asked carefully. 'About how your father died?'

'Bits of it.' Those weeks and months following the dog attack were a jumble of disjointed events, a jigsaw puzzle with most of its pieces still rattling around in the box.

'Maybe I'd better start at the beginning, then. It might help you understand. Not just about your father, but about why I felt compelled to hide your great-grandmother's letters.'

She let her gaze roam across the courtyard, and dragged in a deep breath.

'Late one Sunday afternoon I was cleaning up after a barbecue. Your father had been entertaining some of his bikie friends.' Mum's voice turned hard with disapproval. 'They'd been drinking all day, but no one seemed to care about that as they got on their bikes and rode away, least of all your father. He was drunkest of them all. They'd been teasing Boozo—' Mum looked at me. 'Henry didn't believe in chaining dogs, so he kept Boozo in a large enclosure in the backyard, only taking him out to go hunting. Anyway, Henry and I had words. I'd gone off my head about him getting drunk around you children. You see, Ruby, your father changed when he hit the bottle. It made him pigheaded and stupid. That day was no different. He told me to stop nagging, and so I did. I knew better than to cause a row, especially when you girls were playing so happily in the garden. There was no point spoiling the day.'

Mum got to her feet and collected her secateurs. She began to clip random leaves off the nearest lemon tree, and I saw that her hands were trembling.

'I'd gone into the house,' she continued. 'I forget why. Probably to do the washing up. My hands were wet, because when I heard the scream I rushed to the door to see what was happening, and I clearly recall wiping my hands on my apron. Funny, isn't it,' she said looking at me, 'how you remember the insignificant things, while the more dramatic moments are often a blur.'

I knew what was coming; my fingers went halfway to my shoulder, but I forced them down.

'Do you want me to stop?' Mum asked.

'No, I'm okay. Dad let me go into the enclosure, didn't he?'

Mum nodded. 'Bloody idiot that he was. Anyway, the dog must have snarled and startled you, because you let out a scream. You used to love old Boozo, you were always reaching through the wire to pat him on the head or tug his tail, and ordinarily he was tolerant. But that day he was in no mood to be petted.' She cut a withered branch from the base of the tree, then stared at the wounded trunk.

'By the time I'd reached the enclosure, your father had scooped you up. There was blood everywhere, your poor little shoulder was open to the bone. I took you in my arms while Henry ran inside to call the ambulance. We sat on the verandah. While I staunched the blood flow, I kept telling him to get the rifle and go out to the pen and put Boozo down. I said if he didn't, then the animal-welfare people would. But he refused point blank.'

'I remember you arguing.'

'We argued for days. All the time you were in hospital.' Mum shuffled into a gap of sunlight. The secateurs hung loose from her fingers. She was lit from above, frailer and older and more beautiful than I'd ever seen her.

'A week passed,' she went on. 'Henry still refused to do anything about Boozo. Finally, I took matters into my own hands. Henry was out in the garage, fixing his Harley. I unlocked the rifle safe, loaded up, and went out to the enclosure. I was a fair shot in those days, thanks to your father's insistence on giving me lessons. I engaged the lever, took aim at Boozo and was about to pull the trigger when Henry came around the side of the house and rushed at me, yelling. He swung a punch, to throw off my aim, but instead he knocked the rifle upwards and it exploded in his face.'

Silence wedged itself between us.

Mum's skin was ashen, her eyes huge and glassy. I had the urge to go to her, to push beyond the barriers of our mutual mistrust and find the loving mother who I knew must be in there somewhere. But all I could do was sit in the cold stillness, and wait for her to continue.

When she didn't, I found myself asking, 'Did you love him?'

Mum looked startled. 'In my way.'

'I always thought you were unhappy because you missed Dad.'

She turned back to the lemon tree, and pruned off another branch. The tree was taking on a stunted look, bare of foliage now, skeletal.

'I was unhappy because after your father died I understood something about myself. Even though his death was finally ruled by the police as accidental, I was tormented by doubt. You see, later, whenever I thought about him, this dark feeling would bubble up inside me. No matter how I tried, I could never seem to summon up any feelings of remorse. I was sorry for what I'd done, but there were days when I was so very glad for it, too.'

The courtyard dimmed as the sun went behind a cloud. The scent of lemons sharpened the air.

Silence tiptoed around us. Mum's shoulders were shaking; her head dipped forward and she hid her face in her hands. Again I wanted to go to her and pull her into my arms, tell her that everything was all right – or at least that it would be, if we faced it together . . . whatever 'it' was. But another, wary part stayed put. Mum and I had never faced anything together. We were all that was left of our family, the opposite poles of a fragile little unit that had crumbled to dust eighteen years ago. It wasn't that we were different, because differences could be reconciled; it was simply that we were strangers, shackled together by blood ties.

Finally she turned to look at me. Her eyes were shadowed and she seemed, suddenly, terrifyingly frail. Strangers we may have been, but she was still my mother.

'Henry didn't deserve to die.' Her nostrils flared as she inhaled deeply, and her next words came out in a rush. 'He was great with you girls, crazy about you both. He might have been rough around the edges, and weak-willed when it came to the grog, but underneath all the bluster he was a decent man.'

She slumped, turning her face towards the sun. Washed in the soft green light that filtered through the vine-covered pergola, she was like an apparition from one of the turn-of-the-century paintings she so admired: deathly pale, adrift and helpless, childlike.

She stared at the pile of leaves at her feet. 'I used to wonder where those dark feelings of mine came from. Which is why discovering that my grandmother was a murderer scared me so much.'

'So that's what you meant by "bad genes"?'

'Yes.' She crouched and gathered the lemon twigs and leaves and placed them in the bucket. There were dots of red on her palms and knuckles and wrists, bloody smears where the thorns had scratched her.

I got to my feet too quickly, overturning my chair. 'But Mum, it doesn't make sense. You inherit things like hair and eye colour, maybe even the tendency to develop similar sorts of disease . . . but *murder*. That doesn't get passed along.'

'Did I ever tell you why your Grampy James had all those medals? He was decorated in both wars, but not for saving lives. As it turned out, my father never coped too well in peace time, but give him a rifle and a war and a licence to kill, and he was in his element.'

'Mum, this is doing my head in.'

'I believe that a tendency to violence can be passed on, Ruby.'

'So, what are you saying?'

'Just . . . be careful.'

I stared at her, flashing back to how she'd been after Jamie died. Unwashed hair and dirt under her fingernails. Eyes darkened by grief, and a mouth perpetually downturned. Her garden had gone to weeds, and the house always smelled like burned toast. Even when another summer rolled around, it still felt like winter.

'You think I killed her, don't you?'

'Of course not.'

I thought I saw fear surface in her eyes, a slight enlarging of the pupils, a like a shadow crossing the sun. She hid it well, but once seen, something like that couldn't be unseen.

I told Mum I had to be somewhere, and she walked me to the door. We stood awkwardly, me lingering on the doorstep eager to be gone, Mum looking shell-shocked after her disclosure about Dad, stray wisps of dark hair drifted around her face. I pushed through the screen door, but Mum touched my arm.

'Ruby?'

'What, Mum?'

'I read Rob's book. I think he's got it right. Don't let the past drag you down. Put it behind you, and do your best to move on.'

Without really knowing why, I kissed her gently on the cheek.

'Goodbye, Mum.'

Before she could reply, I hurried along the path, carrying with me the burden of her confession, and the lingering odour of lemons.

That afternoon I walked along the riverbank towards the granite formation we had explored as kids.

It was on the edge of the national park adjoining Lyrebird Hill, a cluster of mammoth boulders that flanked a stretch of river, squeezing the fast-flowing water into a narrow channel. Several metres downstream, the riverbed abruptly dropped away, creating a surge of waterfall that thundered into a deep pool far below. We'd been warned as children about playing here. It was well known as a dangerous place; I'd heard of inexperienced canoeists being killed after their canoes jettisoned over the falls. Bushwalkers, too, had slipped on the rocks and gone into the deadly rapids, their bodies washing up on riverbanks kilometres away in the park's dense heartland.

For the most part we'd stayed away, but from time to time we would be drawn back here like bees to the hive. Then, as mysteriously as it had arisen, our obsession would ebb and we would forget again, almost as though the rocks had taken from us what they needed and then returned to their primordial realm.

Hopping from rock to rock, I made my way up to the big flat outcrop where eighteen years ago my mother had found my sister's body. My only memories of this place were happy ones: picnicking with Jamie in the early days when we were friends, and sometimes Mum had come with us, supervising our explorations in the stony caves that honeycombed this stretch of the embankment.

These ancient stones had fascinated us. The huge granite formations congregated closely together, their smooth surfaces mottled with bright green moss and black or yellow lichen. Deep crevices carved between the stones where they banked shoulder to shoulder, creating gaps that seemed to vanish into black nothingness below. Mum had warned us about these gaps. The rocks were slippery when wet – drenched either by river spray or rain – and she'd heard of people breaking bones when they fell.

I made my way along a flat shelf of granite until I came to an assemblage of tall stones pushing skywards. I was tempted to sit at the base of one, to rest back against it and watch the sunset, but being here made me uneasy.

The sun was sinking behind the trees, and pink clouds gathering on the horizon. Below, the water pounded the rocks as it gathered momentum towards the cascade. Behind me, higher up the embankment, shadows congregated among the trees. It was May, and while the days were still warm, night-time brought an iciness that heralded the approaching winter.

I went over to the water. Looking down, I watched the rapids swirl and froth between the half-submerged stones. Jamie used to say that the river was magic and sometimes, if you listened hard, the rush of water sounded like a woman singing.

I listened now. Curiously, it wasn't singing I heard, but my sister's distinctive musical laughter . . .

There was a noisy splash, and squealing. Another splash, and Jamie laughing some more.

I inched along the bank, determined to see what she was doing. Climbing up on a wedge of granite, I peeked over the top. The river was washed in golden light, with sunny speckles dancing on the water, and half-submerged boulders pushing through the surface. Along the bank grew maidenhair ferns and soft lemon-green grass.

I saw them lying in the shade of a gnarly old casuarina. Jamie had her arms wrapped around the neck of an older boy, one I didn't recognise. They were kissing. Not just pecking away, but really going for it. Yuck.

Jamie sat up suddenly and scrambled to her feet. 'Hey, Bobby,' she called, 'look what I found.' She flung up her arm, and something bright and glittery dangled from her fingers.

Bobby, I wondered. There was only one Bobby I knew of, and that was Bobby Drake. I shifted, trying to get a better look at him, but the sun was in my eyes.

'Hey, give that back,' Bobby said, springing after Jamie.

'You'll have to catch me first,' she teased.

Bobby charged, but Jamie leaped with Tinkerbell-like grace up onto a high shelf of stone, where she taunted Bobby with her trinket, swinging it to and fro as though trying to hypnotise him.

'You little thief,' Bobby accused, half-laughing. 'Give it back, or I'll have you transported back to Newcastle.'

I frowned. What was he talking about, transported back to Newcastle? A grimy feeling came over me and I shifted uncomfortably in my hiding place, trying to get a better look at him. He was tall and thickly built, and his hair might have been fair but it was hard to see in the dazzling brightness.

Bobby climbed the rock and made a lunge for Jamie, but she only trilled and sprang away. Of course, Jamie had done four years of ballet, and if Bobby Drake thought he could catch her so easily, he was in for a surprise. Which he was anyway, because Jamie scrambled nimbly to higher ground, nearly to the top of the tall boulder that jutted out over the river. The rapids gushed beneath her, sending up rainbow sprays of mist.

Out went Jamie's arm, the silvery trinket dangling from her outstretched fingers.

'Dare me to throw it in?' she said in her teasing voice.

'You wouldn't have the guts.'

Bobby turned, but with the sun behind him he was still just a shadow. He climbed the rock and ran towards Jamie. She laughed as he caught her and pinned her against him, trying to grapple the trinket out of her hand. The chain winked in the sunlight and the pendant gleamed like a silver raindrop. Where would she have got something like that?

Jamie shrieked, and I shifted position the better to see. Bobby's back was blocking my view of Jamie, but I caught a sharp little motion as Jamie elbowed Bobby in the ribs and twisted out of his grasp.

'Oh, really?' she said, sounding annoyed.

She whirled, a funky sort of pirouette on her nimble fairy-feet, and somehow landed on an even higher ledge of stone.

Her hand shot out and her fingers splayed and then there was a splash in the water below.

'What'd you do that for?' Bobby yelled.

Jamie lifted her shoulders and looked down her nose at him. 'I just did you a favour. Sooner or later your mum would have found it, and then she'd know it wasn't that weirdo brat who took it, but her own darling Bobby-boy.' She laughed and gestured at the water. 'This way, there's no proof.'

'Hell, Jamie. Mum loved that locket!'

Jamie pouted. 'More than you love me?'

Bobby went over and glared into the river. Then he slumped on the sun-warmed stone and dropped his face into his hands. 'Aw, crap. I'm stuffed if she finds out it was me who took it.'

'She won't find out now.'

When he didn't reply, Jamie danced silently up to him, turning out her feet, still doing the ballet thing. She kicked Bobby lightly in the back, and when he still didn't respond she kicked harder. 'What's up, Bobby-boy. Crying for your mummy?'

Bobby gave a yell and grabbed her ankle.

'You'll be the one crying, once I'm done with you.'

Jamie shrieked and tried to twist free, but her foot slipped on the mossy stone and she crashed onto her bottom. In an instant Bobby was on her, pinning her beneath him, covering her slender body with his own large one.

Sliding back behind my rock, I sat heavily on the ground as understanding came to me. The locket Jamie had just tossed into the water had glittered in the sun like something valuable, because it *was* valuable.

At least, it had been to Mrs Drake.

The memory had left me feeling jittery.

Suddenly, my palms were damp and I kept wanting to look over my shoulder. Crouching, I ran my hands across the smooth surface of the granite, collecting particles of lichen and moss, trying to regather myself. I had hoped that returning to this place would jog my memory of Jamie's death and, now, after my flashback about the stolen locket, I felt close. Too close. The vault had opened, but I wasn't ready. Perhaps I should come back when I felt stronger, when my heart didn't pound so painfully, when my limbs were not so weak and prone to trembling.

And yet I lingered, as if the rocks had cast their spell on me once more and trapped me here. Except tonight – and it was almost night, I noticed as the sun began to swan-dive into its ocean of deep pink clouds – it wasn't the joyful spell Jamie and I had experienced as children. There was something dark about the place, as if the sun-warmed granite beneath my feet was vibrating, rumbling like an ancient beast on the brink of waking from long hibernation.

The trees and bushes that flanked it swarmed with shadow. I searched the dark-infested trunks, seeing figures crouched or standing, as if someone was watching.

I looked back along the track I'd taken to get here, and willed myself to walk towards it, but I couldn't move. The fragment of memory thrown up by my hypnosis session rushed back around me, terrifyingly real.

There had been a struggle. Jamie had crashed backwards against the upright wall of stone, hitting her head. Her scream echoed around me, amplified and shattered into, not just one scream, but many, and then the sound was no longer erupting from the throat of a girl, but somehow blaring out of the stones around me—

Dragging in a breath, I tried to shake off the hallucination, but the screams continued to rise around me. I covered my ears and began to run, wanting only to leave this place and return along the track to the safety of the farmhouse. As I neared the edge of the rocky shelf, the toe of my runner caught in a crevice and I lurched forward, hitting the rocks with full force. My head rang with the sudden silence. I tried to move, but I was locked against the ground, immobile, as if the granite had somehow seeped through my defences and turned my limbs to stone.

Sometime later, I woke in darkness. I was no longer on the flat shelf of stone overlooking the river. The roar of the rapids was dim, muffled, as if in the distance. A smell lingered in the air: dampness and the powdery scent of lichen, the sharpness of animal dung. Somewhere overhead a branch creaked like a rusty hinge, but there was no other sound.

Vaguely, I remembered crawling. My body was stiff and sore after my fall, and I had wanted to find somewhere out of the wind to rest until I recovered enough to walk home. I had rested against a large boulder, but then something shifted; the embankment had given way and swallowed me.

I became aware that I was curled on my side, and that stones were digging into me. My joints ached, and the skin of my elbows and knees stung as if I'd been bitten by fire ants. Worse was the feeling that something enormous crouched over me – not an animal, but a large mass the size of a planet. Stretching out my arm, I reached up and my fingertips grazed damp stone.

That was when I became aware of the cold.

My shoes were gone, and I'd lost my cardigan, too. I was shivering, my thin jeans and tank top useless against the chill. I groped around. I seemed to be lying in a dirt cavity; a cave hollow or grotto.

I crawled towards where I believed the opening to be, but I bumped my head on a sloping bank of earth. It seemed to take forever, wriggling around the base of my hollow, seeking an opening, not finding one.

Finally, I curled into a ball to contain my body heat, but I was already shivering uncontrollably. Lying very still, I breathed deeply and tried to stay calm. My panic over the vision that had swamped me on the rocks had dimmed, replaced by a new fear.

No one knew where I was.

My body was jarred, my ankle swollen and sore.

And I was cold. Very, very cold.

Even if by some miracle Pete *did* come searching for me, how would he ever know where to look? He couldn't know about the rocks, or that Jamie had died there. He couldn't know that I'd returned here in search of answers.

Squeezing shut my eyes, I tried to find the doorway into sleep. Instead, I found myself sliding into the silvery twilight of the past. A riverbank, and my sister casting her shadow across the rocks as she leaned out over the water, a glittering chain swinging from her fingers . . .

When I found the place where Jamie had thrown the locket in the water, I stripped out of my clothes, folded them, and laid them on a dry rock. Then I waded into the river.

The water was icy. My body prickled all over with goosebumps. When the water reached my knees, my breath left me. When I was waist-deep, my teeth started clacking like castanets. When it slapped my chest, I sucked in a gulp of air and let out a groan.

Then dived under.

A watery world folded around me. I groped among the pebbles on the riverbed, my fingers throbbing with cold. Sharp fragments of quartz cut into my feet, and my knuckles bruised against water-smoothed knobs of granite and jasper. The freezing water stung my eyes, but I all I could think of was finding that locket and proving to Mrs Drake and everyone else that the Wolf was innocent.

Something string-like slithered between my fingers. I made a grab for it, but it was just a length of old fishing line, the catgut festooned with sparkly air bubbles. I yanked at it, hoping to snap the line, but it whipped across my palm and drove the hook into the fleshy base of my thumb. I wriggled it, wincing as the barb worked deeper under my skin, and then somehow my frozen fingers fumbled it free.

I was about to toss it back in the river, but stopped. What if it caught in the throat of a platypus or some other poor animal whose only crime was being thirsty? I wanted to keep looking for the locket, but maybe the fishhook was a sign that I needed to rest for a while and warm up?

Halfway back to the bank, I saw a shadow dart from the trees.

Two shadows. The sun was in my eyes, but I knew who they were.

'Well, well,' Bobby Drake said. 'Check it out, Jamie – it's the Little Mermaid.'

Jamie's laugh sounded like birdsong, only there was something sharp in it. I bobbed neck-deep under the water and glared at them, willing them away, mortified to be seen naked, even if one of the people seeing me was my sister. I didn't have much to see, but somehow that felt even worse.

Jamie slid something from her pocket, dangled it in the sunlight. It spangled, the chain reflecting liquid light, the bauble on the end winking pure silver.

'I don't suppose you're looking for this?' she asked.

I stared at the locket, astonished. 'How did you—'

Jamie twittered. 'You silly nong! I didn't really throw it in. What do you take me for, an idiot?'

'But I saw something go in the water.'

'I knew you were spying, so I threw a pebble to get you off our scent. Stop following us – and if you tattletale to Mum, you'll be *really* sorry!'

She whirled away, her dark hair swinging behind her as she strode off along the embankment and vanished into the trees.

Bobby came to the water's edge. I squinted into the glare, but with the sun behind him, he was a dark featureless blob.

'Spying little brat,' he said nastily. Picking up a stone, he skimmed it across the water. I jerked out of the way, which made him laugh. Then he went over to where I'd left my clothes, and kicked them into the water.

'Quit following us,' he warned, 'or you'll be in deep doo-doo. That's a promise. I got rid of your weirdo friend, and I can get rid of you, too.'

Vaguely I registered that I was dreaming – the chill of river water, the icy wind on my bare skin, and the fear that tiptoed through my bones.

But then the dream turned warm – at least it did along one side of my body. In my mostly-asleep state, I imagined it was Pete lying next to me. I nestled against his body heat, wishing he would raise his arms around me and hold me close, because the side of my body he *wasn't* pressing against felt frozen. At least I'd stopped shivering. At least sensation was finally starting to circulate back into my hands and feet.

I snuggled closer.

A whine came from the dark. Then a wet tongue licked my face. I became aware that the air in my cramped prison had changed. There was still the damp mustiness of stone and earth, but I caught a trickle of cool night air. I breathed it greedily, and again I felt the sinewy wetness on my cheek.

Through the grey fog of sleep came awareness: this wasn't Pete. The body I was curled into wasn't even human.

'Bardo?'

The kelpie whined and licked my face again.

I let out a moan, and then as if a lifetime of terror had never been, I rolled into her and wrapped my arms around her warm body, buried my face in the soft fur of her neck, and wept.

When I woke, Bardo was gone, but her warmth remained. I was gripped by a terrible desolate panic, fearing she'd abandoned me here in the dark. But then I heard barking. It was distant at first, but soon it drifted nearer.

'Bardo?' I had meant to shout, but my throat was so dry I barely made a whisper.

There was a scuffling nearby, and then Bardo was back beside me. She nudged me with her nose, and I understood that she wanted me to follow her. She disappeared again, and I could hear a furious scratching, soil sifting and stones thudding against other stones. Again the dog darted back to my side, nudged me, and then went back to her digging.

Following the smell of fresh air, I crawled across the cave floor. Bardo had dug away the mouth of the hole, which was now easily wide enough for me to crawl through. From beyond the hole drifted an eerie quietness . . . broken suddenly by the sound of footfall.

'Ruby!'

'I'm here,' I called huskily, and Bardo began to bark.

Pete's face appeared in the hole opening. His lovely, pink-cheeked face, with scowl lines cutting into his brow.

'Hell, Ruby – are you okay?'

'My head hurts,' I rasped, 'but nothing's broken.'

'Take hold of my arm. I'm going to slide you out slowly. Tell me the minute you feel pain of any sort, and I'll stop.'

I gripped his forearm, felt the muscles bunch and tighten under my fingertips. I tensed and Pete began to slide me through the opening. Stones bit into my belly and I heard a tearing sound as my T-shirt caught on a splinter of stone, but then I was out in the air, and Pete was cradling me tight against him.

The dogs yapped and circled us, rubbing their flanks against our legs and whining in anxious pleasure – but rather than flinch away or break into a sweat as I would once have done, I welcomed their nearness. And as Pete held me tight and safe against him, I felt the cosy warmth of love surround me.

18

Brenna, July 1898

Rain streaked the window as the train drew into Armidale. The carriage was damp and a chill had settled on me. By the time I stepped onto the platform, I was shivering.

A boy rushed towards me. He was scrawny and hollow-eyed, stooped like an old man, his clothes swimming on his bony frame. My gaze slid past him, then back.

With a jolt I recognised him. 'Owen!'

He didn't smile, just lifted his arm and gave a jerky wave. He was holding Fa Fa's favourite black hat. As he approached I saw the hat brim was dusty and the crown battered out of shape. The blue kingfisher feather in the band was tattered as if moths had made a meal of it.

I rushed at my brother and gripped him by the shoulders. 'What's happened? Where's my father?'

'At home,' he said in a dead voice.

'Is he all right?'

Owen nodded, but didn't meet my eyes.

'Why did you bring his hat?'

The boy's elbows tucked against his ribs, and he moved the hat out of view behind his leg. 'I don't know.'

I took his free hand, found it ice-cold. Chafing it between my palms, I said gently, 'Please tell me. Is Fa Fa terribly unwell?'

Owen pulled his hand from my grasp and looked along the platform.

'We'd better get back,' he said in that same lifeless voice. 'Do you have your baggage ticket?'

I fumbled the slip from my pocket. 'Alone? Why is he alone? Where's Millie?'

Owen flinched, and snatched the docket from my hand. Pulling Fa Fa's hat onto his head, he darted away and ran the length of the train to the freight carriage. He stood patiently while the attendant checked the tickets and retrieved carpet-bags and hatboxes and travelling cases. Finally my battered trunk emerged and Owen seized it and surrendered the ticket.

We hurried outside and down the hill to the carriage. The horses were restless in the rain, their flanks wet and streaked with mud. I noticed that one had a red sore on its eyelid. Owen threw my bag in the dray, then fumbled one-handed with the tethering rope and released the horses. He checked the yokes and harnesses, and made to slip past me and up onto the driver's bench, but I grabbed his arm.

'Owen, you must tell me what's wrong.'

He wound the leather reins around his hand but said nothing.

'It's Millie, isn't it?' I persisted.

Owen nodded, but made no attempt to elaborate. Finally he met my gaze, and the empty desolation I saw in his young eyes tore my heart.

'Please, Owen, I'm dying of worry. I demand you tell me.'

He paled. The dark in his eyes swallowed him. He stared up at me from under the brim of my father's hat.

'Fa Fa told me not to.'

'Why?'

Pulling from my grasp without answering, he escaped up the carriage steps and took his seat, staring straight ahead.

I climbed up after him and settled my skirts, then gently took the reins from his frozen fingers. The horses quivered and snorted, blowing rain from their nostrils as we headed uphill from the station. Turning onto the Bundarra Road, I set them to a trot, all at once aching to be home and yet fearful of what awaited me there.

My father's wolfhound Harold met us at the gate.

Like Owen, the old dog appeared diminished; his bones jutted knife-like from his flanks, and his coat was unkempt and crusted with mud. He darted skittishly around my feet as the I alighted and hurried into the house, leaving Owen to drive the buggy to the barn and tend the horses.

Bursting through the back door, I ran from room to room. The once-gleaming floorboards were trampled with mud, my aunt's prized rugs littered with debris and kicked askew. There was a sickly smell in the air that grew stronger as I approached the kitchen.

'Millie?'

The benches were cluttered with unwashed dishes. Crusts of bread and spilled food and bowls of curdled milk lay about the benchtops, and a branch had smashed one of the windows, letting in a puddle of rain.

'Millie! Where are you?'

Drifts of dog hair and mouse dirt and breadcrumbs littered the dining-room floor. Leaves had blown in from outside, and the tabletop was silty; a bird had made tracks through the dust at the head of the table where my father liked to sit.

My father's study was empty, his desk in disarray, the curtains drawn, and a stale smell in the air like spilled brandy and perspiration. I ran upstairs and knocked on his bedroom door, pushing it open.

'Fa Fa?'

He was hunched on the edge of the mattress, his elbows on his knees, his head resting in his hands. As he looked up and saw me, I gripped the doorhandle to steady myself. The skin hung from his cheeks, and his eyes were hollow. His hair had thinned and grown long, the faded curls now shot through with silver.

I rushed to him and settled beside him on the bed, wrapped my arms around his shoulders. His bones felt brittle through his shirt, like those of an old, old man.

'Where's Millie?' I said gently. 'The house is in a dreadful state. You and Owen looked half-starved, and even Harold is skin and bones. What's happened?'

A thin hand reached for me. 'Millie is gone, Brenna.'

'Gone?' I blinked. Black spots swarmed behind my eyes. 'Where has she gone?'

Fa Fa covered his face with his hands. 'Get me a brandy, Brenna girl. And a pair of tumblers. I will tell you, my sparrow, but you must prepare yourself. I fear you are going to need a bellyful of drink to bear it.'

'It happened soon after dusk. Millie had served dinner and was just bringing her own plate to the table when we heard the screams.'

My father paused to wipe his mouth. He gazed at the strong cup of tea I'd laced with brandy, but he made no move to touch it.

'We went onto the verandah. There was smoke in the air, and far off in the distance we saw the glow of a blaze. At first I thought it was bushfire, and that the shouts we could hear were to warn us of the blaze. But something made me go upstairs and load my rifle. Owen left first. His horse was already saddled and tethered to the post at the front of the house. I tried to call him back, but—' Fa Fa's eyes were pleading. He took my hand. 'What poor Owen saw that night has addled him. They are all dead, my Brenna. The clan is gone. Men came to the encampment, just as they did all those years ago. They brought their swords and guns and wreaked bloody murder.'

My back flushed ice cold, while my face and hands were on fire.

'Jindera?' I managed to whisper. 'Mee Mee?'

My father shook his head. 'Gone, my little love. All of them, gone.'

I slumped back as if struck in the face. My thoughts were scrambled. I wanted to clutch for a logical explanation, an escape from the horror, but I was in a maze of fear; everywhere I turned, my way was blocked. I moaned softly. My skin was clammy. I swayed forward, willing myself to slide into unconsciousness, willing the ache in my chest to somehow drag me under.

Finally, I found my voice. 'Is there a chance that Jindera or any of the others might have escaped? Like they did that other time, when they hid in the cave along the riverbank?'

My father stared towards the window. He was wide-eyed, as if he had just woken from a nightmare, his nostrils flaring, his breath coming short and sharp.

'I saw the pyre,' he said, his voice cracking with grief. 'The men lit it and dragged the bodies into the flames, but they didn't tend it well. It never burned, just . . . just—' He stared fixedly into the shadows. 'I am to blame. They are gone. Our people are gone. And I am to blame.'

'No,' I whispered, wanting to reassure him, but my voice jammed in my throat. Fa Fa spoke his bitter words from the unreliable standpoint of his grief, but it was clear to me that he bore no blame for what had happened. Clear to me, too, that while guilt ate away my father's kind heart with the ferocity of acid, the real offenders had escaped without reproach.

Owen entered the room and hurried to my father's side. He lay at his feet without a word to either of us, and closed his eyes. He began to cry quietly, but when Fa Fa reached down and placed his hand on the boy's head, Owen became still.

Beyond the open window the sky blazed blue. The grass was golden, and leaves gusted through the winter air. By all appearances, life was going on. Out there, out in the world, the destruction of my small family had made no impact; and yet here in my father's quiet, familiar room, the very heart of time had come to a standstill.

My father let out a great shuddering sigh. Lying back on the bed, he rolled to face the wall and dragged the coverlet up to his ear. He began to sob – dry, wretched gasps that echoed after me as I shut his door and descended the stairs on shaky legs.

Dawn lightened the sky across the mountains. I sat in the dappled sunlight beneath the red gum where once wallaby skins were hung to dry. Where once, on a sunny afternoon, my grandmother had scattered a handful of black seeds onto her grindstone, to pound into flour for cakes.

Where once I had stood with Jindera, promising to return.

The shady encampment was now a blackened scar of land. The huts were gone, the campfire had been scattered. Despite the passage of weeks, the smell of burned flesh lingered in the air.

I found the site of the pyre that my father had described. Nothing remained of the bodies that had been burned there. The ground had been raked clear, the debris dragged away, the corpses buried. I wondered what it had cost my father to see the ruin brought upon the people he had loved so dearly.

Everything. It had cost him everything.

I lay down at the centre of the scar and looked up at the sky. Clouds drifted past, and the sun blazed in my eyes, forcing me to close them. Blood-red behind my lids. After a while I drifted – not into sleep, but into a sort of waking dream.

Jindera stood before me. The favoured yellow dress that Aunt Ida had once given her was gone. Instead, she wore a large wallaby skin blanket around her shoulders, its ragged hem reaching past her knees. Around her neck she wore a necklace of snake vertebrae, each fragile bone bleached salt-white.

Approaching, she held out her hand.

A small silver object gleamed on her palm. She gestured for me to take it, but when I tried to grasp the object, it puffed through my fingers like smoke.

No cross water, Bunna. Danger there. Bad spirits.

I thought of my journey to Tasmania, of the months I'd spent at Brayer House. Jindera had been right; I did not belong under that distant roof, confined like a caged bird. And yet I couldn't help wondering where I would be now if I had listened to Jindera's warning. Would I have been able to prevent the massacre? Or would I now be resting in the nearby ground, my body charred, consumed by the same flames that had consumed hers?

I stood up. My clothes were streaked with charcoal and dust. I began to walk without knowing where I was going. I don't remember taking the track down to the river, but sometime later I found myself on the rocky embankment overlooking the rapids. The water had receded from the banks, exposing pebbles and turning them dull with silt. Looking along the mud bank, I saw a half-moon-shaped impression.

The mark of a horse's shoe.

Further along, I found more tracks. They continued on the mud bank for a while, before disappearing higher up the verge. I knelt beside one of the indentations, dipping my fingers into the curve. A rider had come this way, perhaps in pursuit of someone. I looked along the riverbank, but saw no sign of any cave or cleft in the rocks that might serve as a hiding place.

The sun went behind a cloud and the horse tracks turned dark with shadows.

All the time I was away, I had daydreamed about the moment I would tell Jindera what I'd learned from Aunt Ida and from my father. I had envisaged her face as I spoke the words that acknowledged her as family. She would beam, her round face alight with pleasure. We would laugh, and she would clasp me tightly against her, and our joyful tears would wash away the sorrow and loss she had buried inside herself the night my mother died.

The sun emerged again, and the shadows shrank away.

A glimmer caught my eye.

I searched the ground until I saw a soft glint beneath a feathery brown clump of winter tussock. I pushed back the grass and stared at the object partly submerged in the dust.

It was a silver chain, attached to a dirt-encrusted locket.

I picked it up. An expensive treasure, to be lost out here by the river. One of the riders must have dropped it as they gave chase along the embankment.

The sun retreated behind a cloud and the shadows shifted again. Opening the locket, I stared at the miniature portrait.

The woman's ash-blonde hair was pulled into a loose knot on the top of her head. Her pale blue eyes were framed by lashes so fair they were almost invisible. Her cheeks were plump and pink, and a wreath of yellow flowers adorned her hair. She was smiling prettily, almost dreamily.

'Mama,' I whispered.

For a long time I stared at her likeness, so pleased to see her familiar features that a lump formed in my throat. But as the minutes ticked away, other feelings arose. Unease. And the queasy sensation that I stood on the brink of some terrible realisation.

Why was my mother's portrait out here in the dust, fallen by the riverbank, so close to the horse tracks I'd found? Had my father dropped it when he'd buried the bodies of the clan; had he wandered beside the river in a daze, as I had just now?

I snapped the locket shut, and rubbed away the dirt. A design emerged. A stylised representation of a lyrebird's tail, the long feathers curved into a decorative harp.

My queasiness became a solid lump, cutting off my air. I couldn't breathe. Blood thundered in my head as the truth settled over me. I had seen this locket before. Not in my father's possession, but sitting on the writing desk in my bedroom at Brayer House.

It had gleamed in the lamplight, and at first I had mistaken it for a fob watch. My husband's fob watch. Only, it hadn't been a watch at all.

I closed my fingers over its ornate face, gripping it so tightly my knuckles popped. I struggled up the embankment on shaky legs. When I finally reached the encampment, I started to run.

Through my tears, I could see Carsten's face, that night in the library. Carved through with devastation, hollowed with shock and hatred. He had glared at me with dark eyes and made a promise, that now rang ominously in my ears.

You'll all be sorry you crossed me—

'No, no.' I tripped and hit the ground, but climbed unsteadily and stumbled on. *Michael told me Florence had a baby that year*, he had said. *I thought she was—*

She was the woman in the locket.

Florence. My mama. The woman Carsten had once loved, but lost to another man. To my father.

Your father took my money to save his godforsaken land . . . by God, he has a bloody hide . . .

Fa Fa would know. He would know how to make sense of the words, the snatches of memory, my mother's likeness in the locket. If anyone could explain what I'd found, it was my father.

I pounded upstairs to my father's room, then paused. The house seemed very quiet. Too quiet. I knocked, and when there came no answer I put my head in and called softly.

'Fa Fa, are you awake?'

He lay where I had left him, curled towards the wall with the sheet drawn up to his ear. Tufts of hair spread like grey smudges on the pillowcase, and one hand was flung palm-up on the coverlet.

There was a stillness in the room that made the air seem cold despite the sunlight drifting through the window. The tea I'd poured for him yesterday sat untouched, a thin film of scum floating on its surface.

The chair creaked as I sat down. My father didn't stir. I touched his shoulder. It was cold, unyielding. My fingers crept to his wrist, and then gently to the hollow beneath his ear, but I could find no pulse.

'Oh no . . . no, *no.*'

I took his hand, gripped his rigid fingers. His skin was fragile and smooth, clammy under my touch, cold. I buckled over, resting my forehead on his knuckles, trying to swallow the black desolation so that I could, at least, whisper goodbye.

I don't know at what stage I remembered Owen. Only that when my tears dried and my shock had frayed into numbness, I became aware of sounds beyond my island of misery. A rooster crowed in the yard. A possum bounded over the roof. The clock chimed in the parlour. Once, twice. Three times.

With profound effort, I sat up and tried to collect my thoughts. There were things I must do. Send Owen to fetch the minister, the doctor, the undertaker. Find my father's best suit. Notify his solicitor and write a letter to the bank.

Getting to my feet, I kissed the top of Fa Fa's head and shuffled across the room. Closing the door gently behind me, I made my way along the hall and then downstairs. The old house creaked, the roof ticked as the iron expanded under the sun's heat. A flock of black cockatoos flew overhead, their screeching cries violating the quiet.

I paused a moment, breathing the air into my lungs.

Then I went to find my brother.

Owen wasn't in the house. I searched the yard, looked in the chook pen and all his usual haunts around the garden, and ran along the riverbank calling his name. Harold, who shadowed Owen just as the boy had shadowed my father, was missing, too.

Owen must have already found my father dead, and fled into the bush to grieve in private. My heart gave a painful twist. Fa Fa had been Owen's world; how could he bear to lose him?

I ran through the yard, calling. The silence and stillness was eerie, and I had the disconnected sense that I was stumbling through a dream. As I neared the stables, I saw that the tall doors had been dragged shut. I pounded my hand on the sun-warmed wood.

'Owen? Are you in there?'

The only reply was a warning growl from Harold.

Dragging aside the stable door, I stepped into the stuffy darkness. Harold let out another rumble, and I heard something shift on the straw. Several heartbeats passed before my eyes adjusted to the gloom.

At the far end of the stable, in the darkest corner behind the row of stalls, I saw Owen standing on a chair.

'What are you doing?'

Harold whined, but Owen didn't answer. He seemed very still. I took a step nearer.

'Owen?'

My throat was already tight with grief, but it had suddenly gone dry. I shuffled nearer the stalls, unable to shift my gaze from my brother.

That was when I saw the rope. Ice went through me and my legs buckled as I stumbled across the dim space towards him. Harold rushed at me from the dark, barking. When I tried to shove past him, he sank his teeth into my hand.

'Owen!' I screamed.

The sound of my voice drew an anguished yelp from Harold, and then he started to bark, great drawn-out crying noises that echoed off the stable's inner walls and drowned out my sobs.

Owen hadn't been standing on the chair. He had simply used it as a stepping-off point. I grabbed his legs; his body seemed so pitifully small, yet it was too heavy for me to lift. I tried to untangle him from the rope, but the loop he'd tied in the end of it would not release him. In the end I let him go, and he swung away from me. I cried out and stumbled across the straw-littered floor, slamming into the wall where a row of tools dangled from their nails. Grabbing a curved knife, I rushed back to my brother and climbed the chair beside him, held him against me while I hacked through the rope. When the last strands finally frayed and gave way, Owen's weight dragged me from the chair and we landed together on the floor.

I gathered him to me, my fingers finding his throat, seeking the pulse I already knew would not be there. Harold stretched beside us, licking Owen's face. I tried to shut my ears to the old dog's wretched grieving, but the voice in my head was worse.

Please, not Owen. Not my gentle little Owen who swam naked in the river like a fish and blushed crimson when the clan girls teased him. Not the little boy who clung to my father like a shadow and tripped us all up in his eagerness to be loved. Not Owen . . . please, please – not my dear Owen.

In a box under my bed I found the revolver Aunt Ida had given me, and a carton of brass cartridges. The weapon was heavy. It took forever for me to find the catch that hinged open the frame. The cylinder had been cleaned and oiled, and the shells slid easily into their hollows.

Downstairs in the yard, I placed a row of pinecones along the fence. Walking back twenty paces, trembling hard, I wasted a full chamber of rounds to shatter only two pinecones. Reloading the gun, I slowed my pace. Breathing deeply, I took control of my tremors. And instead of seeing pinecones, I envisioned my husband's face.

Six shots rang out, and six times his countenance shattered to dust. When my shells were spent, I returned to the house. Upstairs in my room, I wrapped the pistol in burlap and secreted it in the false lining of my travelling trunk, covering it with clothes. As I was packing it, I found the pouch of wolfsbane flowers I had picked that day in the glade. The deadly blossoms were withered now, and would crumble easily to powder. I slipped them into my pocket, and then stood in the dimness, hugging my arms, breathing the scent of wildflowers and perspiration-stale clothes and gunpowder, as I planned my return to Brayer House.

19

Belief in limitation breeds unhappiness.
– ROB THISTLETON, *EMOTIONAL RESCUE*

Ruby, May 2013

A few days after my ordeal on the rocks, Pete drove me into Armidale to have my ankle checked by the doctor. The swelling had mostly gone down, but Pete was insistent.

'Just in case,' he told me. 'Besides, I'm going in anyway, I've got a delivery of seedlings to make to the Landcare group's nursery. And,' he added with a grin, 'I'm becoming quite addicted to your company.'

I rolled my eyes, but was secretly pleased.

'Hey, I'm serious,' Pete insisted. 'I'm hooked, Ruby . . . and and so are the kelpies.'

I glanced over my shoulder at the cab window. Sure enough, two pointy brown and tan faces with lolling tongues were gazing raptly back at me. A few weeks ago, I would have shuddered at the sight; but a funny thing was happening. I was moving through tolerance, and into the first shallow waters of acceptance.

And I had the sneaking suspicion that they knew this. Lately, both dogs had turned deaf to Pete's commands to leave me alone; they followed me wherever I went, flopped beside me when I sat on the verandah, and gazed, besotted, up at me when I reached towards them to tickle the tips of my fingers over their silky ears. I hadn't quite progressed to rolling on the ground and cuddling them – as Pete often did – but it was a start.

Half an hour later we drove through Clearwater and my phone made a succession of chirps. I checked the register and found eleven missed calls; two were an unknown number, the rest were from Rob. I deleted them all, glad I'd been out of range. Which was why, when we reached the Armidale town limits and my phone began to warble, I was reluctant to answer.

'Hello?'

'Is that Ruby Cardel?' a woman asked. 'We've been trying to contact you for several days. My name's Anne Arding, from New England Solicitors. I was hoping to arrange an appointment with you to discuss a matter regarding the estate of Esther Hillard. How soon can you be available to come in?'

I did an internal double take: Esther's estate? My good mood plunged. Had someone complained about me staying at Lyrebird Hill, a long lost family member who had somehow gotten wind of my extended visit?

'I'm in Armidale now, if today suits you?'

We agreed on a time, and Anne explained how to find her office. I hung up, and slumped.

'I think I'm in trouble,' I told Pete.

'I couldn't help overhearing,' he replied, and a secretive little smile touched his lips. 'Was that Esther's solicitor?'

'She wants to see me.' I looked at him worriedly. 'Can someone get sued for overstaying their welcome?'

'That depends.'

His serious tone made me look at him more closely. He was studying me, not exactly smiling, but there was a hint there, as if he was on the brink of a laugh.

'What?' I asked.

The laugh finally erupted. Suddenly Pete was all teeth and twinkling sapphire eyes, and a merry gaze that locked onto mine – and even though I clung fiercely to my annoyance, I felt the quiver of a smile take hold, and then the bubbling urge to laugh along with him. How did he do that?

Pete leaned back in his seat. 'I hope she's left you something amazing.'

A flush of warmth filled me, but as I made my way along Rusden Street in the direction of the solicitor's office, the anxiety oozed back. I hoped Pete was right. I remembered the book Esther had mentioned to me that night in the gallery, and how she had insisted it belonged to me. It wasn't Jamie's diary, because that had gone into the ashes years ago; but it could be an old volume of fairytales, which – considering the memories that had been trickling back in the past weeks – would have been a most welcome memento of Granny H.

The solicitor's office was in the central mall, an old building with an echoey foyer that led upstairs into a tiny cluttered room.

The solicitor, Anne, got straight to the point.

'Esther has named you in her will to receive her farmhouse and the surrounding three thousand acres of land known as Lyrebird Hill.'

I hovered on the edge of a heartbeat, hardly daring to breathe. When I found my voice, I blurted, 'But I hardly knew her.'

Anne smiled warmly. 'When my associates witnessed this will, Esther explained that you had lived at Lyrebird Hill as a child, and that you'd been neighbours. She said she was fond of you, and since she had no other relatives, she wanted the property to go to you. There's also this.'

Taking a paper-wrapped parcel from her drawer, she passed it across the desk to me.

It was a book.

While I sat stunned, Anne explained that probate would take a month, after which time the deeds and related documents would transfer to me. She would then send me a letter when the documents and spare keys were ready for pick-up.

I thought I'd better come clean about my extended stay at the property, in case it impacted the legals, but Anne reassured me that since I was there at Esther's invitation, and there were no living relatives to question my presence, she could see no reason why I shouldn't continue to stay on.

I left the office in a daze, stumbling along the street to where Pete's Holden waited. I got into the car and sat silently, hugging myself as I stared through the windscreen.

'Are you okay?' Pete wanted to know. 'You seem a bit out of it.'

I held aloft my parcel. 'Esther gave me a book.'

'That's great,' he said, frowning. 'What else happened in there?'

'She also left me the farm. I barely knew her, and she left me a three-thousand-acre property.'

Pete blinked, then broke into the giddiest smile I'd seen so far. He let out a delighted howl, which inspired the dogs into a barking frenzy.

'I knew it, bless her,' he declared, thumping his palm on the steering wheel. 'Oh the darling old girl, if she was here now I'd give her one of my famous bear hugs.'

'You seem pleased.'

He beamed. 'Of *course* I'm pleased.'

My brain was still trying to untangle the complicated idea that in a month's time Lyrebird Hill would belong to me. I looked at Pete with his wild dark hair, and the blue gaze now fixed steadily to mine. He and Esther had been close, and Pete had always been there to help her. I felt a rush of protectiveness for him.

'Of all people, I would have thought she'd leave the farm to you.'

He shrugged, and hammed up the wide-eyed puzzlement. 'I've got my own farm.'

'But . . . she should have left you *something*.'

'She did.'

Clearly, I'd slept through the part about Pete's inheritance. I frowned and shook my head, mystified. 'What are you talking about?'

He grinned, buckling on his seatbelt, and leaning towards me so his face was a handspan from mine; his eyes crinkled at the edges and gleamed like gemstones.

'Ah, Roo,' he said in a softer voice. 'It'll be just like the old days, only better. We're going to be neighbours.'

It wasn't just any old book in Esther's parcel, it was a large leather-bound journal.

And not just any old journal. It had been written by my great-grandmother, Brenna Whitby, recording events that had occurred between March 1898 and her imprisonment in August that same year.

The book was full of beautifully detailed botanical paintings. They were clearly rendered by the same hand that had decorated the letter to my grandfather as a baby. Native orchids, ferns, gumnuts and blossoms – all accompanied by notes about their medicinal uses.

But most intriguing were Brenna's personal entries.

It is dawn, she had written towards the end of the book. *I am sitting on a blackened scar of land. Tears stream down my cheeks as I write, splashing onto my words and making the ink bleed. Once, a humble dwelling occupied the patch of bare dirt where I now sit. But the people who lived here are gone, their ashes swept away by the wind. I searched for them all day yesterday, and late into the night. But they are gone.*

From the moment we got back to Lyrebird Hill, I immersed myself in Brenna's world. As her story unfolded – as the pages turned, and as I became more entangled in the web of mystery surrounding Brayer House and the shadow it had once cast over Brenna's family – I found myself desperately hoping that she had been innocent. I wanted to know the truth – but I wanted it to be a truth that led to redemption, and not one that marked her as a murderer.

But as I reached the journal's last pages, I couldn't help feeling disheartened.

I could understand Brenna's grief, and how it had driven her over the dark brink of endurance. But still, the question shadowed my mind. Was I like Brenna, after all? Did the potential for murder lie buried in me, just as it had in her?

'This calls for a celebration,' Pete declared, as we sat on the verandah later that afternoon. 'I'll fire up the barbie, and we can relax with a glass of wine or three and bliss out under the stars. What do you say, Ruby?'

'I say, *absolutely*.' I tried to smile, tried to force up a festive mood – but I was still feeling overwhelmed by the enormity of Esther's bequest and the uncertainty inspired by Brenna's journal. I gazed across the rambling disorder of the garden, and down the slope to the river. Through the grove of casuarinas, I could see the water babbling over the stones, and kingfishers swooping for insects, and above it all, an endless vista of blue sky.

'I'm still wondering,' I told Pete. 'Why me?'

He reached for my hand and gave my fingers a gentle squeeze. 'Esther liked you, she used to talk about you a lot. Maybe she thought you deserved a break. You know, after your sister.'

Twining my fingers in Pete's, I examined his hand. It was a broad square hand, the knuckles nicked with scars and the skin lightly freckled from time spent outdoors. Despite all the gardening he did, his nails were short and clean; not manicured, like Rob's, but somehow honest and real. Looking back,

I wondered how I had ever been satisfied with anyone who wasn't . . . well, *Pete*.

He shifted closer, his warmth radiating against me, the friendly aromas of eucalyptus and dog hair wafting from his shirt.

'Do you remember,' he said quietly, 'how Granny H always used to rework the story? One of her favourite tales was *Beauty and the Beast*, but she never told the ending the same way twice. We must have heard that story a thousand times, but each time Granny told it, Beauty changed – sometimes she was tomboyish, other times a priggish little princess. And the poor old Beast got uglier, more wretched with every telling. Sometimes he turned out not to be the handsome prince after all, but the evil witch in disguise.'

'That was the best part,' I said, smiling through my tears. 'Not knowing how it was going to turn out. She always kept us guessing. We were never sure whether the ending was going to be happy or sad, do you remember? I suppose she liked to keep us on our toes, so things never got boring.'

Pete looked at me a long time. Then he leaned forward again, and this time pressed his lips ever so gently against the corner of my mouth. 'A bit like life, wouldn't you say, Roo?'

I pondered this. And then, inexplicably, I began to shake.

It started in the vicinity of my diaphragm, subtle at first, as if I'd grown a second, tinier heart right in the middle of my body and it was beating out of time with my real heart. The little heart sped up, began to race. And then, like ripples spreading outward from the centre of a lake, the tremors took hold.

Pete gathered me into his arms and held me tightly, stroking my hair, whispering against my scalp. And I rained tears onto his chest, overwhelmed that a woman I hadn't known since childhood had given me a gift of such resounding love.

Later, I lit a fire in the donkey burner and waited for my bathwater to heat. I was looking forward to immersing myself in a tub of steaming water; my neck muscles were tight and I felt strangely restless. Good news always seemed to have that effect on me; rather than bubble over with joy, I tended to brood.

As I sat on the rim of the bath, I gazed up into the trees. I had hoped to find answers here at Lyrebird Hill, and I *had* – but they still weren't slotting as neatly into place as I had hoped. Rationally, I understood that life was not that simple; not every question had an answer, and you could do your head in trying to find one.

But buried in the dark folds of my logical mind was a granule of frustration; it niggled and nagged, an irritating particle that refused to go away.

Jamie's killer was still unknown.

I turned on the tap. The water that rushed out was still cold. I huffed, impatient. Withdrawing my hand, I wiped my fingers on my jeans, but didn't turn off the tap. Water gurgled down the plughole. It was a waste to let it run, but there was something about the sound of it that made me uneasy. The splash and patter as it drummed the base of the bath, the noisy burble as it flowed away down the drain; and now the quiet thrum of my pulse in my ears, that made it sound almost like—

Rain.

I stared glumly at the window. It had been pouring all day, all last night, too. It was Saturday, and the yard had turned into a bog.

Mum and Jamie and I were trapped inside together like a trio of bedraggled battery hens, cranky and ruffled after harsh words from Mum at breakfast when she'd managed yet again to burn the toast.

Rain always seemed to draw out the smells. Aside from burnt toast, there was woodsmoke from the stove, and Jamie's wet hair, and the earthy pong of the root crops Mum had harvested yesterday. Huge yellow potatoes, fat purplish turnips, long skinny parsnips with bulbous heads, and a grotesque Jerusalem artichoke that would later add the stink of our farts to the mix.

I sighed and turned my mind back to my jigsaw. Because of the rain, I had been allowed to set it up on the kitchen table. Mum had lit the old Warmbrite, which sent wafts of smoke curling into the room whenever she opened the door to stoke the fire. It took the damp out of the air, though, and sometimes – when Mum had her act together, which, after the burned-toast fiasco, obviously wasn't today – she baked bread or carrot-and-walnut muffins, or cooked stew on the stovetop.

My jigsaw was an old birthday present from Jamie, given before she had become an insufferable snob. We'd spent a ridiculous amount of time together in those days, our heads bowed over various jigsaws, nattering or absorbed in contented silence. This one was one of my favourites – a thousand-piece mind-bender depicting a bunch of swans – and I had hoped Jamie might remember that we'd once been close, and maybe show some remorse for how she'd been treating me . . . and more importantly, over her part in Bobby's betrayal of the Wolf.

No such luck.

Jamie sat by the window gazing out at the overcast sky, as if nothing else in the world existed. Her normally perfect face was puckered in a frown, her brow as bumpy as an old piece of corrugated cardboard. I knew she was mooning over Bobby, probably planning to meet him that very afternoon. She'd been acting a bit cuckoo the last few days; doing a lot of window-gazing, rolling her eyes behind Mum's back, trying on all her clothes then complaining she had nothing to wear. She didn't look as pretty as she normally did, either. Her face was always pale, and she was developing a permanent frown line—

'Ruby?' Mum was standing in the kitchen doorway, watching me.

'What?'

'I'm off to the market now. Don't forget to check the rain gauge at nine o'clock and make sure it's written in the book.'

'Okay.'

I frittered around in my room after she'd gone, then spied on Jamie for a while; she was still hunched at the window. I went back to my room, and when nine o'clock arrived, I dragged on my gumboots and was just about to head out to the rain gauge when I noticed that Jamie was no longer moping by the window.

Not bothering to slip off my boots, I ran out to Jamie's room. It stunk of deodorant, and the perfume that always made me think of insect repellent. She'd left her jeans and sweatshirt in a heap on the bed. I looked in the cupboard – sure enough, Jamie's new dress and her best black sandals were gone.

Rushing to the window, I searched the yard outside. Jamie was nowhere, but there on the lawn, cutting through the wet grass, was a trail of footprints.

'Bugger the rain gauge,' I muttered, rushing along the hall to the back door. I burst outside and squelched over the wet grass, following my sister's trail down the slope to the river.

Steam was rising from the release pipe on the donkey burner; the fire had burned low. Pulling myself back to the present, I twisted on the tap. This time, there was no eerie patter of half-remembered rain – just the regular gush of scalding river water as it filled the tub. I added cold, then dipped in my toe and deemed it perfect.

Taking off Esther's locket, I slipped it into my dressing-gown pocket. Now that I was brave enough to bathe naked, I abandoned my clothes on the wrought iron chair and sank into the tub, sloshing water over the rim and onto the granite pavers.

This afternoon I had lingered in front of my dressing table, examining my reflection and thinking about Brenna. My features showed no trace of an Indigenous heritage, no evidence that I was anything other than what I appeared to be: a thirty-year-old woman with brown eyes and brown hair. But if I turned my thoughts inwards I could feel a sort of double-beat inside me. One that whispered of the people whose blood I shared, and another for the land that had claimed me as its own.

Closing my eyes, I sank deeper into the bath.

Water dripped from the tap. Butcherbirds sang their afternoon serenade in the apple gums. Bees mumbled in the rosemary. Waves of bliss washed through me. If I wanted to, I could stay here forever—

'Hey, babe.'

Yelling in fright, I shot out of the water, scrambling as my wet limbs slid from under me. As I fell backwards into the tub, hot bathwater washed up and engulfed my face, leaving me blinded by a curtain of wet hair. I knuckled the water out of my eyes and sat up, trying, without much luck, to cover my naked-ness with a washcloth. I glared at the man sitting on the end of the tub.

'What are you doing here?'

Rob reached into the water, grasping my ankle firmly in his large fingers. He must have meant to steady me, but his touch had the opposite effect. I flinched away, causing another tidal wave.

Despite all the water, my mouth was dry with nerves. I looked past Rob to the entrance of the bottlebrush hedge.

'Where's Bardo?'

Rob looked at me, puzzled. 'Who?'

'She always sits in the doorway over there when I have a bath.'

'Doorway?' Rob's brow shot up and he shook his head, amused. 'God, Ruby, next you'll be getting around in an Akubra and flannelette shirt. Aren't you tired of all this rustic crap? When are you coming home?'

'I *am* home.'

Rob fixed his gaze on me, and his mouth downturned. 'You're making a mistake, Ruby. You're throwing away everything we built together, and for what? To wallow in the past out here, rather than standing up in the real world and facing your problems. I never picked you as a coward, babe – but now I'm starting to wonder.'

His words had a toxic affect on me; three years of frustration bubbled up. Rob's veiled criticisms over the years, the self-satisfied way he always pointed out my failings – and me falling for every word of it.

'You cheated on me,' I said, not bothering to keep the venom out of my voice. 'Worse, you lied about it. You can think what you like, Rob, but I don't want anything more to do with you.'

'Hey, I understand you're upset. I made a stupid mistake.' He lifted his hands as if in surrender. 'I'm only human, Ruby.'

'I don't care what you are,' I growled. 'This is my property now. I want you to leave.'

Rob's smile vanished. Springing to his feet, he stared down at me. He didn't exactly frown, but a narrow look came into his eyes. His gaze roamed over my nakedness; he seemed to regard me from a great distance, a bird of prey considering his quarry.

Abruptly, he leaned forward and dashed his hand in the bathwater, splashing my face. '*Your* property,' he said nastily. 'Who the hell do you think you are, Ruby Cardel? Miss high and mighty, you sound just like your stuck-up bitch of a sister.'

I was shaking so hard my teeth wanted to clatter together, and my pulse hammered my eardrums; but I tightened my jaw and held my ground.

'Please leave, Rob.'

His mouth screwed up in scorn as he gave me a cursory once-over, then he turned on his heel and stalked away.

Staring after him, I waited until I was sure he was gone. Shakily, I climbed out and wrapped myself in the relative privacy of my dressing gown. For a long time I stood in the sunlight, waiting to hear Rob's car start up and drive away – but all I could hear was the short rapid rasp of my breathing.

Finally my trembling subsided. I slid my hand into my dressing gown pocket, and drew out Esther's silver locket. Sunbeams spangled on its ornate face, picking out the intricate design as it swung back and forth, back and forth, liquid bright. Then the light and warmth faded. In their place, the overcast sky of a rainy day; and drifting in the damp air, a smell: sharp and sweet and vaguely artificial, almost like insect repellent. It made me think of Jamie.

Miss high and mighty, Rob had called her.

A glimmer; a question. How could he know—?

And that was all it took for the vault to crack open and spill forth my last remaining memory.

They were standing on the flat granite shelf overlooking the river, caught up in a heated argument. They couldn't see me hiding behind the boulder, but I had a clear view of them.

Jamie, and Bobby Drake.

My sister had her back to me, but for the first time, I saw Bobby clearly. He was tall and heavyset, with stubble on his pale cheeks and a dark gaze that was fixed intently on Jamie. His hair was lank and mousy, curling over the neckline of his football jumper.

'Where is it?' he was saying. 'Mum wants it back.'

Jamie said something I didn't catch, and it seemed to infuriate Bobby further. He stalked away from her, then turned on his heel and came back.

Jamie went to sidestep him, but her sandals slid on a patch of moss. Bobby took her arm to steady her, but she jerked away from him.

'Leave me alone, you idiot.'

She started walking along the rocky embankment, back towards the track that led home. Bobby lunged after her and spun her around to face him. Gripping her shoulders, he gave her a shake.

'Just tell me what you did with the locket.'

'I hid it.'

'Mum wants it back.'

Jamie pulled free. 'You shouldn't have nicked it in the first place. Besides, you said your mum originally got it as a present from my great-grandmother.'

'Yeah, years ago. So?'

'So it's rightfully mine. I'm keeping it. And if you hassle me about it anymore, I'll tell everyone you're a thief.'

Bobby made an angry sound in his throat, and shoved Jamie. The action sent her off balance again and her sandals skated on the mossy surface and skimmed from under her. She hit the rocks on her hands and knees, gasping in pain.

Bobby laughed.

Jamie flushed beet red. She struggled to her feet and rushed at him, swinging her fist into his face. Bobby grunted and stumbled back. Blood began to stream from his nose and seep over his lips. He wiped his mouth with the back of his hand, and when he saw the blood he looked at Jamie. Just looked at her for the longest time. Then he grabbed her by the arms, pinning them to her sides as he swung her around and shoved her against the tall granite boulder.

Jamie's head hit the stone. Bobby pushed her again, and she started screaming.

'Shut up,' Bobby hissed.

He shook her really hard then, over and over, as if to wake her from a dead sleep. Each time, her head bashed into the rock. Then her scream cut out midway, and her head wobbled forward. She began to cry, and a bubble of blood came out of her mouth.

I flew from my hiding place. I was trembling so hard I could barely stand, but I charged at Bobby, digging my fingernails into his arm, trying to drag my sister away from him. Bobby elbowed me in the head, bringing stars to my eyes, but he released Jamie. She staggered against the boulder and then slid onto her bottom. Wheeling around, Bobby walloped me across the side of the head and I went skating backwards across the boulder, sliding over the edge onto the rock below. My shoe caught in the gap between two stones, and I couldn't get it out, so I wrenched my foot free and left the shoe there. Scrambling back up the boulder, I found Bobby crouched beside my sister. Jamie sat crumpled on the ground like a ragdoll, her legs crooked beneath her.

'Jamie,' I said kneeling beside her, 'are you okay?'

She didn't look okay. Her face was greyish-white and streaked with grubby tears. Her hair stuck to her face, and when I lifted it away I saw that her ear was full of sticky black liquid. A handful of seconds passed before I realised it was blood.

'Jamie?'

She looked at Bobby. 'They're here somewhere,' she said in a trembling voice. 'They're my best sandals, I don't want them getting lost. Help me look for them, will you?'

Her voice sounded strange, slurred, the way Mum's was after Dad died. Worst of all, her sandals were on her feet, right where she should have been able to see them.

'Where are they? What have you done with them?'

'Jamie,' I said, touching her arm, 'we better go home now.'

She looked at me, but Bobby tugged her around to face him. 'Hey Jamie – you fell, remember? If anyone asks, tell them you fell. You understand?'

Jamie's mouth dropped open and blood trickled out. She must have bitten her tongue. She touched her fingers to her lips, then stared at them as if she'd never seen blood before.

I tried to get her to stand up. Her hair was matted and wet, and all I could think was: *Maybe she should stay here and not move?* Her head was gashed, I could see the wetness through her dark hair. She might even have to go to hospital.

Her eyelids fluttered. She looked – not quite at me, but not quite anywhere else, either.

'Get Mum,' she said in a weird voice. She started shivering, I thought with cold, so I dragged off my cardigan and tucked it around her shoulders. She was still looking at nothing, moving her lips now. I leaned closer but her words were too mumbled to understand.

Bobby was looking at me in a shifty way, and I was suddenly wondering why he hadn't already run for help. Jamie was hurt, badly hurt ... Why was Bobby just standing there, staring at her?

'You have to tell them you fell,' he said firmly to Jamie. 'That's what you've got to tell your mum. You fell, okay? And don't say I was here. You can't tell. You know what I'm saying, Jamie? You have to say you fell.'

My mouth opened.

No, I wanted to say. *No, that's not what happened. You did this, Bobby Drake. It was you, you hurt her.* But the words stayed within me, bottled up and, trapped by the lump that was suddenly lodged in my throat.

Bobby took a step towards me. His lips were wet with spit, and his brown eyes seemed to bulge, as though the pressure in his head was building. He glanced down at Jamie, then his hand shot out and he grabbed hold of my T-shirt. He dragged me up close to his face, and said sharply, 'She fell, okay? That's what happened. And if you say anything different, I'll tell them *you* did it.'

That was when I saw the stone in his hand. I looked at that stone, and then I looked back at my sister. She hadn't moved, but a puddle of blood had seeped from the gash on the side of her head and made a black stain on my cardigan.

I looked back at Bobby. My lips were numb, my tongue felt swollen, but somehow the words slipped out.

'I saw you hurt her. I'm going to tell.' Twisting like an eel, I tore free of his grasp and stumbled away. Regaining my footing, I raced across the slippery granite shelf towards the safety of the trees.

Mum would be home by now; she'd know what to do. Mum would tell the police, and they'd go and talk to Mrs Drake, and Bobby would be in serious trouble—

A gust of air rushed past my ear.

Then pain, an explosive pain that I'd never experienced before. It started in the base of my skull and erupted outward, sending shockwaves like broken bits of glass shattering through my veins and bursting out of my skin until I was no longer Ruby but a glowing fiery angel, an angel of pure, molten, blindingly brilliant pain. Wings burst from my shoulder blades and unfurled around me, easily lifting me off my feet and carrying me up, up into the wide blue sky. For a while I circled like a bird, gazing down with only mild interest at the three small figures on the broad granite embankment below. Then I breathed my newfound strength into my wings and soared away.

20

Brenna, August 1898

Late on Tuesday afternoon, I arrived back at Brayer House. As my hired carriage drew into the drive, I met Adele and Quinn hurrying across the gravel towards the black dray that awaited them. The dray was attended by one of the stockmen, I noted, and was packed with several large carpet bags.

'I'm on my way to Launceston,' Adele explained, holding me close in a warm embrace. She rattled out a cough and touched her handkerchief to her lips.

'You are unwell,' I said.

She nodded, then frowned and held me at arm's length. 'But look at you, my friend. You are troubled, I can see it in your face. What's happened? How is your father?'

I was not yet ready to speak of Fa Fa or Owen, so instead I asked, 'Where's Carsten?'

Adele coughed again, her thin frame shaking. 'In Hobart. He's due back in a day or so. He was furious with you,' she added quietly. 'And with Quinn and me for helping you escape. After you left, he sank into one of his darker moods. I feared he would rush after you and try to bring you home, but he just kept saying that you would return soon enough.' She squeezed my fingers

333

and searched my face with worried eyes. 'You've been crying. And you're trembling. I will cancel my trip and stay here—'

'There's no need.' I glanced at Quinn, who had walked over to the carriage to speak to the stockman. I drew Adele into the shadow of the house. Taking the locket from around my neck, I held it in my palm.

'Do you recognise this?'

She frowned. 'It's Carsten's. Where did you find it?'

'At the Aboriginal encampment at Lyrebird Hill. Carsten was there, Adele. Just as he was there twenty years ago, committing violent acts against helpless people.'

Adele's eyes grew large. She looked at me for a long time, then took her handkerchief from her pocket, and held it against her mouth. She began to cough, and tears sprang from her eyes. Once the fit had passed, she seized my hand.

'My brother was always so deeply bothered by his conscience,' she murmured, her face blanched of colour. 'Now, after what you've told me, I understand why – and I fear for his soul.' She looked at me closely. 'How you must hate him, Brenna. Why have you returned here, knowing what he's done?'

I thought about the pistol hidden in the false lining of my suitcase, and decided Adele did not need to be burdened by my plan.

'I came back for you,' I said simply, fastening the locket back around my neck. 'And for Lucien.'

Adele looked at me sharply. 'Lucien has gone.'

'Where?'

'No one knows. I suppose he wanted to wait until his wounds healed enough for him to travel, but Quinn came in a few weeks ago and said that he was gone.'

Kissing Adele's cheek, praying I was right, I said softly, 'I think I know where to find him.'

Running between the trees, I headed for the south-west corner of the garden and the track that led to the glade. The grass was damp beneath my feet, the air tasting faintly of frost.

'Lucien,' I called, my voice as soft as the hoot of an owl. 'Lucien, are you there?'

He must have been camping in the forest, always nearby; I had known he would not leave without me. He must have seen the arrival of my carriage this afternoon, and perhaps guessed that I would have picked this place to meet him.

A restless shadow broke from between the trees and came towards me, barely visible among the narrow-trunked trees that caged the glade. He hesitated, but when I rushed at him and flung my arms about him he swept me up and crushed me against him. He was trembling, and his closeness made me tremble, too.

In a jumble of words and tears I related to him what I'd told Adele – the horrible devastation of my family and the clan I loved so dearly; the evidence of Carsten's locket on the riverbank, and the picture of my mother it contained.

'Your mother?' Lucien drew away. 'Why would Mr Whitby have a picture of your mother?'

I recalled the yearning I'd seen in my husband's eyes whenever he gazed at his treasure, and a shiver rushed through me. 'He loved her once. He wanted to marry her, but she married my father instead.'

Lucien gripped my arms and held me at length, examining my face. 'And he married you? Why?'

I dragged in a breath. 'I have spent the last weeks trying to understand. Our marriage was an arrangement to benefit both Carsten and my father; Fa Fa needed to save his farm, and Carsten wanted a son. But I have come to believe that his motivation was darker than that.'

Lucien nodded. 'He wanted to take you from your father, just as your father took your mother from him.'

I shut my eyes, wanting desperately to be away from this place, to be at home where I could find a way to repair the shattered fragments of my life.

'I'm returning to Lyrebird Hill,' I told Lucien. 'Will you come with me?'

Lucien's smile was slow, but when it arrived it lit him like a beacon. The moon's shifting light toyed with his features; one moment he was a man, his angular features as fierce as any bird of prey; the next he was a wide-eyed boy, his brows pulled in, his mouth aquiver.

'I would go to the end of the earth for you,' he whispered. 'I would go to the brink of death and back again, just for a glimpse of your sweet face. Is it true, then? Do you really want me to return with you?'

'Yes. But first there's something I need to do.'

Lucien frowned then, his gaze sharpening on my face. 'If I were in your shoes, I would seek to destroy any man who killed my family. I can see it in your eyes, Brenna. You're planning something, aren't you?'

I couldn't speak. My loathing for my husband was a bushfire raging out of control in my heart. My despair over what he'd done to my family was intolerable; the pain of it had set me alight and was relentlessly burning me, consuming me. How could Lucien ever understand? He had sought and found forgiveness in himself for the man who had scarred him so terribly as a boy. How could I ever expect him to comprehend my darkness, when his own heart was only full of light?

Turning away, I started along the track towards the house. I'd barely walked two paces when Lucien was at my side. He took my hand, drew me to a stop.

'Brenna, wait.' Tucking a strand of hair behind my ear, he smoothed his thumb across my cheek. 'I'm sorry about your family.' He frowned at the dark track that led back to the house, then returned his gaze to me. 'But I want you to promise me something.'

'What?'

He tightened his lips against his teeth, the way my father used to. 'Promise that when we walk away from Brayer House, we truly leave it behind us. When we forge a new life together, we will find a way to forgive what has happened.'

I flinched. 'Forgive?'

'You must. If you don't let go of your hatred, it will fester and grow in your heart. It will destroy you. Eventually, it will destroy us both.'

How could I tell him that it had already festered, already grown beyond what I was capable of containing? My hatred had become a living, breathing entity within me – a second, more powerful self; a master whose bidding I had no choice but to carry out. But Lucien was watching me with his stormy eyes, and somehow – at least in that moment – I was swayed. I did not want my hatred to poison my heart. I saw clearly then that my plan to avenge what Carsten had done to my family would not heal my pain. Rather, it would only add another blight upon the burden I already carried.

Lifting my hand, I cupped Lucien's damaged cheek. 'For you, love . . . I will find a way to leave it behind.'

His face filled with longing. Grasping my hand, he brought it to his lips and kissed my palm, my fingers, my inner wrist. Love shone from him like lantern light, and it made him beautiful. It beamed out of him and bathed me in its warm glow, dissolving the shadow that had eclipsed my heart and finally, fiercely and compellingly, setting me free.

The grass was soft and moist beneath us. Lucien made a bed of our clothes and we lay on them in the darkness. The night air was cold, but Lucien's skin was hot. It kept me warm as I cradled him, as I wound myself around him, caressed him with all the tenderness I'd kept hidden from him for so long. He moaned softly as my fingers found his scars, as I memorised their location with my touch so my lips would know where to find them.

Afterwards we lay curled together, using my cloak as a blanket. Lucien whispered in my ear, his voice lulling me. He spoke of our future together at Lyrebird Hill, the beautiful garden of roses he would build for me, the milking goats and dogs and possums, and eventually the children who would share our happy home.

He fell silent, nestling against me. I knew it was time to leave. There may have only been a few hours left before dawn, but I sensed that Lucien was as reluctant as I was to break the spell of our lovemaking, to pollute the memory of it just yet with the ordinary necessities of travel.

Soon, the cold settled upon us.

We dressed hurriedly, I re-pinned my hair while Lucien shook the leaves from his. As we set off along the track back to the house, Lucien took my hand.

'Wait for me in the stables. I'll collect your belongings and we can be away before the rest of the household wakes.'

'Make sure you get my brushes and paints, my paper and drawings. They're all in my trunk under the bed. And Lucien . . .' I stopped walking and drew him to me, forcing him to pay me careful attention. 'There is a false lid in the trunk. If you prise it away, you will find my father's firearm hidden there.'

If Lucien was surprised at my disclosure, he didn't show it. He nodded, and lifted my hand to his lips and kissed my knuckles. 'Don't worry, love. I'll bring everything that's precious to you.'

We reached a fork in the path. One branch led back to the house while the other would take me to the stables.

Lucien pulled me back against him. 'Soon we'll be on our way,' he whispered into my hair. We kissed quickly, then he hurried into the darkness and out of sight.

I slipped my hand into my pocket, touched the pouch of desiccated wolfsbane flowers. When I heard the scullery door click shut, I knew Lucien was inside. I paused, imagining him climbing the stairs, moving along the upstairs hallway in the dark, treading on silent cat feet to my room.

Deceiving him sat uneasily with me, but I knew there was no other way for us to escape. Carsten would never let me go. Nor would his pride allow Lucien to follow me. And if he came after us, found us – worse, found us together – his rage would know no bounds.

My fingers tightened around my pouch of herbs. A grain would slow a man's heart, a larger measure might send him into an uneasy sleep; a pinch, and he would never wake.

Doubling back along the path, I unlatched the French doors and went in. The air was cold inside, far colder than it had been in the garden. Moonlight washed through the tall windows, puddling on the marble floor and splashing shadows into the corners. I had come to despise this dank house; it would be a relief to escape its dreary confines forever.

When I reached the library, I slipped quietly through the heavy oak door and shut it behind me. Only then did I dare to light a candle.

The decanter of sweet sherry sat on the sideboard, a quarter full, the sickly wine glinting red like blood in the candlelight. I removed the crystal stopper. The scent oozed out, making my stomach roll and twist. I raged inside to think of the nights I had shared with Carsten; the man who had murdered my mother, and whose actions had eventually led to the destruction of my family.

I tipped a measure of Wolfsbane into the sherry, swirling the liquor until the powdery grounds dispersed. Then I settled the decanter back on the tray, wiping up a sticky droplet from the stopper with my sleeve. Adjusting the empty glass, I turned back to examine the room.

Everything was in order. It was time to go—

Footsteps approached along the hall.

I blew out the candle, realising I had lingered too long. The footsteps paused. Then the door swung open. A tall figure crossed the threshold. His shadow leaped violently in the light of the lantern he held aloft.

Carsten's face twisted when he saw me.

'I knew you'd be back. What are you doing here in the dark?'

I retreated behind the desk. Carsten followed, but I made a move towards the open door. Carsten reached into his waistcoat and drew a revolver. Pulling back the hammer, he took aim at my head.

I unclasped the locket from around my neck, and held it in the light. 'Look what I have found,' I said, unable to stop the violent shaking in my fingers.

Carsten flinched, and the weapon wavered. 'Hand it over.'

'Not until you tell me how it came to be by the riverside, at Lyrebird Hill. Near the destroyed Aboriginal encampment.'

He took a lurching step towards me, and tried to swipe the locket from my grasp, but I darted out of his reach. A dark light came into his eyes.

'Your father stole Florence from me. I wanted to strike a blow against him that he'd never recover from.'

'By marrying me? By killing the people he loved?'

Carsten's mouth worked, as if his words had left a sour taste. 'I blamed Michael for Florence's death. The last time I saw her, she was hollow-cheeked, her beautiful hair lank, her spirits low. She was about to be married and should have been flushed with happiness, but I knew Michael was sneaking off to the encampment, crawling into that savage's hut, when he should have been on his knees, thanking Florence that she had agreed to be his bride. Michael had what I wanted, but cared nothing for it. It made me sick. Sick to my stomach, and sick at heart.'

'You were there in seventy-nine,' I said harshly. 'And a month ago, you returned. You helped murder innocent people.'

Carsten's lips were raw and the reflected lantern light blazed wildly in his eyes. He gripped his revolver and adjusted his aim, taking an unsteady step towards me.

'When I saw Michael last month, I couldn't forget what you had told me. My old resentments resurfaced. That night I went to the tavern and sat with a group of acquaintances who shared my hatred of the blacks. We got talking, and the drink fired us up. We agreed that something had to be done, and all of a sudden we were the men to do it. It was an hour's ride to Lyrebird Hill, and we reached the encampment by midnight. The savages were asleep, but their dogs began to bay at the sound of our horses. Within moments, several males burst from their huts bearing spears, and rushed at us.'

The blood froze in my veins. My hands went hot, and my heart began to race unsteadily. 'There were women,' I said, my voice thick with grief. 'And little ones—'

Carsten went to the decanter and poured a glass of sherry, drained it in a gulp. Almost instantly, his gaze sharpened on me. His hand went to his mouth. He looked at the glass in his hand. I could see the question dawn in his eyes – suspicion at first, as his tongue darted along his lips, suddenly aware of the unfamiliar burning, tingling, of the sensitive skin. Then dark realisation, a blink of fear.

He dashed the glass to the floor, and swept the decanter after it. Sherry splashed around him, pooling on the wooden boards before seeping quickly between the cracks.

'What have you done?' His voice was ragged, as if the poison had already begun to etch away his vocal cords. 'What in God's name have you done to me?'

I backed away from him. 'You killed my mother and her people. You destroyed my family. Did you really think you would get away with what you did?'

Carsten stumbled towards me, taking aim.

I lunged to the door and wrenched it open. Before I could slip through, Carsten fired. Splinters exploded from the floorboards at my feet and I staggered back, hitting the wall. Blinded by the gunpowder flash, I covered my face, expecting the next shot to rip into my body.

Carsten let out a wretched, broken sound. Shadows carved lines in his face, scooped the flesh under his eyes, making him gaunt. To my flash-blind eyes he looked thinner, diminished; a knife-edge of a man, lost in a wilderness of his own making.

I stood tall. 'If you can't shoot me, then let me go.'

Carsten wiped a sleeve across his face and seemed to gather himself. His gaze burned into me, and he shook his head.

'I'll drag you with me into the grave rather than let you walk away.' His cheeks glistened, his hands trembled, as he pulled back the hammer a second time and fingered the trigger. Slowly, as though moving through the quicksand of a dream, he raised the weapon again and lined me in his sights.

The door burst wide. Lucien stood in the threshold. Snug in his hand was my aunt's revolver, aimed unwaveringly at my husband's head.

'Drop your weapon, Mr Whitby.'

My heart caught. Lucien was no killer; despite his flogging, he still respected Carsten, and would stay his fire in the hope of a peaceable outcome. I rushed at him, shrieking his name, meaning to shield him with my body—

A shot rang out. Then another. And another.

Starbursts of gunpowder-flash blinded me. For a moment I wouldn't allow myself to accept what I was seeing.

Lucien fell to his knees. My aunt's revolver, loaded and cocked but unfired, clattered to the floor beside him. He swayed. His gaze found me in the lantern light. Then he crumpled.

I flung myself at him, gathering him into my arms, touching his face, his throat, his chest. My fingers turned red with his blood. More blood bloomed on my skirt, my white blouse, splashed my sleeves. Shadows fractured and broke apart. A void opened up and I felt its dark energy drag me towards its brink. It was easy to let myself slide, frighteningly easy. I released Lucien and groped on the floor, blindly seeking the weapon he'd dropped.

On my knees now, I gripped my weapon with both hands and took swift aim. There was a click. A roar, and a yell. The violence of the shot pushed me backwards, filled my head with smoking light and the sharpness of gunpowder.

Carsten stared at me, his eyes wide. His mouth moved but no words came forth. He let out a strange moan. Blood splashed his lips. He took a step. The gun fell from his fingers. He seemed to teeter forever, as though poised at the edge of a high cliff, knowing that his next step would carry him into eternity.

When he finally fell, he hit the ground almost without a sound.

For a long time my arm wavered before me, my finger frozen tight against the trigger, as if in some dark part of my soul I was still shooting and would carry on shooting, was condemned to keep shooting for as long as my heart continued to beat.

But then my body gave way. Dropping the weapon, I slumped over Lucien. Pressing my cheek against his, I whispered his name.

'Love, can you hear me?'

His eyes fluttered.

'Rest for a moment,' I told him, 'then we must leave this place. We've a long ride ahead of us. In the morning we sail.'

Lucien searched my face. Reaching for my hand, he closed his fingers around mine. His skin was slippery with blood.

'Tell me,' he said on a breath, 'tell me again about the flowers you love.'

I drew near, holding his hand against my chest as I peered into his face, my tears raining on him, washing rivulets in the blood that smeared his face.

'Flowers?' I asked, confused.

He drew a shaky breath, and a look of pleading came into his eyes. 'Tell me how good they smell . . . in the rain.'

I grasped his hand. 'You mean yellow-buttons, with their furry grey leaves and gold button-heads that quiver in the breeze?' I tried to smile. 'You'll see them soon enough, love.'

'Tell me.'

I tried to smile. 'After it rains, the air smells wonderful. You want to keep breathing it in, until your lungs are full to bursting. But then the scent fades and you forget about it for a while. A day goes past, sometimes a week. Then, your nostrils flare and it's there again, sweet and sharp. You try and hold it in your lungs for as long as possible, memorising it, wishing it would . . . wishing it would last forever.'

He was quiet.

'Lucien?'

I kissed him tenderly, and kept kissing until I felt his lips soften . . . until his breath ceased flowing into mine. Even then I could not bring myself to withdraw from him, for that would mean facing a life without him; breathing the air of his absence; dwelling somehow in a world where he no longer existed.

How could he be gone, when his fingers were so warm in mine, and his scent still drifted around me? Pressing my face to his, I breathed him in. Horses and sun-warmed hay, old leather and bootblack, thyme oil and fresh perspiration.

And blood.

So much blood.

Then, the bitter odour of my despair quickly engulfing it all.

This will be my last entry. It is midnight. I am hunched on the cold floor of the library, scratching these words by the light of a candle stub. Wind rattles the panes, and the smell of gunpowder sharpens the air. Far off in the distance, a dog barks. I expect that one of the stockmen has heard the shots from the house. He will go to a neighbour's, or perhaps ride the short distance to Wynyard.

I might have a half-hour, an hour at most. Then the men with guns will come, and they will find me.

But the wider world does not interest me now. All that matters are my last remaining moments with Lucien. And the promise that one day, not far from now, we will meet again on the other side of death.

21

Ruby, May 2013

I stared at the silver locket dangling from my fingers. A lifetime ago, my great-grandmother had found it on the riverbank and come to understand a terrible betrayal; years later, she had given it to her young neighbour, probably glad to unburden herself of its memories. Doreen Drake had treasured the locket, until it was stolen from her two decades ago, and the blame pinned on a twelve-year-old foster child from Newcastle.

But Pete had been innocent.

The real culprit, Doreen's son, Bobby, had stolen the necklace to impress my sister, but perhaps also to rid himself of the orphan boy his mother had taken under her wing. But Bobby's deception had escalated and ended in tragedy; at least it had for Jamie, and for those of us who loved her. Meanwhile, Bobby Drake had drifted away without blemish, enjoying success after success, creating a life based entirely on falsehood.

'Oh Rob,' I whispered. 'How could you?'

346

The sixteen-year-old street kid under the bridge; the broken bottle; the mysterious voice telling him to let go and live; the best-selling books; the smooth, charming persona. All of it, lies. Rob Thistleton was a shiny apple on the surface, but rotten all the way to the core.

Closing my fingers around the locket, I headed back to the house on shaky legs. Disjointed images flew through my head faster than I could process, but my mind kept returning to Bobby Drake. To Rob. To the lie he'd built his life around.

And to his murder of my sister.

I stumbled, nearly fell. Somehow made it onto the verandah.

'Pete?' I called, but my throat was like sandpaper. 'Pete, where are you?'

Then I remembered he had gone to his traps early, hoping to get a few rabbits, and release any native animals lured into the cages; he wouldn't be back for another hour. He had promised to cook dinner, something special to celebrate – but my brain had gone into overdrive and I couldn't for the life of me recall exactly what it was we were celebrating.

The house was dark. My eyes were slow to adjust, after the brightness outside. My heart felt so heavy I could barely walk. As I trod along the hall, I kept trying to gulp air into my lungs, but it wasn't until I stood in the doorway of the bedroom I'd once shared with my sister that I was able to breathe again.

That was when I noticed the sharp smell.

I went in and looked around. Everything was in place. The smell seemed stronger near my bed. There was a frothy puddle on the floor, which seemed to be the source of the smell. I checked under the bed and when I saw the motionless body lying in the dust, my heart began to gallop.

'Bardo!'

Reaching towards her, I stroked her leg. She didn't move. On hands and knees, I crawled into the shadowy space. My sides were suddenly slicked with sweat and my breath came harshly, but this attack of nerves had nothing to do with my fear of Bardo . . . but rather my fear *for* her.

'Bardo . . . what's happened, old girl?'

To my relief her feathery tail twitched, and then began to thump feebly against the floor sending up wafts of dust. I ran my hands along her sleek body, searching for an injury. She was warm, and her fur satiny, but she was unable to move. Lifting her head, she gazed around at me, but her eyes could not focus. Gently I gathered her and dragged her out from under the bed, then lifted her onto the mattress.

There was froth on her muzzle. I pulled up her lip, and examined her gums. They were greyish white, when they should have been pink.

Poison. 'Oh God.'

Dark panic swamped me. I lay over her, wanting to shelter her with my body despite knowing the damage was already done. She was breathing, but there was no way to know how much poison she'd taken – or how long much longer she would survive.

I kissed her sleek head, and when her tail lifted briefly to acknowledge the show of affection, a knot tightened in my throat. If someone had suggested a month ago that I would develop a bond of love for a *dog*, I would never have believed it; but here I was, quaking in fear and sick at heart to think that this beautiful, gentle creature might die.

Covering her with a blanket, I considered my options. Esther's car was in the barn, the keys in the kitchen. Bardo needed to be kept still; if I brought the car nearer the house, I could avoid unnecessary movement of her—

Poison?

It struck me that I hadn't heard Rob's car start up. Slowly, understanding crept over me, followed by a dark tide of fear. Rob was still here. Had he known how close I was to remembering his true identity – and what he had done to Jamie? Had he anticipated I'd waste no time taking my story to the police?

Everything Rob did was carefully orchestrated; nothing was ever random. He liked to be in control, and he liked to win.

I gripped my face in my hands, trying to think. What was he planning? This man I had trusted with my secrets, the man I had held and loved and clung to; how could he be the same man who had, eighteen years ago, so brutally stolen my sister's life?

I buckled over, burying my face against Bardo's furry neck, breathing her sweet, clean canine scent. She whined, and her body twitched as she offered up another feeble tail-wag.

'Oh Jamie,' I whispered, and a tremor went through my body, shaking loose my last defences. My three years with Rob had not merely been a lie; they had been a cruel deception. Rob had known who I was; all along he had *known*. And yet he had continued the pretence – listening to my fears, soothing away my nightmares, assuming a sympathetic face as he watched me battle my guilt over Jamie's death, and mourn my deteriorating relationship with my mother. Meanwhile he had been feeding, feeding ... drawing my sorrow into himself like sustenance, growing strong on my weakness.

Whispering a final reassurance to Bardo, I left her and ran along the hall. In the kitchen I pocketed Esther's car keys and wrote a note for Pete, then crept to the door. It was shut; had I closed it when I came in? I glanced over my shoulder. The hallway was dark, and suddenly the house seemed cavernous and riddled with hiding places – the lounge room with its book-lined walls, the vacant upstairs bedrooms—

I opened the door and looked outside. A trail of smoke curled lazily into the blue sky above the donkey burner. The yard was deserted, cut through with black afternoon shadows. I ran silently down the steps and around the house to the barn. It was a matter of moments, but that short dash seemed to take a lifetime. Every shadow twitched and morphed onto a man-shaped threat; every noise was a footstep; every gust of wind was a sigh or a whisper, or the soft, seductive calling of my name.

I dragged the barn door open as noiselessly as I could, and stepped into the vast, cool space. I ran over to where I had parked Esther's car. Climbing in, I dug the keys into the ignition, but the engine failed to kick over. I kept trying, but nothing happened. Gripping the steering wheel, I fought an oncoming rush of panic. The Morris had been working at the start of the week when I'd driven it into Armidale; now, the motor was totally dead, as if a vital connection had seized up . . . or been cut. I gave it another try, pulling out the choke and pumping the gas to the floor, but again the motor failed to engage.

Dark waves of adrenaline pulsed through me, fogging my senses. Bardo might not have much time left. I was at a loss. There was a landline at Pete's cottage, but that was a good twenty-minute hike at least. It wasn't ideal, but it might be all I had right now.

As I got out of the car, a prickle of awareness drew my attention to the old stable stalls.

A man stood motionless in the shadows. He'd been watching me, and as he stepped into the muted light, he fixed me with his most seductive gaze.

'Hey, babe. Going somewhere?'

A jolt of shock. Seeing him now, knowing what he had done to Jamie, understanding the enormity of his deception, made me want to rush at him and claw away his smug smile.

'No,' I said in a ragged voice I barely recognised, 'but you are, *Bobby*. You're going to jail for what you did to my sister.'

Rob's smile didn't alter, but his eyes hardened. 'Sorry to disappoint, Ruby. But you're the only witness. And if you're not around to blab, then no one will be the wiser.'

My lips parted. My heart squeezed one almighty beat, then stalled. Until that moment, I had believed that uncovering the truth about my sister's murder would somehow heal me; but as

I stood in the fading gloom of the barn – with my gaze locked on the man I had once loved, the man who had betrayed me in the most devastating way – I finally understood what he'd been trying to tell me all along.

Leaving the past behind wasn't merely a catchphrase that he used to sell books; it wasn't a new age principle that he promoted to help people turn their lives around; it wasn't even a deeply held personal belief.

It was a warning.

My stalled heart began to race. I wanted to take a step back, but my legs were suddenly numb, my entire body locked in place. Even my voice, when I finally found it, came haltingly.

'Why are you here?'

Rob took a step towards me, the muted light playing across his features. 'Call it asset insurance,' he said, pausing to glance at the wide entryway. 'Now you know who I am, I'm not safe. I've got too much to lose.'

Numbness crept through me. Memories of my sister batted my conscious mind like moths against a lit window – her head hitting the stone, her eyes losing focus; the blood in her hair, and in her mouth, staining her teeth pink. I had seen what Rob was capable of as a young man; how much more brutal might he be now, when all he valued was at stake?

The ground beneath me swelled like a sea tide, then sank away, leaving me adrift. I clutched for something, anything, to anchor myself; my mind threw up a lifeline of anger and I grabbed it gladly.

'So, what'll you do?' I said harshly. 'Kill me – the way you killed my sister?'

'You've left me no choice.'

Barely ten paces stretched between us. I glanced to the doorway, assessing the distance. If I tried to bolt, would I make it? If I could stall him, keep him talking; if I could escape into the bush, I had a chance.

'You took a risk, being with me,' I told him, shuffling back a step. 'You must have known that sooner or later I'd remember.'

He was watching me attentively, as if enthralled by my trembling, by my wide-eyed stare, by the sharp scent of the nervous sweat I could feel pouring out of me.

He licked his lips. 'I was curious to see how long it would take. How long I could keep you in the dark.' His jaw tightened. 'This afternoon, when I watched you in the bath, I could see you still hadn't recognised me, but you were close. And once you finally joined all the dots, I knew you'd run straight to the cops.'

Despite what I now knew about him, his words dug under my defences. My logical mind judged his actions and found him abhorrent – a man who hurt others to preserve himself, perhaps even to entertain himself – but there was a small corner of my heart that was slower to make the transition from love to loathing.

'It was one big lie, wasn't it? Us, I mean. Everything you did and said for three years – all of it, lies.'

Rob shifted and a beam of light struck his face. 'Not everything. I enjoyed you for the most part. But then, a while back, you started getting edgy. Having nightmares again. Getting moody, restless. I knew something was brewing, that your memory was getting ready to resurface.'

I risked another shuffling step nearer the doorway, but the light beyond the barn's gloom seemed no closer. When I focused back on Rob, he'd grown more alert, his breath coming faster than it had a moment ago.

'You had it all worked out, didn't you?' I said. 'From the start, you knew who I was. You knew it would come to this.'

He nodded. 'It was always on the cards, Ruby. We were never forever. Eventually, something I said or did would have triggered a memory, and then the whole lot would've come pouring back.'

Never forever. How had I not seen through his lies? Why had I ever believed that he genuinely cared?

I could see him more clearly now, the ghost of the young man my sister had written about in her diary; who she had met on the riverbank, and kissed, and teased as she danced in the sun. The young man who had, in the end, left her to die on the rocks in a pool of her own blood.

'Why didn't I recognise you?'

'Eighteen years is a long time,' Rob said, running a hand over his mouth. 'People change.'

'That's not it. You're . . . *different.*'

He stepped close, eclipsing a stream of dying sunlight. 'Maybe it was the broken nose,' he said simply. 'A footy accident that scored me a metal plate. It flattens things out, changes the planes of your face . . . just enough. Besides, you only ever saw me once or twice at the river with Jamie. By the time you Cardels had moved to Lyrebird Hill, I was living in Sydney. I did my final years at boarding school, then I went to uni. My visits home were pretty infrequent. That is, until I met your sister.'

'But I remember you now,' I said, grappling to make sense of it. 'The instant my memory returned, I knew who you were.'

Rob palmed the back of his neck. 'I was at the core of your amnesia. You blocked out a year of your life because of me, because of what happened that day with Jamie. For most of your life, you *wanted* to forget me.'

'But you never forgot me.'

He rubbed the side of his face, contemplating me with hard eyes. 'You and your sister haunted me for years. I did everything to put that time behind me. I even changed my name. It felt good to be free of Bobby Drake. I hadn't realised until then how much your sister's death weighed on my conscience. I started thinking about how good it would feel to be *really* free. As in, free of the worry of ever being found out.'

This took a moment to process. When understanding dawned, it bloomed in me like an ink stain, quick and dark and indelible. 'And the only person standing in your way,' I murmured, 'was me.'

Rob almost smiled, and then he blinked, a slow deliberate reflex, as if capturing my shock on an internal camera. 'I thought you'd forgotten about Bobby Drake. Eighteen years passed, I thought I was home free. But when you rang my publicist wanting to organise a book event, I got worried. I had to meet you in the flesh, find out what you remembered.'

'Is that all I was to you – damage control?'

'At first, yes.' Rob moved nearer. 'You intrigued me. Not just your amnesia, and your terror of remembering. You reminded me of Jamie. I couldn't resist getting close. But after a while, I fell for you . . . or rather, I fell for the vulnerable part of you.' Rob moistened his lips with his tongue, and smiled. 'Do you know how that feels to a man, Ruby? To know you've won the trust of someone so untrusting? Pure intoxication.'

His words seeped into me like poison. I felt the slow burn of shame rise to my face, but from deeper down came a rush of white-hot anger.

'Why aren't you in jail?' I cried. 'Didn't anyone think to question you after she died? How did you slip through the net?'

'I *was* questioned. But no one knew I was her boyfriend. I came home a couple of times a month when I could get away from uni, and Jamie and I always met in secret. She said your mother was strict and would have stopped her from seeing me.'

I glanced at the doorway. I was close enough that I might make it if I ran, but the questions were hammering at me, and I needed to know. 'You were there the day she died. Why didn't they suspect you?'

A tremor went through Rob's body, not quite a shudder. In a sudden motion, he raised his hands and clawed his fingers across his scalp.

'When I left you and your sister on the riverbank, I went home and drove straight back to Sydney. Mum was away, and no one knew I'd been anywhere near Lyrebird Hill. I made sure I was seen on campus that weekend. My alibis were pretty much watertight. And anyway, because of the way your dad died, your mother was a major suspect in Jamie's case. She stole the limelight from everyone else.'

Despite my trembling, I couldn't stem my anger. 'I'm going to tell them everything. You're finished, Rob. You're going to jail.'

Rob's lips drew back, his smile was all teeth. 'I don't think so, babe.'

I sensed a sudden shift between us. My heart began to jack-hammer. I turned and ran, but Rob caught me from behind and swung me around to face him, then dragged me over to the wall. My spine thudded into a post, and I was momentarily winded, but I managed to thrust my knee towards his groin. He recoiled and his grip weakened. Twisting my torso, I wrenched free my arm and, making a half-fist, rammed the heel of my palm up under his chin.

His head snapped back. He grunted, and blood bloomed on his lower lip. I tore loose and sprang away, but he seized a handful of my hair and hauled me back. This time when he drove me against the wall, my head cracked on a beam and lights exploded behind my eyes. Rob slammed me backwards again – and suddenly my heart was swelling in fear because I was there again, on the rocks with my sister and Bobby, with the river rushing by and the sun glaring through the storm clouds. But instead of Jamie's hair and scalp matted with blood, instead of her eyes staring in that unseeing way, instead of Jamie's face contorted in pain . . . it was mine.

From far away, someone shouted my name. Rob heard it too, because he let out a growl and looked around.

'Ruby?' Pete called from outside. 'Where are you?'

Rob shoved me to the ground and whirled towards the door, grappling at the small of his back. I caught a flash of steel and, as I struggled to my feet, I registered his weapon.

'Pete,' I tried to call, but my throat was tight with fear. I dragged in a breath to try again, but Rob lurched over to me and struck me across the head with his fist. I staggered and tripped, falling against the side of the Morris.

'Pete,' I yelled. 'He's armed!'

A shadow flit across the dying sunlight that was pouring its last rays through the door. A familiar silhouette appeared. He saw me, and started to run towards me. From the corner of my eye, I saw Rob raise his arms and take aim.

There was no time to shout a warning. The crack of gunfire shattered the air, and Pete reeled sideways and slumped against the door. I threw myself across the barn, clutching for him, crying out when I saw the blood spreading across the front of his shirt, a dark saturating bloom. I gathered him to me, running my hands over him, seeking the damage, finding the slow sticky ooze of blood just below his collarbone.

'Run,' he told me, his voice harsh and full of urgency. 'Go to my place. Take the ute.'

'I'm not leaving you.'

There was a snarl behind me. I twisted around, saw Old Boy spring at Rob and knock him sideways. Rob shot off a round and the old dog let out a harsh human-sounding howl of rage and pain, then drove his teeth into Rob's forearm. Rob bellowed and went to his knees under the weight of the animal.

I hauled Pete to his feet and got him through the doorway and out into the dying light. As we struggled uphill, there was another gun blast, and Pete moaned. Locking his arm around my shoulders, his hefty weight buckling me nearly double, I managed to get him across the dry expanse of open grass and away into the trees.

The cave was dark. When we ducked into the cool space where we had, only a week ago, visited the lyrebird's nest, Pete crumpled. I lowered him to the ground and settled him against the wall.

He had bled a frightening amount as we fled up the hillside, and the wound in his chest was still oozing. Tearing off his shirt, I wadded it against the flow, praying we'd lost Rob on the other side of the tea-tree forest.

Pete clutched my hand. 'Where's Old Boy?' he rasped. 'Did he make it?'

My body trembled so hard I could barely form the words. 'No, Pete.'

His eyes searched mine, his face drained of colour. 'Ah, God. Bardo?'

'Rob poisoned her.' My words caught in my throat, and I had to gulp a breath of air to loosen them. 'She was alive half an hour ago, but I don't know what he gave her. I'm sorry, Pete. I'm the one Rob wanted, now you're hurt and the dogs—'

Pete's jaw tensed and he gripped my hand. 'Rob? *Your* Rob?' Understanding dawned in his eyes. 'The guy in the barn . . . that was Bobby Drake.'

I nodded. 'It was him all along, but I'd blocked him out. Even when I had all those flashbacks, I never managed to see his face clearly. Until this afternoon. We argued, and he mentioned Jamie. It rang my alarm bells, and then everything flooded back. It was Rob on the rocks that day. He killed my sister.'

Pete lifted a trembling hand and traced his fingers along the side of my face. 'And now he's come after you?'

I nearly lost it, then. Three of the beings I loved most in the world were slipping away from me. Old Boy gone, Bardo's system failing, and now Pete—

Please, not him. Take anything else . . . I'll give anything, my life. Just not him.

'I'm going to your place,' I told him. 'I'll call for help, then come back here. We'll be safe in the cave while we wait. Rob won't find us here.'

Pete's expression turned fierce. 'Forget coming back. Here,' he said, his voice ragged. He fumbled at his pocket. 'Get my keys, will you?'

I dug in his pocket and took out the keys. 'I'm not going to abandon you. Not ever again. You understand?'

He shook his head, his gaze fixed to my face. 'Go to my place. Take the ute to Clearwater, to the general store. Call the cops from there once you're safe.'

A sob stuck in my throat. I had been alone all my life, but the emptiness had never ached as acutely as it did now, knowing what I stood to lose.

Pete's cheek was smeared red where I'd touched him with my bloody fingers. His blood was all over me; I could taste it on my lips, feel its stickiness on my skin.

I took his face in my hands. 'Hang on, Pete. Please hang on. Old Boy saved us. Don't waste that.'

He shut his eyes for a moment, and when he opened them again his pupils had engulfed the blue. 'Hey?'

'What?'

'I love you, Roo.' His hand shook as he reached out and cupped the side of my face. 'Always have.'

I crushed his fingers against my lips and kissed them hard. 'Don't you dare say goodbye,' I said hotly. 'If you freaking die on me, I swear I'll never forgive you.'

He drew me near, and I clutched the wild mess of his hair and pressed my face against his.

'I love you, Wolf. Stay alive for me, will you?'

As I kissed him on the mouth, I prayed it wouldn't be for the last time. Then, getting to my feet, I stumbled from the cool shadows of the cave and into the blinding afternoon light, swiping away my tears.

The Beast was out there, stalking me. The game was on, for real this time. And the prize was something I simply could not bear to lose.

The sun was sinking fast. The western horizon had caught alight, fire-pink behind the blackened outline of the trees.

I raced downhill, veering through the thick scrub towards the river, my runners thudding the ground in time to my pulse. Pete's cottage was on the opposite bank, hidden up among the trees, twenty minutes' walk. I might make it in ten. I had read that gunshot wounds were best treated within an hour, but out here that time frame was impossible. Emergency services would respond immediately to my call, but there was the drive from town, then the search for our cave . . . and the risk of Rob finding us first; meanwhile Pete's life was bleeding away.

Ahead was the track that led down to the farmhouse, a narrow avenue cutting through the bush. As I crossed it, I glanced along its length, but there was no sign of Rob. Soon the incline became steep, and as I slowed to navigate the rocky ground, I heard a bellow from the direction of the house. Rob would be searching the grounds, perhaps already scouting the undergrowth that bordered the garden. I imagined him circling like a cat, moving in wider and wider loops until he found a footprint or a scrap of my torn T-shirt or a red droplet of Pete's blood clinging to a leaf—

I forced myself to move. My body trembled so hard my footing was unsure. My pulse hammered the back of my neck, and a painful sickening fear clouded my senses, dulling me when I most needed to be sharp.

I heard Rob yell again. There was a wildness to his voice, and I imagined his face raw with anger, his eyes dark and determined. I skirted north-west, anchoring my bearings on the natural bridge of stepping stones that would take me across the river to the cottage.

I broke through the cover of trees onto the riverbank, and stood panting in the shadows. I checked the bank in both directions, then silently picked my way down the steep verge to the water. The current rushed past here, deep green, dark with sunken logs and frothing around the partly submerged stones that formed the bridge across.

As I leaped onto the first rock I heard the crash of branches behind me. I spun a look over my shoulder; the trees were motionless, the bushes benign in the twilight – but somewhere beyond, Rob was on my trail and fast closing ground.

Within minutes I had traversed the stepping stones and bounded onto the far bank. From here the track that wound up to Pete's cottage was well trodden, but I didn't dare expose myself by running along it. Pushing through the trees was slower, but I couldn't chance being seen. My senses had taken flight; adrenaline coursed through me, making every sound a threat. Finches called shrilly in the bushes, the song of the rapids had turned deep and full of menace. My panicked breath rasped in my throat; dots jumped across my eyes, and the pressure in the back of my skull pounded like a drumbeat.

I stumbled up the steps to Pete's front door and burst inside. Going straight to the phone, I dialled triple-0 three times before I got it right, then wasted a full minute holding my breath for an in-control voice to answer and reassure me that emergency services and police were on their way.

Then I realised the line was dead.

I wasted more time rattling the cord, checking the connection. Then I remembered that Rob had grown up on the next property over, and would have known about the cottage. In typical fashion he had covered all bases and effectively cut me off from any link to the outside world.

Slumping against the wall, I closed my eyes and dragged in breath after breath, trying to find my calm centre so I could think. Pete's keys were in my pocket, but it was likely

Rob had immobilised the Holden, just as he'd done with Esther's Morris.

As I stood trembling in the darkened room, breathing in the scent of books and dogs and Pete's comforting presence, the tension in my head momentarily eased. A tiny window opened, and the breeze of a thought blew in. I looked at the cupboard under the sink. Went over and opened it.

There on the top shelf sat a small bright yellow device: the personal beacon Pete had told me about the morning after Esther's death.

If only she'd carried the PLB, she could have signalled for help.

I grabbed the beacon, then found a first aid kit. Filling a bottle with water, I stowed the lot in a haversack, which I slung over my shoulder.

The track that led back to the river looked clear, but again I ducked into the trees and ran silently downhill, my bag banging against my side. I allowed myself a moment of relief; I was going to make it, I was nearly home free. But as I rushed towards the shoreline, I heard footfall behind me. Rob shouted my name.

Panic took hold and I veered directly down the bank, crashing onto the pebbly beach, stumbling into the shallows as I tried to create distance between us. Of course he would have known I'd try to use Pete's landline. Now he was close, but I couldn't risk hiding, couldn't risk getting cut off from the stepping stones that bridged the river. My feet and jeans were wet and my runners slid on the smooth rock, but within moments I reached the opposite embankment.

Rob's voice rang sharp and loud behind me and I chanced a look over my shoulder. He was closer than I'd hoped, already bounding across the rock islands that glistened wet with my footprints. I saw his shoe skate on the slippery surface, then as he righted himself, the dying light caught a metallic flash in his hand. He stopped mid-river and raised his arm, took swift aim.

I turned and stumbled up the bank, climbing onto the granite shelf that jutted above the rapids, half-hoping to find the overhang I had taken shelter in the night Bardo had found me.

The crack of gunfire made me hit the ground. I lay trembling on the damp rock, gasping the scent of rotting vegetation that wafted from the crevices that carved between the stones, fear seizing control of my limbs. This was real. Rob meant me harm. Big gentle Rob with the warm smile was gone, his mask removed; in his place, the killer I had been trying to forget for most of my life.

Another shot blasted out, and shards of stone exploded nearby. Rob had crossed the river and was running along the shore towards me. His face was pale, but his eyes were dark hollows in the dimness, and his chest rose and fell with his ragged breathing.

I scrambled backwards and somehow got to my feet, my wet shoes leaving water trails on the granite. I kept my gaze fixed on Rob, but saw, on my periphery, a cluster of boulders nearby. Dark shadows gathered between them, gaps that might provide me shelter. But I was too slow, my reflexes dulled by panic; Rob swiftly climbed onto the shelf and strode towards me.

'Hey, babe.' His shirt was smeared in blood, torn along one sleeve. His gaze was fierce in the gloom, and as he levelled his weapon at my head, his hands shook. 'I guess it's goodbye, after all.'

'So much for all your letting-go crap,' I said, my voice harsh with nerves. 'You might have gotten away with it. But you couldn't forget her. That's the real reason you were with me, wasn't it?'

Rob hesitated. The handgun wavered. His eyes narrowed and he appeared to consider my words. 'You're so like her,' he said after a while, and his voice softened. 'You never quite understood how much you resembled her.'

'And now you're going to kill her all over again.'

He shook his head, parting his lips, baring his teeth in a grim smile. 'If it means saving the career I've worked so hard to build, then yes. I'll hate myself for all eternity, but that's a price I'm willing to pay.'

I shuffled backwards, my whole body quaking, my breath coming in gasps.

Rob watched me, and I saw the excitement in his face, the way his gaze sharpened to absorb my distress. As I retreated, a distance grew between us, but then, slowly, he began to walk towards me. I continued to take small steps, keeping the cluster of boulders on the edge of my vision, noting how the dusk now enveloped them in shadows. I wanted to run, but fear made me stumble and I only managed a few steps before I tripped and fell.

Rob moved suddenly, readjusting his aim, but as he shifted his balance his brogue skated across the wet trail of footprints I'd left behind. His foot went from under him and drove sharply downwards into a gap in the rock. He let out a yell and tried to pull free, but his foot appeared to be jammed fast. There was an awkward angle to his leg, and he was hunched over himself, the handgun gripped loosely, almost carelessly now, as he focused on his trapped foot.

He let out an animal noise of frustration, then swore loudly. 'Ruby, don't just stand there like a frigging post. Get over here and help me.'

I climbed to my feet. 'I don't think so.'

Rob's lips were white, and his face grey as the stone we stood on. Judging by his twisted grimace, he was in horrible pain.

'You cold-hearted bitch, help me.'

I shook my head, backing away. 'I'll let rescue services know you're here, but I'm not coming near you. Not now, not ever.'

My stomach knotted, but I forced myself to turn and walk towards the edge of the stone plateau; towards the safe shadows of the tall rock formations.

'Ruby, get back here.'

I looked back. Rob swung the gun and aimed it at my head, gripping it with both hands. Sweat glistened on his forehead. I knew the pain in his ankle must be inching up to near intolerable. The hollowness in his eyes had grown darker, his skin was grey.

'Stay where you are,' he said, his voice cracked and hoarse. 'I'll finish you, Ruby. I'll shut you up for good.'

'Your ankle's swelling fast. It's jammed tight in that crevice. You're already in a lot of pain. In twenty minutes you'll feel as if your leg is being crushed in a vice. Even if you were able to wrench it free, there's no way you'd make it across this terrain with an injury like that. Especially now it's getting dark. I'm your only hope of survival. If I die, you die, too.'

'But if I let you walk away, you'll tell them about Jamie.'

'Yes.'

He raised the gun. 'I'll take my chance.'

Time slowed. I thought of Pete in the darkness of the lyrebird cave. His pulse slowing, his blood seeping through the compress. How long did he have? Maybe he was already slipping away.

I looked at Rob, the man who had once held over me a magnetic power I'd been unable to resist. All I felt for him now was pity. He had built a smokescreen around himself – respected psychologist, bestselling author, advocate for emotional freedom – but his life was based on a lie. And a life based on lies, as I'd learned the hard way, was no life at all.

'I'm going to signal for help,' I told him. 'Try to keep still until the medics get here.'

'Ruby, don't you dare leave me here!'

I walked across the flat rocks, shakily retracing the steps I'd taken eighteen years ago as a frightened twelve-year-old. My fear was ebbing, leaving in its wake a sense that time was speeding up, that the clock had recalibrated and had started ticking forward again.

A shot rang out.

I stumbled and fell. The granite was warm under my palms, hard under my knees. The world seemed to vibrate. I waited for the pain, for the blaze of understanding to lift me upwards and carry me into the wide dark sky . . . but it never came.

Slowly, I got to my feet.

I stood for a long time, breathless. Listening. Any moment now, his voice would shatter the stillness, his words ringing over the rushing hiss of the river. He would call.

Ruby, don't leave me.

In my mind's eye, wings sprouted from my shoulder blades and carried me up into the wide blue. Through the eyes of a bird, or an angel, I saw two small figures on the granite embankment below. One stood shakily, frozen in place, unable to look back; the other was slumped, his heavy frame listing to one side, his face – his beautiful, treacherous face – now forsaken to shadow. Beneath him a black pool was spreading, slowly darkening the stone, seeping into the crevices, finding its way down through the granite into the rushing water below.

By the time I reached the lyrebird cave, the sun was sinking. I stumbled around in the gloom for ten minutes before I finally located the cave entrance. When I did, I placed the PLB on the ground and activated the satellite connection that would alert a chain of emergency services and give them our position. Then, pushing my way into the cave opening, I fell beside the dark shadow huddled against the wall.

'Pete?'

He was shivering. Stripping out of my jeans, I placed them over him as a makeshift blanket. Settling beside him, I put my arm gently across his chest and pressed close for extra warmth.

'Roo?' His voice was barely a whisper, but when I gripped his hand he held firm.

'I'm right here,' I said. 'Help's coming. We're going to be okay.'

As the last rays of daylight dissolved, the darkness in the cave deepened. Pete's body grew warm beside me, and his breathing steadied. As I held him, I could feel myself sliding into that other world that existed in the cracks of this one; a mythical world where beasts roamed moonlit hillsides, and wolves wore masks, and stories spun out like spider webs to trap you in their sticky threads.

Pete murmured, whispered reassurance, and moved closer. Warmth began to spread between us where our bodies touched, and as I drifted in the hazy twilight, I clung to the steady rhythm of his breath. My heartbeat slowed and, somehow, a lifetime's worth of guilt and self-blame began to ebb away. For the first time since that day on the rocks twenty years ago, my sister's ghost settled back into the past and finally found peace.

22

The mask you wear might be grotesque, or quirky,
or plain; or it might be one of extraordinary beauty –
but it's still only a mask. If you peel it away and look
in the mirror, who do you see gazing back?
– ROB THISTLETON, *LET GO AND LIVE*

Ruby, September 2013

I trailed my fingers over the dusty book spines until I found
what I wanted. A slim volume bound in red leather, its
face embossed with silver patterns. After reading Brenna's
journal, I recalled glimpsing the book when I'd scanned Esther's
bookshelves soon after my arrival here.

It was *Aucassin and Nicolette*.

Inside the cover was written: *To my beloved Adele, from Father.*
Christmas 1891.

The pages were heavy and the print had the slightly
crooked uniformity typical of an old printing press, each
black letter embossed in the fibre of the paper. As I flicked
through the pages, a letter fluttered out. It was tattered and
well-thumbed, the folded edges torn as if it had been read and
reread countless times. The handwriting was spidery, clearly

written in haste and barely legible; tiny drops of ink splashed the page, and many of the words were smudged or ran together. I checked the signature, intrigued to find it had been written by Adele Whitby.

9 July 1899

My dearest Brenna,

The light is fading and I am growing weary. Sleep will come soon and I will surrender to it with a glad heart, but first I must beg your forgiveness. I hated deceiving you, but I knew that you would never agree to my plan.

I wasn't being selfless.

It was simply a waste of life to let you die.

Dear one, you may have wondered at my visits to Launceston, and perhaps noticed the many tonics I habitually took. There is a herbalist who lives on the hillside among the rocks and trees of the wild western shore. She runs a small sanatorium for those, like me, who suffer weakness of the lungs. Her salt baths and herbal tinctures did me much good and even now I swear they prolonged my life; but even those marvellous concoctions had not the power to recover a system that was clearly failing.

My time had run out.

Which is why I convinced Quinn to help me free you from this dreadful place. To her credit, she didn't question my order, but even as we made plans to drug you and steal you to safety, tears leaked continuously from her eyes. She raised me, you see, from a tot, and she loathed for us to be parted.

It was our favourite tale of Aucassin and Nicolette that gave me the idea. Do you remember how dear Nicolette dressed as a troubadour to reignite Aucassin's love for her? Their story has provided inspiration for me since I first read it as a swooning girl; now, it has inspired me one last time, so that I, like Nicolette, may serve someone I love.

Quinn used a measure of laudanum in the syrup I delivered to you, that day in the prison – just enough, you understand, to make you groggy and disoriented. Once your eyes began to drift shut, it was easy to convince you to shed your threadbare coat and don my heavy fur-trimmed mantle; it was one you'd long admired, and the cell was so very cold.

Once the drug took effect, I called to the guard and said you were ill. I stood in the shadows weeping – a pretence I'd planned, but, when my moment came, there was no need to pretend. My tears flowed freely. I wept for joy that you would soon be safe, and I wept with sorrow knowing I would see you no more.

Quinn was waiting in the guard room to collect you, and hurry you to the hired carriage beyond the prison gates, where baby James was swaddled in the arms of a trustworthy associate of Quinn's. From there – by which time I had calculated you would be fully under the effect of the laudanum – the carriage took you and Quinn and little James to Devonport, and then onto the steamer bound for Melbourne. In Quinn's possession was my birth certificate, which I knew would enable you to lay claim to what is rightfully yours. Destroy this letter, my dear. Let your identity die with me, and grant my last wish by taking my name. Take it to protect yourself and your child, and to benefit from my brother's estate – to which you are rightfully entitled. Knowing you, my dear, you will rail against my plan, but I beg you, Brenna, if you cannot do this for yourself, then please do it for your little one. And do it for me. It is my gift, given in love and gratitude by a lonely, grieving woman whose life was so greatly improved by knowing you.

God bless, travel safe, and always remember – whenever you feel the sunshine on your face, whenever you hear the whisper of a breeze in the treetops, or catch the sweet scent of those bush flowers you so dearly love – remember that someone in heaven is thinking of you.

Your friend and sister,
Adele Whitby

The letter trembled in my hand. Going over to the window, I stood and gazed out across the landscape of flowers and trees and stark outcrops of granite, then down the grassy slope to where the river ran over boulders and stones and forged its journey inland.

Brenna had made it home after all.

The woman whose sorrowful face I had once studied in an old album, the woman my mother remembered as Nanna Adele, had in fact been Brenna Whitby, my great-grandmother.

Meanwhile Adele, in a gift of love, had taken Brenna's place in the prison cell so that her beloved friend could have a new chance at life.

I was glad. So very glad.

I folded the letter and replaced it in the little book and closed the covers back around the secret it had held for over a hundred years.

And as I hung my head and wept, my tears washed clean the darkness that had for so long shadowed my soul, and I felt Adele's gift of life and love renew me, too.

Months had passed, but at times I could still hear him.

In the morning when the rush of the rapids was loudest; and in the afternoon when the sun's heat lifted the scent of lichen from the stones; and again at dusk when the wind moaned in the casuarinas that grew along the river, and the memory of what had happened that day was strongest.

Ruby . . . don't leave me.

Last night I walked down to the riverbank, certain the voice I heard was real. Bardo trotted at my heels as she always did since her ordeal; we were both worse for wear, jumpy and prone to nightmares. But, as Pete liked to say, we were birds of a feather, Bardo and I – far stronger than we appeared at first glance.

As I stood on the embankment staring into the darkness, an owl cried in the casuarinas above us and Bardo whined softly.

Heavy rains near the coast meant the river was up, and the black water rushed past, swollen high along the banks. The water was ink, the starlight so frail and the night so dense that there was nothing to see. I stepped nearer the edge, drawn by the soft call of the wind.

Ruby . . . Ruby, don't leave—

I felt the squelch of mud underfoot as I neared the water. The current dragged at my legs, drawing me deeper.

I slid my hand into my pocket. Drawing out the silver locket, I held it in my palm. Apart from the diary, it was my only link to my great-grandmother; the only object I owned that connected us.

Beside me Bardo whined again and I whispered reassuringly, as much for myself as for her.

The locket had grown warm from the heat of my skin. I took a breath, and before I lost my nerve, I threw it into the darkest, deepest part of the river. It disappeared silently, joining the tumble of stones and water weeds and silt and fish eggs that the river carried on its back as it carved its way ever inland from the sea.

In October, Mum had another exhibition. Looking radiant, she rushed over to greet me as soon as I walked in the door.

We hugged, and then she took my hand.

'Thank you for giving me Brenna's diary. I loved my grand-mother, but there was always a sadness about her that I never understood. If only I'd known she was an artist, I might have encouraged her to paint again.'

'Do you think she stopped painting to protect her identity?'

'No . . . I think it was more personal than that. I suppose it reminded her too painfully of the loved ones she'd lost. I'm only grateful I persisted with my art, because my passion for painting has healed me.'

'I'm happy for you, Mum.'

She beamed. 'Now that I know what Brenna went through, it's given me a new perspective on my own life. I feel at peace for the first time since your father died – and I have you to thank for it.'

Slipping her arm around my shoulders, she gave me a quick squeeze. Just before she pulled away, I felt a rush of warmth and found myself hugging her back.

Since the inquest into Rob's death, and my witness statement describing my memory of how my sister died, the tension between Mum and me had eased. There was still a vast chasm between us; we were basically strangers linked by blood; but our new, gentler treatment of one another had given me hope.

Mum left me to attend to a patron, and I wandered over to the perimeter. The gallery was smaller than the one she'd exhibited in at the start of the year. Her paintings had changed, too. They were still huge, but they were no longer realistic depictions of house interiors.

Each canvas bore great starbursts of crystalline colour, with intricate centres – flowers, I thought at first – captured within swathes of blue–white and filmy turquoise, clear pinks and carnation-blooms of palest yellow.

Her last show had sold out, and I saw that already most of these new works had red dots stuck to the wall beneath them.

One painting in particular caught my eye.

It was smaller than the other canvases, less vibrant. I went closer. It was a tiny portrait, the size of an orange. Wisps of dark hair framed the girl's oval face; she had pointy cheekbones and a sweet rosebud mouth, and wide golden eyes.

I stood spellbound. Her name formed on my lips, but I was suddenly too breathless to utter it. Part of me felt like crying, while another part wanted to toss back my head and laugh. Joy and sorrow battled in my heart . . . and the joy won. I bent closer to read the printed legend attached to the wall at the base of the painting. *Jamie, 1994.* She would have been fourteen.

I moved along the wall, re-examining the other paintings with fresh eyes. More tiny faces peered from billowy starbursts, and from the centres of gold and tangerine carnation-blooms. All were dark-haired and achingly pretty – only the ages differed. Some showed the chubby-faced toddler I'd never known; others portrayed the Jamie I remembered most – the teenager who had it all: beauty, brains, popularity, attention from boys, and most significantly, Mum's unconditional approval. The paintings were a celebration, I realised – of the daughter Mum had loved, and of the sister who had once meant the world to me.

A waiter swept past with a full tray, and I grabbed a mineral water. Smiling at the glowing portrait, I lifted my glass.

'Here's to you, big sister. From now on, may all our memories be happy.'

When November rolled around, a parcel arrived early for my birthday. It looked like a big flat box, quite heavy, but when I shook it nothing rattled.

It was one of Mum's paintings, a portrait of two girls with their arms around one another. Both were dark-haired, one a little taller than the other. The taller girl was wearing a pink floral tank top and hippy pants; the younger girl wore an identical outfit, only in green. On their heads were crowns of wildflowers, and they were beaming happily, almost deliriously, as if posing for a photo.

Jamie and me.

Turning the painting over, I was surprised to find an inscription written neatly on a piece of paper glued to the canvas backing.

For my precious girl, Ruby
Love Mum

My eyes filled, and I tried to smile but my lips were suddenly trembling and hot happy tears were flowing over my cheeks.

For so long I had doubted; for so long I had believed that my mother had chosen to love one of her daughters, and not the other. In a flash of insight, I saw how wrong I'd been. Mum had loved us both with all her heart; the sense of emptiness I'd carried in me for the last two decades was not her doing, but mine.

Later, Pete had a present for me, too. We were sitting in his cottage by candlelight, picking at the remnants of my birthday cake – chocolate mud, with fresh cream and blueberry roulade. Roky Erickson's *Forever* played softly in the background, and Bardo and the new puppy slumbered peacefully on the floor at our feet.

Inside the silver wrapping paper I found a gorgeous white vintage nighty, full length, similar to the one I'd once worn on my midnight forays with the Wolf. I held it up and shook out the creases, admiring the exquisite lace cuffs and décolletage.

'It's wonderful! In mint condition, too. Where on earth did you find it?'

'It was Esther's. A present from her mother in the forties when she got married. Esther always preferred pyjamas, it's never been worn. She would have wanted you to have it. And wear it,' he added mysteriously. Then he leaned over to kiss me on the lips, and dropped a second parcel into my lap.

Inside was a wolf mask. The pointed face was rubber, but the back of the head and the ears were faux fur; the mouth hung agape exposing large white fangs.

'Oh,' I said, then felt a smile creep up. 'This does put a more interesting slant on the evening.'

Pete laughed huskily and took the mask, went to slip it on – but I plucked it from his fingers before he had the chance.

'No you don't,' I declared. 'This time around, *I'm* wearing the wolf mask.'

Pete shook his head. 'Hang on, Roo. You're the beautiful one. Beauty gets the nighty, remember? Beast wears the mask.'

He went to take it back, but I waved it out of reach.

'Not in *this* game, he doesn't.'

Pete made a sulky face, but his eyes were alight, glowing like sapphires in the candlelight. 'Yeah, well,' he muttered darkly, 'there's no way I'm getting togged up in Granny's nighty.'

Laughing, I took his hand and led him outside. We sat on the grass and gazed up, my fingers linked warmly in his. The air was fragrant, scented with the spicy tang of wildflowers. Overhead the sky had disappeared behind a luminous galaxy of stars.

'I don't want this to end,' Pete said softly.

'What makes you think it will?'

Lifting my hand to his mouth, he kissed my fingers one by one.

'You're like a dream, Ruby. An incredibly beautiful, sexy dream. But in my experience, dreams always end. I guess I'm scared you'll get tired of living out here in the middle of nowhere. You'll go back to the coast and forget all about me.'

I pulled him close and kissed him. 'There won't be any going back. The new Busy Bookworm is thriving in Armidale, and Earle loves the tablelands climate. Besides, I'm becoming quite addicted to your company. You're stuck with me, old thing.'

Pete beamed and drew me closer for another kiss, but I laughed and wriggled out of his arms. Unzipping my dress,

I soaked up his wide-eyed appreciation of what I wore underneath: black boy-leg undies, and a slinky black lace bra. Placing
my hands on his shoulders, I guided him back onto the moonlit
grass, then slipped the wolf mask over my head.

'Welcome, dear Beauty,' I said huskily. 'Welcome to my
humble abode.'

Acknowledgements

When I began *Lyrebird Hill*, Selwa warned me that the second novel is always the hardest. I was sceptical; after all, I had a bottom drawer full of rejected old manuscripts – surely they counted for something?

But Selwa is always right.

I made several messes of this story before it finally incarnated into a novel I feel proud of, and getting there took the help, advice, and guidance of a talented and dedicated team. I would like to express my deepest gratitude and thanks to the following people.

Number one on my list is my agent, Selwa Anthony, my wish-fulfilling jewel. She believed in me from the start, and stood by me for many years, always incredibly wise and kind and strong. The rumours are true, she has the ability to make dreams a reality!

Many thanks as well to the brilliant crew at Simon and Schuster for all their care and hard work, in particular Larissa Edwards and Lou Johnson; the wonderful Anna O'Grady, for getting my stories noticed; and my editors Claire de Medici, and the saintly and tireless Roberta Ivers, who always helps me weave more magic (and logic) into the tale.

A special thank-you to my German publisher, Goldmann, for their enthusiasm and faith in my stories. Knowing my books will be read in the language of some of my favourite authors is the thrill of a lifetime.

Thanks as well to Bolinda Audio, and the talented Eloise Oxer for bringing my characters to life in such a beautiful and compelling way. Heather Gammage for her skilful research and story input. Brian Dennis, Linda Anthony, and Drew Keys for their behind-the-scenes support over the years.

Russell Taylor for his steadfast love and friendship. Dan Mitchell for teaching me about the bush, and for being a wellspring of inspiration. Bet and Norm Mitchell for our wonderful Sundays. Rusty Lawson and Di Luxford-Lawson for reminding me to believe in myself. Stuart Ruthven for insights into character motivation, and Hailey and Luke for their love and passion.

I would also like to acknowledge and thank the Kamilaroi and Anaiwan people of the New England regions around Armidale in NSW, whose history and culture inspired some of my favourite scenes in *Lyrebird Hill*.

A very heartfelt thank you to my mum, Jeanette, for teaching me to love books; my dad, Bernie, who I miss every day; my sister Sarah for her loyalty and friendship; and my sister Katie for her pride in me, and for always cheering me on.

And finally my readers, who continue to brighten my life with their good wishes and encouragement.

My love and thanks to you all.

Anna Romer
2014

Exploring my Writing Process

For me, a novel begins a long time before I sit down to write. I always start a project with a new notebook. Over many months – or years – I fill it with photos, newspaper clippings, articles, and random scribblings. I make lists and timelines, draw maps, create detailed dossiers for my characters and build histories around them. I currently have about fifteen of these notebooks on the boil, each containing the raw ideas of a future novel.

As the bones of a story begin to emerge, I pick over my favourite themes – forbidden love, obsession, scandal and family secrets, and the lies we tell to each other and to ourselves. I never consciously try to work my themes into the storyline, but they are always brewing away under the surface, helping me to stay focused.

I also choose a fairytale that resonates with me, and think of ways I can weave it through the plot. In *Thornwood House* I played with the idea of Bluebeard, and his mysterious locked room which eventually tempted his wives to their deaths. The manifestation of this theme in the final story is very subtle, but it inspired the sense of curiosity and danger that I wanted to convey – both for the back bedroom of the house at Thornwood, and for the old settler's hut near the gully.

When I finish brainstorming, my pile of notes is thicker than a telephone directory. I rarely look at these notes again. The story seeds have been planted; now it's time to let them germinate and grow in the dark garden of my subconscious.

Meanwhile, I dive into the research, which is another great way to peel open further layers of story.

My research involves a lot of travel to soak up scenery and get a feel for local people and families and their fascinating pasts. For *Thornwood House*, I needed to know what life was like in the Fassifern region of Queensland during the 1940s, and how a small rural community was impacted by the war. I studied old newspapers, maps and photographs, and explored the landmarks in my story, such as Boonah's historic Lutheran graveyard, and a spooky old settler's hut I discovered in a forgotten paddock.

I also read heaps of war correspondence, as well as wartime memoirs and diary entries. Mum gave me a bundle of airgraph letters that were sent to my grandmother during the Second World War. These letters documented a young pilot's longing for home, and made the war experience all the more personal for me.

By this stage I'm usually impatient to start the plotting process, which I really love. For me, there's nothing more enjoyable than sitting at my 'plotting table' with a thermos of tea, and assembling the skeleton of a new story.

I love making a mess with scraps of paper, jotting down ideas for scenes and plot points and possible twists, and then puzzling them all together like a huge unwieldy jigsaw. The plot is always organic; when I start drafting, the story flies off on tangents and I invariably write myself into a corner. Back I go to the plotting table and re-shuffle my paper scraps until the problem is solved, then I return to my embryonic story and redraft. This phase of the process goes on for many months, and is a mental and emotional rollercoaster ride!

Some scenes – endings in particular – are more difficult to write. I enter avoidance mode: gardening or knitting or brushing the dog, or collecting wildflower seeds for my various regeneration projects – meanwhile freaking out over the gaps in my story, worrying myself into a state of creative agitation. By the time I'm ready to write my most challenging scenes, I'm a mess . . . but that's good! Angst and chaos are part of the writing process, too, and are frequently the catalyst for better work.

Often I write to silence, but some scenes require that I work from a place of heightened emotion. If this is the case, on goes the music – Mumford and Sons, Will Oldham, Yma Sumac, Roky Erickson, Loreena McKennitt. For especially dark brooding scenes I play Espers, Six Organs of Admittance, PG Six, Nick Cave; for the ending I'll crank up Muse, maybe a few Metallica tracks, or some weird obscure 70s folk rock. At some stage during a critical scene I'll pull out Evanescence and have a great old cry.

Understandably, after all this intense focus, the story lines begin to blur; it becomes easy to overlook mistakes. One of the most exhilarating (and terrifying) parts of the process is handing over the novel draft to my agent and editors . . . and my eagle-eyed sister. They are the ghosts in the novel machine, and without them the story would be a shambles. An editor's job is to pick apart a story and then send it back for the writer to fix. If someone points out that part of the plotline or a character doesn't work, I gladly make the changes, knowing the story will be better for it. It's a daunting process, but my 'behind the scenes' team always gives me deeper understanding and insight – not just into the novel we're working on, but more importantly, into the craft of storytelling.

Another vital part of the process – especially after slogging towards deadlines – is clearing the brain fog. For me, this usually involves vanishing deep into the bush never to be heard from again . . . well, at least not until dinnertime! I'll swim in the river, or climb into the hills and daydream on a bed of wildflowers. When I finally return to the world with the peppery scent of yellow-buttons clinging to my clothes, my brain and body are fully recharged.

One of my favourite quotes comes from Joseph Campbell, who said, 'Follow your bliss.' For me, the process of creating a novel is very much about following the trail of ideas that I find most intriguing and inspiring . . . a strategy that works well for writing in general, and also for life.

Anna Romer
2014

HAVE YOU READ THORNWOOD HOUSE?

Anna Romer's first novel is an enthralling, haunting tale of obsession, love and courage.

Read on for a peek at the prologue and first chapter . . .

When you're all that stands between the murderous past and the fate of those you love, how far would you go to save them?

When Audrey Kepler inherits an abandoned homestead in rural Queensland, she jumps at the chance to escape her loveless existence in the city and make a fresh start.

In a dusty back room of the old house, she discovers the crumbling photo of a handsome World War Two medic – Samuel Riordan, the homestead's former occupant – and soon finds herself becoming obsessed with him.

But as Audrey digs deeper into Samuel's story, she discovers he was accused of bashing to death a young woman on his return from the war in 1946. When she learns about other unexplained deaths in recent years – one of them a young woman with injuries echoing those of the first victim – she begins to suspect that the killer is still very much alive.

And now Audrey, thanks to her need to uncover the past, has provided him with good reason to want to kill again.

Prologue

On a sunny afternoon, the clearing at the edge of the gully resembles a fairytale glade. Ribbons of golden light flutter through the treetops and bellbirds fill the air with chiming calls. The spicy scent of wildflowers drifts on a warm breeze, and deep in the shady belly of the ravine a creek whispers along its ancient course.

But then, come dusk, the sky darkens quickly. Shadows swarm among the trees, chasing the light. Sunbeams vanish. Birds retreat into thickets of acacia and blackthorn as, overhead, a host of violet-black clouds roll in from the west, bringing rain.

Here now, in the bright moonlight, it's a different place again. Nightmarish. Otherworldly. The open expanse of silvery poa grass is hemmed in by black-trunked ironbarks, while at the centre stands a tall, fin-shaped boulder.

I'm drawn towards the boulder. It seems to whisper, shadows appear to gather at its base. I go nearer. Shivers fly across my skin. I stumble in the dark and pause to listen, straining to hear the sound of a voice, of a muffled cry or sob – but there's only the tick of rain in the leaves and the ragged rasp of my breathing. Further down the slope wallabies thump unseen through the bush, and something meows overhead, probably a boobook owl.

'Bron . . . are you here?'

I don't expect an answer, but when none comes my sense of panic sharpens. I cast about for a broken bough, a trail of flattened grass, a familiar scrap of clothing abandoned on the ground . . . but there's nothing of my daughter here, nothing of the man who took her.

I search the shadows, trying to see beyond the tree-silhouettes that shift and sway around me. Lightning illuminates a dirt trail that cuts uphill through the undergrowth. I edge towards it, then stop. A chill skates up the back of my neck, I sense I'm not alone. Someone's near, it must be him. Hiding in the trees. Watching. I imagine his gaze crawling over me as he speculates how best to strike.

When he does, I'll be ready.

At least, that's what I keep telling myself. In truth, I feel as though I've relived this scenario a thousand times, hovering in this desolate glade waiting for death to find me, but each time floundering at the critical moment.

The air is suddenly cold. Rain trickles off my face. The trees bow sideways in a damp gust and gumnut flowers spin from high branches, carrying forth the sharp scent of eucalyptus.

A twig cracks, loud despite the rain; a violent sound like a small bone being broken. I whirl towards it. Lightning threads through the clouds, brightening the glade. A solitary shadow catches my eye on the other side of the clearing. It breaks from the greater darkness and moves towards me.

I recognise him instantly.

He's a big man, his features a pale blur in the dimness. His skin shines wet, and something about the sight of his face makes my blood run thin.

'Hello, Audrey.'

And it's only now that I see the axe handle grasped in his hand.

1

Audrey, September 2005

T he sky over the cemetery was bruised by stormclouds. It was only mid-afternoon, but already dark. A large group of mourners stood on the grassy hillside, sheltering beneath the outstretched arms of an old elm. In the branches overhead, a congregation of blackbirds shuffled restlessly, their cries punctuating the stillness.

Crows. Darkness. Death.

Tony would have loved that.

I swallowed hard, wishing I was anywhere but here; anywhere but standing in the rain, shivering in a borrowed black suit, silently saying goodbye to the man I once thought I'd loved.

Bronwyn stood beside me, her dark blue dress making her fair hair and complexion all the more stark. She was eleven, tall for her age and strikingly pretty. She held an umbrella over our heads, her thin fingers bloodless around the handle.

Despite the rain, despite the glances and hushed talk behind our backs, I was glad we'd come. No matter what anyone said, I knew Tony would have wanted us here.

The coffin hovered over the grave, suspended from a steel frame by discreet cables. Nearby, a blanket of fake grass was draped over a mound of dirt that would later fill the hole. Huge wreaths of white lilies and scarlet anthuriums carpeted the ground. They looked expensive, and my handpicked roses seemed out of place among them.

Everything glistened in the rain: the coffin's brass handles, the garlands of lilies, the clustered umbrellas. Even the minister's bald head gleamed as he intoned the scripture. 'Deep from the earth shall you speak, from low in the dust your words shall come forth. Your voice shall rise from the ground like the voice of a ghost.'

The ancient words were muffled by the rain, spoken with such solemnity that they seemed to drift from another time. If only they were true. If only Tony could speak to me now, tell me what had driven him in those last desperate days.

Lightning flickered, and thunder rumbled behind the clouds. The crows lifted from their perch and flapped away.

Bronwyn shuffled closer. 'Mum?' There was panic in her voice.

The pulleys suspending the casket started to move. The long black box began its descent. I grabbed Bronwyn's hand and we clung together.

'It'll be okay, Bron.' I'd meant to offer comfort, but the falseness of my words was jarring. How could anything ever be okay again?

I grasped for a memory to latch on to: Tony's face as I most wanted to remember it – his cheeks ruddy, his dark hair on end, his sapphire eyes alight as he stared at the tiny bundle of his newborn daughter cradled in his arms.

'She's so beautiful,' he'd muttered. 'So beautiful it scares me to look away from her.'

Bronwyn tugged me closer to the edge of the grave and together we stared down at the coffin. It seemed impossible that a man who had once embraced life with such gusto now lay in the boggy ground beneath a mantle of rain. Impossible that he of all people had given up so easily.

Bronwyn kissed the parcel she'd made for her father and let it drop onto the coffin lid. It held a letter she'd written to him, a package of his favourite liquorice and the scarf she'd been knitting for his birthday. I heard her whispering, but her words were lost in the rain. When her shoulders began to quiver, I knew tears were brewing.

'Come on.' We turned away and started down the slope to where I'd parked my old Celica. Heads pivoted as we passed, their faces pale against the cemetery's grey backdrop.

Ignoring them, I slid my arm around Bronwyn and kept walking. Her sleeve was damp, and through the fabric I could feel the coldness of her flesh. She needed to be at home, cocooned in the warmth and safety of familiar territory; she needed soup and toast, pyjamas, fluffy slippers . . .

'Audrey – ?'

I looked up and a thrill of shock made me release Bronwyn. My nerves turned to water, my mouth went dry. Silly, such fear. I took a breath and summoned my voice.

'Hello, Carol.'

She was stony-faced, the strain showing around her eyes. Her hair was coiled at the nape of her neck, and as usual I was struck by her beauty.

'I'm pleased you came,' she said quietly. 'Tony would have wanted you both here. Hello Bronwyn, dear . . . how are you holding up?'

'Good thanks,' Bronwyn answered dully, her eyes on the ground.

I rattled out my car keys. 'Bron, would you wait in the car?'

She took the keys and plodded off down the wet slope, the umbrella bobbing over her head. At the bottom of the hill, she wove through a line of parked cars until she reached the Celica. A moment later she disappeared inside.

'How is she really?' Carol asked.

'She's coping,' I said, not entirely sure it was true.

We were alone on the slope. Mourners were hurrying out of the wet, back to their cars. The cemetery was nearly deserted. Carol was gazing down the hill, so I stole a closer look – marvelling at her perfect face, her expensive clothes, the way she held herself. She wore a black dress, fitted and elegant, and at her throat was a chip of ice. A diamond, probably. Fine lines gathered at the edges of her eyes, but they only seemed to intensify her loveliness. No wonder Tony had given up everything to be with her.

Carol caught me looking and frowned. 'I know what you're thinking. The same thing everyone else is thinking . . . But you're wrong. Tony and I were getting along fine, our marriage – ' She drew a shaky breath. 'Our marriage was as strong as ever. Things were good between us, they had been for a long time.'

'You weren't to know, Carol.'

She shook her head, her eyes glassy. 'But that's just it, isn't it, Audrey? . . . Of all people, I *should* have known.'

'What Tony did was no one's fault. You can't blame yourself.'

'I just keep thinking if I'd done more . . . noticed more. Been more attentive. You see, the night he left, I knew something wasn't right.'

I frowned. 'How do you mean?'

'Well . . . we were in the lounge room at home. I was watching TV and Tony was flipping through the paper. For some reason I looked over at him and he was staring into space . . . All the colour had drained out of his face. He got up, folded the newspaper and went to the door. He kept saying "They found him. They found him." Then he went out. I heard the car start up, heard the wheels crunching over the gravel in the drive. And that was the last time I saw him.'

'What did he mean? Found who?'

Carol shook her head. 'I don't know. Later I scanned the paper he'd been reading, hoping for a clue . . . but there was nothing. Nothing that made any sense to me – as you can imagine, I was distraught.'

'Didn't he call?'

'No, but the police did, ten days later.' Carol shifted closer, her eyes searching mine. 'I'll tell you now it was the worst shock of my life. Tony was dead, just like that. When they told me his body had been found in Queensland outside a little town called Magpie Creek, I thought they were talking about someone else. But he . . . he – God, it was so sudden, so unexpected. I never even knew he owned a gun – '

I flinched, and Carol's eyes went wide. A single tear trembled on her lash.

'I'm sorry,' she said, 'it was a horrid thing to say . . . but that's the most confusing part of all. Tony was terrified of guns – he hated any sort of violence, didn't he?'

Since hearing about Tony's death from a mutual friend, I'd been wondering the same thing. Wondering why Tony – ever the advocate for peace, love and goodwill to all – had chosen to end his life so viciously and leave a legacy of devastation to those of us who'd loved him.

To my surprise, Carol grasped my wrist. 'Why would he do that, Audrey? How could he have been so selfish?'

The sudden fervour of her words shocked me. I groped for something reassuring to say – as much for myself as for Carol – but she rushed on, digging her fingers into my arm.

'You were always so close to him – early on, anyway. Did he ever tell you anything – a childhood trauma, something that might have come back to haunt him? Had he ever been ill when you were together? He wasn't taking anything, not that I know of . . . but he might have been trying to protect me. Unless there was another woman? Oh Audrey, no matter which way I look at it, I can't make any sense of what he did.'

Her eyes were haunted, rimmed by delicate rabbit-pink, the skin around her mouth blanched white. I understood what she was saying – outwardly, Tony had appeared to be too level-headed to ever succumb to depression or self-pity. Yet I couldn't help remembering our years together – the happy days so often overshadowed by his recurring nightmares, his abrupt mood swings, his episodes of broody silence. His almost phobic horror of violence, blood. And his passionate hatred of firearms of any kind.

'Tony never talked about his past,' I said. 'Whatever secrets he had, he kept them from me, too.'

Carol looked away. 'You know, Audrey, if we'd met under different circumstances, you and I might have been friends.'

I dredged up a smile, knowing it was her grief talking. Carol Jarman and I were just too different to be anything other than strangers to one another. We moved in different circles, came from different worlds. She was poised, elegant, beautiful, and enjoyed the sort of lifestyle I'd only ever dreamed about. If it hadn't been for Tony, our paths would never have crossed.

Carol slid her hand into her shoulder bag and withdrew a small parcel wrapped in fabric. 'I found this in his belongings. I thought it was something you might like to have.'

I recognised the fabric at once – it was a scarf Tony had brought back from a trip to Italy, the first year he'd flown over for the Venice Biennale. Wrapped inside was a Murano glass paperweight with an electric-blue butterfly preserved at its centre.

'Thank you.' A buzz of warmth. I locked my fingers around the object's cool hardness, flashing back to the days when Tony and I had been happy.

'I might not see you again,' Carol said, 'so I should tell you now, rather than let you hear from the lawyer.'

I looked up from the paperweight, still aglow with bittersweet memories. 'Tell me . . . ?'

'Tony left instructions for the Albert Park house to be sold. I hate having to ask this of you, Audrey, but you'll need to vacate within twenty-eight days. I won't kick you out if you need longer . . . but I'd like to start renovating as soon as possible so I can put it on the market.'

I could only stare at her. 'Twenty-eight days?'

'Don't worry. Tony wouldn't have dreamt of leaving you homeless. You and Bronwyn will be well provided for,' she added cryptically. She seemed about to say something more, but instead gave my arm a quick squeeze – gently, this time – then turned abruptly and hurried away.

I watched her glide down the hill. Her friends gathered around her; a couple of them shot me furtive glances. Then they bundled her off towards the line of waiting cars, where she ducked into a glittering Mercedes and was whisked away.

Twenty-eight days.

I clutched the paperweight tight. Tony had never actually lied to me about his past, but his stubborn refusal to talk about it had always been hurtful, as if he didn't consider me worthy of his trust. Now, as I glared up the slope, I felt the burden of his silence shift around me, stirring up all my old doubts and inse-curities. In that moment I wanted nothing more than to climb back up the hill and hurl the paperweight into the grave as a final, bitter farewell. But it was raining again. The ground was sodden and the slope looked slippery.

I shoved the parcel into my pocket. Alive, Tony had brought me nothing but trouble; now he was dead, I refused to allow him the same opportunity. With that promise firmly planted in my mind, I picked my way back down the hill to the Celica and my waiting daughter.

In other parts of the country, September heralded the begin-ning of spring. Here in Melbourne it still felt like the tail-end of winter. Weeks of rain, chilly nights and mornings. Endless grey skies. There were days – like today – when it seemed as though this drab, gloomy purgatory would never end.

Albert Park, the sought-after heritage suburb where we lived, seemed even colder and drearier than everywhere else.

Tony's funeral had left us in a low mood. We were shivering as we pushed through the front gate and unlocked the house. It was dark inside. I stalked through, cranking up the heat and switching on the lights until the place glowed like a furnace. Bronwyn refused soup and toast, but hovered in the kitchen while I made her a mug of hot Milo. Then she fled to the haven of her room.

My own bedroom was icy. I buried the Venetian paperweight under a pile of clothes in a bottom drawer, then threw my damp suit into the washing basket. Dragging on soft jeans and an old T-shirt, I wandered out to the lounge room and stood gazing through the window.

Silvery raindrops cascaded across neighbouring rooftops, making haloes around the streetlamps. Lights shone like beacons from nearby houses, but out over the bay the water was lost beneath a shroud of premature darkness.

Drawing the curtains, I stood in the centre of the room, hugging my arms. Getting my head around Tony being gone. Wondering, for the millionth time, what had possessed him to load up a gun and end his life in such a violent way. Tony had been many things: a charming and wildly successful artist, a brilliant father to Bronwyn, a sufferer of nightmares . . . and in the end, a selfish two-timing bastard; but I'd never pegged him as a man who'd willingly devastate the people he cared about.

I wandered out to the dining room. He was gone, I reminded myself. No amount of speculation was going to bring him back. And there was no point feeling abandoned by a man who'd already deserted me years ago. Even so, I could feel my old resentments creeping back. Bronwyn and I were about to be torn from our home, a home that Tony had promised would be ours as long as we wanted. He'd bought it in the early days, after a string of sell-out overseas exhibitions. Later, I hadn't bothered to argue when he'd suggested it remain in his name. I was just glad to continue living in it rent-free. I'd been young, full of pride. Angry at Tony, and stubbornly opposed to feeling indebted to him.

But now I ached . . . ached for my daughter and the grief she would carry with her for life. Ached for Tony, whose suffering must have run deep; and for Carol, whose world had revolved around him. Ached for my own selfish longings that sometimes whispered in lonely unguarded moments that perhaps – by a miraculous twist of fate – he might one day come back to me. And I ached with the burden of questions he'd left behind. Why had he rushed out that night, then driven for days to some little backwater? What had finally pushed him over the edge?

Carol said she'd checked the paper, but had been too distraught to properly focus. I remembered that Tony had subscribed religiously to the *Courier-Mail*. He'd grown up outside Brisbane – one of the few morsels of background info I'd managed to prise from him – and had liked to stay abreast of Queensland news.

I booted my laptop and went online.

It took a while to sift through the search results for the *Courier-Mail* dated just before Tony's death. Nothing leapt out. My neck started cramping from peering at the screen and I was about to log off, but as a last resort I punched in the name of the town where they'd found Tony's body, 'Magpie Creek'.

A single search result filled the screen.

DROUGHT SOLVES TWENTY-YEAR-OLD MYSTERY
BRISBANE, Fri. – For most people, Australia's current drought – called the worst in a thousand years – has been the cause of deep concern. For the small community of Magpie Creek in south-east Queensland, it has brought an unexpected solution to a mystery that has baffled the town for twenty years.

On Wednesday last, a group of conservationists were taking water samples from the near-dry Lake Brigalow Dam, 24 kilometres from the town, when they discovered a vehicle submerged in the mud. Fire and Rescue Services retrieved the car, only to discover inside it the remains of a human body.

Magpie Creek Police have linked the car to a local man who was reported missing by his family in November 1986. Positive identification of the remains will necessarily await the results of forensic examinations and post-mortem.

I sat back and stared at the screen until my eyes blurred. Maybe I was clutching at straws, but I couldn't help wondering. Had Tony known the missing man, been close to him? Had the man been a one-time friend, a relative? Someone whose death had mattered enough for Tony to walk out on his wife with barely a word and travel 1600 kilometres into a past he'd so obviously put behind him?

In 1986, Tony would have been fourteen. His father, then? Reported missing by his family; by Tony's family. A family that Tony had – in the twelve years I'd known him – steadfastly refused to acknowledge. Shutting my eyes, I tried to restrain my rampaging thoughts. It was unlikely, probably just coincidence. Probably nothing more than connections made by a brain fuelled with exhaustion and grief.

Logging off, I went out to the kitchen and looked in the fridge. It was crammed with food, but my hand reached robotically for a Crown Lager. The beer was icy, deliciously wet on my grief-tightened throat. While I drank, I stared at the black square of window. In it I saw the woman the past five years had caused me to become: hollow-eyed and gaunt, with shadows beneath the pallid skin where there should have been a healthy flush. I would be thirty this year, but my face wore the grey resignation of someone much older.

I rubbed my palms over my cheeks, then smoothed my hair. It had escaped the neat ponytail I'd forced it into for the funeral, and reverted into a shaggy seventies-style bob. I recalled Carol's restrained elegance, and grimaced at the small, boyish person reflected in the window. The pinched little face stared sullenly back at me, silently accusing: You see why he left? You see why he wanted her and not you?

Turning from the window, I went along the hall to Bronwyn's room and knocked lightly. There was no response, so I cracked open the door. Her lamp was on. She'd fallen asleep on top of the bedcovers – her fair hair fanned over the pillow, her face was blotchy from crying. She was wearing the pyjamas her father had given her a year ago, too tight now, and faded from overuse.

'Bronny?' I whispered, stroking her hair. 'Let's get you under the covers, sweetheart.'

Up until six months ago, she'd seen Tony every Sunday without fail. Just as the church bells began to chime across the waking city, Tony would pull his dazzling black Porsche into the driveway, honking the horn as Bronwyn ran down the path to greet him. Meanwhile, I lurked in the front room, my lips pinched tight, spying on them through the shutters. Six or seven hours later I'd hear the familiar honking, and Bronwyn would rush in brimming with news of what a fabulous time they'd had, cooing over the presents he'd bought her, eyes aglow and cheeks flushed pink with joy.

Then, six months ago, the visits ground to a halt.

Tony stopped showing up for their Sunday outings. He forgot to ring, sending expensive gifts in lieu of a visit. Without explanation, he disengaged himself from her life. I watched helplessly as the sorrow grew in her like a sickness, turning my bright little girl into a forlorn shadow-faced creature who moped around the house as though, rather than living in it, she was haunting it.

Bronwyn sighed and rolled over. Tucking the blanket around her, I laid a whisper of a kiss on her brow. She smelled of honey and chocolate, of fresh washed laundry and lemon shampoo. Safe, familiar smells. I was about to tiptoe out when I caught sight of a photo propped against her night lamp. I hadn't seen it for years, and it brought back the past with a pang of sadness.

Tony sat on a low concrete wall, the National Gallery's water-curtain doors in the background. His eyes glinted behind his glasses and he was smiling his famous heart-stopping smile. He wasn't traditionally handsome – his face was too bony, his nose too large, his teeth a fraction crooked – but he had a compelling quality, an intensity that was both guarded and beguiling.

I switched off the bedside lamp and took the photo out to the kitchen, leaning it against a jar of peanuts on the bench so I could study it in full light. It felt good to look at his face, to pretend he was still out there somewhere, moving through life, perhaps taking a moment to gaze up at the stars and think of me.

It almost worked.

Then I remembered the coffin. The boggy slope, the yawning grave beneath the elm. By now the cemetery would be dark, its poplars and cypresses sagging beneath the weight of rain, the sky raked by fingers of lightning.

Though I hadn't seen Tony for months, suddenly I missed him unbearably. With him, I'd been different – strong, capable. I'd laughed more, worried less, opened up and found pleasure in unexpected places. When he left I pulled back into my shell – escaping into my work, neglecting my friends, desperate to lose myself. Tormented by the knowledge that the man I loved no longer loved me.

The only light in that dark time had been Bronwyn. Despite her own confusion over Tony's leaving, she'd been a chirpy little girl, seemingly wise beyond her six years. I'd thrown myself into mothering her, and been rewarded by moments of closeness we'd rarely shared before. Even as a baby, Bronwyn had gravitated to her father – she was the tiny moon that orbited Planet Tony, worshipful and constant. She'd run to me for scraped knees, for a bandaid and a pat . . . but afterwards she'd always hobble off to Tony, knowing he was the only one able to kiss away her pain, calm her vexation, tease a laugh from her baby lips.

But then, after Tony left, we connected. Bronwyn would giggle madly and fling her arms around my waist, insisting that I was the prettiest, the best, the nicest mummy in the whole entire world . . . and those moments had saved me.

I sighed. 'Dammit, Tony. Why did you have to go and die?'

I'd met him at art school. At seventeen I'd been critically shy, but determined to establish myself as a photographer. I'd grown up with my Aunt Morag, and after she died I'd found a Box Brownie camera in her belongings. I quickly became obsessed, and when I realised there were people who made a living by taking pictures, I was determined to count myself among them. Not knowing where else to start, I enrolled at the Victorian College of the Arts.

Tony was in the painting department, and a few years ahead of me. He was talented, mysterious, popular, funny . . . yet oddly – and enticingly – vulnerable. We'd been rubbing shoulders at the local watering hole for nearly six months before I drummed up the courage to speak to him. To my baffled delight we hooked up quickly. Within a year I was pregnant. I deferred my studies, unable to think of anything but Tony and the baby. As our child grew within me, so did my confidence. Tony loved me, and the world was a happy place to be. Commissions for photographic work trickled in, and for the first time in my life I felt as though I belonged somewhere – truly belonged.

Tony's success came swiftly. He began selling his paintings through a top-notch gallery, building a name for himself, working harder than ever. He got invited to the Venice Biennale, a career highlight for him at the time, and also a memorable milestone in our life together. Bronwyn was born soon after his return, and it seemed that life couldn't get any better. It was so dreamily good, so fairytale perfect, that it made me nervous. That was when the decay set in. Slowly, so slowly at first that I barely noticed.

Tony began spending more time away. He was working at the studio, he said, preparing for a big group show at the National Gallery. Over the next few years a pattern developed. The more Tony withdrew into his career, the tighter I clung to him ... and the tighter I clung, the further he withdrew.

I chewed my fingernails to the quick, spent nights prowling the house, unable to sleep. My photos became dark and somehow disturbed: hollow-eyed children; solitary old people feeding pigeons or gazing out to sea. Bare trees, derelict buildings, empty playgrounds. Fear nibbled at my happiness, creating holes I could find no way to fill. On the surface, life went on as usual. We took Bronwyn to the beach, or for long country drives; we helped organise school concerts, attended ballet then netball like the doting parents we were ... But privately, we were both wretched.

We argued all the time. Money became an issue. We stopped making love. So when Tony started coming home later and later – and then not at all – I knew the end was near.

How wrong I was. Unknown to me, the end had already been and gone.

The phone shrilled on the kitchen bench, jolting me from my thoughts. I allowed it to ring, waiting for the answering machine to splutter awake. An entire evening of wallowing lay ahead and I intended to make the most of it. But then, at the last minute, I panicked and made a lunge for the handset.

'Hello?'

'Ms Kepler, it's Margot Fraser here, Tony's lawyer. Sorry to call so late in the day, but there's a pressing matter I need to discuss with you. Are you free tomorrow?'

I stiffened. Tony's lawyer? My mind began to scramble, stirring up a muddy froth of guilt and alarm. My long-dormant survival instinct bubbled forth. Say anything, it warned; blurt any excuse to buy more time.

'Tomorrow's Saturday,' I informed her lamely.

'It's regarding Tony's will,' the woman explained, 'and rather urgent. I'll be in the office tomorrow until four o'clock, but I can drop by your house if that's more convenient?'

Fear laced through my stomach and tied itself in a knot. The last thing I wanted was anyone on official business coming here. Crazily, I had the urge to tell her about the spare room – all the boxes of books I'd stored there, Bronwyn's old bike and the piles of untouched sewing that had been gathering dust for years. Surely she wasn't going to insist we vacate the house immediately?

'Ms Kepler, are you there?'

'Yes, tomorrow will be fine. I'll pop into the office.'

She gave me the address, then said, 'Sometime after lunch, let's say two o'clock? It won't take long, but if you've got any questions it'll give us time to be thorough.'

'Great,' I said hurriedly, ever the chicken-hearted. 'See you then.'

'Here's one.'

Saturday morning, the kitchen smelled of toast and fresh coffee. Rain bucketed down outside. The windows were fogged, cutting us off from the rest of the world. Usually I loved hearing rain hammer the roof and hiss along the guttering. Today the sound was unsettling, a reminder that the secure little world we'd created here was about to end.

Bronwyn elbowed me, tapping her finger on the rental section of the newspaper she'd spread across the table in front of her. 'What do you think?'

I blinked at the sea of print. Sleep had foxed me again last night, luring me to the brink of much-needed unconsciousness, only to skitter away the moment I began to drift. I kept seeing Tony's grave, surrounded by sodden flowers and fast filling with water . . . and I kept hearing Carol's fretful words: 'Why would he do that, Audrey. Why – ?'

I took a gulp of coffee. 'How much?'

Bronwyn made an approving sound. 'Three-ninety a week. Second bathroom. Looks nice.'

The coffee burned my throat and I let out a weak little cough. A second bathroom was all very well, but three-ninety? Our rambling old house had its drawbacks, but it was rent-free. Tony had never paid child support; I'd refused him that satisfaction. Instead, I'd agreed to stay on at the old house after he moved in with Carol. In the five years that Bronwyn and I had lived here alone, I'd saved a substantial nest egg that would go towards buying a home of our own one day. All I needed was a few more years . . .

'Is there anything cheaper?'

'That's about the cheapest, Mum. Unless we cram into a bedsit.'

I rubbed my eyes, seeing my nest egg swiftly sucked into the vortex of someone else's mortgage. 'Maybe there'll be something in tomorrow's paper.'

'Tomorrow's Sunday.' Bronwyn's finger moved expertly down the page as she continued to scan. 'They don't do real estate on a Sunday.'

I gazed at her, wondering how an eleven-year-old knew these things. Wondering how she managed to stay so calm, while my stomach was twisting itself into knots. I checked the clock above the fridge. Only a few more hours of torture to go. The muscles in the back of my head were as tight as rubber bands. I rolled my shoulders to ease the strain, then tried to focus on my daughter's finger as it snailed through the maze of potential new homes.

The finger stopped abruptly. Bronwyn peered into my face. 'You keep checking the clock. Are we going somewhere?'

'Your father's lawyer wants to see me this afternoon. It won't take long. I'll drop you at netball and be back in plenty of time to pick you up.'

Bronwyn's eyes widened. 'He's left us something?'

I shrugged, not wanting to get her hopes up. 'Carol might've changed her mind about the twenty-eight days. She could want us out of the house sooner.'

'I'm coming with you.'

I hesitated. The Sundays Bronwyn had once spent with her father were now passed in her bedroom – the door locked while she pored over photos of the two of them, shuffling through her mementoes, refusing to eat anything until early evening when she'd re-emerge red-eyed and solemn as a priestess. She'd been grieving for him long before his death, I realised.

'Please, Mum?' She gazed up at me, her eyes blue as springwater.

'It'll be boring.'

'Please?'

I sighed. Carol had hinted that Bronwyn would be well provided for. Whatever Tony had left her, it wasn't going to repair the damage he'd done by withdrawing from her life. On the other hand, it might offer a welcome reassurance. I prayed that he'd left her something wonderful, so she'd know he really had cared.

'All right,' I conceded. 'Just don't get your hopes up.'

'Magpie Creek?'

My heart kicked over. Tony had died there, and I knew with a sudden pinch of apprehension that the little town must have meant more to him than a random port of call. I remembered the *Courier-Mail* article about the man's remains found in the dam ... and wondered if I'd dismissed the connection too hastily.

I cleared my dry throat. 'That's in Queensland, isn't it?'

The woman sitting behind the vast oak desk – Margot – smiled warmly. 'It's an hour or so south-west of Brisbane. Quite pretty, I'm told. Mostly farmland, but it boasts spectacular volcanic remnants that draw a lot of tourist interest. The town is small, but there's a thriving art community and several award-winning cafes, as well as the usual amenities.'

Bronwyn sat on a leather chair beside me, perched forward, gazing raptly into the lawyer's face. She looked older than her eleven years: maybe it was the dark blue dress and smart black sandals she'd insisted on wearing. Then again, perhaps it was simply that she'd brightened on hearing the news of her father's bequest. A considerable trust fund accessible when she turned twenty-one, and a huge delicate watercolour of a robin that she'd long admired.

Most astonishing was what Tony had left for me.

'A house,' I marvelled, shifting awkwardly. I couldn't help wondering if there was a catch. 'What about Tony's wife?'

Margot nodded. 'Carol is satisfied with Tony's decision; she's informed us that she won't be contesting the will. Now . . . Tony left keys in security with our office. The probate process should take about a month, after which time the keys and all documentation will pass into your hands. In the meantime, perhaps you'd like to hear a little more about the property?'

'Sure.'

Margot opened a folder. 'Thornwood originally belonged to Tony's grandfather, but I expect you already know that?'

I shook my head. 'This is the first I've heard of it.'

'Well, you're in for a treat,' she said, drawing out a large colour photo and placing it on the desk before us. 'That's the homestead – gorgeous, isn't it? It was built in 1936, a classic old Queenslander with four bedrooms. It's fully furnished – I'm assuming Tony decided to keep the place intact for sentimental reasons. There's a vegie garden, orchard, creek access . . . Also, hidden up in the hills surrounding the property, there's a small dwelling that was probably the original settlers' cabin, most likely built sometime in the late 1800s.'

The photo showed a magnificent residence skirted by a shady wraparound verandah. Stained-glass panels curved out from twin bay windows, and iron lacework festooned the eaves. The garden surrounding it was a maze of hydrangeas and lavender hedges, with a brick path meandering up the grassy slope towards wide welcoming stairs. Dappled sunlight danced across the lawn, where a magnificent old rose arbour sat smothered in crimson blooms.

'The house itself is quite a feature,' Margot went on, 'but as with any property, the true value is in the land. The total land size is 2500 acres – that's just over a thousand hectares. The property adjoins two other large farms, but most of it backs onto the Gower National Park. You have 200 acres of grazing pasture, with rich dark soil, dams, fencing, a permanent creek . . . and according to the report, the views are stunning.'

Bronwyn sighed. 'Mum, it's perfect.'

'We're not going to live there,' I said hastily.

'But Mum – '

'We'll sell it and buy a place of our own here in Melbourne.'

Bronwyn gave me a mournful look, but I ignored her and resumed my inspection of the photo. After Tony's death I'd vowed to forget him . . . for Bronwyn's sake as well as my own; how could I do that if we were living in his grandfather's house? The old homestead looked huge and rambling and mysterious. Probably full of secrets, riddled with ghosts, haunted by other people's memories.

Tony's memories.

Margot drew out another photo: an aerial view that showed the property as heart-shaped and densely forested. A section of cleared grazing land rolled along the southernmost quarter, a verdant patchwork stitched with fences and dotted with brown dams. Central to the photo was the homestead – a rectangular patch of iron roof, surrounded by sprawling gardens that rambled uphill and vanished into bushland. A ridge of hills swept to the north-west, mostly heavily treed, but there were curiously bald areas where stone formations pushed through the rust-red earth.

'If you did change your mind and decide to live at Thornwood,' Margot told us, 'there's really not a lot to do. The paddocks are mostly in agistment, which means you'll have additional income from farmers grazing stock on your land. The rest is natural bushland, so aside from general maintenance near the house, it's the sort of property you can simply sit back and enjoy.'

She collected the photos and slid them back into the property file. 'Now, I expect you're keen to know how much it's worth.'

Shadows were creeping across the room; the light filtering through the window had taken on a grey tinge. My chair creaked as I shifted my weight. A rundown old house on a chunk of wilderness, miles from anywhere; a few grazing paddocks, some muddy dams. Nothing to get too keyed up about, surely?

I nodded.

Margot wrote on a notepad and tore off the top leaf, then placed it reverently on the desk in front of us.

Bronwyn gasped.

The lawyer smiled approvingly. 'Certainly worth the trouble of a quick look, wouldn't you say?'

About the author

A nna Romer grew up in a family of book-lovers and yarn-tellers, which inspired her lifelong love affair with stories. A graphic artist by trade, she also spent many years travelling the globe stockpiling story material from the Australian outback, then Asia, New Zealand, Europe and America.

Her first novel, *Thornwood House*, published in 2013, reflects her fascination with forgotten diaries and letters, dark family secrets, rambling old houses, and love in its many guises – as well as her passion for the uniquely beautiful Australian landscape.

When she's not writing (or falling in love with another book), Anna is an avid gardener, knitter, bushwalker and conservationist. She lives on a remote bush property in northern New South Wales.